# Peace & Quiet & The Falling Rain

Raymond S Flex

DIB Books

# PAIN AND CHAOS AND THE BLAZING SUN

E verything was black and a dull ringing filled my ears.
I was lying face down with my eyes shut.

I could feel a welt on my forehead the size and shape of a chicken's egg. The welt throbbed with a life of its own, seeming to grow in diameter with each beat of my heart. A nagging voice at the back of my mind told me not to open my eyes.

Not quite yet.

I obeyed.

I felt a tremendous heat on the backs of my shoulders, like I was in a reptile pen at a zoo. My mind was wrestling with the idea that the Earth was spinning at a thousand miles per hour and that it was somehow supposed to keep up. The rest of my body was having similar issues if my churning stomach was anything to go by.

I coughed.

One of those retching, bottom-of-the-lungs, clear-everything-out coughs.

I tasted a bit of everything:

Blood.

Alcohol.

... And something else, too ... something sour, like body odour, sweat ...

As I breathed in — too deeply and too quickly — I took in a mouthful of sand.

This led to more coughing.

Spluttering, gasping, I tried to spit out as much sand as I could.

The way my brain was pounding at the confines of my skull, it felt as though I was suffering from a potentially lethal combination of hangover and sunstroke. The welt on my forehead stung as if it was a tiny beast that I had awoken and angered.

Taking things slowly, as my delicate condition demanded, I straightened my arms.

A sharp pain danced up the inside of my left arm.

I bit my lip, trying to absorb the pain.

I shifted my weight onto my right arm, which was — thankfully — in full-working condition, if a little stiff ... it felt as if I'd done a full-week of office-droning although my current situation hinted that a computer keyboard, mouse and bad posture weren't to blame for the ailment this time around. Once I'd levered myself up into a sitting position on the sand, feeling an ache just above my tailbone even despite the soft surface, I decided it was time to open my eyes.

To see what I'd got myself in for.

I was sitting on a beach.

I'd gathered that much from my other senses.

Flawless sugary sands.

Turquoise waters which turned azure as they got deeper.

A big blue sky with a few scattered puffs of white cloud for variation.

In other words, paradise.

Behind me, there was a veritable forest of low-growing, scrubby trees; a half dozen palm trees sprouting up through them, straight-backed, elegant giants among hunched-over, decrepit pygmies. Although I couldn't see the other side of the island for the trees blocking the view, I guessed it couldn't be much larger than a school playing field.

I would've been surprised to discover a metropolis on the other side, put it that way.

If only it hadn't been for the incessant nausea, the constant ringing in my ears, the welt competing with my skull for space under my skin, and the great unease brought on by the amnesia surrounding just how I had ended up here, I might've enjoyed the view.

There was also the matter of the overbearingly humid tropical heat that sweated me from every pore, of course ... one of the things that's always put me off beach holidays.

I'm more of a room-temperature kind of guy.

The clothes I was wearing said as much because I wasn't dressed for the beach.

I had on what could only be described as a suit. A white shirt, with a now-tattered jacket over a pair of smart, black formal trousers. When I inspected my aching left arm, I realised that the sleeve of my jacket was damp. When I touched it with my other hand, my fingertips came away with the unmistakable trace of blood. Although I've never been that squeamish about blood I'm not a glutton for punishment, either.

There would be time enough later to examine battle scars.

At least I thought so ...

I was also wearing a pair of leather shoes. They looked fairly new, apart from the fact that they were now covered in scuffmarks and battered from whatever journey I had just been on. I could feel a strange sensation at my left heel and when I inspected the sole I saw that there was a large hole, with the bottom of my sock poking through.

It went without saying that everything I was wearing was covered in sand.

I reached up for my hair.

Sand.

My fingertips brushed my inner ear.

Yep ... sand.

As I brought my hand down, I knocked the welt on my forehead.

It sent a sudden fizzle of pain directly through my frontal cortex.

I sat still for a couple of seconds, eyes clamped shut, absorbing the sudden unpleasant sensation. Even though it looked like there was no one else around, I tried my best not to swear. And although my intentions were good, a particularly filthy word did manage to sneak out between my lips. No more than a husky whisper, but it was there.

Initial assessments finished, and the worst of the stinging pain on my forehead dealt with, I tentatively opened my eyes once more. Heart thumping my ribs, skull squeezing my brain, I hoisted my knees up to my chest in a kind of sitting foetal position and lost myself in the mystical sparkle of sunlight across the surface of the water. It was as if nature itself was trying its best to hypnotise me ... to return me to a former place or time in my mind. The ringing in my ears was becoming weaker, or I was growing more used to it, because I started to notice ambient sounds.

A calm, refreshingly cool, breeze rustling the leaves.

Some tropical bird trilling.

The sea suckling the shoreline.

It would've been the perfect place for someone who makes those relaxation CDs to come and record; the CDs that are always found on pop-up cardboard racks at petrol stations and other unlikely locales.

I let loose a long exhale and dared to take a really deep breath for the first time since I had woken up. What I smelled on the air snapped me back to reality. And nipped any sense of calm that had descended over me firmly in the bud.

Smoke.

I jerked away from the placid scene, pushed myself up onto my feet, forgetting about my afflicted left arm as I did so. Somehow the welt on my forehead was also offended by this unexpected movement and pain once again jangled through my nervous system. I swore again — this time loudly — and rubbed at the bloody spot on my shirt sleeve while scowling uselessly up at where I imagined the welt to be on my forehead.

Clenching and unclenching a fist with my left hand, I did my best to take my mind off the aches and pains. I experienced a slight wobble as my mind went another round in its argument with the Earth's rotation but I managed to stay on my feet.

And then — just like that — it was as if someone sparked a match.

Images flickered through my brain.

Visions framed by convex glass.

4

The sky.

The sea.

The island.

Everything too close.

And all at once.

Then a scream.

... *Crunch*!

Blackness.

My pulse ticked through the welt on my forehead and I restrained the urge to rub at it.

That would only make the pain worse.

I took a shuddering breath.

Looked in one direction and then the other.

A pristine, empty beach.

That was all.

But then I saw ...

Smoke coiled up from behind the tree line.

Faint.

So grey it was almost transparent.

Almost lost against the brilliant blue sky.

But it was there.

With loping, drunken strides, I lumbered along the beach, finally seeing where the smoke trail led. A small plane with a single propeller, the blades of which were either bent beyond repair or snapped clean off as a result of the impact, had crash landed upon the shore. Its nose was half-buried in the sand and it had landed at a forty-five degree angle so that one wing stuck up into the sky while the other was submerged beneath the surface of the water. There was no sign of any wheels and I supposed they had either broken off upon landing or else sunk into the sand. The back end of the plane continued to float, fishtailing slightly in the current; the plane's nose keeping it anchored to dry land. Smoke rose from just behind the propeller.

Perhaps it was my imagination but I was certain it was getting thicker.

The plane was big enough for maybe two people with a small space for suitcases behind the pilot and co-pilot seats. The fuselage was painted white and was blinding in the bright sunlight. I couldn't help but notice the simple sketched-on decal of a semi-circle with five lines fanned out evenly ... a crude — albeit accurately executed — image of a rising sun. One of the plane's chrome fixtures caught a sunray and the full force of the UV light struck my eyeballs.

It felt as though the welt on my forehead had been struck by lightning.

I brought my forearm up to shield my eyes from the glare.

The plane put me in mind of a beached beluga whale.

As if all it needed was a small push back out to sea.

Back into the depths.

Where it would once more go about its life unnoticed by humans.

Able to take care of itself.

Now I knew what that smell had been.

The one I had thought was body odour, sweat ...

So sharp that it was undeniable:

Kerosene.

Footprints in the sand led away from the downed plane, leading into the trees.

For a couple of seconds, I scoured the foliage thinking someone had escaped the wreck. But then — my thoughts drooling through my mind like honey off a spoon — I realised they had to be my footsteps.

I couldn't remember leaving the plane.

But there was no other explanation.

It looked like — in my confused stupor — I'd got disorientated and wandered off into the trees. And then passed out on the other side of the island.

As if in confirmation, the welt on my forehead twinged.

A woman's voice brought my ponderings to an abrupt halt.

She was calling my name.

"Marc! Marcus!"

I snapped my full attention back onto the plane.

Through the cracked tinted glass I made out the form.

The silhouette within.

How had I got here?

How the *hell* had I got here?

And who was that?
The smoke was getting thicker now.
Darker.
Blacker.
There was the flicker of a flame.
Another.
And another.
My heart beat at my temples.
And the welt on my forehead throbbed with a pulse of its own.
A life of its own.
My stomach clenched.
There was no time to lose.
I took off down the beach.

*WEEKS EARLIER*

# TECHNOMANCER

I screwed up my eyes, massaged my temples and gripped the phone tighter in my fist.

And then I allowed myself to fold over my desk.

When my forehead made contact with my computer keyboard, I felt the cool, slightly damp surface against my skin. The accumulated perspiration of a long day of entering customer details. I wondered what might happen if I just stayed here for a while.

Would someone eventually ask if I was okay?

Most likely not.

It was past five o'clock on Friday afternoon and I was conscious that everyone had already left or was in the process of leaving. The general sense of cheer and the palpable fuck-it-leave-it-till-Monday feeling. Soon I too would leave this stale, air-conditioned prison and venture back out into the real world for a couple of days.

I thought about the beers sitting in my fridge at home.

Waiting for me.

I could almost taste their yeasty, hoppy goodness.

But I wasn't there yet.

I was trapped on the phone with some lady from Market Harborough.

I was talking to her about Imagick, the flagship product of LifeWare, the software company where I worked as a technical support advisor.

Her voice re-entered my immediate consciousness.

"... and when I click on the icon all I get is a spinny circle, it's like it's stuck or something. Do you think it's stuck? Should I shut down my computer and turn it back on? But if I do that I might break something, mightn't I? ... Could I lose some of my photos if I do that? When I ..."

I opened my eyes.

Took stock of my computer screen.

The unread messages in my inbox were past three figures.

For some reason that I'd like only to think of as a mental reflex, I recalled an appraisal with my manager Lucas a few months ago. One of the goals "we" had set together was for me to better stay on top of my inbox. "We" had set a goal for me to turn around all messages within twenty-four hours. And that goal had lasted all of twenty-four hours ...

The problem I have with emails is that once I start responding people reply right back.

It's virtual-reality Whack-a-Mole.

I loosened the knot in my tie. I undid the top button of my shirt. That made it feel like I was closer to the weekend — *fractionally* closer — but closer all the same.

My gaze wandered across the pin board I had behind my computer monitor. There were still several photos of myself and my ex-girlfriend Olivia. The two of us cuddling together, grinning, in a variety of settings.

At a local pub with a pair of pints.

A Cambodian jungle.

On the Norfolk Broads.

I should have taken the photos down by then.

We had broken up weeks ago.

"... Hello ... hello?"

Realising I had tuned out completely — again — I returned my full attention to the lady on the line. "Hi, I'm sorry ... I missed that." I thought for a second and then decided to add, "The line cut out for a few seconds."

The lady gave a heaving sigh that plainly said she was unfortunately used to dealing with incompetents such as me. "Who am I speaking with?"

"Marcus," I said.

The lady remained silent and then with a jibing tone that suggested she might be writing this down, added, "Surname?"

"Raisin."

"Raisin?"

"Yes, you know, like a ... dehydrated grape?"

I waited for the titter of laughter on the end of the line which almost always followed this witticism, but ... nothing.

Tough crowd.

And on a Friday of all days.

Spirits should've been flying high.

For some reason it has always been inordinately important to me for people to laugh at my jokes. Maybe it's the same for all guys but ... nah, I think I'm definitely more needy than most. I still cling to the childish dream that I will one day leave all this behind and make a career in comedy. And that spark of hope keeps me going in even my darkest hours. The fact that I have never shared so much as a single line of the measly few pages of material I have produced in over thirty years of life doesn't make any difference to my inner child.

Somehow it doesn't show this dream up for what it is.

And what it will always be.

A *dream*.

Perhaps if it had been earlier in the week, or there had been any management still hanging around, I might've been slightly concerned about what the customer was going to say next. As it was, though, I only ached to get out of the office as soon as humanly possible.

Faster if I could.

On the other end of the line there was a multitude of clicking and some humming before, "I think the issue might have resolved itself, Marcus. When I click on the icon now, it seems to be working. The program is opening up and it looks like I have all my photos."

It felt as if some phantasmal beefcake had lifted a great load from my shoulders. I actually felt a smile sketch itself upon my lips. "Great — I'm so glad to hear it ..."

I waited, still hearing the lady's breathing on the other end.

One of LifeWare's "Guiding Principles" was to never hang up on a customer.

*Customers are the only ones who do the hanging up around here ...*

That was one of my boss Lucas's favourite phrases.

"Oh," the lady said, and then, "I see ..."

I glanced to the clock again. It had gone five past five now.

There was nobody left in the office at all. I could hear the cleaning lady rustling about in the maintenance cupboard. Soon she would shoo me out so she could vacuum the floors and wipe down desks. She would want to get out of here just as badly as I did.

Unless, of course, she was some kind of psycho:

A workaholic cleaner ...

I made a mental note of potential material.

I could almost *smell* those beers.

I could feel the slight resistance when I tugged at the ring pull.

I could hear that beautiful *hiss* as pressurised air escaped the can.

The forecast this morning had said it was going to be pleasantly warm all evening. An "Indian summer" some people were calling it, although people are always generally looking for ways to rebrand, reframe and brighten up the drab, increasingly cold-and-dark, back-to-school month that is September. When I got home, I could clamber out of the skylight window of my attic flat and stretch out on the roof tiles to savour the late-afternoon sunrays.

I might even get a bit of a tan.

"No, no, no ... I can't see it. Sorry? ... Hello? Hello?"

"Hi?" I replied.

"I'm missing one of my photos. Can you recover it for me, please?"

I shifted back to my computer screen, gladly minimising the bombsite that was my inbox, bringing open the client-side window which showed the lady's account. Her photo thumbnails were blurred out so that they resembled mosaics — a fairly basic privacy feature that our company director was overly proud of ...

*LifeWare takes customer privacy extremely seriously ...*

I flicked through the images. Usually when a customer has deleted one of their images, the thumbnail will remain but appear greyed out for thirty days before it's permanently deleted from the system. And even then there might well be a way of recovering it ... but that was above my station and would require me calling in favours.

Something I wasn't all too keen to be doing.

Especially not at this time on a Friday.

I took a deep breath. "You didn't ... delete it by mistake, did you? It's not one of the greyed-out images?"

"No. Why would I have done that? It's a photo that I'll cherish until the day I die."

At past five o'clock on a Friday, I couldn't help but hope silently to myself that that particular day would come sooner rather than later.

"I'll tell you what," I said, "I've found a few deleted photos here. I'm going to restore them all. They won't be greyed out anymore. Maybe if you have a proper look you'll find what you're searching for?" With a few clicks, I did as I had told her and watched the grey mist lift.

There was silence on the other end of the line, and then, "No, no, it's none of *these*. I'm with my granddaughter. *Angelica*. At her *graduation* ceremony. It's where she's getting her degree in Human Resources with Emphasis in Talent Acquisition *and* Development."

"I'm sorry," I replied. "It's just that I can't really see your images properly. They're all kind of a blur on my screen ..."

"What do you mean they're 'a kind of a blur'?"

She made it sound as if I was insulting her. "I ... It's a privacy thing. Look, you wouldn't want someone looking at your private photos, would you? So we can't see them. We just see a few blurry colours. And the file name. We can see if there are deleted photos there. That's about it. Have another look through those photos I've just restored. Are you sure it's not one of those?"

The lady was silent for another few seconds. "No, definitely not." Another short pause, and then, "Could I speak with your manager, please?"

I looked around, although I already knew the answer.

There was no sign of Lucas.

"He's already left for the weekend. You could try calling back on Monday?"

"Do you think you will have found the photo by then?"

I considered my options.

In theory, all of our conversations are recorded and kept *somewhere* for someone to scrutinise at some later date. I often wondered if there might not come a day when upper management would come along and haul someone up from their desk to explain a call they had had with a customer months ago. To back up some outrageous claim they'd made. Or to explain some just-below-the-customer's-hearing sweary exclamation that had snuck out.

In reality, though, I knew it was paranoia. The only reason for Life-Ware to record any of our conversations was to cover themselves in case of a lawsuit. Nobody had the time to listen to conversations lasting hundreds of thousands of hours unless something went to court for some reason. That way they might find evidence to blame the employee rather than the company.

I stared hard at my monitor, knowing it was definitely at least five fifteen by now. "Yes," I replied. "I'm certain the photo will have turned up by Monday."

With the strap of my messenger bag thrown across my chest, I hastily hit Shut Down on my PC, eyeing the week's jetsam across my desk. Several disposable coffee cups, grainy sops at the bottom. One of the cups had a banana skin rudely stuffed into it.

I swept my arm across my desktop, collecting up all the cups, scraps of paper, and other assorted messes, and deposited them into the nearest bin, which was already overflowing. As I straightened up, I caught the eye of the cleaning lady who had emerged from the maintenance cupboard. She was built like a fridge and wore a pinstriped apron strapped around her front. She gave me a glare as if I was responsible for the sorry state of the entire office and not just my own desk. In truth, she was fully justified in being vexed. An empty office after leaving time on a Friday is a decidedly weird place to be.

When I returned to my desk, I eyed the photos featuring me and Olivia. I wondered if today was the day I took them down. I was surely past the point of surreally believing we would somehow get back together. Even though we'd only been together two years, it was difficult to recall a time when we hadn't been an item.

The weirdest thing was how hard it was to picture her in my mind.

Without the photographs before me, seeing her black hair, cropped to just above her shoulder line, her walnut-coloured eyes, freckled cheeks, I couldn't ever quite bring all her features together. It made me think that a large part of her had only existed in my mind at the time and had been lost soon after our break-up.

I was about to take the photos down, tear them in half, put them into the confidential waste bin to be shredded, when I noticed the message etched across my computer screen:

*Error – report to system administrator*

I blew out a long exhale, my lips making a rasping sound as the air escaped.

"Shit," I uttered under my breath.

Another of LifeWare's Guiding Principles is that employees take full responsibility for their computer systems. To log in and log out. An employee will be held directly responsible for any and all activity on their account.

Authorised or unauthorised activity.

And that includes any activity logged over a weekend.

I clicked about on the screen.

Attempted to close the error message by clicking "Ok" innumerable times ... but the message stayed where it was.

My finger hovered over the hard reset button.

I jabbed it.

The screen went black. It went through its splash screen. A monogram of the LifeWare logo — a globe with a cable snaking out of it — flickered across the monitor.

And then the message again:

*Error – report to system administrator*

The cleaner started the vacuum and a hum filled the air. I caught a whiff of the smell of warm electronics as the machine went about its work, guided by its human operator.

At the heart of it, the issue wasn't so much the message, but what the message meant.

I had to go face the system administrator.

And the system administrator would definitely be in his office ... he always was.

Even at this time on a Friday.

I had never really thought of myself as being a proud guy but I'd always found it difficult to handle people who manage all their human interactions through sarcasm. Okay, so I might not have bothered to go get a degree in computer science before getting a job at a tech company but at least my emotional intelligence has passed "pre-pubescent teenager" ... or so I hoped.

If I wanted to go enjoy my weekend guilt-free I needed to do the hard thing right now.

Otherwise I'd only have to face him on Monday.

And explain to my boss Lucas why I had left my account unlocked all weekend ...

With a heavy heart, I glanced to the cleaning lady, seeing that she was off in her own little world, earbuds poked in, clearly not unhappy, a neutral expression on her face.

As I went to confront my destiny, I wondered if she hadn't uncovered some secret to balancing happiness — if not fulfilment — with paid work.

And that was a major miracle in my book.

I rapped my knuckles a few times on the open door, glancing at the name plate as I did so. Although it had his name and role etched on the metal — John Horsham, Systems Administrator — this had been covered up with a crudely torn piece of paper. Written in a flamelike script, the kind you might use for a tattoo or stencil onto the bass drum of a heavy metal band, was the word:

"TECHNOMANCER"

It was difficult to tell if it was a joke that one of his friends might have played on him and he had either found amusing and left there or else hadn't noticed at all. Maybe he didn't have any friends and the explanation was simply that he had done this himself and put it there. There wasn't any satisfactory explanation which wasn't wrought with weirdness or that didn't rake up an infinite heap of unanswered questions. What did it even mean? That he was a kind of necromancer of IT? Bringing old hardware back to life when it seemed to have long ago descended into the digital grave? He always had a high opinion of himself.

There was something else to the name, too. Like a kind of living pun, I could hear the low mechanical melodies of techno music rattling away within.

For a few seconds, I savoured the sound.

It sounded like the weekend.

I couldn't help but wonder if me and John Horsham — Technomancer — didn't have more in common than I had first thought.

There was no light in the room except for the eerie bluish glow from the various computer monitors. The flickering orange, blue and green lights from the banks of servers stacked up on one side of the room like nocturnal creatures in a midnight forest. Maybe I didn't have a degree in computer science, but I knew that the problem lay behind one of those blinking lights in one of those servers.

There were half a dozen cardboard pizza boxes stacked up against the wall and I caught the not-completely-unpleasant scent of molten cheese mixed up with salty pepperoni and hot sauce. This scent was unfortunately tainted by the underlying reek of body odour and flatulence. I guessed the pizza boxes remained where they were because the fire safety inspector was unable to hold his nose long enough to set foot in the room.

I had always thought the room kind of small and pokey, but I realised a large amount of space was taken up by the pizza boxes, the servers and Technomancer himself. There was a blackout blind which — presumably — concealed a window to the outside world. A good decluttering and proper lighting would have made it seem a much larger space, or so they claimed on those countless home-improvement programmes my ex Olivia used to enjoy watching.

I imagined Technomancer had the place exactly how he wanted it.

I eyed the back of his chair. Although it was by no means an unsubstantial chair, I could make out the folds of Technomancer's shoulder and waist fat protruding around the edges. As he always did, he was wearing a black button-down shirt with questionable stains on it. His greasy black hair was thrust into a scrawny ponytail. I could see from this angle that he had a tattoo on the side of his neck, poking just above his shirt collar. I had never noticed it before, but, then again, I was in the business of limiting my interactions with Technomancer as much as I could. I certainly didn't want to set any ideas racing around his head by gawping at his skin. The tattoo was a straight-forward geometric drawing of a sun rising on the horizon:

A semi-circle represented the sun.

Five straight lines — sunrays — fanned out from it.

"Hello?" I said.

Technomancer didn't turn in his chair to acknowledge me.

It was nothing personal.

He didn't acknowledge *anyone's* existence unless he absolutely had to.

"Uh, hello?" I said, deciding to try again.

Still nothing.

I eyed the computer screens, wondering whether Technomancer was busy in a world of code, unable or unwilling to lower himself to the level of mere mortals until he was done. Although I'm far from a computer expert, it didn't *look* like anything was happening on the screen. When I checked my watch, I saw it was coming up to five twenty-five.

Piece by piece, my weekend was being eroded.

"It's my computer," I said, as if there might be some other reason why I'd come here. "I'm trying to shut down but it's giving me an error? It says I need to speak with the system admin? I just need to log out, really. So if you're able to do that remotely we can always look at the problem again on Monday?"

Still nothing.

I took a step into the room.

Another.

I felt my heart bobbing in my throat. Just what was I afraid of? That the scary computer geek was going to make fun of the stupid customer service rep?

Well, actually ...

I squared my shoulders, breathed in deep and then ... noticed the computer tablet lying on the desk in front of Technomancer.

My heart stopped completely.

It was hard to take in at first. As if my eyes were lying to me. It just seemed so out of place. It jarred so horribly that it couldn't possibly be true.

But there was no denying.

It was the face of Olivia.

My ex-girlfriend.

In a trance, I stepped closer, fixated upon the image. I recognised it well, of course. It was one of the many sexy pictures Olivia had sent me during the course of our relationship.

... Towards the beginning of our relationship.

I thought about the many times later on, when things were clearly winding down between us, when she had casually mentioned those photos, waiting for me to fill in the gaps, to confirm that I had deleted them. But I never had.

And then we had broken up.

To tell the truth, I had forgotten I even had them.

Or, well ... they hadn't been at the forefront of my mind ...

Who am I trying to fool? I'm a creep and I know it.

In this particular photo, Olivia had been trying on a black bikini she had bought for our holiday in Greece. And she'd thought to send me a snap ... only it seemed that the bikini top had slipped slightly ...

My mind caught up with the present.

And a fiery ball twisted in the pit of my stomach.

"What the ... *fuck*?"

I expected Technomancer to startle.

But he didn't react.

He didn't spin around in his chair.

Jabber some ridiculous explanation.

He remained where he was.

The tablet still in front of him.

The photo of Olivia still very much in line of sight.

I got closer, wanting to see his face.

And that was when I saw.

Even though I had never seen a dead body before, there was no doubt about it.

He sat slumped, shoulders hunched, chin tucked into his chest. His glasses had slid all the way down to the tip of his nose. His eyelids were slightly open. He looked as if he had drifted into some sort of a daydream. Or if someone had sedated him.

But I could tell he was dead.

A sort of coolness emanated from him like he was made of squidgy marble.

I looked to Technomancer, and then back to the tablet, my mind still attempting to reconcile the situation. I slid the tablet across the desk, minimised the image, returned to the main menu. For several seconds I remained there, stunned.

I realised that I was looking at the home screen of my mobile phone.

That at least solved one of my far-fetched questions.

Technomancer hadn't started seeing my ex-girlfriend and she hadn't suddenly started sending him sexy photos from several years ago intended for another guy.

Admittedly that did leave the question of how in *hell* he had hacked my phone but I supposed that was something a degree in computer science taught you.

In the corridor outside, I heard the vacuum cleaner getting louder.

I knew time was limited.

I glanced to Technomancer again, ensuring that he was definitely dead. Then I clicked the tablet into standby mode. As I did so, the symbol of the sun — the same as the one tattooed onto Technomancer — showed up on the screen.

When the screen had gone black, I slipped the tablet into my bag.

And left to get help.

# HOME COMFORTS

It was past seven thirty in the evening when I finally got back home. Although the paramedics had shown up promptly, the police had kept me and the cleaning lady for questioning for about three quarters of an hour. They had taken down our details and said they would get in touch if they required anything further.

I jabbed my key into the lock. As I tried to turn the key, it jammed several times.

I wiggled it about.

The trick to getting the lock to open is a supple wrist.

The door finally opened with a creak of hinges that a haunted house would've been proud of.

I was on the top floor of a house which'd been converted into four flats. There was a basement, two intermediate levels, and then the attic where I lived. It'd been advertised as a "penthouse" but this was at the very least false-advertising — and at the worst borderline criminal — considering it was smaller than all the other flats.

I had distinguished myself during my first week living here by coming home raging drunk and passing out in the front garden. The nice old lady, Mildreth, who lives in the basement flat, had offered me tea and crumpets when I had stirred lying sprawled on her patio on Sunday morning, covered in dew. After our impromptu tea party she had re-marked in delighted tones about my sudden recovery before politely pointing out that I had vomited in one of her pot plants. She had told me not to worry about it — she had three sons of her own.

The sun was setting in the attic windows and the sky was like a bruise caught between its greenish-blue and purple-pink stage. Both windows were wide open and a pleasant breeze was blowing in. My flat isn't much. It's a studio with a sofa bed that I have to fold out every night, pack up every morning — whenever I feel up to it. Considering the fact that the sofa bed was still folded out, I guessed I hadn't felt "up to it" that particular morning.

There's a kitchenette off to one side and an adjoining, windowless bathroom with just about enough room for the shower, toilet and basin squeezed inside.

I allowed my messenger bag to drop at my feet, forgetting momentarily about the tablet computer I had stowed away there. My bag landed on the threadbare carpet tile with a thunk.

I thought for a moment about the police.

Should I have told them about the tablet? The thought of telling the police simply hadn't occurred to me at the time. Or maybe it had briefly but I hadn't wanted them to confiscate the tablet and go prying through the contents of my phone.

... We all have our secrets, okay?

"Sparky Raisin? You home, Sparky?"

It was Riko.

He was the only one who still called me "Sparky Raisin" after all these years.

Actually, thinking about it, he was probably the only one who had ever called me "Sparky Raisin" in the first place.

I turned to look. He had popped into view, resting his elbow on the open fridge door. He was wearing a black polyester gym shirt and matching shorts, the material of both fuzzy and frayed after repeated washes. His feet were bare. His dark-brown hair was buzzed short and the stubble on his face was beginning to sprout into a beard. Riko has a Japanese mother and a British father. The particular way in which the genes had interlinked had made him an extremely handsome bastard, with the combination of his mother's darker features, high cheekbones; his father's square jaw, green eyes. We had become best friends when

25

we met at university, about ten years ago. And we still were now, in our early thirties.

A couple of weeks ago, Riko had been "let go" by the insurance firm he had worked for. When his housemates had learned this, they had gone straight to the landlord and got Riko kicked out. It turned out he hadn't paid rent in months. As I'd mostly been spending my time at home moping about my break-up with Olivia when he'd asked to stay, I had said it would be fine for him to crash on my kitchen floor for as long as he wanted.

I had thought the company would be nice.

After the first week or so, though, I had started to regret the total loss of privacy.

And now — several weeks later — I was beginning to wonder if he would ever leave.

"I thought you were going to your parents' this weekend?" I asked.

"Well, it's nice to see you too," Riko replied.

I rolled my shoulders, making a vain effort to ease some of the tension I'd worked into them throughout the week. I collapsed onto the still-unfolded sofa bed. As I dropped onto the mattress, I caught the unmistakable scent of another man and knew that Riko had been napping there. Whatever ...

"Is there a story?" I asked, suppressing a yawn with the back of my hand.

Riko shrugged. "Nah, not really. Just my dad being an arsehole. You know? The usual."

"What is it this time?"

"Oh, he wants to know 'the plan' ... you know how it goes."

"I thought you had a plan?"

"Nah, not really."

I didn't think to press Riko on this. I told myself that I'd give him another week before I floated the idea of him paying some rent ...

To tell the truth, I felt kind of sorry for him.

The place Riko had been working made it seem like I had my feet up all day.

It had been a company called Titanium Securities.

Riko told me that every morning they needed to "check in" with their line manager in keeping with the company's "dedication to employees' ongoing mental wellbeing" programme. In practice, this involved filling out a questionnaire which included marking on a one-to-ten scale such items as "professional fulfilment" and "improvement areas". These numbers all summed up into a weird pseudo-scientific daily score defined as a "positivity index". According to Riko, the "positivity index" was supposed to show how positive the employee felt about the day ahead. It was rumoured among Titanium Securities employees that if anyone averaged below an eight for more than a ten-day period, they would be swiftly whisked off to a "mental wellbeing and professional fulfilment" meeting with HR.

It wasn't all bad, though.

They could wear jeans one Friday a month.

And every three months they had "Team Bowling".

As always with Riko — whenever he makes his mind up about something — his resignation had to be sudden and spectacular. On the chosen day, he had turned up for work as usual, going through the positivity index process as he always did. However, that particular day, in the daily meeting with his line manager, he had asked to be scored an "eleven" in each category on the questionnaire. He told me how his line manager had smiled wryly as he had scribbled down a ten beside each criteria.

The scale only went up to ten.

Riko had noticed this and insisted it was corrected.

In fact, he had insisted and insisted until the situation had become very uncomfortable.

As Riko had related the story to me, the details had started to get hazy, but one thing was certain. At some stage, he had started to take off his clothes.

Whenever Riko relayed what he referred to as his "leaving story", I was always blown away by the whole matter-of-factness of his delivery. Not so much as a hint of redness flushed his cheeks. His voice never hesitated, not for a moment, as if each ensuing action was merely a logical progression in a preordained sequence.

27

It seemed that Riko taking off his clothes was the ultimate wildcard. Nobody knew what to do about it.

Riko had simply left his clothes in a pile in the meeting room, calmly strolled out of the office, caught the bus, and gone back home.

He told me later that he believed leaving his work clothes behind had been something akin to a snake shedding its skin. To allow the new skin to show through. To stretch the metaphor to breaking point, I supposed this new skin was what Riko referred to as "the plan".

I took the fact that Riko spent his days prancing about my flat in gym wear as part of a sort of journey to spiritual recovery. He was cleansing his spirit and renewing his sense of self. One thing was for certain, he would never return to Titanium Securities.

Or anywhere else that required a professional reference.

To tell the truth, some days I wondered why I didn't have the courage to do something similar at LifeWare. Blow everything apart.

Except maybe without inflicting my ball sack on innocent bystanders.

Riko slammed the fridge door shut. He held a chocolate yoghurt that I was sure I had bought for myself a few days ago and forgotten about. It was only because my memory was hazy that I failed to question Riko about it. Or that was what I told myself.

"And how was your day?" he asked.

I closed my eyes and then pressed the heels of my hands to my eyelids, giving them a quick massage. When I opened them again my vision was all blurry. Although I hadn't really had time to process what'd happened a few hours earlier, I realised I felt kind of nauseous.

My craving for beer had subsided.

"The system administrator dropped dead."

Chocolate now spread all about his mouth, Riko stepped closer, focused on the yoghurt pot. His tone was nonplussed. As always. "No shit?"

"Yeah. And guess who discovered him?"

"You?" Riko replied, licking the back of the spoon.

"That's why I'm late. I had to speak to the police."

"What time is it?"

"After seven. Seven thirty."

"P.m.?"

"Uh huh ..."

Riko chewed on the spoonful of chocolate yoghurt for several seconds, mulling things over. He focused his gaze back onto me. "That the first time you seen a dead body?"

"Yup." And then, because the silence was becoming awkward, I responded, "Have you ever seen one?"

Riko looked slightly offended for some reason. "You think I'm a serial killer or something? Did the police send you?" He exhaled loudly, a few flecks of chocolate yoghurt ending up on the carpet tile. "Of course I haven't seen a dead body. What sort of a life do you think I lead, man?"

I sighed.

Riko returned to his chocolate yoghurt. "So, what happened to him?"

"I dunno, heart attack?" I replied. "It happened so quick. When I got there, he was already gone. He could've been dead hours and no one noticed. I just ..." — my mind immediately flashed to the tablet I had discovered on Technomancer's desk, and the scantily clad photo of Olivia — "... guess I happened to walk in at the right time. The *wrong* time. I mean, it's a good thing I didn't see him die. But it was too late for me to save him. You get what I mean?"

"Is it true what they say about the smell?"

"The overriding odour was pizza and old farts."

"Ah, a man of culture. Like all IT men," Riko replied. "Then what happened?"

"I phoned the police, and they came. They brought an ambulance, too."

Riko wrinkled his forehead. "An ambulance? That seems kind of pointless."

"Why?"

"I dunno." Riko thought some more. "Maybe they thought he was still alive. That they could save him. Those ambulance people think they're miracle workers, don't they?"

I felt as though I was about to be sucked down into invisible quicksand.

That was how I usually ended up feeling after a conversation with Riko.

"Do they?"

Riko jabbed his spoon at the air to emphasise his point. "I mean, if a guy's dead, he's dead, right?"

"I would've said he was dead, that's what I told the police ... but I'm not a doctor or whoever has to confirm it."

"Yeah, well, they could've just sent a doctor or whoever. There's like a shortage of ambulances or something, isn't there?"

I breathed in deeply, feeling another swill of unease in my stomach.

I wasn't sure if I was really up to a dose of Riko's crazy after the day I'd had.

"Is there?"

"Sure. Resource management." Riko gave a wide grin as if this was some sort of code word that explained everything. "You gotta take care of what you've got, haven't you? It's all about arrogance, you know. People's egos. You've gotta put your foot down somewhere, huh? These ambulance people think they can do anything. But it costs money too. Gotta live in the real world."

A headache bit my frontal lobe. I closed my eyes and massaged my temples — just like I did back in the office when I felt like my head was going to flip its lid.

But I was supposed to be home now.

I should've been relaxed ...

I decided that if this was the hill Riko wanted to die on then I was going to leave him to it.

And I wasn't about to call an ambulance, either ...

"Yeah, I guess," I replied, finally.

In the near distance, I heard Riko crunching the yoghurt pot in his fist then tossing it into the bin; the vaguely violent action apparently meant to draw a line under the point he had just made. I heard the fridge door open again. A brief but pleasant rush of cool air wafted across the room and brushed my cheeks. "You want a beer?" Riko asked.

Just the thought sent a quiver through my stomach. "Nah, I'm okay for now."

"Ah ... good."

I stirred from my introspections. I sat up straight. Opened my eyes again, casting my glare off in the direction of the kitchenette. "Why 'good'?"

"'Cos we're all out."

"Really?" I replied, getting up from the sofa bed where I was sitting, knowing for a fact that I had been out and bought beer the previous evening — as I always did on a Thursday night. It was a system I had so I could be sure that, without fail, there would be a cold beer waiting for me when I got home from work on a Friday.

I trod over to Riko in the kitchenette, my brain slopping against the sides of my skull, seemingly doing its best to break out.

Sure enough, the fridge was empty.

I shifted my gaze to the bin.

Four cans had been crushed and deposited inside.

I caught Riko's eye.

And the two of us understood one another perfectly.

No need for words.

Riko held up his hands. "Okay, okay. I'll admit it. Julie came over, see?"

"Julie?"

"Yeah, you know? The girl from the coffee shop? Frothy Cups?"

I took a moment. It was difficult to use any portion of my imagination after ten-plus hours of office-droning. Me and Riko had gone to Frothy Cups about a week ago. As whenever I go anywhere with Riko, he had ended up chatting with a girl. In this particular case, it had been the one behind the counter. The barista.

I pictured Julie in my mind:

Purple hair. Dyed, of course.

An eyebrow piercing.

A tattoo which ran up her bicep.

... She had also had large breasts, accentuated by the tight-fitting burgundy polo shirt all employees at Frothy Cups had to wear.

I jumbled the pieces together just in time to make sense of the vague dampness and strange odour clinging to the sheets of the sofa bed I had been resting on moments before. "Oh, fucking hell!" I said, the dead beers a fading memory. "Really, Riko?"

Riko knocked the spoon off the kitchen counter and it tinkled at our feet on the checkerboard tiles. I guess I surprised him. "What?" he said. "What is it?"

"Over there!" I pointed at my sofa bed. "What the fuck? I have to sleep here, man! You could at least have changed the sheets." I chewed my tongue, trying my best to keep my anger in. I did pretty well considering, muttering only a dampened, "*Jesus*" at the end.

Riko shifted through a whole host of expressions. I could almost see the cogs turning in his mind as he attempted to manipulate the situation to his advantage. In the end, it looked like I had rumbled him, and I got something that is so rare I had begun to believe it was extinct.

Something resembling an apology.

"I'm sorry, Sparky," he said. "... It just *happened*."

"Stop fucking calling me Sparky! I'm not a bloody electrician!"

Riko rolled his eyes and held up his hand as if he was being the reasonable one. "I'll take care of it, okay? Just calm down. Where'd you keep the spare sheets?"

"I don't *have* any spare sheets!"

"Then how am I supposed to change them?"

I glowered, started to throw up my hands, but only got as far as my shoulders before realising that any show of anger with Riko was in vain. "Argh! It's just a form of expression." I took a deep breath. "When I need to change my sheets, I get up early, stick them in the wash, then hang them up to dry so they're ready by the time I go to bed."

Riko pouted. He has a disarming manner of keeping a cool head when everything around him is kicking off — not unlike his resignation from Titanium Securities. A knack of removing emotion and reducing everything to pure, cold-headed logic.

Or making it *seem* logical.

He's probably some sort of high-functioning sociopath.

"Why don't you just buy some spare sheets, man?"

I resisted the bait. I couldn't help realising that Olivia had once put the same line of argument to me. Logical. There wasn't really a coherent answer except to say I had never been bothered enough to do anything about it.

Maybe *I* was the sociopath …

I managed to keep a lid on my emotions. "Look, Riko, I've had a … a fucking *traumatic* day — I really don't need this." Even though I managed to sound halfway convincing about this, my hesitation took something of the essence away.

To tell the truth, I was either numb to what I had witnessed, or I had taken the experience a little too comfortably in my stride.

Maybe this is how all adults feel.

Nothing shocks them anymore.

Not really.

"Okay, okay," Riko said, his eyes widening as if I was the one acting like a petulant teenager. "I'll take care of it." He brushed past me, out of the kitchenette and to the sofa bed, beginning to strip the sheets. "The way you're carrying on, anyone would think that you bloody killed the bastard!"

I followed him out of the kitchenette and back to the front door.

I bent over my bag and slipped my wallet out from inside.

I made a mental note that I needed to be more careful around Riko.

Who knew what else he was up to behind my back.

"I'm going to the pub," I said, my hand on the front door latch. "There's no beer and I can't be arsed to cook."

Riko wagged his head from side to side as if he was being scolded by a parent. "Don't piss yourself, mate. I'll have it all sorted when you get back. You won't even know anything untoward took place. I promise."

# THE STREET SERMON

As the last of the sun disappeared behind the trees and houses, casting the road in shadow and approaching night, I eyed the wooden sign creaking back and forth on its hinges above the doorway to the pub around the corner from my flat.

Written out in gilt letters below the illustration was the name of the pub:

*The Street Sermon*

The sign had seen better days. The pub had too.

The wood on the sign had had chunks taken out of it, either by careless passing lorries or punters in high spirits who had either hurled heavy objects at it from ground level or else taken a leap and struck it with some blunt weapon. What remained of the sign was rotting away steadily.

The illustration itself was still clear, although its colour had faded greatly in the sun.

The scene was set somewhere around the turn of the twentieth century and depicted what might have once conceivably been the street where the pub was situated. The streets were cobbled and the upper storeys of the Tudor-style, timber-framed buildings leaned in towards one another like spent mattress springs. In the foreground, his back to the viewer, a manic Catholic priest thumped a tatty bible and barked at the people gathered before him. The priest's collar was torn and dangled from his throat. His robes, too, were ripped to shreds. Among those gathered to hear the sermon, I counted merchants, a pair of noblemen's wives, a scattering of street urchins. There was a shabby

34

horse and cart a little way back while, in the far distance, an orange sun blazed, setting on the horizon. In idle moments at work my mind often drifted back to this scene, as if I might garner some extra layer of meaning from it following intense thought.

The bouncers on the door were about what anybody might expect from bouncers. They were dressed in black, bald and measured a solid head and shoulders taller than me.

They were also roughly twice as wide as I was.

I wasn't interested in finding out whether that extra width represented fat or muscle.

I stepped between the pair of them with a sheepish smile, worried that they might ask me for ID, even though the last time I'd been asked for ID must've been five or six years ago.

I guess I was getting old.

Or at least starting to look old.

The wrong side of thirty and all that.

It being a Friday, the pub was totally rammed.

A strong smell of sweaty armpits and perspiring feet greeted me. This mingled with lashings of perfume and aftershave. A heavily distorted electric guitar solo crackled from tinny speakers. Droopy, faded curtains were drawn back from the windows, harnessed by scuffed and dented brass fittings. It had just gone dark out and no one had drawn the curtains so the windows reflected back everything going on inside the pub as if there was some parallel shadow world just beyond the glass. A black mirror.

I tucked in my elbows and weaved through groups of clustered-together office workers in the direction of the bar. A man wearing a red football shirt and tracksuit trousers was leaning over the counter, shouting something possibly abusive at the barman. The barman was currently stooped down at one of the fridges, his back to the man, either unable to hear or actively ignoring him.

The bouncers on the door were taking no interest.

But then again I don't know why I was surprised.

Given all I've seen at the Sermon I knew that a boozed-up, slightly lary man isn't an issue ... until he starts to get physical.

Once the barman was through with the man in the football shirt, I ordered fish and chips. Even though the barman was clearly flustered keeping up with the nonstop activity tonight, he still flashed his eyebrows in surprise at me when I ordered a fizzy orange drink instead of something alcoholic. It *was* Friday, after all. And on any other occasion I would've indulged Friday to the full, only I didn't quite trust my gut to handle adult beverages after the day I'd had.

I flashbacked to the scene.

Treading into Technomancer's office.

Mingled odours of pizza grease, perspiration, flatulence, cardboard.

Olivia's photo on the tablet computer.

*Him*.

Dead.

I halted my train of thought.

The barman handed me a wooden spoon with the number seven scrawled on it in black marker pen. I spotted an empty table in the corner. There were no chairs at the table so on my way over I swiped a chair from beneath the departing behind of a lady in her late forties or early fifties. She was wearing a tight red dress which exposed a lot of wrinkled cleavage. As I backed into my corner, chair in hand, she cackled her way out of the pub on the arm of a lardy bald guy about the same age wearing a black shirt stuffed into a pair of jeans.

Sometimes I wondered if happiness was actually as simple as it looked.

I speared the spoon into a wooden block on the table which also efficiently housed tomato ketchup, vinegar, brown sauce, salt and pepper, and mustard. There was a set of cutlery wrapped up in a paper napkin which was a nice surprise. I wouldn't have to risk giving up my table to go scouting for a knife and fork.

Happy that I had marked my territory, I did what any self-respecting millennial minding his own business does — I slipped out my mobile phone. After about five minutes, someone interrupted me.

"Hey."

To begin with, I thought it was the waitress bringing my food to the table. I sat up straight and looked up from my phone with expectation.

Disappointment quickly followed.

It wasn't the waitress.

And the woman standing there didn't have my fish and chips.

However, I did recognise her.

I took stock of the blue eyes, the delicate pink mouth and the jagged blond hair which bobbed sharply as she moved her head while speaking.

It was Kelly from work.

Kelly is a software engineer. Although there would've been little reason for a tech support advisor like me to be interacting with an engineer, last summer LifeWare HR had had the bright idea of setting up "multi-disciplinary collaborative collectives" throughout the organisation with the target of "fostering inter-departmental relationships".

This had brought the two of us together.

The way the scheme had worked in practice was that groups of five or six members were set up throughout the organisation and each group was given an abstract noun that they were supposed to use as inspiration. Our abstract noun had been "satisfaction".

What each group was expected to deliver was deliberately left flexible. In practice, however, most groups had ended up cobbling together a slide deck summarising their findings. When I had floated the idea of an "interpretative dance" so that we might stand out a little, my joke — it wasn't a good one, granted — had soared over the heads of everyone except Kelly.

Our collaborative group had been obliged to meet for an hour each Friday at 11am. Thankfully, we didn't have anyone who was wildly enthusiastic about our group's aims and so our sessions were mostly reduced to everyone making small-talk and droopily nodding their heads over coffee, sneaking glances at the clock to check how many hours it was before home time.

If nothing else, the group allowed me to see that I wasn't alone.

That work was an equal and universal torture for everyone — no matter their role.

The whole "multi-disciplinary collaborative collectives for fostering inter-departmental relationships" thing got quietly dropped after about four months, consequently just after the HR manager, and driving force behind the project, left on maternity leave.

As I remembered from when I'd seen her for our group sessions, Kelly was wearing a slightly baggy satin blouse over a pair of loose-fitting black trousers. Today, the blouse Kelly wore was a faint pink colour, matching her lipstick. She wore her blouse with three buttons opened, exposing the beginnings of soft white skin at her breast. As I remembered from those meetings, she exuded a slight smell of lemon. She also had on a pair of black skateboard shoes. During one of our meetings I had once asked her how she had managed to get away with such a clear violation of a LifeWare Guiding Principle with regards to appropriate employee dress and appearance. She had asked whether I had ever actually set foot in the IT Department and when I told her I hadn't she had explained that just about anything went from cargo shorts to flip-flops to string vests to those plastic hats with straws and a cup holder on either side. One of her colleagues — Ralph — had even come in one day with vodka bottles in each of the cup holders on his hat. Once satisfied he'd got the reaction he was after, he revealed he had emptied the bottles the night before and filled them with water. Which was kind of what everyone had expected ... All the same, I knew that if I'd tried similar hijinks in my own role, my boss Lucas would've taken firm hold of my shoulder and marched me straight off to an HR meeting.

No joke.

The upshot of the conversation was that Kelly definitely dressed on the smarter side of her colleagues and that a pair of skate shoes made no difference to this. She had also explained away the skateboard shoes by telling me that when she had been a teenager she had been into skateboarding. In actual fact, it was far more than that. She had managed to achieve every teen skateboarder's driving dream:

Sponsorship.

However, soon after she'd turned seventeen she had broken both wrists, her left leg in three places, and knocked out her front teeth. She had never fully got her confidence on her board back after this experience. Understandably, in my view.

She had stopped skating and instead decided to do something about her stellar school performance. That was how she had ended up becoming a software engineer.

During one of our meetings, she had told me about her ultimate goal. That she wanted to go fully freelance, jet off to Bali and rent a beach shack. In her new life, she would get up early, code away the mornings then go surfing in the afternoons.

I had to admit that I was impressed with this. Not particularly the details of the plan she had sketched out — although they certainly sounded extremely pleasant — but the fact that she had a plan at all. It was far more than Riko had.

It was far more than *I* had.

Kelly had gone on to explain that one of the legacies from her skate sponsorship was a wardrobe full of complimentary shoes. And since her shoe size hadn't changed since she had been a teenager, she reasoned that it really didn't make sense for her to ever buy any more shoes.

She had skate shoes to last her a lifetime.

"Oh, hi!" I blabbed out belatedly.

"Is anyone sitting here?" Kelly asked.

I looked at the table, realising there weren't any other chairs. "Uh, no. You're welcome to sit if you can snag something to sit on."

Kelly glanced around before settling on a free chair at a table of men in their seventies, or eighties, nearby. They all looked extremely grumpy and especially hard of hearing as Friday night held The Street Sermon firmly in its fist; all red cheeks and furrowed brows and shaking heads. When Kelly swooped down upon them, however, I watched their features soften to find a young woman in their midst. Within their clutches.

I saw Kelly mouth a thank-you to the men as she carefully extracted the chair, taking care not to knock over any of the assorted ambulatory aides leaning up against the wall beside them.

She tucked her chair in and rested her forearms on the table. She clawed her hands up through her blond hair, widened her eyes and said, "Raaah!" in a gruff whisper, a stifled scream of frustration loud enough for only me to hear.

"Is something the matter?" I asked.

It had been months since we had seen one another for longer than just to say hi out in the corridor. There was no reason for us to come into contact any longer now that we were no longer obliged to submit to those particular whims of HR.

I expected it to feel awkward, but it felt strangely natural.

Actually, to tell the truth, this was the best I had felt all day.

"Oh, you know," Kelly said, rising back up, straightening in her chair. "Work stuff. Pressing palms. Nodding. Smiling. Social interaction in general?"

"I don't think I've seen you in here before."

"Mm, I'm not much of a pub-goer. I usually do yoga on Friday nights." She glanced around. "Everyone seems to have pints. Is that what I should have? Should I go and get a pint?" She looked at me, at the soft drink I had ordered. "That's a kid's drink, isn't it? Can I have one of those? Am I allowed?"

"You're *allowed* to do whatever you want. You're an adult. It's part of the rules."

Kelly drew an invisible square with her index fingers. "'There *are* no rules.'"

I smiled at this. "If you're so adverse to pubs then why aren't you doing yoga?"

"Work thing, like I said. Someone had the bright idea that us 'middle managers'" — she actually made wagging quotation marks with her index and middle fingers here — "should meet once a month and *mingle*. The Middle Managers' Mingle, if you'd ever believe it."

I did my best to conceal my smirk but failed in the end.

She fired a glare at me.

I composed myself. "A chance to share tips? Something like that? How to use and abuse your subordinates?"

40

"Sounds like you've got it in one ... if you just shear off anything useful about the whole experience at all and admit that it's a total shit-shooting fest."

"Gossip o'clock?"

It was Kelly's turn to smirk. "You really do have a way with words ... it is definitely 'gossip o'clock' until someone ends up overindulging and efforts turn to stuffing said person in a taxi home."

"Has that ever been you?" I asked.

Kelly leaned back in her chair. "And what makes you think I'd tell you if it was?"

I felt my cheeks redden slightly, only realising that she was joking a hair later as a slight smirk turned the corner of her mouth.

She sat forward in her chair again, closing one eye as if lining me up in her sights. "Anyway, how come you're not climbing ladders, rising to heady heights and such, you know, like the rest of us?"

For a second I was winded by this remark.

She had a point.

We were about the same age.

And Kelly was clearly doing far better in her career than I was.

Then again, she *was* a professional. With, like, actual *marketable* skills. She was a living reminder that my degree in medieval history had been a colossal waste of time.

I didn't even *like* history, medieval or otherwise.

And I suppose my final grade had reflected this ...

I could see the waitress bringing over my plate of fish and chips.

My mouth started to salivate.

The waitress set the plate before me then rushed off someplace else.

Realising I had to answer the question before I tucked in, I replied, "I guess I never wanted it as much as everyone else."

For a second or so, I absorbed the comforting beige colours on the plate.

Golden battered cod.

Thick-cut potato wedges.

Salt sparkling all over.

And then, for variation, a verdant pool of mushy peas on the side.

I breathed in the greasy, oily goodness and my mind was assaulted by an uncontrollable gushing firehose of childhood memories.

All of them featuring fish and chips.

It was impossible to separate one memory from another.

They were all just right there united by the salty, fatty goodness, or badness ... depending on your perspective ...

I hardly had a chance to bask in the warmth emanating from the plate, let alone try to bring one of those childhood memories into any sort of sharp focus, before someone — not Kelly — broke my concentration.

"Marcus?"

I glanced up and saw my boss, Lucas, standing over me.

My stomach fell.

And my appetite dissipated.

Lucas has bleached blond hair, thick sideburns, also meticulously bleached, and wears an earring in his left ear. His figure is trim, although certainly on the skinny side. He relishes detailing his weekend cycling exploits at work whenever he gets the chance. He goes on "rides" with the Retro Giants, a group of men in their early forties who have no family or other personal ties. From what I gather, they mostly dedicate themselves to procuring old-style racing bicycles, doing them up — or employing bike mechanics to do this for them — and then trying to kill themselves on said bikes via physical exertion. This is all painstakingly documented via the usual online social mediums, of course.

Although I wasn't interested at all personally, on several occasions I had caught one of my colleagues, Adriana, browsing Lucas's social media profile during her lunchbreak, flicking through monochrome photos of the Retro Giants' latest outing.

In more than a few of them, the lycra-clad men were photographed stripped to the waist, hairy pigeon chests on show, grinning, sweating, suckling on water bottles in bright sunlight.

I knew I shouldn't have been so bitter.

And I wasn't really.

It was my own fault.

I really needed a hobby of my own.

Just like all the other office workers in the pub, Lucas was still in his work suit which, despite the generally buttoned-up-ness of LifeWare, always carried a sense of bohemian flair.

As always, he wore a clean white shirt. Today, though, he had opted for a dark purple jacket lined with a fine woven pattern that would've looked at home in the sixties. A purple tie hung from his collar with a matching design. He hadn't loosened his tie at all despite it being hours since the office had closed for the day's business.

Lucas was never less than flawlessly turned out. To be honest, I wondered why he had stuck around for so long somewhere so decidedly unglamorous as LifeWare.

Maybe it was good for his ego.

Because neither I, or anybody else, was going to challenge him for Best Dressed any time soon.

Lucas flipped a glance at Kelly, who looked awkward all of a sudden.

His gaze fell upon me.

He smiled lightly, in what I imagined he thought was a paternal sort of way. "I didn't expect to see you here." He looked to Kelly, as if waiting for an explanation. When one wasn't forthcoming, he addressed her. "You didn't get the group message, did you?"

"Guess not?" she replied.

"We thought it best to cancel the meet-up this evening ... given the circumstances."

"Oh," Kelly replied. "What circumstances?"

Lucas caught my eye and his smile faded completely. The control he exercised over his expressions had to border on psychopathic. "Marcus hasn't told you?"

Kelly gave me a weirded-out look. "No? Told me what?"

I flushed slightly, though I wasn't really sure there was anything to feel sorry about.

I'd been speaking with Kelly for a grand total of three or four minutes.

Lucas has a real knack for wrenching every last drop of awkwardness from any social encounter. He jabbed his tongue between his lips, clasped his hands together at his chest, as if in some quasi-religious gesture of respect. "John Horsham passed away this afternoon, unfortunately."

Kelly took a moment to absorb this. Her mouth was kind of like watching a vacuum cleaner in reverse. "...Technomancer?" And then, looking at me. "John?"

Lucas nodded dolefully.

"Jesus," she replied.

"And Marcus, here," Lucas went on, "was the one to find him."

As I felt more heat rising in my cheeks, I sensed the plate of fish and chips before me starting to go cold.

"Really, Marcus?" Kelly said. "That's awful."

All of a sudden I felt quite squirmy, to have these two people making sympathetic faces at me. One of them genuine. I averted their gaze, shifting my attention back to my food. "I just came across him. I was having computer issues — after everyone else had gone home. It ... must've happened a few minutes before I got to him."

Neither Kelly or Lucas said anything.

I wanted one of them to make a joke about me having murdered him or say something to break the tension. But I could tell that neither one of them knew what to say.

So I took it upon myself.

"He wasn't the healthiest of guys, was he?"

Several more seconds of silence followed.

Okay, it hadn't been the most appropriate thing to say ... especially considering that I had a plate of fish and chips sitting right in front of me.

Lucas was first to speak. "No. Still, you've had a pretty crap run if you don't make it to eighty these days."

Kelly remained silent. Her expression stonelike.

More than anything I wanted Lucas to disappear.

I wanted to get on with my dinner, go home, tuck myself up in bed ... which hopefully — by some minor miracle — now had clean sheets.

44

Lucas took hold of my shoulder with his disarmingly strong grip.

I suppose cyclists develop a strong grip from all the clinging on they do ...

"Don't rush it," Lucas said, his tone of voice firm and clearly produced on command from some management training course. "Sometimes these things can be delayed."

I decided that it was one thing for Lucas to walk all over me at work — he *was* my boss after all — but it was quite another for him to do it on my free time. "I hardly knew him," I replied. "What *things*?"

Lucas exchanged glances with Kelly as if he was speaking with a moron.

Perhaps he was.

"Trauma," Lucas said. "Often it will sneak up on you when you least expect it. Flashbacks, that sort of thing. The point is, if you're not feeling up to it on Monday, then don't just drag yourself in on my account, all right?"

I thought about what Lucas was saying. I could remember the one day I hadn't made it into work during my whole time at LifeWare. It had been the middle of December and I'd been struck down by a horrible lurgy and was unable to make it out of bed one Friday. When I had phoned in that morning, Lucas had been all chirpy, happy to accept my explanation, but when I had turned up to work the following Monday, still feeling bunged-up, I'd had to sit in an airless room with him and someone from HR to talk through whether there were any arrangements that could be made to help me in my return to work.

Throughout the whole meeting, Lucas made it seem as though I had got lost in the Amazonian jungle for several months and turned up that day out of the blue.

There was no way I wasn't coming into work on Monday.

Not unless I won the lottery.

I was not going to give Lucas the chance to put a black mark against my name on the mental wellbeing chart, or whatever other "tool" managers used to keep tabs on their staff.

I made a grin-and-bear-it face, hoping Lucas would believe he had got his message across. He let go of my shoulder in any case and checked

45

his watch. Although I don't know an awful lot — or *anything* — about watches, I judged from its all-round chunkiness and the amount of extra dials that it was an expensive one. "I wouldn't be here tonight either if I hadn't been meeting someone," Lucas said, beaming his smile at me and Kelly as if this had been the most pleasurable coincidence in recent memory. "I think I'll go get a drink." He glanced at Kelly, making a drinking motion and raising his eyebrows.

When I looked at Kelly again, I saw she had turned pale.

I guessed she was in shock.

She broke from her daze. Her colour improved slightly. "Oh, no. I'm fine, thanks. Actually" — she freed her phone from her handbag, tapped and then read the screen — "my boyfriend isn't far off. He's having a dinner with the 'boys'." She shot me a look. Found a smile from somewhere. It looked authentic but I was sure there was still a note of sadness there. "I know I shouldn't burst in on a lads' evening but last time it was so hilarious. He made me promise not to do it again. *Ever.*" She dropped her voice so that only I could hear her. "I told them about the time he used my nostril-hair clipper on his arse crack. I guess he thought I wouldn't notice ... except next time I used the clipper it smelled of arse."

I couldn't help but chuckle at this.

Her actions a little too hyperactive to completely convince that she was calm, Kelly got up from her seat. "Gentlemen, I'll see you on Monday."

My heart hung in my throat as I watched Kelly steer her way between the merry Friday-night drinkers, and out of the Street Sermon.

That left me and Lucas alone.

In awkward silence.

Well, silence broken only by scraping chairs, chinking glasses and chuntering, drunken laughter.

"I see you've already charged your glass," Lucas said, nodding to my orange-flavoured soft drink. He looked at his watch again, glanced to the door. "Guess I'll be seeing you on Monday, too. All being well, of course."

"Yup," I replied. "See ya."

Lucas nodded and mercifully pissed off.

I watched him all the way back to the bar.

I had almost forgotten about the fish and chips sitting on the table before me.

My food *was* certainly cold now.

Trying to make the best of a bad situation, I lashed the chips with vinegar and yet more salt before spunking a dollop of ketchup on the fish. I'd chewed about halfway through my mediocre pub supper when I took stock of Friday night at the Street Sermon.

It was unavoidable and I hated myself for it, but my focus lasered in on Lucas, standing at the bar. There was that unshakeable morbid fascination with seeing your boss out in the wild, I suppose. He was wearing that signature smarmy smirk of his. As he always did when speaking to people, he held his shoulders back, puffed out his pigeon chest, and dipped his right hand into his pocket. I suppose he'd learned that from a book or magazine article.

Just like his sense of dress and his retro cycling hobby.

He clasped a pint of lager, fizzing away on the bar counter, speaking with someone.

A girl.

A *woman*.

It took a moment for the observation to properly spark across all the relevant synapses and neurons. To realise that what I was seeing wasn't some sort of illusion.

A *hallucination*.

That this wasn't the single weirdest day in the History of Mankind.

Or, then again, maybe it was ...

Because, standing at the bar, in a cocktail dress the colour of a pickle, was my ex-girlfriend Olivia. Although I knew I must've looked like a prize dick, I couldn't help staring.

She had had her hair cut shorter. It was tighter to her face and sashayed with her movements. As she *touched* Lucas gently on his arm. When Lucas rested his palm flat against her bare back, she made no sign of flinching. It was only when some worse-for-wear office worker, grinning from ear to ear, shoved his face up to mine and knocked on the table that I returned to the present. "Knock-knock! Anybody home?!"

"Hmm?" I said.

"Mine if I take thith chair? Nobody sitting here, istha?"

"No, take it — it's fine."

As I continued to stare at my boss and my ex-girlfriend at the bar, I was only peripherally aware of the man retreating from the table with what had been Kelly's chair.

I pushed my plate away, deciding I had lost my appetite completely this time.

I hoped against hope that Riko had sorted out my bed.

# KNOCK-KNOCK

I wasn't entirely sure why I knocked first before turning the key in the door to *my own flat*. Maybe it was just indicative of good breeding. As if Riko's privacy mattered at all to me.

As if I wanted to give him warning that I had arrived.

On this occasion, though, even with the knocking, he wasn't fast enough.

I suppose beer and sex and an afternoon nap had slowed his reflexes.

The sofa bed was made up.

That was a positive.

Unfortunately I could also see that the same sheets were on the bed.

I'm no expert, but I was fairly sure Riko hadn't had enough time to get the sheets washed and dried during the hour or so I had been out. And then there was the fact that he was lying on top of the sofa bed holding the computer tablet in his hands.

The one I had snatched from Technomancer's office.

He was so engrossed by whatever he was looking at on the screen that he hardly noticed me arrive. I decided to prompt him. "Hey! What the hell are you doing?"

Riko startled.

For a fraction of a second, there was pure panic in his eyes. And then — perhaps noticing it was only me — the look disappeared and the familiar unflustered expression returned. I could just imagine that expression when he'd resigned from Titanium Securities.

"Switch it off — switch it off now!" I said, pacing towards him.

Riko held up a hand. "Relax, it's fine."

"It's *not* fine!" I replied. "I got that thing from Technomancer's office."

"Techno ... *who?*"

"The system administrator. The guy who died. The guy I walked in on dead."

"Oh, so it's stolen?" Riko asked, allowing the tablet to fall slightly in his grasp as if stolen property was infectious.

I thought about the solid reasons I had come up with for swiping it from Technomancer's office. He had got access to my phone.

He had had pictures from *my* phone.

... Pictures of Olivia.

Who I had just seen ...

In the pub ...

... With *Lucas*.

"You feeling okay, bro?" Riko asked. "Look like you've seen a ghost. Want me to call someone? There's a special number for psychos, isn't there?"

I paused my advance, breathed in deeply, sighed out. "Just give it to me. I don't know *why* I took it ... but we shouldn't mess with it."

"Are you planning to give it back?"

"I ... don't know ..." I arrested my reply before I totally threw away my Big Chance "... Yes. Y*es*, I am."

"But the guy's dead."

"I'll give it to his relatives. It might be in his will, for all we know."

Riko switched his focus back to the screen. "Dude, have you had a proper look at what this thing can do? It's amazing. I mean, Jesus, the way you go on about LifeWare it's like it's some brain drain, office-droning shite ... but this thing is awesome. It's like hacking for idiots."

I trod up to Riko, vaguely hoping that by standing over him I might come off as a modicum more intimidating. "I don't think it's the sort of thing that LifeWare would endorse. I'd say this looks more like a passion project." I paused a moment, sniffed the air. "You didn't wash my bedsheets, did you?"

"Uh" — Riko smiled inanely — "I thought about it. You were right. We'll do it tomorrow, like you said. Get up early and get them washed."

"Or you could buy me some new ones? Like *you* suggested?"

"My bank balance might disagree with that idea."

I allowed the tension to fizzle out. Riko was expert at diluting or diverting an argument. I told myself that once I got the tablet back in my hands, and safely out of his reach, we would start into that Serious Chat I had promised myself we would have.

These living arrangements couldn't go on forever.

"Check this out," Riko said.

Telling myself to bide my time, maybe to snatch the tablet out of his hands if the opportunity presented itself, I looked at the screen. "What the hell are you doing?"

Riko had up a computer desktop. It was filled to bursting with icons.

The mess sent my OCD senses tingling.

"What is this?" I asked. "Whose computer is this?"

"Dunno."

"Jesus, Riko, you really are a fount of knowledge."

Riko wrinkled his brow as he jabbed the touch screen. "I'll show you how I did it in a minute, okay? First let me show you what I found."

"This is definitely illegal, Riko. You know that?"

"So's stealing." He carried on speaking before I could correct him. "Come on, Sparky, live a little. We might get rich, or something."

"Or something."

Riko tapped a few times on one of the folders on the computer desktop.

It was ambiguously titled, "Gnomes".

"This is like getting inside somebody else's goddamn mind, Spark. It's some really weird shit, I swear."

The folder had opened out into a series of sub-folders. I saw countless sub-categories of gnomes represented, "Garden", "Festive", "Novelty", among others.

Riko scrolled down. "This is the one I want to show you. Check this shit out."

He tapped on a folder which was titled, "Love".

A mosaic of ornamental gnomes in what seemed like every possible incarnation of the *Karma Sutra* raked my eyeballs.

I actually audibly gasped. "Ahh!"

Riko gave me a playful punch in the chest. "Weird, huh? Told you, Sparky."

I found myself fixated upon a certain couple of gnomes who were performing the sexual position I had been reliably informed was known as the Sixty-Nine.

Aside from the fact that both gnomes had been painted naked — and both were bearded, and so presumably male — it seemed pretty PG.

Well, PG does seem to cover a pretty large field these days ...

Still, the question remained.

"... Why?" I said, the word escaping from my increasingly hoarse throat.

Riko shrugged. "Takes all different types, I guess." He looked at me more closely. "Spark, you've gone all pale. Come on, man? Have you really led such a sheltered life?"

"Whose computer is this?" I asked.

Again, he shrugged.

"Can we go back?" I asked.

He offered me the tablet.

Before taking the tablet, I felt a moment of hesitation. No two ways about it, we *were* handling stolen goods. And Riko had surely broken about a dozen laws doing what he had just done. Although it was un-deniably weird, I didn't think that the person we were spying on had broken any laws. I don't imagine obscenity litigation stretches to cover terracotta. But then again I wasn't a lawyer ... and if I had been I probably wouldn't ever have gotten into this situation in the first place. I would've been living somewhere better.

And probably still have a girlfriend.

And probably have lost touch with Riko ...

You know, the kinds of things that go along with not being a customer service rep at some third-rate software developer.

Riko shifted up on the sofa bed, making room for me. He patted the spot he had vacated as if I was a Labrador he was cajoling to get up and snuggle with him.

Of all the things Riko had talked me into over the years, I was determined not to get myself into any sort of situation which might end up with him spooning me.

All the same, feeling like a Labrador or not, I sat and took the tablet.

A little voice at the back of my mind told me the sensible thing to do was to run off right now. I might not get another chance. And yet, a louder, dumber, voice told me that I should check out just what this thing was capable of ...

"You can go back to the previous folder like this," Riko said, leaning over.

"You're speaking to me like I don't spend all day wrangling with tech."

"Oh, sorry," Riko replied, backing away theatrically, and adding with a deep note of sarcasm, "I forgot you're a computer whizz kid. That's why LifeWare had to have you."

I gave him a fiery, lingering look, daring him to push his luck just a little further. To see just how much further he could lean on me before I finally broke and went berserk.

Everybody else had lost their patience with him at one time or another.

But not me.

Perhaps I'll get canonised.

At the top left corner of the screen, there was a menu icon, three straight lines.

I tapped.

At the top of the screen, an information bar informed me that I was currently accessing "Mildreth Victoria Loaves PC".

"That's the lady who lives in the basement," I said.

Riko arched an eyebrow. "Who ever would've guessed?"

"I dunno. Maybe I had my suspicions."

I never had.

She seemed like a nice lady.

Just a normal, you know, boring lady.

She even made me that cup of tea and was polite about my vomiting right on her doorstep.

I guess that shows me up for the judgemental prick I am.

Riko carried on. "How'd it be if we went out and got some really kinky gnome costumes and just showed up on her doorstep one day? Huh?"

Like a parent doing their level best not to indulge their child, I tried to keep a straight face. But I was struggling. I forced my attention back onto the tablet.

On the menu before me, there were several technical terms I didn't quite comprehend — not that I was going to let on lest Riko think me less of a "whizz kid". In the end, I tapped on the one which read, "Close Session".

The tablet screen flickered back to its home menu.

A little circle spun around itself like a digital worm chasing its tail.

When it finished loading, a list of devices appeared.

Half a dozen in all.

Devices which belonged to other people in this building, I suppose.

Among them, I saw a particularly bizarre name, "R_2_Tha_Kay_Oh_Baby".

I caught Riko's eye.

He just gave me another of his shrugs.

As I saw my own phone — boringly Christened "M L Raisin's Phone" — appear on the list of available devices, something occurred to me.

The pictures of Olivia ...

"Riko?" I said. "When you picked this thing up ... what was on the screen?"

"Why?"

"It's just a question. Answer it."

Riko met my eye, pouted, looked at the tablet. "Nothing. I mean, just that. The home screen. What you're looking at now. All I did was tap on one of the options. On 'Mildreth Victoria Loaves PC'. Thought it sounded like some kinda person from Tudor times, or something."

I couldn't quite read whether or not he was telling the complete truth, but I told myself that if he *had* accessed my phone via the tablet, then he would've gloated about it endlessly. And, anyway, surely my phone would've been out of range while I'd been at the pub. I just had to hope that the tablet hadn't saved anything from my phone on it.

I'd have to take a proper look later.

"What'd we do now, Sparkly?" Riko asked, treating me to another from the long list of his slight variations on my nickname.

I stared at the screen. All the devices there. When I spoke, I was really talking to myself. "It really is hacking for idiots. All we've got to do to get access is tap on any of these devices. Then we're in." I glanced up. "This is definitely illegal. No two ways about it."

"Take it to the police, then. Like you said?"

"Yeah."

I could feel Riko's gaze still upon me. "You should shut it down, too," he said. "Looks like the battery's running low."

I glanced at the battery level in the top corner of the screen.

Riko was telling the truth.

It seemed the longest few seconds of my life as I pressed the Standby button.

As before, the screen went blank.

And that same sun symbol appeared.

Then the screen returned to shiny blackness.

I held on tight to the tablet, still feeling as if Riko might somehow contrive to sneak it away from me if I gave him so much as a sliver of an opportunity. It was time for some strategic distraction. "I saw Olivia at the Street Sermon."

Riko straightened up. "Really? Are you getting back together?"

At first I thought he was concerned. And for a fleeting moment I was somewhat touched that deep down he cared about my wellbeing. I blame the long day for making my reactions so numb. The truth struck belatedly. Of course. What he was *concerned* about was giving up his spot on the kitchen floor. It was the sort of situation Olivia was likely to bring to an abrupt end. I eyeballed him. "No. We hadn't *arranged* to meet up. We didn't even speak. She didn't even see me there ... I don't think so, anyway."

"Why was she there, then?" he asked.

"I don't know. She's a person, you know? Like anybody else. She has a *life.*" I rose from the sofa bed, taking the tablet with me. "I also bumped into my boss. Lucas."

As I busied myself in the kitchenette, hoping to find somewhere to stash the tablet out of sight, Riko stared at the wall, apparently piecing things together. "Sounds almost like they had some sort of surprise party planned."

"Hmm?" I replied, eyeing up one of the cabinets, and wondering if there was a hidden shelf within where I could safely conceal the tablet.

"Yeah," Riko continued, "like it was your birthday or something." A pause. "It's not your birthday, is it?"

Realising my kitchenette was so pitifully small that there was nowhere to hide anything, I straightened up. "No, Riko. It's not my birthday. But thanks for asking."

"Huh," Riko said, clearly stumped by this unsolvable mystery.

I decided to press on. Talking to Riko was better than speaking to a brick wall.

But not by much.

"Olivia was with Lucas at the bar. They were ... it looked like it was a date."

Riko blinked rapidly. As if clearing a delusion. "Really? That doesn't add up."

"Dunno. Stranger things have happened. We do all live in the same city. Boy meets girl. It's not impossible."

"Weird, though."

It took some effort to keep my voice firm but I managed it. "Definitely."

I decided not to say anything about seeing Kelly at the pub.

I hadn't mentioned her to Riko previously and it would only lead to more confusion in his already addled brain. I still held the tablet in my hands, looking increasingly awkward.

Riko picked up on this. "What're you going to do with it next?" he asked.

I had thought things over.

I needed to do the right thing.

"Turn it in. Tell the truth. Or ... well, something like the truth. I'll say Technomancer came over to fix something on my PC — that he left it behind. I was in shock so ... I just stashed it in my bag, took it home."

"They'll understand that."

56

"Hope so. It's pretty much the truth."

"Sparky?"

"Uh-huh?"

"You don't need to bother hiding the tablet. I won't do anything else with it. Go ahead and leave it in your work bag. I won't touch it. Promise. I was wrong to take it out in the first place. Sorry."

I looked at Riko, half expecting to see some wry, sharp sarcasm in his eye, but he actually seemed to be speaking sincerely. That was a first. Riko giving me something like an apology. He put me in mind of a repentant child trying to make good with a parent.

He came across as almost ... endearing.

Was this how he acted around his *actual* parents?

Jesus. Where did that leave me?

With a sigh my shoulders drooped and my stomach gurgled. In retrospect, I probably shouldn't have left my dinner unfinished at the Sermon.

I plodded over to my work bag and slipped the tablet inside.

I told myself that even if Riko was playing me for a fool, there was a limit to the damage he would be able to do. The battery was nearly dead and I hadn't had the brainwave to pilfer a charger along with the tablet.

"Okay," I said. "I'm gonna turn in."

Riko remained where he was.

On the sofa bed.

Unmoved.

Stuck in a world of his own.

"Riko? The sleeping mat's in the kitchen. That's where you're sleeping. Remember?" I sighed again. "At least at night."

Riko bounced up with the sort of vigorous energy that can only come from satisfied sexual desire and a lack of work-related stress.

*Lucky bastard.*

Once I'd undressed, got in beneath my smoothed-over but still-soiled sheets, I listened to Riko's rhythmic heavy breathing, getting deeper and deeper. The aural sensation was a little homoerotic for my tastes. I was surprised when he spoke, thinking he had drifted off minutes earlier.

I was almost asleep myself. His voice breached the very fringes of my consciousness but it was definitely there.

"Spark? Are you asleep yet?"

I mumbled.

"Thanks for taking me in. It means a lot. You're a true friend." He paused, as if the sense of cringe was too much for him to go on. He managed to compose himself, however, as only Riko seems able to do. "Trust me, if things are ever different, I'll do the same for you. I promise. Just like I'm not going to touch that tablet." Another pause. "Are we good?"

I turned over, catching an unpleasant whiff of Riko's body odour. It was mixed in with the smell of coffee and jasmine, which I imagined Julie from Frothy Cups was responsible for. There was also the hint of the sweet, plasticky smell of condom mixed up with body fluids. I grimaced a moment, waited for my stomach to settle and then replied.

"Uh-huh."

# THE ROUTINE

I t was one of those dreams which is annoyingly lucid. One of those dreams where you know that you are definitely dreaming and yet you're unable — or unwilling — to wake up and bring it to a halt. I suppose with these sorts of dreams — half-remembered memories of something that happened a long time ago — there's a morbid sort of fascination around finding out whether it's all going to end just like it did in real life or if your subconscious has some — hopefully happier — resolution to put forward.

It was the first year of university.

Cheap lager cut through the air amid the buzz of university students' conversation.

Everyone was thoroughly enjoying their Tuesday evening at Union Station, the bar area of the University Student Union which also provided a cultural venue for all manner of student events throughout the week and at the weekend. More often than not that took the form of an Open Mike Night. Long-locked boys in their late teens, early twenties, warbling away while strumming an acoustic guitar on the raised platform that served as a stage was not an uncommon occurrence.

I wouldn't normally turn up at those nights. I've never been much of a musician, although I went through a phase of playing guitar when I was about fourteen, fifteen years old. And the thought of performing in front of other people has always sickened me to the stomach. Or so I had thought until I had spotted the poster pinned up to the noticeboard as I had been leaving a lecture on the Medieval Warm Period in my second week at university, several months ago.

I had stopped dead in my tracks, in fact.

My action had been so sudden, so unexpected, that someone had bumped into me from behind. They — I didn't deign to even look at them long enough to ascertain whether it was a man or a woman — had apologised profusely even though I was clearly at blame. I guess people who choose to study Medieval History are the same type of people who tend to be conflict-averse which is ironic given the quantity of bloody battles involved in studying the subject.

It was the poster headline which caught my attention:

*Comedy Night*

It had triggered something further back in my memory.

And I wondered why not ...

This was university, after all.

A new start.

Nobody knew me here.

And I could be whoever I wanted to be ...

The comedy urge had happened when I had been about sixteen years old.

I'm not really sure where it came from.

I had been on study leave, revising for my exams, going through my textbooks for the thousandth time, committing everything I possibly could to memory so I could later regurgitate it upon my poor, unsuspecting exam paper. I guess my examiner was to be pitied the most seeing as he or she would eventually be the one to have to look upon my exam paper and attempt to draw out some kind of meaning.

One day, as I had been cracking through my revision, my mind had drifted.

This wasn't an uncommon occurrence.

However, this particular time my reaction *was* uncommon.

While I would usually find myself reaching for whatever book was my current bedtime reading and flipping through a few more pages, or else tapping away at some video game or other, this time I found myself scratching away on my notepad.

*Writing.*

Drawing thoughts directly from my brain and depositing them on paper.

It took me a while to realise exactly what I was writing.

When I reached the bottom of the page, there was no doubt about it, though.

It was a stand-up comedy routine.

I had no idea where it had come from.

I'd never been all that interested in comedy. I guess I always enjoy a good stand-up segment, and I had gone through a particular phase when I had been borderline obsessed with a comedian called Heinrick Lee who mostly riffed off his mixed-race German and South Korean ancestry. I'm not totally sure why his comedy chimed with me so well given that I'm neither German or South Korean, or anything other than a typical Anglo-Saxon male.

Maybe it was the funny voices?

In any case, that obsession had reached its peak and fizzled out back when I had been fourteen or fifteen, around the time when I had put the guitar down for the final time.

I hadn't spent much time listening or otherwise interacting with comedy ever since.

However, as I had sat back in my desk chair, my biology textbook discarded to one side, forgotten for the time being, I speculated that this experience had been akin to automatic writing.

Or maybe even some form of therapy.

The stuff had just poured out of me.

I did wonder for a few anxious moments whether I might be channelling some sort of unquiet spirit, sitting on my shoulder, whispering *stuff* into my ear.

Thankfully, though, even by that age, I had studied enough science — enough to last me a lifetime — so that my critical-thinking skills were pretty well honed. I knew in my bones that it was at best fanciful to believe in ghosts and at worst delusional.

As I had read over what I'd scribbled down, I chuckled to myself a few times.

Once I even broke into a full-on belly laugh.

My mum soon came knocking on my bedroom door insisting I stop whatever it was I was doing and return to my revision. Because revision was a serious business.

No laughter present or required.

To tell the truth, I wasn't sure what was worse. That I wasn't doing revision or that I was laughing at my own jokes ... In the end, I had returned to my biology revision, but that page remained. All that *stuff* which had poured out of me.

I had taken a year out before going to university. I had worked at the local post sorting office, living at home and raising money for my studies. During the day at that monotonous job, sifting through birthday cards, bills and court summons, I would find myself imagining bits and pieces to add to that page. The page, which I had dubbed — of course only to myself — The Routine, I had folded up and safely inserted at the back of a dusty, unused hardbound dictionary. The dictionary had been signed and dedicated to me by Uncle Egbert on the occasion of my baptism. I had no recollection of Uncle Egbert and he had one of those names which made you think twice before asking your parents ...

Throughout that year, I had come home, post codes still branded upon my mind's eye, and scribble down another line or two to the bottom of The Routine.

As the year wound on, I ended up with three, four pages of material — two double-sided pieces of A4. Sitting back one Saturday, at a bit of a loose end having just completed the latest instalment of Dragon Queen, my favourite gaming franchise, I looked over The Routine and realised that I needed to work it up into some sort of structure.

Something which made sense.

On the internet, I read about basics of formulating a comedy routine but that all seemed so sterile. I watched more of Heinrick Lee's routines, watching for patterns of how he set things up and then knocked them down ... how he sprung surprises.

There was a lot of scribbling over those pages of A4.

Several looping arrows and more than a handful of crossings-out.

About halfway through my year out, working at the sorting office, waiting for the spectre of university to descend, I felt as though I had put together something that worked.

It was around that time that I realised I needed to practise out loud.

It was all very well to have it written down but — as I had learned from observing Heinrick — so much was down to how you said it rather than what you said.

And so, when I was certain nobody was in earshot, I took to practising in my bedroom mirror. Why I wanted to look myself in the eye while reciting The Routine, I'm not quite sure, although I kind of think the idea was that I was performing for a one-man audience.

One day, believing I was alone in the house, and seeing this as a golden opportunity to get in some practice on The Routine, I had gone to my bedroom mirror.

I had been going for about five minutes — complete with shouting and some screaming — when I heard a flushing toilet in the distance of the house.

Footsteps on the landing.

In my bedroom doorframe appeared my older sister Edwina's boyfriend, Ted.

Believing I was alone, I had seen no point in shutting the bedroom door.

To say Ted wore a startled expression was an understatement. He looked truly traumatised ... as if he had walked in on me ... well, doing something else entirely. "Uh, are you ... okay, Marky?" Ted had said.

I can still recall the jolt up my spine as I had taken stock of him standing there.

The look of total surprise spread across his features.

He was wearing a white V-neck t-shirt over a pair of blue jeans, his long, pale feet jabbed into a pair of flip-flops. His eyes fell upon the piece of paper in my hand — The Routine — and he scratched the top of his head as if in deep thought. "Jesus, Marky. I was on the pot and thought you were having a fit or something."

Finally, I got over the shock. "I didn't realise Edwina was here ... I didn't think anyone was ..."

"Oh, hey!" Ted said, eyes wide, taking a step back, "She's not here ... I mean, she was this morning but I ..." He went slightly red.

I knew that although Ted had started staying over at some unspecified time in the past year, it hadn't exactly been cleared by my parents. In fact, I was fairly sure that I had unwittingly stumbled into some sort of an omertà when I had gone down for a glass of water one evening and spotted my sister letting Ted in through the back door.

Ted composed himself and carried on. "I stayed over last night. Over-slept a bit. She'll be back later." He closed one eye in a weird, TV-actor wink. "You're not gonna say anything to your parents, are you?"

"It's okay," I replied, "I'm seventeen, I'm not twelve."

Ted nodded at this, clearly relieved.

My sister, Edwina, was studying a vocational course in lighting design at the local regional college. That was where she had met Ted who was taking a carpentry course. Their plans, or so my sister's monologues declared whenever she managed to get me on my own long enough to dish them out, detailed plans for the two of them to start a company de-signing film sets or other kinds backdrops, you know, for photo sessions, weddings, things like that just in case Hollywood didn't come knocking. As with most teenage ambitions, though, things hadn't quite worked out.

My sister was now a middle-manager in a recruitment firm in the city while the last I had seen of Ted was when I had come home a couple of years later one Christmas from university. As I had emerged from the train station I had seen Ted dressed as a parking warden clearly musing the question of just where he was supposed to stick the parking fine he was dishing out to a scooter. Although I didn't stick around to find out, I assume he had eventually pasted the fine to the seat ... that seemed the obvious place to me.

Maybe that was why I was at university and he was a parking warden.

Or perhaps it had something to do with Ted being chilled out and not some geared-up academically minded weirdo ... Somewhere in between probably lay the truth.

That particular day, the day that Ted heard me going through The Routine, Edwina told me later that Ted had called in sick to his classes so he could go and rehearse with his band Savage Packages ahead of a gig they had had that evening.

In the end, Savage Packages had failed to get a record deal and had disbanded.

Ted had also failed to graduate from his carpentry course, scuppering his and Edwina's dreams for their company and launching Edwina on her path into recruitment.

"What were you ... ?" Ted began, his eyes falling onto the paper once more. "Is it like a ... a song or something?"

A flush filled my cheeks.

I set the page down on my desk.

Did my best to smile.

"Nah, it's nothing. Just a ... a .. revision technique?"

My tone of voice hardly sounded convincing but it was too late ... I had already spoken.

"I thought you took your exams last year?" Ted asked.

Self-satisfied me, I had smugly believed that Ted had left mainstream education and promptly forgotten everything about it.

Apparently not.

"Retakes?" I responded, not sounding at all convincing.

Ted gave a kind of half nod. His mouth latched open briefly as if he was going to say something to this but instead he hooked his thumb in the direction of Edwina's bedroom. "I'm, uh, gonna go get ready for practice, okay? Sorry to, you know ... butt in like this. Shouldn't have said anything. I ... it's not good when you don't realise there's someone else in the house, you know?"

"Yeah ..." I replied.

Finally the cringe proved too much for either of us to bear and, flashing an apologetic smile, Ted shifted out of view. That was probably the last thing resembling a conversation I had had with Ted. Probably one of the last times I'd seen him, the whole parking-warden scene apart. As I had flipped on my bedroom TV I had tried not to think about how the first thing that Ted was bound to do was tell my sister what he had caught me doing.

The lighting in the bar was white.

Too bright and too even.

It was all a little too much like being in a classroom.

I imagined the university used the same bulbs in the bar area as they did for the rest of the campus. That saving on a bulk order probably sent a tingle through the ball sack of some management accountant in the university's finance division. The windows in the bar were all fogged up with condensation and provided an otherworldly matte reflection of the room.

The figures within were presented as mutilated variations of their true selves.

Stretched or squashed ... their faces blurred.

On my lonely walk here, a few snowflakes had fluttered down and the sweater I'd pulled on had proven insufficient protection against the elements. Now I was back indoors it was completely different, though. It was hot — so hot I'd long ago shucked my sweater. Cold hasn't traditionally been much of a problem for me, but I never deal well with heat.

The black shirt I had buttoned on about half an hour earlier, in my bedroom in university halls, stuck to my skin. I was all too aware that whenever I sweat my face takes on a waxy sheen. Once at school, on a particularly hot day, playing games out on the school field, someone had told me I looked like a department store mannequin.

I never quite pinned down why the comment stuck with me so long.

Was there something even to take much offence at?

I suppose department store mannequins have some positive features.

They're extremely stoic.

Of sound mind ... if not beating heart.

It was coming up to Christmas so some attempts at brewing a festive spirt had been put in at the bar; only in that slacker, half-arsed style so distinctive of students. There was a shabby Christmas tree that looked as though even this early in the season had already been knocked about during the course of several drunken nights. The wreaths hanging from the walls were on the wonk ... either hung carelessly or treated with the same disrespect as the Christmas tree. Then there was the sad string of fairy lights nailed high up on the walls. The lights faded in and out ... a kind of lethargic shifting between lit and unlit that made a mockery of the dance music's throbbing rhythm pulsing from the bar speakers.

I glanced around the room, trying to pick out familiar faces.

There wasn't anyone I knew at first glance.

That had been the plan. I had wanted to make absolutely, one-hundred-percent sure that there would be nobody here I knew to see me ... do what I was about to do. In the end, the fact Comedy Night happened on a Tuesday night was what had finally swung it for me — what had given me the prod I needed to get over the precipice.

I was going to stand up before a room full of people and do The Routine.

This was the step I had to take if I ever wanted to find out just what it was that I had in me. Or whether — as I had always suspected with a growing sense of dread — there really wasn't anything within me to find after all. That I was condemned to live out my life in an open office "pinging" emails and "liaising" with customers on a telephone headset, hating myself a little bit more with every passing day.

The bar was maybe half full.

There were a couple dozen aluminium tables with matching chairs haphazardly arranged around them, five or six to each table. The surfaces of the tables caught the sharp even light from the strip bulbs with a kind of accompanying multi-coloured twinkling madness from the disco ball sitting on top of the DJ decks.

The people who were here were clearly taking Tuesday night drinking seriously, judging from the mouths torn at the corners with laughing. There was one group, over in the corner of the bar, where a girl was standing on the chair and downing what looked like a metre-long test tube of some blue liquid while her friends clapped their hands and stamped their feet out of jubilation.

I felt a quiver pass through my stomach and turned away, not quite sure what to do with myself until the compere arrived and proceedings commenced.

A guy with bleached blond hair spilling out from beneath his baseball cap bumped past me, splashing a little lukewarm beer on my shirt sleeve from the four plastic pint glasses he was carrying. "Sorry, mate," he mumbled, without so much as looking at me, making towards the group in the corner with the girl downing the strange blue liquid.

It wasn't too late to turn around and go home.

I had told no one I was coming here.

Anybody could get up on stage and give it a go.

There was no list of names — nothing like that.

Nobody would ever know.

And yet I remained standing where I was.

Awkward as hell.

Deciding that it would give me the excuse both to burn some time and ensure that I didn't know anybody here, I wormed my way between the tables and chairs in the direction of the bar. As the barman straightened up from where he had been squatted on his haunches, tending to the empty glasses beneath the counter, I realised that I recognised him from the first week at university. I had decided to give joining the university football team a go and he had been the trialist I had been paired with while the captain of the team gave us a passing-over and decided who might have a chance of making the squad. It being a fairly open process, I knew that in reality they couldn't stop anyone from playing who desperately wanted to, but for me it had been the talk of the "initiation" ceremony in which inductees were required to down a pint of their own urine in order to secure their place on the team that eventually turned me against joining.

A ripple of panic passed through my chest as I wondered if the barman might recognise me ... however, the empty look he gave me told me that I was in no danger. I guess that's the blessing of being eminently forgettable. Or perhaps it's just that everybody forgets what happens in the first week at university anyway ... as if it's something which simply takes place in an alternate timeline, safe from the One, True Passage of Real Time.

Once I'd got my order in — settling for the same pissy lukewarm lager that guy had spilled on my shirt sleeve — I told myself that I was being irrational to be afraid of what was about to take place. I had been listening to a lot of self-help audiobooks during my significant down-time at university and most of them came back to the same message which read something along the lines of, "The only true freedom is achieved by not caring what others might think" ... but probably a lot more succinctly. I guess "self-help guru" is never going to be my gig.

Because it seemed a decent enough way to deal with my nervous energy, and more specifically the urge to fidget, I stood with my back to the bar, resting my elbows on the counter. I looked over the room, seeing that an Indian girl with dyed, bushy red hair and a tight striped black and red t-shirt was making her way to the stage.

Or what passed for a stage here.

She was on the chubby side, the extra weight at her sides spilling out over the top of the tight waistband of her jeans in a way that I actually found quite sexy.

I've always had a thing for girls with curves.

I guessed this was Agatha, as mentioned on the Comedy Night poster as being the compere.

Agatha proceeded up onto the stage, with a confidence I could only dream of possessing, approaching the DJ. She gesticulated to him and he gesticulated back, bending down within the DJ booth and retrieving a clipboard which he handed over to her.

From somewhere she had produced a mike which she fumbled with, finally flicking the switch and sending a squeal of feedback all around the bar.

Over in the corner at the table with the girl downing the test tube and the guy who'd spilled beer on me, I heard someone say, very loudly, "Fucking hell!"

To be honest, I identified with their sentiment.

Finally, the squealing stopped and Agatha's husky voice came out through the barroom speakers. "Evening everybody and welcome to Comedy Night."

"Shut up!" someone from the corner cried out.

Laughter gargled in response from the same area of the bar.

Agatha glowered in their direction and went on, unabashed. "Anybody who'd like to come up and do a slot is welcome. Everybody gets fifteen minutes." She held up the clipboard. "Come over and I'll put you on the list." With that, she switched off the mike, slipping it into the back pocket of her jeans, and going back over to chat with the DJ.

"Comedy! Comedy!" someone from the corner shouted out. "Hills, mate, you should *fucking* do it — you're *fucking* hilarious mate!"

I looked over to the group in the corner, seeing "Hills" — an unassuming, stick-thin guy with glasses dressed in a green hoodie — smirking and shaking his head as his friends surrounded him.

"Go on, Hills!"

I could tell that it was the same guy who had bumped into me while carrying the beer who had spoken. He had worked his baseball cap around backwards as if we had all somehow been transported back to the mid-nineties.

"Why don't you bloody do it Niall?" another member of the group put in, addressing the guy with the baseball cap who had been carrying the pints.

"I'm not funny, am I?"

"Yeah, but you've got a big fucking mouth."

A peal of laughter stirred the group.

Looking around the room, I was starting to have misgivings.

But I was here now.

If I retreated I would only be breaking a promise with myself.

... Nobody else would ever know.

But I'd have to live with myself.

"Okay, okay," Niall said. "I'll bloody do it if Hills does it — you can be funny, can't you Hills? Go on, Hilly boy!"

I had to admit that I was impressed by Niall's abilities at manipulation.

What he had wanted was for "Hills" to get up and do a comedy slot and that was what he was going to get.

I supped on my pint, looked over to the stage, seeing that Agatha was now sitting on the edge, dangling her feet in a childlike manner, clipboard lying across her lap, tapping away at her smartphone. I put my plastic pint glass down and strode over to her, my heart knocking at my tonsils and my lungs appearing to be operating at half their usual capacity.

"Name?" Agatha asked, not looking up from her smartphone screen.

For a second, I considered giving an alias ... but thinking on my feet has never really been a part of my skillset. "Marc," I said, and then, because I naturally try to make everything as awkward as possible. "Marcus Raisin."

Agatha sniffed a laugh.

Glanced up at me.

"It's all right," she said, and gazed about our surroundings. "I'm not police and I don't reckon we'll lose you in the crowd."

I reddened and thought about backing away.

But she had my name ... *both* names.

Well, actually, she had written down "Mark R", spelling Marc with an "K" rather than a "C", not that I did anything to correct her. Things were awkward enough without me spooling out a conversation a second longer than it needed to take.

"You okay to go on first?" she asked.

"Hmm?"

She looked up at me again. "It's all right," she said. "I always start things off myself, do a little five minute bit, then it's the first off the list. That okay with you?"

"Uh ... yeah," I replied, feeling a little stunned at how fast everything was happening.

It had taken me the best part of a year to put all my material together in The Routine, and several weeks and months — let alone the hours and hours of deliberation about whether this Tuesday would be *the* Tuesday I came along to Comedy Night ... and now I was finally here.

She narrowed her eyes and tilted her head to one side as if she was staring at a particularly complex maths puzzle.

I had decided that Agatha was devastatingly beautiful ... not that that was anywhere near enough to soften the pain from the enormous embarrassment I was clearly about to put myself through.

"This your first time here?" she asked. "I don't think I've seen you around."

"No," I replied, and then, "I mean, yes ... first time here, I'm saying."

Agatha's lips were slightly parted as if speaking to me induced a slight sense of disbelief. She closed her mouth, returning to the room once again. "There's the Comedy Society. You might be interested in joining. We had a stall set up in Fresher's Week but there's so much going on then that you probably walked right past it."

I felt another quiver through my gut and I couldn't help wishing that I'd brought my plastic pint glass with me just so I might have something to do with my hands.

But my pint was all the way back there on the bar counter.

In proximity to the barman who I'd attended the Football Trials with.

"Yeah, probably," I replied, finally, scratching the back of my neck.

"Well, you can join," she said. "Just have a look on the clubs part on the university website. We get together a couple of times a week. Watch routines. Go for coffee. Even go out for drinks. Talk about what we're working on."

It was as if some sort of inner child within me was stirred by what she was saying ... but at the same time there was the other Marcus Raisin, too.

The Sensible Marcus Raisin.

The one that told me I was to stick to the straight and narrow.

The tried and true.

I kind of made a pact with myself.

If tonight went well then I'd join the Comedy Society.

If I had something then I'd throw myself in at the deep-end.

But I needed some assurance first.

"Sounds ... good," I replied.

Agatha shrugged and gave me a pretty smile. I found myself somewhat distracted by the way her breasts rose and fell with her deep breathing — expanding and contracting. I did my best to put it out of my mind. "Just if you're interested, you know," she said. "I know how some people are against joining clubs, societies, for whatever reason. Especially with something like comedy. You get all sorts of non-joiners. *Outsiders*, you know, that sort of thing."

I wasn't completely sure what Agatha was talking about but I found myself nodding along all the same. I guess that my mind was fully occupied with worrying over The Routine, soon to be performed live and in front of an audience, because I seemed to miss the cue Agatha gave me that I was to wait my turn. And I was only made aware when Niall tapped me on the shoulder, and with the dirtiest, shit-eating grin ever, asked me if my name was really so complicated that it took that long to write down.

I could have died laughing ...

I stepped out of the way and let him, and the apparently hilarious Hills, through to sign up on Agatha's clipboard. As I took up my position at the bar once more, now starting to tremble — I was sure visibly — I witnessed a girl and another guy sign up on the clipboard too. While sipping away at my pint, I couldn't help but notice that the bar was starting to fill up even more. That during the course of my conversation with Agatha, about ten or more people had filtered into the bar area. And I couldn't help noticing that one of them was a medical student who had a room in the same halls of residence I occupied.

Just why this made much of a difference — I had never said anything more than "hello" or "goodbye" to this girl — I wasn't quite sure. I think it was just because there was the assumption that this person was just too close to where I lived for comfort.

I told myself I could still back out.

This was probably my last opportunity.

As the level of chatter in the bar rose above the not-insignificant volume of the music, I watched as Agatha dropped off the stage and then made her way up the steps, the clipboard firmly in her grasp, my name — or at least a shortened edition of it — scribbled there.

There was no time now.

Partially aware of Agatha taking the mike from the DJ, putting her clipboard to one side for the time being, I dug into the back pocket of my jeans, produced the scrunched-up ball of paper.

As I uncrumpled it, I immediately saw that there was an issue.

The blue pen I had used to scribble out some notes had got wet and had smudged into the paper after my walk through the drizzle to get here.

Not a single line was legible.

My heart rose to my throat.

And my ribs seemed to squeeze the air from my lungs.

Was the world spinning or was it just my imagination?

... I hadn't had that much to drink, after all.

I breathed in deep, trying my best to ignore the heady mixture of perfume and cheap ale and disinfectant. I knew that under normal circumstances I would've had no trouble at all remembering The Routine. God knows, I'd been through it in my head enough times to see me through a lifetime. Just about any moment when my mind was idle, my stray thoughts would pick up and play with The Routine ... and yet ... now it just wouldn't come.

I couldn't find the first point.

The music dropped away.

Agatha took to the centre of the stage.

Someone — I wasn't sure who, the DJ? — flipped on a spotlight and shone it upon Agatha. Her face looked more beautiful in the bright light. I wondered if it was her natural looks or as a result of that thing which has always been a mystery to me:

Make-up.

Everything was happening too quickly.

I realised more people were coming into the bar.

It was about nine in the evening now, I guess that I should've known — just considering my own habits — that students tend to go out later than the general population.

A sparsely populated bar at eight in the evening was never a guarantee of a dirge of a night on a university campus.

All of the tables without exception had two or three — or more — students sitting around them. Everybody had got their drinks in ... this was almost without exception the cheap lager I was drinking. It was then that I twigged — somewhere at the back of my mind — that I had seen publicity about campus, perhaps weeks ago now, talking about a promotion ...

Wasn't it a pound a pint, something like that?

It was just like me to be so oblivious that I hadn't even given the cost of my beer a second thought. And it was also just like me to lean over the bar and ask the barman, after he had served his latest new customer, how much the beer was.

He gave me a scowl which I probably deserved. "A pound a pint, mate." And with that he shot off, with raised eyebrows, to serve his latest customer — a girl in a low-cut top.

So that was it then ... it was going to be a packed house tonight.

The trembling only got harder to control.

And for better or worse — most likely worse — I ordered another pint in the hopes that it might steady my frayed nerves. Every time that Agatha finished a sentence, it felt like an invisible man was punching me in the gut. Although I didn't hear the words — a persistent ringing now filled my ears — I was all too aware of how the audience broke out in increasingly raucous bouts of laughing as Agatha finished with her latest quip.

And I was supposed to follow this.

Because there was no doubt in my mind that what I was watching was a skilled practitioner — someone who had done this many, many times before.

I wondered how I could've been so stupid as to believe that going through The Routine in front of a mirror might be any sort of adequate preparation for performing in front of a live audience. What was I thinking getting involved in comedy? I wasn't really interested in *anything* ...

not really ... and anybody who wanted to be a comedian, to make people they didn't know laugh, had to be downright dedicated to their art.

That made it even worse.

That meant I was an imposter.

Before I really knew what was going on, I heard my name resound about the bar.

With applause and wolf whistles, Agatha picked her way carefully down off the stage, standing to one side while she watched me closely. As I passed her by, she spoke in a husky whisper that sent a tingle through my blood.

"Just do it how you've practised — it'll be fine."

I sort of turned my head in her direction before catching myself.

Telling myself that I was rising up, taking the inevitable path to the gallows.

I suppose there are worse ways to die than by comedy ...

The floor creaked beneath my feet and was more unsettling than it would've been ordinarily. I realised I had my back to the audience, that I was focused upon the DJ booth — currently bereft of its DJ — and yet I also knew that I was incapable of turning around.

That some sort of Medusa with those eyes that turn you to stone awaited me.

But I knew I had to turn around.

I couldn't stand up here all night.

So I turned around.

It wasn't what I expected.

For a start, the spotlight shining upon me rendered the audience as nothing more than a series of strange celestial beings bathed in golden sunrays.

As if I had an audience of angels.

That twisted the corner of my mouth in a smile.

Someone in the audience chuckled and I realised that they were laughing at my expression ... as if I had made that face intentionally.

That sent a weird thrill through me.

Something like ... power?

From the audience someone — maybe Niall? — called out.

"You all right up there, mate? You look lost."

A couple of nervous laughs from the audience — wilder laughter from the back of the room with the group of Niall and his drunk friends.

"Shaking like a leaf, man," the guy continued. "Want a glass of water? Got Parkinson's or something?"

More delirious laughter from the back of the room.

I glanced down and saw Agatha scowling off into the crowd with a maternal fire.

My cheeks flushed.

And my throat felt dry.

I realised I'd left my pint on the bar counter.

I peered at the microphone in front of me.

It was as intimidating as looking into the round black hole of a loaded gun.

But I knew that I had to approach it ...

As I took my first step forward, my eyes fell across the medical student — Brucie? — who lived in my halls of residence. I told myself that I would have to get over people finding out about my comedy sooner or later ... and even though my logical mind was in no doubt about this fact there was something deeper in me which resisted this.

Something which told me that I could keep this secret forever.

It wasn't too late.

I realised that now.

Close enough to speak into the microphone, so that the whole room could hear my voice, I said, "Sorry," and promptly plodded my way across the stage, down the steps and straight out of the door into the chilly night.

Nobody would ever know what had happened.

Nobody except me.

... And, well, Brucie ... or whatever he was called.

As it turned out I never spoke another word to him ever again.

# MONDAY MORNING

Monday wasn't a normal day.
  Not that it ever is.
The whole mental anguish of getting back into the grind following the respite of the weekend is always borderline physically painful. My body protesting against its continued existence.

Outside it was grim and grey. There was no sign of the fine weather from Friday night continuing into this week. A mizzle was falling as I trudged to the bus stop to join the others with similarly dismal expressions, wearing suits, ties, work blouses, skirts ... although not all at the same time, of course.

I was wearing my thick duffel coat, the strap of my messenger bag squeezing my shoulder, the added weight of the tablet within like some sort of half-hearted life-coach giving me a "geeing-up" before I stepped over the threshold to do battle in the area of the Adult World once more. I'd always thought that the main task of a life coach is to trick you into believing that your life has some sort of meaning or focus. I guess delusions can take you a long way — as far as you're willing to let them.

The main excitement that morning had been burning the roof of my mouth with the instant coffee I had "brewed" to go along with the rest of my breakfast — a pot of sour-tasting yoghurt. Thinking about it in the cold light of day that yoghurt had probably passed its use-by-date several weeks ago ... I had had to root around right at the back of the fridge to retrieve it.

While everyone else tapped away at their mobile phones, bleary-eyed as they silently conversed with friends, relatives, lovers, or else just flipped through news headlines, social media feeds, I just stood my ground in the queue, sort of going for an existential stare at the curb. I usually brought my headphones with me so I could listen to music or a podcast or — if I was feeling especially erudite — an audiobook for the duration of my commute.

Not today, though.

Apparently I was happy for my skull to be a silent steel chamber for a little while.

Before those voices started to fill my head again.

All those *customers* with their never-ending streams of queries, complaints, well-meaning suggestions.

By the time the bus rumbled into the stop, hydraulics hissing and creaking with a kind of anthropomorphic disappointment, I was pretty damp from the persistently falling rain and my non-waterproof duffel jacket. The bus shelter had clearly been built in a different era. When it hadn't crossed the mind of the City Council — or whoever decided these things — that the ballooning population of the city might mean that more than half a dozen people might want to wait for a bus. I was one of the ten or eleven unfortunates who had failed to arrive in time to snag a place beneath the bus shelter's plastic refuge. I consoled myself with the fact that I was saving myself from the grubby, mucky, pissy smell of the bus shelter ... let alone the conjoined body odours of my fellow commuters. Still, I was feeling pretty damp, there was no question about it. And I knew that given the harsh air conditioning that blew about the LifeWare office rain or shine, snow or hail, I had no choice but to remain damp for the rest of the day. Until I got back to the relative dryness of my flat ... assuming that Riko didn't spike a water pipe in the course of the day and cause a localised flash flood that was.

It was clear to tell from its muted arrival that even the bus didn't want to be here (let alone the bus driver). Its bright orange lights showing number and destination reminded me of those fake professional smiles that would be awaiting me once I ducked my head in through the LifeWare entrance. I always thought it an amazing feat of human perseverance that meant the average office worker could spend in excess of forty years keeping up appearances before descending into the blissful solitude of retirement.

*Roll it on*, was all I could say ... at least to myself.

I cranked out the canned cheer, smiling with a corner of my mouth and muttering a muted, "Morning", at the unsmiling bus driver as I flashed my pass beneath the red eye of the scanner. It gave a contented little bleep and with a nod that the driver — with his thousand-yard stare — didn't appear to register at all. I wondered whether I should try for one day — just one day — being a total arsehole to everyone and anyone I came into contact with.

Or maybe just strangers.

That would be okay ... nobody would ever know ... most likely I'd never see them ever again. I wondered if that was how narcissists always managed to become so successful, because, to put it bluntly, they just didn't give a *fuck* ... my problem, though, was that I was quite definitely not a narcissist. Already I was feeling a creeping dread that my morning greeting to the bus driver might've sounded ironic in some way and that it might've dampened his mood. No, I was always worried about how what I was doing might affect other people. And that, I was pretty sure, meant my fate was sealed — at least professionally — to be a kind of hapless loser.

I took a seat on the upper deck of the bus.

There's always been a childish attraction to occupying the high ground, or maybe even something *feline* about the whole thing. There's a good, confident feeling of control you get from being able to easily see your surroundings. Not that through the steamed-up windows or the pasty veil of mizzle beyond I could see very much of anything.

But it was the thought that counted.

Once everyone was aboard, and the bus had huffed its way out of the stop and into the sluggish morning commuter traffic, I felt my eyelids begin to droop. A couple of times, I woke with a sudden start, with that feeling of falling, followed by the self-conscious realisation of vulnerability that I always get whenever I'm in danger of falling asleep in public. Then again, I suppose that genetically speaking it was more of a feature rather than a bug as if potentially prevented someone knifing me in my sleep ... if I ever do get knifed then I'd like to be conscious. At least then I'd have the outside chance of managing to get in contact with the relevant emergency services in a timely manner. Maybe even with time enough for them to save my life.

Deciding that I needed to do something to occupy my mind, to stop my brain anticipating and reacting to the day of drudgery which stretched out before me, I dug about in my messenger bag, producing the tablet from within.

I perched it on my knee, and then because I'm a paranoid sort of soul, I cast a glance over my shoulder. There was nobody I recognised among the sleepy, puffy faces bobbing along in their seats. Nobody from work. I returned my attention to the tablet.

I had told Riko that I was going to turn it into the police. It was potentially evidence ... or, well, if not evidence then property of the deceased ... of Technomancer ... John Horsham. It still felt weird to think that he had died. Although I hadn't known him at all — or wanted to know him any better than I already did — it felt strange to think that he was no longer of this world. That he had slipped off his mortal coil, or whatever it is they say ...

Still, I thought about that picture of Olivia that had been on the tablet screen when I had come across him. He had been hacking into my mobile phone. Just as Riko had hacked into one of my neighbour's computers the night before.

There was no way that this thing could be legal. Or at least whatever program, app, whatever, Technomancer was running on it couldn't have been legal.

Maybe I was at a weird point in my life where it just seemed as though I should take some more risks, but I found myself tapping the power button, switching the thing on again. The screen was bright enough that the raindrops clinging to my duffel coat glinted. I looked around again — still nobody I recognised, although I wondered just why I would be so worried. As far as I was concerned the only person that even knew of this tablet's existence was Technomancer ... and now me.

The splash screen showed.

That same monogrammed sun.

A few seconds later, it disintegrated and I was confronted by the home screen.

And a list of devices.

I noticed that my own mobile phone was there:

Marcus Raisin Mobile

Looking at the myriad other devices in the vicinity — "Ad_the_Ladz Earbox", "Jemma's Jewels", "Purple Dragon" — I couldn't help but note that the name I had baptised my phone with seemed just a little, well ... *beige*. Was I really a mother in her fifties trapped in a thirty-year-old man's body? I continued scrolling through the list, marvelling at the power that Technomancer had once possessed, and which, through his death, he had passed on to me, and I wondered where I should start. Or if I should start at all.

There was no doubt in my mind that this *was* illegal.

I recalled vague bullet points about "computer misuse", or something similar, from my LifeWare corporate induction.

But I wasn't at work right now.

Not quite yet.

As I carried on scrolling through the list of available devices — in the same way that you would choose which wifi network you want to connect to — my focus fell upon a particular device:

EndoLine Transportation

That was the name of the company which managed the bus service — their logo stickers splashed about the bus at various strategic places.

I decided to give it a tap.

Although I doubted that there was all that much dishy waiting to be discovered on the bus's hard disks, or whatever it was that I was accessing through the tablet ...

I was aware that we were about halfway to the bus stop where I got off each morning on the way to work. The bus was ambling its way up the steady slope of the bridge, its engine rising to a nasal whine and its higher frequency vibrations throbbing through my seat. When we reached the crest of the bridge, I glanced through the steamed-up windows and veil of mizzle, making out the faint shape of the slate-grey river which slashed through the city in an apparently random pattern.

As we began to go down the other side, following in the wake of the similarly sluggish traffic, I switched my attention downwards once more to the tablet.

This time, instead of the desktop I had seen while Riko had been accessing my neighbour's PC, there was what looked like a virtual set of controls.

I furrowed my brow.

Peered closer.

It was a dashboard of what looked like the bus. There was a speedometer, rev counter, all of which appeared to be rising and falling in time with the bus's machinations. There was a gearbox. And there was a virtual steering wheel which was shifting from side to side as the bus driver made minor corrections to our course to keep us straight on the road.

Right at the bottom of the screen, of the dashboard, there was a red button with the text, "Virtual Override Inactive" scrawled across it in white writing.

What was a virtual override?

And what happened when it was activated?

Once again — because I am *that* paranoid — I looked around me.

Nobody was the slightest bit interested in what I was doing.

And why would they be?

I was just as unassuming as any other commuter packed onto the bus.

Maybe even more so than average.

Deciding that if I was intending on going through with the whole plan to hand in the tablet to the police anyway that I might as well satisfy my curiosity while I still could, I breathed in and tapped the override button.

For about five seconds everything went on like normal.

Then I sensed the bus gaining speed.

Rolling along faster and faster down the hill.

I glanced up, sensing the reaction of others sitting nearby.

People straightening up and stretching their necks to get a look at the road out ahead.

I shifted my attention back down to the tablet.

To the controls in front of me.

It seemed impossible that this was happening.

But ... there didn't seem to be any other way of explaining it.

I had control of the bus.

Through the tablet.

It was then that I thought to rise in my seat.

To peer our through the front window of the upper deck.

And to the road out ahead.

We were coming up behind a car — its brake lights lit up like a pair of beady red eyes.

The tablet clutched in my hands, my eyes danced across the screen.

I identified the button for the brakes.

Glanced up to the approaching back end of the car.

And then realised what I needed to do.

I tapped the override button again ... waited for the bus to return to the control of its trained operator — the driver sat at the steering wheel below.

The bus braked hard.

Then swerved sharply.

I was thrown out of my seat.

Someone behind me screamed.

Outside I could hear horns blaring.

The bus engine had stalled ... fallen quiet.

Feeling numb, realising that I was lying on the floor of the upper deck, my head just beneath one of the seats, I gently eased myself up onto my elbow. At first I thought that I'd hit my head in such a way that it had set me off-kilter with the world.

I wondered if the damage would be permanent.

And then I had the more obvious realisation.

That the bus had climbed the pavement and had come to rest at a slight angle.

The bus floor was all I had ever dreamed it would be.

Slightly sticky.

A strange sweet smell mixed in with mud and dank rainwater.

And a sharp edge of disinfectant.

Someone reached their hand out to me.

I clasped their palm, feeling my bones ache as they yanked me up to my feet.

It was a man a few years older than me, dressed smartly in a suit and tie. Judging from his grip I guessed that he visited the gym four or five times a week. "Bloody bus drivers, huh? Think it shows sometimes the people they get to drive these things never finished school."

My head ringing and my heart throbbing in my eardrums, I breathed in sharply. I hadn't blacked out. Nothing like that. It had just been the sudden, jarring motion of the bus banking onto the pavement that had thrown me off my feet.

I guess that's why they advise against standing on the upper deck of buses ...

Blushing — in the way that beta-males do when they know they are in the presence of one who is clearly overwhelmingly *alpha*, despite whatever abhorrent views they might hold — I thanked him ... and was somewhat grateful he didn't deign to snap me in half like a dry twig. The suited man snorted, shook his head, and then waddled over the bus steps in the way that only people who have muscular thighs are required to do.

Despite the violent evasive manoeuvre, the bus appeared to mostly be in one piece. When I breathed in a little deeper, I was sure I could smell a sort of metallic burning scent. That smell of an overheated engine, or radiator, or whatever part of a vehicle goes through anguish when it's misused.

"Hey, mate? I think this's yours."

I turned my head.

Saw that there was a boy, about fourteen, fifteen, dressed in a school uniform holding the tablet up in the air. My eyes snapped onto the screen, wondering whether the bus controls might still be visible. However, the screen was blank. As the boy handed it back to me, I thought it remarkable that it was still in one piece. But then as I held it up to the light, I noticed a tiny hairline crack splitting the middle of the screen. It was almost unnoticeable ... not that the school boy thought this. He was of the generation that had grown up with smart phones, and their screens about as robust as egg shells.

"Sorry, mate," the boy said. "It was like that when I picked it up — promise. It was the impact that done it, I reckon."

I must've remained straight-faced, serious, staring at the screen a few seconds too long because there was a look of genuine panic on the boy's face when I replied. I managed to raise a smile from somewhere, despite the ringing in my ears, the swelling I could feel at my lower back and side. "It's okay," I said. "Don't worry about it."

Clearly conditioned by his school teachers to seek to take the blame wherever possible, the boy beamed at me before following the suited man down the stairs to the lower deck. I clutched the tablet in my hands — staring at the black screen, with the slight crack through its centre. I only snapped back to the real world when someone excused themselves, asking to get past.

Just like any other Monday morning at the LifeWare offices, phones were going off all over the place. The office was a flurry of fingers across keyboards, mouse buttons clicking madly, gentle tones of voice emanating from half-awake customer service reps ... pure muscle memory.

My ears had stopped ringing and the pain was almost gone from my back and side from where I had fallen on the bus. I wondered if it would return later that evening, or if I would feel terrible tomorrow. Was it the weirdness of what had just occurred with the tablet which was currently distracting my nervous system from my physical afflictions?

I had been driving the bus ... well, sort of ... I had taken control of the bus away from the driver for just long enough to cause a minor accident ...

I had trod past the wide-eyed bus driver, who was apologising profusely to each and every passenger as they alighted, shaking his head, an unlit cigarette squeezed between his fingers. He had muttered something or other about, "losing control", about it being, "the damndest fucking thing", and that the bus had a, "mind of its own".

I had been of half a mind to take him to one side and explain what had happened.

As if that would put his mind at ease.

As if it wouldn't have made me look like a complete and utter maniac.

Despite the issues with my commute that morning, I wasn't any earlier or later than usual. I guess I must've left the house earlier than I had realised. True, I was never the first to work ... but neither was I ever the last. That honour always went to Filseek Geepara who sat at the desk beside mine.

Filseek — or "Fil" as he asked everyone to call him — would arrive to the office every day, without exception, precisely thirteen minutes late.

Never earlier, never later.

Fil had had endless "one-to-one" meetings with our manager Lucas. When the problem persisted, these meetings were escalated so an HR representative was involved. Finally, LifeWare had put Fil into some procedure to get him to change his habits or else face formal disciplinary action. He had managed to comply for a day or two at a time before falling back into the same old pattern. Thirteen minutes late. Without fail.

Every. Single. Day.

In the end, a decision had been made, or not made, as the case might be, to allow things to continue as they were. Despite the tardiness, there wasn't anything wrong with Fil's job performance. He was enthusiastic, competent, professionally turned out, friendly with everyone. And he was always sure to make up the thirteen minutes he lost every morning at the end of the day, leaving at five thirteen rather than the standard five o'clock.

One day, while we had been having lunch together, he had revealed the reason for his lateness. It was the same thing he had told Lucas and HR in confidence. He told me he lived with his mother and his younger sister; his father had died several years before. Fil was about nineteen or twenty and I got the impression that his sister was much younger; seven or eight. Each day his mother started work early, and so it fell to Fil to take his sister to school. As they didn't have a car, they had to take the bus across town. Once at school, Fil would drop his sister off before catching another two buses to get to LifeWare. A quirk of bus timetables made it impossible for him to arrive on time. If he left the house any earlier to drop his sister off, the school wouldn't even have opened and he would have to leave his sister unaccompanied outside the closed gates before catching his next bus. That just wasn't an option. So the earliest he could leave school was as soon as they opened their gates.

To tell the truth, more than anything, I was impressed by the punctuality of city buses; evidenced by the fact that Fil was always *exactly* thirteen minutes late to work. If I'd been smarter, and I'd worked for the bus company, I might have been able to spin Fil's story into some sort of case study marketing campaign.

I was still shaking slightly as I sank onto my computer chair at my desk. I had stashed the tablet back inside my messenger bag. I knew it was just my imagination, but I couldn't help thinking that my bag felt impossibly hot pressed up against my shins as it sat beneath my desk. I shrugged my damp duffel coat off onto the back of my chair. A group email was waiting for me at the top of my inbox from Lucas when I had logged in. It was concise and said only that there was to be a meeting at ten a.m. to discuss a "delicate matter".

I was already filled with dread.

Even more so than usual.

This email appeared to serve as a signal to the office that it was okay to speak about the news everybody already seemed to know. And which — unhappily — involved me.

The upshot of Fil's lateness that particular morning was that by the time I had got through with all my wide-eyed colleagues telling me just how sorry they were that I had witnessed something so terrible, I had already had my fill of kind-hearted sympathy and wasn't in the best of moods. Their concern was just a façade, of course. All anybody really wanted to know was the gory details. As with any office, gossip was its lifeblood.

The worst irony of all that morning might have been the fact that my computer seemed to be in perfect working order. I wondered if Technomancer's soul had been unable to "cross over" until he had taken care of all the open support tickets.

Unfinished business, something like that.

Bringing back hardware long ago thought to be obsolete, destined to pass through those binary gates in the sky en route to the digital dumpsite.

The idea of an IT-savvy poltergeist tickled me and I made a mental note, thinking that it might be a decent addition to the stand-up routine I had been working on for ten years and which, after all that time, consisted of about two minutes of material ...

Not that I would ever perform it.

The fact my computer was back functioning meant I could use work as a legitimate distraction. I managed to get out of my colleagues' probing attempts by smiling and looking altogether more cheerful than normal before busying myself with my inbox, frown lines etched across my forehead. However, this tactic didn't quite work with Fil.

He sat at the desk beside mine and wasn't infected by the same slimy subtlety as the rest of the office. "Hey Marcus," Fil said, hanging his coat on the back of his chair.

"Oh, hey. Morning, Fil," I said, flipping him a glance and the shade of a smile.

He glanced about his desk, shuffled a piece of paper out of the way with the back of his hand, and then fixed his gaze upon me. His eyes looked more bulbous than usual. "Adriana just told me what happened. On Friday. That's *awful*."

Adriana sat in front of me. I shot a fiery look at the back of her head. She didn't turn around upon hearing her voice being mentioned, but

I could see her ears burning beneath the telephone headset she wore. Her ears had almost gone the same shade of red as her dyed hair.

Although many members of the office found Fil's unchecked enthusiasm annoying, I tried my best to be patient. To act in any other way would've been like kicking a puppy.

"Yeah ..." I said, replying to Fil, "I didn't see much. I arrived at the wrong time ... the *right* time." I sucked in a deep breath, pissed at myself that I still hadn't quite managed to work out a formulaic response to the question everyone had been asking me all morning. I guess that inability to think on my feet — or "to bullshit" — was one of the reasons why promotion had so far eluded me. In the end, I settled on, "It was too late when I saw him."

"Are you feeling okay?" Fil asked, giving me a look of genuine grave concern. "I mean, do you feel all right being here?"

I turned this question over in my mind — just as I had done the other dozen times I had been asked it that morning. I wished I could be one of those people who reacted instinctively in conversations. That replying to someone was as natural as flinching when someone hit you on the kneecap with a rubber hammer. But for some stupid evolutionary reason I have never been capable of it. Some stupid switch in my brain forces me to treat each and every question put to me in excessive detail.

The answer was still the same, though.

That was the depressing part of it.

Surely it said something about me.

That I really felt nothing at all.

Not even that *numbness* people talked about following trauma.

I just felt *normal*.

... It was the world around me that had gone crazy.

And why shouldn't I feel normal? Technomancer had had no impact upon my life whatsoever ... except for the fact that he had fixed issues with my workstation a handful of times or that he had hacked into my phone to perve at pictures of my ex-girlfriend. It was somewhat unpleasant to think that Olivia's raunchy snap might well have been the last image which'd passed through his mind.

"I feel fine, Fil," I replied, eventually. "Really."

Fil gave me an unsure look. "Okay, but they always say things like this can have a delayed effect. If you ever want anyone to talk to then you can count on me."

Even despite the constant harassment which'd come at me from all sides that morning, Fil's sentiment warmed me from the inside. Because, unlike the others, I could say without a shadow of a doubt that it was genuine. "Thanks, Fil, that's nice of you to say."

When I returned to work, I couldn't quite shift the sense that people just outside my field of vision were constantly eyeballing me. For some reason, I started to feel self-conscious of the tablet I had stashed away in my bag, under my desk, as if someone was going to come marching over any second and ask me to explain why I had it in my possession.

But of course nobody did.

I was on the phone when I noticed the clock had ticked over to ten in the morning.

Although my call was wrapping up, I did my best to keep it going as long as possible.

I sensed that everyone else in the office had finished their calls and had come out of the loop. Phones weren't ringing any more. I was the last person who was still speaking to a client. I also noticed that Lucas had appeared in the doorway of his office.

And that Kelly was with him.

That was strange.

I was speaking with a charming man in his nineties, who happened to live in a nine-bedroom mansion, now all on his own (although he had six children, twelve grandchildren and had gone through four wives). I never would've guessed that he was out of his sixties if he hadn't said anything. I sensed he was beginning to tire from the way his delivery had slowed and the odd yawn crept in here and there. But he continued to relay the latest fascinating anecdote about an army squadron he had been a part of in his youth (before he had become mayor of some small fishing town which he had eventually turned into a magnet for culinary tourists by providing grand incentives for talented chefs to set up shop there). As he told me all of this, I had attempted to fix the red-eye correction feature on his copy of Imagick. I say "attempted" but I had actually successfully fixed the problem about ninety seconds into the call. Everything else had been me playing for time. Unlike some of my colleagues, who were interested in furthering their careers within LifeWare, I had no interest in ending my calls as efficiently as possible to boost my CQR ("customer query resolution") figures.

Across the room, Lucas surveyed the office before his focus came to rest on me. He paced in my direction. My stomach dropped. The soles of his shoes made no sound as they brushed the carpet. There had always been something of the night about him.

I knew his plan.

I had seen it play out so many other times before.

Although it was certainly beaten into members of staff that they weren't ever to *hang up* on customers, there was also, conflictingly, such a thing as taking too long to settle an outstanding query. Solid company man that he was, Lucas was keen to guard against such incongruences.

Realising I had no other choice with Lucas standing close enough to hear me, I wished the gentleman well and read him out the standard patter; that he was to contact us again in the case of experiencing any further issues with Imagick if the information on the website turned out to be insufficient to solve his problem.

When I put the phone down in its plastic cradle, I felt Lucas's hand on my shoulder.

I suppose he intended his grasp to be reassuring — in a "trained empathy" sort of a way — but he was clearly not used to making physical contact with other humans. His grip was just a touch too strong. Too insistent.

Or maybe that was his intention.

Although I had my back to him as he continued to clasp my shoulder I knew he would be raising his eyebrows up into his forehead, like a head teacher addressing a hall full of school children. It was uncomfortable to feel the whole office staring at me and Lucas as if this was some sort of impromptu theatrical performance.

Then again, maybe that's not too far away from what it was.

An especially *arduous* theatrical performance ...

"Good morning, everyone," Lucas began. "I thought I should bring us all together to discuss what occurred on Friday evening. I'm sure you have all heard rumours, here and there, but I thought we should set the record straight."

I caught Kelly's eye across the room.

She gave me a faint smile and the slightest of nods.

What I wouldn't have done for a bomb to come whistling down through the ceiling at that exact moment. Wiping everybody and everything out in a single, merciful explosion.

But there were no bombs in sight.

Lucas continued. "Tragically, John Horsham, our Systems Administrator, passed away on Friday evening."

There was an appropriately deathlike silence across the whole office.

I heard Lucas give what I was certain was a stage-managed swallow. As if he was struggling for the words. "And even more tragic still, Marcus, here, was left to discover John after everyone else had gone home."

I waited for a wave of emotion to hit.

But there was nothing ...

What a heartless bastard I am.

Lucas went on. "He managed the situation admirably and I wish for his good judgement to be recognised. A true example of calm-headedness for anyone else — *God forbid* — unfortunate enough to find themselves facing similar circumstances."

Lucas gave a dramatic pause. He took a wrenching breath and squeezed my shoulder even tighter. I was waiting for him to stop touching me. I wondered if there wasn't something in my employment contract that prohibited unnecessary physical contact.

Probably just my human rights, thinking about it.

"I wanted to make everyone aware that there is help available. Our HR team is able to offer advice and support, or to refer you to counselling if necessary. Please let me know if you require any further details and I shall pass it on."

I couldn't help thinking that this was one of Lucas's infamous tests. He was daring someone to come forward and claim that they were "disturbed" in some way by the death of a colleague. Their personnel file would be pulled and forever black marked.

"Are there any questions at this point?" Lucas asked.

One hand went up.

Fil's.

"Yes?" Lucas said.

"When is the funeral?"

I felt my stomach squeeze.

"The family will inform us when a date has been fixed for the memorial service."

I saw Fil blush slightly.

Perhaps he realised he had used the word "funeral" a little too freely.

"Any other questions?" Lucas asked, and I imagined his eyes scanning the room. "No? Then, there remains the question of who shall cover such a pivotal role following John's untimely departure."

I looked over to Kelly, who was smiling shyly.

"IT has allowed us the services of Kelly on an interim basis while a substantive replacement is sought."

If any single expression could've summed up the feeling in the room, it would've been an eye-roll. It was an open secret among everyone who worked at LifeWare that anyone who covered a role "on an interim basis" — almost without exception — ended up in said role full-time. Whether or not Technomancer's role was a step up for Kelly, I really had no idea.

Or interest in knowing, to tell the truth.

She seemed happy enough, though.

So I was happy for her.

I gave her a smile back. I had to admit I was glad that from now on it wasn't going to be an ordeal whenever anything went wrong with my computer. Now there would be an actual fully functional human being to speak to who wouldn't make me feel like a brainless worm.

"Okay," Lucas went on. "If there're no further questions ..."

Nobody said anything.

Lucas pressed on a smile. "Do your best, everyone!"

Whispering conversations picked the former silence apart and before long the noise levels in the room rose to what they had been before Lucas had started speaking.

Finally, Lucas released me from his grip.

I focused on my computer, hoping to get back to something resembling normality.

But then I heard Lucas's voice again.

A near whisper.

And unnervingly close to my ear.

"A minute in my office, Marcus?"

Reluctantly — *oh so reluctantly* — I backed away from my computer and followed.

Lucas's office was what I termed — at least in my own mind — a "starter office". It had the most basic, and yet the most prized — most precious — of all things in the twenty-first century workplace:

Privacy.

Four walls. A ceiling.

A *door*.

Granted, the wall which looked out across the rest of the office was transparent, made of soundproofed glass, but still this space was the sort of thing that any ambitious Company Man might aspire to. I took my place in the stiff-backed chair opposite Lucas's desk.

He had a swanky, high-backed articulated chair for himself with added lumbar support.

Today, he was wearing a light-grey suit with a pink tie. He had matching silver cufflinks with salmon-coloured stones. On his desk, he had one of those expensive-looking pendulums with ball-bearings at the end of metal rods. I knew it had a name but I couldn't bring it to mind. If I'd had to guess, I would have said that Lucas wouldn't know what it was called either. I imagine he had taken just about as much interest in physics at school as I had. Perhaps we had more in common than I wanted to believe ... maybe that was why we had both attracted Olivia ... and, great, now I was sounding like a voiceover for a nature documentary ...

Lucas pressed on a smile. "How're you *feeling*, Marcus?"

I shrugged. "Fine, I guess."

Lucas steepled his fingers and rested his palms on the desk. He had a blotter like my dad used to have in his home office. I didn't realise they were still a thing. "I've arranged for us to speak with someone about ... what you experienced on Friday night."

For some reason, my mind immediately flashed onto the *other* thing that had happened on Friday night. This was the first time we had been alone since I had seen him with Olivia at the Street Sermon. Somehow my brain was still struggling to accept the truth.

As if it had been an illusion playing out before my eyes.

But, no, it had definitely been real.

And then I remembered the *other* thing from Friday.

The guy who had died in his boots.

I looked him in the eye. "A therapist?" I asked.

"No, not a therapist, but someone who has training for this kind of thing."

That would be someone from HR then ...

Lucas lifted his hands up off the desk and clasped them in his lap. As he reclined slightly in his chair, his eyelids narrowed to snakelike slits. "LifeWare can arranged a therapy session if you would like?"

"No," I replied, a little too quickly. "I don't think that will be necessary."

Lucas tilted his head to one side, averted my gaze. "All right. If you change your mind, let me know. There's nothing shameful about asking for help. It wouldn't leave these four walls. It would be just between you and me."

I had very little faith about that.

"This afternoon. Four o'clock," Lucas said.

"What about my calls?"

"It's fine. Someone will cover." An uncomfortable silence draped down upon us. Lucas took a subtle breath in through his nostrils, arching his shoulders and rising in his chair as he did so. "Sorry to ask again, but I want to make completely sure. Do you feel up to being here today?"

This time I took care to be more emphatic. "I feel fine. Completely fine."

Lucas bowed his head as if submitting to the chaotic yet iron will of a child. "Okay."

I expected him to dismiss me.

But Lucas allowed the silence to drag on.

I felt an uncomfortable stirring in my stomach.

An ominous feeling.

"There was something else I wanted to mention," Lucas said. "And I would please like you to let me know if you think this crosses a line."

I had to admit I felt a touch disarmed by his tone.

It took me off-guard.

I couldn't recall another time he had come across so sincere.

Perhaps he had been on a new course recently.

"Cross a line how?" I asked, feeling my gut tighten.

"Between the personal and the professional."

And then I knew what was coming.

I felt speechless.

Lucas attempted a wry smile, but it slipped. "This morning, when I called everyone together, I couldn't help but notice those, uh ..." he waved his hand in the direction of the office as if he spoke English as a second language and had briefly forgotten the correct vocabulary "... photographs. The ones pinned up at your workstation?"

The room was spinning. I was glad my hands were down at my sides because I was bunching them up into fists, my fingernails pressing so hard into my palms that it stung.

Lucas met my eye briefly then looked away.

To his desk pendulum.

And then through the glass wall to the office outside.

97

Fil caught Lucas's eye and rapidly snapped his attention back onto his computer.

Adriana, too, had been watching and she started desperately clawing at the number pad on her phone.

Lucas continued. "It might not be anything. It might just be that, I don't know ... they look very similar. Stranger things have happened, but when — "

I sucked in a breath, deciding it was time to be a man.

To speak up.

"Her name's Olivia," I said. "We broke up weeks ago."

This stopped Lucas cold. "Ah," he said. "I see."

I noticed he had coloured slightly, clearly caught off-guard by my candour.

"That's her name, isn't it?" I asked.

Lucas stared at a spot in mid-air, his thoughts seemingly a million miles away. "Hm? Yes, yes. That's right."

"It's fine," I replied. "It won't be an issue. Really. I should have taken those photos down weeks ago. I don't know why I haven't."

Lucas appeared to regain some of his former professional composure. Maybe he had recalled the exact part of LifeWare policy which dealt with a matter such as this one. He met my gaze again. "I suppose everyone handles ... *breakups* differently. Sort of like, well ..."

"Denial?" I suggested.

Lucas made an odd sound at the back of his throat.

It was the first time I had ever seen him be something close to speechless.

I swallowed hard. Told myself to be cool. "Thanks for this chat," I said. "I really appreciate it. Was there anything else?"

Lucas flashed an unconvincing smile.

For the first time in our relationship it felt as though I was in control.

I told myself to savour the sensation because it would be no longer than momentary.

"Uh, no," he said. "Nothing else, no."

I got to my feet and left Lucas's office.

As I walked across the office, I would've been able to hear a pin drop.

Nobody said anything.

Nobody was even on the phone.

And although nobody would meet my eye, I could tell they were all staring when my back was turned.

They wanted to see me break down.

They wanted to see a show.

They wanted to tell their families about something "weird" that had happened at work that day. Just so they would have something to say at dinner.

I sank back down in my chair.

Waited out a few seconds.

A phone rang across the office.

And then another.

One by one, everyone was returning to work.

Suddenly becoming *busy*.

I looked over to Lucas in his office. He, too, was speaking to someone on the phone, looking out of the window, to the outside world.

I took stock of my workstation again.

Saw the photos of Olivia stuck up there.

I unpinned them, placed them in a neat pile, then tore them into strips before depositing them in confidential waste ... not that there was anything to be confidential about.

Everyone would know soon enough.

Gossip like this wouldn't just die.

I didn't turn in the tablet.

To tell the truth, by the time five o'clock rolled around I had completely forgotten I even had it. And by then I was so eager to get away from the office, and the exceptionally awkward meeting I'd had with the HR rep and Lucas later that afternoon, that I almost blew Kelly off as I was on my way out of the gate.

I had just given Geoff the Security Man my usual grunt of greeting/farewell when I heard Kelly calling out to me across the company car park.

That day she was wearing a turquoise satin blouse over black trousers. As always, she was wearing skate shoes. She trotted towards me, her work bag bouncing off her hip. When she reached me, she was flushed. I wondered what was so urgent that couldn't wait for tomorrow. Maybe she'd found out about the tablet.

"Hey!" she said, smiling widely.

Seeing her pleasant expression was enough to spark something positive in me.

I managed to raise a smile although I felt like a husk.

I told myself I was just hungry — that I'd feel better once I got some dinner down.

"Sorry we didn't get a chance to chat today," she said. "Guess your computer's running fine?"

"Huh? Oh, yeah. I mean, it was working fine the minute I got into the office this morning."

"Hmm. Tech support from beyond the grave? A smart ghost?"

I felt a warmth in my chest and couldn't help smiling. "Guess so."

Kelly's own smile slipped into a grimace. She glanced back over her shoulder as if someone might have been listening in. "I shouldn't be making jokes like that. Sorry. He's not even in the ground yet."

"I guess when he is it'll permanently disable his wireless feature."

Kelly choked on a laugh, balling her fist in her mouth as if stifling a cough.

The laugh lines around her eyes gave her away, though.

"How was your first day in Technomancer's shoes?" I asked.

She sighed.

Long and hard.

"Oh, you know how it is your first day on the job. Like poking around inside someone else's brain. Everything looks like a mess because it's at odds with the way you think about things."

"I'm guessing Technomancer wasn't all that keen on documentation?"

"No ... although you would've thought John would've taken more pride in his life's work. Whenever we interacted he always had a high opinion of himself."

"Maybe he wants to remain an enigma in death — as he was in life."

"An enigma, that's one way to put it."

"A pizza-enhanced enigma."

Kelly smirked.

There was something in the air. It was like our brief conversation had blown away all the cobwebs inside my skull. Made everything seem a little less dull. I decided that I should trust my instincts. "You, uh ... don't fancy a cheeky Monday drink, do you?"

She parted her lips, forming a reply.

Then her phone buzzed in her bag.

She slipped it out, read the screen.

Tilted her head to one side and frowned.

Then I recalled what she had said in the pub on Friday. That she wasn't much of a drinker. Before I could catch myself, I found myself saying, "Or, you know, we could go see if we can find a yoga café. I never did want to end up with a posture like Nosferatu in my early-thirties."

She didn't reply for so long that I was worried I would have to repeat my offer. Or apologise for having brought it up at all ... for having made everything so awkward.

Every second that passed by my stomach knotted a little tighter.

And the cringe factor increased.

From somewhere, a little voice told me that it was only as awkward as *I* made it ... I wondered if I hadn't read that in one of the multiple self-help books I had consumed.

Finally, she looked up from her screen. There was no trace of a smile, no humour in her expression now. "Uh, sorry, Marcus. My boyfriend's picking me up in a minute."

When she smiled this time, it was an apologetic one.

It wasn't anything like the other smiles.

This one hollowed me out rather than filled me up.

Back to being a husk again, I guess ...

Apparently sensing the dampened tone, Kelly brightened her voice. "I have to wait for him on the corner. Over there. You know, like a hooker?"

It was my turn to laugh. The sense of good feeling — or at least a trace of it — returned. Even if she had just made the joke to soften the blow to my pride, I was glad.

In some ways, I suppose the joke was on her.

I don't consider myself to *possess* any pride.

Even so, I was blushing. "Okay. I'll see you tomorrow."

Kelly gave me another quick smile, waved farewell then marched off up the road.

"Don't worry about it, mate."

I flinched then turned.

I had forgotten that Geoff the Security Man was even there.

Sitting in his booth, he had fluffy grey sideburns and wore half-moon glasses. He perched on one of those footstools you see in supermarkets — the ones that employees use to reach the top shelves and which they dissuade customers from using. Someone had once said that he preferred to "perch" like this rather than sit in a conventional chair because he had issues with back pain. Maybe I should invite *him* to go find a yoga café ... if that was even a thing .... As always, he wore the navy-blue shirt of his uniform with two or three buttons too many undone. This showed off the tanned hide of his chest and the wiry white hairs sprouting from his skin. It also showed off the golden medallion dangling from his neck. Geoff leaned in closer. "Whenever I see 'er and 'er boyfriend come by in their car, they're always arguin'. You want my advice?"

I did actually ...

"It's just a waiting game. Bide your time. Your chance'll come." He tapped his nose as if he had just imparted some grand wisdom.

For all I knew, he had.

# SIMPLE SUN

T hankfully, the rest of the week wasn't as arduous as Monday had promised it might be. In fact, by the time Friday rolled around, I could almost close my eyes and pretend nothing at all had happened. That John Horsham — aka Technomancer — still walked -*waddled?* — the Earth ... just that LifeWare was no longer his stomping ground.

I didn't dare to so much as touch the tablet again.

But neither did I turn it into the police ...

I found a secret spot in my flat and stashed it away.

One pleasant side-effect of Monday's meeting with Lucas was that he more or less left me alone. It was almost as if he was trying to avoid *me* rather than it being the other way around.

Perhaps something positive might come out of him dating my ex-girl-friend.

On Friday afternoon, I hung back at the office, hoping to catch Kelly when she emerged from what had been Technomancer's office. By the time it had gone five twenty and I'd said goodbye to Fil, who as always left at five thirteen, I decided it was best for me to go too. For all I knew, Kelly was waiting for me to leave, thinking that I was some kind of weirdo-stalker freak.

Maybe I was how weirdo-stalker freaks get started ...

Mainly to make myself feel better, I told myself she was busy with work. She had to take full advantage of the fact that she was currently in a grace period. That owing to the manner of demise of the former sysadmin, there was some goodwill built up which would allow her time in dealing with the backlog of support tickets.

On top of that, she had to get to grips with *being* John Horsham.

And I knew that on no level could that be a pleasant thing.

At least beyond the limitless supply of pizza ...

Following our conversation on Monday, every time I passed Geoff the Security Man on my way into work or on my way home, he clicked his tongue and winked at me.

I told myself it was good to have somebody on my side.

Somebody fighting my corner ... whatever my corner represented ...

I plodded out of the office, brained by a long week and looking forward to a couple of days off. It was as I headed to catch the bus back to my flat that I realised I could hear a car engine lightly droning on my heels. I halted, turned back, expecting to see a car stuck behind a cyclist, the driver growing increasingly irate as they sought to pull ahead.

However, there was no cyclist.

Just a car.

It was following *me*.

There was nothing remarkable about the car. It was shaped a bit like an abbreviated sardine tin. The paintwork was a sun-faded pea-green except for the bonnet which was a stark mauve, clearly transplanted from another vehicle. There were also several dents in the side, a webbed crack in the windscreen, and given that a steady drizzle was falling, I couldn't help but think that the sunroof had to be stuck permanently open.

There was a driver and passenger within.

Nobody that I could see in the back seat.

In apparent acknowledgement that I had seen it following, the car sped up and drew up alongside me, its indicator flashing as it signalled to pull over.

The window wound down on the passenger side.

The passenger had acne so bad his complexion resembled a gnawed slab of raw meat. If it hadn't been for the mirror shades, I might not have believed he was human at all.

"Get in the car, Marcus."

Although the words were clearly intended to be threatening, the voice was nasal, nerdy. The kind of voice I would have attributed to someone who solved algebraic functions for fun. All the same, my heart started to pound in my ears.

It isn't every day I get threatened by strangers in the street.

Especially ones who know my name.

I bent over to get a proper look inside.

I could make out the driver beyond the passenger and almost gave myself a heart attack. His face was almost identical to Technomancer, John Horsham. He had the same oily hair strung down to his shoulders. The same pinched wrinkles at his brow. He would have been identical except for one thing. He was stick thin.

Passenger and driver were both dressed in black ... black jeans with black t-shirts featuring what I believed were metal bands from the artwork.

I had never been all that into metal, to put it mildly.

"What do you want?" I asked, my words calmer and stronger than I intended.

The passenger was dumbstruck a moment. He pushed his mirror shades up onto his forehead, revealing intense blue eyes. "We need to talk with you. Get in please."

"Can't you talk to me out here?"

The passenger glanced over his shoulder, as if they might be blocking the road for the traffic behind. But there were no other vehicles in sight. He shifted his attention back onto me. "This is a delicate matter. It cannot be discussed out in the open."

I calculated my options.

Even though I was hardly a beefcake, I fancied my chances in being able to overcome these two ... unarmed, that was. They did look the types who might just have ornamental Samurai swords mounted on their bedroom walls or nun chucks in their sock drawers.

"Thanks," I said, with a quick smile, backing away from the car. "But, no thanks."

I guess that old piece of parenting advice was well-lodged in my brain.

The one about not getting into strangers' cars.

Even well into my thirties it was keeping me out of trouble.

105

I carried on walking along, hearing the car still droning alongside like a stray dog gingerly limping at my heel begging for some scrap to be thrown its way.

This time it was the driver I heard speak up.

"Marcus, please. It's about John. It won't take long. I promise."

My heart sunk in my chest and I looked back into the car.

The two of them looked truly pathetic.

Anaemic complexions.

Weedy, muscle-free bodies ... and I'm not exactly Mr Universe ...

"Don't you want to know how we know your name?" the passenger asked.

I wasn't certain about this argument.

It had a certain not-so-veiled threat attached to it.

I sighed long and hard. "Are you guys going to keep stopping off here every day after work until I speak with you? Is that the sort of persistence we're dealing with here?"

Neither of them said anything ... but their silence told a story.

I looked up the road to the queue of a couple dozen bored-looking people waiting at the bus stop. There was no sign of the bus. I thought about the prospect of squeezing onto a crowded bus, holding on for dear life while tucked in beneath someone's armpit with the radiators blowing full-blast. I decided that there might be somewhere we could meet in the middle. "Do you reckon you could give me a lift home?" I asked.

The passenger turned away, mumbled something to the driver, who mumbled back.

"Okay," the passenger said. "We will drive you home. Once we've had a chat."

I thought about it a moment more.

Glanced to the bus stop queue.

And decided.

These guys were harmless.

Or that was what I convinced myself as I reached for the door handle.

No sooner had I sat down, brought the door shut behind me, than the driver gunned the engine. The passenger swivelled in his seat to face me. He bore a black canvas bag in his hands — like the ones that get popped over prisoners' heads before getting water boarded.

"Put this on," the passenger said.

I looked at the bag. "Uh, not bloody likely ..."

Up ahead, there was a traffic jam. The driver drummed his fingers on the steering wheel as he slowed down, glowering at me in the rear-view mirror. I waited for the car to come to a complete stop behind the stationary traffic and then reached for the door handle.

It looked like I would have to endure the bus after all ...

"Wait!"

I paused.

Looked at the passenger.

"All right, all right!" the passenger said, resigned, allowing the hood to drop at his feet. "Don't worry about it."

"Where're you taking me? ... And at such a leisurely pace ..."

"Headquarters," the passenger said, neatly sidestepping my jibe.

"Is that where you take all your victims?"

"Victims?"

As the light changed, the traffic began its slow shuffle forward.

"Nobody would ever accuse me of being a social butterfly," I said, "but I don't usually insist guests put a bag over their heads before they come round."

The passenger sat back in his seat, knuckles resting against the window, peering out beyond the glass, straight-faced. When he replied, he sounded slightly disappointed. "No, I suppose not."

It was then that I noticed the mark on the back of his hand.

A tattoo.

It was the same geometrical outline of the sun I had seen sketched on Technomancer's neck. The same logo that appeared on the splash screen of the computer tablet.

I addressed the driver this time. "You look a lot like him."

"Like who?" the driver replied, as if it wasn't obvious.

His voice was gruffer than I had anticipated.

But the tone was like raising the dead. As if Technomancer himself had lurched free of his extra-large casket in the funeral parlour.

"Like John Horsham," I said.

An uneasy silence squeezed the car.

I wondered whether these two had seriously believed I wouldn't notice the resemblance. Perhaps they thought everybody who walked the Earth was thick.

Except for them, of course.

I got the impression that — like John — they were IT People.

The driver snorted. It might've conceivably been to hide a sob, or he might just have been suffering from a lingering cold. "You're the one that found him."

"That's right. Is that why you want to talk to me?"

Neither of them said anything.

The car was trundling along at maybe five miles per hour now, stopping dead every half minute or so, behind the seemingly never-ending Friday-night traffic. We came to a complete halt which was just as well as the driver seemed to be worse for wear.

The driver swallowed hard.

This time there was no question about it, his eyes sparkled with tears.

For the first time in this whole ridiculous situation, I felt bad.

"I was ... his half-brother," the driver said.

I breathed in deeply.

Felt strange.

It was the first time I had experienced any sense of sadness at Technomancer's death. Perhaps it was the first time I had even considered that he might have a family, as everybody at work did. "I'm sorry for you loss."

More silence.

The driver stared at his wing mirror for a long time, examining his own reflection, and then shifted around in his seat. He looked me in the eye. And then stretched out his hand. "I'm Toby," he said.

108

I shook his hand.

There was a long, awkward gap before the passenger realised we were waiting for him to speak up. "And I'm Daymian," he said, finally.

"Damian?" I replied.

He shook his head. "No, you're not pronouncing the 'y'."

Ahead, the traffic shifted forward and we nudged towards the junction.

The driver — Toby — flipped the indicator.

From the passenger seat, Daymian with a "y" spoke up. "John's passing was a shock to all of us. Nobody was expecting it. He was ... larger than life."

There it was. That all-too-familiar platitude.

If John Horsham had been female, the phrase would've been "bubbly". There's something about euphemisms for the bigger-bodied that I've always found a touch sickening.

Toby turned off down a narrow side street and before I could fully take stock of the direction we were heading, I realised we were out in the countryside. I thought back to how Daymian had wanted to "bag" me and wondered if I really was in total possession of my mental faculties. However, the moment of panic passed when I reminded myself that I had my smartphone on me. It wasn't like I was going to get lost. And, anyway, didn't tech companies store all their users' activity in data warehouses somewhere?

At least that would make the murder investigation more straightforward.

All the same, I tapped out a quick message to Riko:

*If I don't respond in half an hour call the police.*

There, that settled it.

Now I just needed to be completely sure that — one — Riko had his phone with him — two — that he would actually read the message and — three — that if he actually read the message he would do something if I didn't respond.

Ah, well. It had been a kind of okay life ...

☼

"Headquarters" turned out to be located on an out-of-town business and retail park called Harper's Lake. Harper's Lake was from around that time when city developers nationwide decided it would be "all the rage" to offer companies space out in the countryside. They could offer leases at a fraction of the going rate in the city centre and make money on previously underutilised real estate. Of course the economy had taken several hits since then and most businesses that had once featured on Harper's Lake, or other places like it, had either got out where they could or gone bust.

Only the survivors remained.

I reeled off their names in my head as we passed them by in the car like the roll call of gnarled veterans they were:

*Hal's Car Exhausts*

*Fridges2U*

*Stair Lifts to Heaven*

Despite the otherwise shabby surroundings — most storefronts had their steel shutters permanently drawn down, graffiti daubed on top — the manmade lake remained quite charming.

Given the lack of regular gardening services, the area had had a chance to "rewild" and now long grasses rose up to chest height, swaying in the gentle breeze. Through the crack in the sunroof, I could hear quacking ducks. A gargling stream. The drizzle was a fine mist which made miniature ripples on the surface of the lake. Yes, there was something to be said for Harper's Lake.

Something poetic, even:

Peace and quiet and the falling rain.

As the car slowed, apparently approaching its final destination, the drizzle strengthened into pellet-sized raindrops. They arced in through the open sunroof and spattered my cheeks. I caught a particularly jagged one in the eye. "Doesn't it shut?" I asked.

"Hmm?" Daymian replied, having slipped off into a world of his own some time ago. He caught my eye, saw where I was looking, and glanced casually up at the sunroof. "Oh, nah. I think it's stuck."

The car jerked to a sudden halt.

Toby ground on the handbrake, switched off the ignition.

He flipped his thumb over his shoulder.

"Went to Hal's Car Exhausts about it but he wasn't able to help." The slightest smile traced his lips. "Guess the clue's in the name, huh?"

"Guess so," I replied.

As the three of us got out of the car, a dark cloud smothered out the last remaining sunlight.

The first peal of thunder rolled overhead.

Talk about omens ...

Rain scored the concrete, turning the industrial grey dust to a mulchy brown mush. There was a light chinking sound whenever a raindrop happened to strike one of the many pieces of broken glass on the ground. Toby and Daymian both popped an umbrella.

It didn't appear that they had brought one along for me.

Then again, I was their "prisoner".

Not having anything else to shield me from the rain, I clasped my hands over my head. I don't know why I chose that particular part of my body to attempt to keep dry — it's not like I ever put any product in my hair except for the cheapest shampoo on offer.

Maybe it's some primal instinct.

Don't they say that you lose ninety percent of your body heat through your head?

Or is that a touch melodramatic?

I hung back at the open car door, feeling the rain beginning to soak into my work shirt and trousers. My work shoes hadn't been waterproof for a long time ... but hopefully we'd get into the dry before too much longer. I reasoned with myself that I could always leave them to dry on the radiator over the weekend ... working on the assumption that my flat was still standing. Any day now I was expecting to return home to find the whole building a pile of cinders with Riko standing beside it, a perplexed look on his face:

*"So that's what happens when you put cardboard in the toaster ... "* or something to that effect.

With the thought of Riko, I checked my phone.

I'd texted him about twenty minutes ago.

He still hadn't replied to me.

I wondered if I should update him.

Probably not worth it, all things considered.

The clank of metal on metal cut off my train of thought.

Daymian was fiddling with the padlock which clasped the shutter closed.

The shutter was one in a long row of abandoned industrial units.

... At least the fact that they were smashed in suggested they were abandoned.

It seemed that each shutter in turn had been ram raided or sledge-hammered, or both, and then as a final act of humiliation been daubed with spray-painted profanity.

I guessed that whoever had tried to break in hadn't exactly been the sharpest knife in the drawer. The evidence of just how much of a thankless task it would be to break into one of these units seemed to be ... well, *evident*.

Beneath the grime and graffiti on the shutter Daymian was fiddling with, I spotted the familiar logo. The logo from the tablet splash screen. And the tattoos.

What else did I expect?

"Simple Sun," Toby mumbled over his shoulder, apparently having seen me staring but his face now hidden as he was stooped over digging through the back of the car.

"What's Simple Sun?" I asked.

"It's a company," Toby replied.

"Company?" Daymian responded, still working tirelessly at the pad-lock. "Really, it's a bit more than a *company*. It's a *movement*."

There was no way I'd been off target with my thinking that these were IT guys.

Completely unwarranted sense of superiority — *check*.

I stood between the two of them, telling myself that old chestnut about "divide and conquer" ... but it appeared that any chance of a conflict dissipated with Toby's sigh as he stooped back over the open car boot and carried on. He produced a rubber welcome mat which he dropped over the open sunroof. Apparently this was the measure he took to keep the sunroof sealed while it was raining and the car was parked.

A bright idea struck me.

"Maybe you should invest in some duct tape?" I said.

Toby met my eye.

"You know," I went on, unperturbed, "so you can stay dry while you're driving?" I paused, and then added, "Or so you can tie your victims up more effectively?"

Toby continued to eye me.

It's an expression people often aim at me — the one which tells me unambiguously that the person is trying to work out whether or not I'm being serious.

"I'll get it fixed one of these days," he said finally. "Or get someone to shut it for good. I dunno how it even got stuck there, really. I never used to open it. It was like that after ..." his voice fell away for a brief moment but he recovered "... after John had been driving it."

I felt a jab in my gut.

I always get that feeling when I rake up someone's emotions unintentionally.

I've never got a kick out of being a bully, making people feel bad, and especially when I do it without meaning to ... I reminded myself that someone had died.

And that Toby had been his half-brother.

I needed to tread carefully.

Thankfully, the awkwardness was broken when Daymian finally snapped the padlock free.

The shutter whipped open, springing upwards to reveal a slightly anticlimactic — but perhaps not entirely unexpected — brick wall with a door in its centre.

I had to admit that I was feeling somewhat intrigued.

Daymian produced another key, unlocked the door and went inside.

Toby, the perfect gentleman, gestured for me to go first.

Still feeling bad about invoking his sorrow, I accepted the honour.

When Toby brought the door shut on my heels, I had the uncomfortable, and unmistakable, feeling of being trapped. Perhaps it was the total lack of natural light. The fact that the only light source was the fluorescent lightly buzzing strip bulb overhead.

Simple Sun Headquarters turned out to be the single room that I was currently standing in. Well, it wasn't *quite* a single room. Towards the back of the room, there was a pair of doors; one of which I supposed led to a toilet and the other to a storage cupboard.

The first of my assumptions was confirmed as correct as with the flushing of a cistern Daymian emerged. Seeing both me and Toby standing there, staring at him, he apparently felt the need to provide some explanation. "I have a very sensitive digestive system," he said.

Simple Sun hadn't invested in any sort of interior décor. The floor was bare concrete and the walls were cinder blocks. There weren't even any posters stuck up on the walls in a half-arsed way. The only furniture in the room was three beaten-up desks, each with two computer monitors perched upon them. Cables snaked all over the floor, with no plastic ties to tame them. The most expensive items of furniture looked to be the desk chairs which were that special ergonomic kind.

Apparently, IT people take their sitting posture seriously.

I stayed where I was, afraid of breaking anything ... even though there really wasn't much for me to touch let alone break.

"We've been renting this space for ten years now," Daymian said, as if I had asked the question. "At first, we wanted somewhere we could have LAN parties."

I must have looked bemused because he grinned.

Toby had mercy on me. "A LAN party is when we come together to play video games. Everyone has their own computer. Their own monitor. Like online gaming only everyone's in the same room. A local connection. Not internet."

I couldn't recall the last time a tech-savvy person had given me such an effective potted explanation as Toby had just done. I wondered if he was looking for a job ... The stark similarity of their appearances apart, it was difficult to believe Toby and Technomancer were related at all.

"Simple Sun was our clan," Daymian continued.

"Our gaming team," Toby clarified.

Daymian shot Toby a smouldering glare. "Soon, though, we decided we could do much more. We outgrew *playing* games. We decided we could *design* our own."

Daymian's tone was more than a little like a precocious child.

It seemed the world had failed to give him the knock around the head it gives all ego maniacs sooner or later, bringing them back down to some semblance of reality.

Maybe his knock was coming ...

"You wanted to make money?" I ventured.

Daymian scowled as if the mere mention of money was so base that I might as well have spit in his eye. All the same, he went on, "John had much grander ideas. He wanted to broaden scope. Even back when we were gaming, he got us into other projects. When we started to make some decent money on the side, we paid him more attention."

"Okay," I replied, looking from Daymian to Toby, back again, and then to the office space surrounding us. "But I guess the money didn't stretch to limos or Jacuzzis?"

Daymian made a sort of huffing sound as though he was a whoopee cushion someone had strangled the last scrap of air from. "This is the very *least* of the business," he said, enigmatically before adding — malignly — "The very *least* of the movement."

"But you still have day jobs?" I asked.

Neither of them said anything but they wouldn't meet my eye.

And I decided to let the matter drop.

It was impressive enough that they had their own office ... what did *I* have to show for my thirty-something years of effort? I waited a polite couple of moments, and then decided I should get the ball rolling if I wanted to get home in time for tea ... and beer. "What does all this have to do with me? Why did you bring me here?"

Daymian took a step closer and I sensed more than just an undercurrent of menace. His breath stank of raw sewage ... and he seemed to emit body odour from every pore.

"You were the last one to see him," Daymian said, his eyes never leaving mine. "John was working on something — something important. Something *secret*. He held it over us. He was always talking about it like it was going to be some grand invention. Something that would change everything."

"Get you out of your day jobs?" I suggested, a little too blasé for my own good.

I couldn't help but think that Daymian was talking about the computer tablet.

The one stashed away at home.

Safe, or so I thought ...

There was a grinding sort of noise.

A whiff of an electrical fire.

Something caught the corner of my eye.

A blue spark?

I pivoted.

Saw Toby — standing a few strides away to my right — holding something down at his side. A device the size and shape of a Dictaphone. Realisation struck me.

A stun gun.

Like the ones police carried.

A cold wave washed over me ... I realised just how much of an idiot I had been to get myself into this situation. As if my phone shared my thoughts, I felt it vibrate in my pocket.

Someone calling me.

Riko?

"We've looked around his place," Daymian went on as if nothing had changed about the situation, "but we couldn't find anything. You, however, had access to his office. And you were the last one to visit his office ... before the police showed up. It must have been there. He must have kept it with him. Until the end."

My mind flickered to the tablet once more.

And — inevitably — to those pictures of Olivia.

My heart skipped a beat.

I stared at the stun gun a few moments.

How had I been so stupid to think that I could handle this pair of nutters?

Didn't all maniacs start out as seemingly harmless eccentrics?

That was why when they interviewed the neighbours, they always said things along the lines of, "It was completely out of his nature", or "He was such a well-behaved boy".

I snapped back onto Daymian. "I didn't see anything," I said. "Nothing out of the ordinary. Isn't the most likely thing that the police have it now? ... Whatever it is?"

I hoped that my tone of voice was convincing ... drama has never been my forte.

Daymian exchanged glances with Toby and then turned his full attention back to me. "For your sake, you'd better hope they don't."

What he did next would've been comical if it hadn't been for what had come before. He indicated his eyes with two fingers before pointing those same two fingers at me. "We'll be watching you, Marcus. If you remember anything you let us know. Is that clear?"

I glanced at the stun gun Toby still held down at his side.

"You know where we are," Daymian said. "It'll be up to you to come find us."

There was another long pause.

Then I said, "Are you guys going to drive me home now?"

# SAFE ... FOR NOW

The trip back home was nothing if not an anti-climax.

It seemed that we weren't going to be in for a dramatic thunderstorm after all — the clouds having taken on a lighter tone since we had driven away from Harper's Lake. As it was getting on for seven in the evening, and we were still on summer time, there was every chance that the sun might burst through at some point for one last hurrah.

I'm not completely sure what I expected getting into the car with Toby and Daymian once more but I guess that after the threatening scene which'd taken place at Simple Sun HQ there would at least be some low-level small-talk.

Threatening or otherwise.

As it was, though, neither Toby or Daymian (with a "y") said anything beyond asking me where I wanted to be dropped off.

I might've been stupid enough to get into a car with a pair of strangers, but my self-survival instincts kicked in on at least one level to warn me from giving away my precise home address. Then again, as these were IT people, I imagined that they probably had ways of finding out where I lived if they so wished. Or they thought they could find out if they wanted.

In the end, I chose the Sermon as the drop-off point.

I reasoned with myself that while I wanted to preserve the secret of my exact address, I also wanted to strike a balance of not walking *too* far back home.

I waited for the car to purr its way around the bend before proceeding to my flat up the road. As I climbed the stairs, I couldn't help but feel that something was *off* ... it's a kind of tingling in my nostrils, a hollow sensation in my gut, that I have baptised my "Riko sense".

It was mostly a fairly useless sense given that it didn't offer any sort of preventative protection against whatever it was that Riko might or might not have done but — being the most average of all average Joes — I guess I had to take my super powers where I could find them. And so I turned the key in the door to my flat and went in, dropping my work bag at my feet.

Before my very eyes, the sofa bed was drawn open, and there were two forms lying there, the bedsheets draped over their prostrate bodies. It took me another moment to realise that they were sleeping; that the sheets were rising and falling with their gentle respiration.

First I took in Riko — lying on his side, lightly snoring — an uncharacteristically stern expression on his face. And then I took stock of the person — or more precisely, *woman* — lying beside him. The woman was lying face down and so her most notable feature was her purple hair.

It took me a second or two to make the connection, but the penny did drop eventually.

Julie.

Julie from Frothy Cups.

As if the visual realisation released my other senses, I breathed in that overpowering, sweet-sour smell of sex ... and almost lost my lunch.

I considered my options.

The idea of giving them a rude awakening appealed to me but in the end I decided that I didn't have the stomach for another potentially violent scene this evening, or any kind of confrontation for that matter, and so I headed for the kitchenette.

I hesitated at the kitchen counter, and specifically the half-full glass of water left sitting on the side — violet lipstick smeared on the rim — and briefly thought of tipping it over the drowsy lovers ... thinking better of it only when I reminded myself that I would need to sleep on the sofa bed that night and — call me old-fashioned — I've never enjoyed sleeping on damp bedding.

I had stashed the computer tablet just above the oven in the kitchenette.

I saw that it was right where I'd left it so I slipped it out of its spot, headed back across the flat, shaking off a loose brassiere caught on the toe of my shoe as I went.

When I made it back to the front door of my flat, standing on the welcome mat in the hallway outside, I hesitated, wondering if I should just be the diligent, long-suffering friend that I had always been to Riko. Apparently I decided against this, because I brought the door shut with an almighty slam.

As I descended the stairs, headed back out to the fresh air, and the street, I listened to the panicked flapping of startled birds rapidly departing their tree branches outside.

I don't really know why I chose the Street Sermon of all places.

I suppose that it was a Friday and so I was probably drawn to it out of a sense of ... I'd like to say loyalty, but it's probably deeper and sadder than that ... more like *habit*.

As I sat down with a hoppy pint of ale at one of the few empty tables in the corner, I tried to remember the last Friday that I *hadn't* ended up here.

I wasn't going to get into too much introspection, though (there would be time enough for me to do that while I was listening to customers' complaints all next week on the phone) and so with my regular Friday night fish and chips order in at the bar I slapped the tablet down on the table in front of me and stabbed the power button with my finger.

I wasn't quite sure just why I was directing my anger — was I angry? — at the tablet, it being an inanimate object, and all ... maybe it was akin to a primate beating a machine with a rock because it's making weird chirpy noises he doesn't understand. All I knew was that this tablet was the reason Toby and Daymian had sort of kidnapped me — certainly *threatened* me — and so it must possess some kind of great value ... beyond perving on people's private collections of gnomic pornography.

The Simple Sun logo splashed across the screen.

I had to admit that I was already becoming more than a little tired of seeing that symbol. It had given me nothing but grief thus far in our acquaintance.

Once the logo was gone, though, I found myself looking over the main screen which Riko had shown me previously. There was a list of devices.

This being a Friday night — and the busiest time of the week at the Sermon — there had to be two or three dozen devices on the list. I glanced up as if someone might know what I was up to and be ready to pounce upon me, or else to scream out for their friends to give me a beating. But everyone was chattering away happily, the warm drunken haze descending like a heavy fog over all patrons. I took another sip of beer to calm my wild thoughts.

Back on screen, I stroked my way down the list, trying to decide who would be my first victim. In the end I settled upon the pubs customer wifi access point:

Sermon Net

I wondered what I might find there.

I gave it a tap.

The tablet did some whirring and I was so focused on the loading circle spinning about that I almost missed the waitress setting my fish and chips down on the table in front of me. Because I'm nothing if not polite to the point of idiocy, I looked away from my "hacking" for a brief moment, gave her my best non-offensive smile and thanked her. From the swift way she turned her back on me I'm fairly sure she wouldn't have noticed the difference if I'd told her to, "Fuck off you stupid cunt". Still, I knew I'd done the right thing.

The tablet was now giving me the view of a computer desktop, much like my neighbour's desktop ... the one which Riko had raided so boun- tifully.

I checked out my options. The folder marked, "BARRED CUS- TOMERS" was too tempting not to have a look at so I gave it a tap. A spreadsheet unfurled before my very eyes.

I suppose that in other — *lower-tech* — times, the list would've taken the form of a series of blurry, grainy Polaroid pictures with scribbled first names beneath them pinned up behind the bar. But the Sermon — proud twenty-first century establishment it was — had leaped into the digital age with both feet.

After about half a minute of perusing the list, I was surprised at just how dry reading it made. There was the customer's forename and surname — several of them had their nicknames listed also — and then there was a concise reason for their ban and the date the ban expired. There was also a link which I supposed led to a photo that'd been cropped from CCTV pictures for whichever barman was on duty to make double sure before having someone thrown out on their ear. I guessed that they probably had an A4 sheet printed out with these photos and stuck up out of sight behind the bar for ease of use even in these post-internet times. What I had found, however, was the master document.

I toyed with my newfound power, a smirk crossing my lips as I considered the idea of adding Riko to the list. This thought, however, ground to a premature halt as I reminded myself that Riko had probably set foot in the Sermon twice in his entire life — and even then I had had to hoist him in kicking and screaming. It was strange because I would've thought that Riko would've had the perfect profile for being a "pub personality" but there was something within him that not only opposed pubs but alcohol too ... in actual fact, if I paused to think about it, Riko was something of a puritan. Or maybe he'd had a rare moment of personal awareness and realised that he was already weird enough without indulging in third-party substances.

I was about to close down the list and turn my attention to something dishier on the pub computer, when I picked out a familiar name:

Mildreth Victoria Loaves

There was a nickname listed too:

"Vicky"

Mysteriously there was no note as to the reason why she had been banned from the Sermon and neither was there an end date to her ban which I took to mean that she was barred for life ... and there I had been a few weeks ago thinking that the person in the basement flat was a sweet old lady. Or maybe it was just a massive coincidence and there was somebody with exactly the same name.

"Excuse me?"

My heart froze and blood hummed in my eardrums.

When I looked up, I knocked my pint glass, splashing some of it onto the already-sticky table. I saw the person leaning over me was a bald man, one of those who clearly waxed his bald head. He was about in his fifties, judging by the bulge around the middle, and the few bristles of white hair sprouting from his otherwise bald pate. He was stocky and had clearly once been extremely well-muscled. Not that I would've had any ideas of messing with him either then or now or in the future. Throughout my life I've taken an evasive approach to physical conflict and it has served me well thus far. He had a Costa del Sol tan and wore a cornflower-blue shirt with a subtle yellow cross-stitch pattern over a pair of what could only be described as "Dad jeans". He stood with his arms crossed over his chest in a self-important way.

It felt as if the tablet I was holding in my hands had become awfully hot all of a sudden. I tried to figure out the best way to minimise what I was looking at without attracting attention but before I could so much as move a muscle the man was talking again.

"You in here last week? On Friday?"

I wasn't quite sure what to make of this question.

The way he said it made me think that he already knew the answer.

I scoured my mind trying to work out whether I had done anything terribly wrong last week ... but found nothing. I decided that I might as well tell the truth.

It was simpler that way.

"Yes, I was," I replied.

He arched an eyebrow and flared his nostrils. "Mind if I ask you some questions?"

My brain tried to escape my skull but just slapped against the side and slid all the way back down. Working as subtly as I could manage, I tapped the Standby button on the tablet, the Simple Sun logo winking at me as the screen disintegrated once more into darkness.

I allowed it to fall into my lap.

He took a seat opposite me.

I realised that my plate of fish and chips was still sitting before me, untouched. It would be cold now — just like last week ... I wondered if that was what this was about.

"Don't know if you know it but I'm the landlord here."

"Ah," I replied, my stomach dipping, and hoping against hope that he hadn't caught a sneaky glimpse of the tablet screen before I'd shut it down ... or maybe he'd been watching a CCTV feed from a back room somewhere.

Perhaps the game was up completely.

Maybe the police were on their way.

"I wanted to ask you about the friend you were with," he continued.

I jutted my lip out in a pout.

I thought about Kelly.

Wondered if I'd seemed like I was her *friend*.

We were work colleagues, but nothing more than that.

Then again, I suppose to the casual observer there's no way of making a distinction ...

"What about her?" I asked.

"Her?" he replied, furrowing his brow. "No, I mean the man — the skinny guy ... had on a pretty flashy suit."

"Lucas?" When I spoke his name it tasted sour and I was fairly sure my tone came across because the landlord looked at me strangely.

"It's the first time we've had him in here — first time that I can remember, anyway."

"Oh?" I replied, genuinely perplexed.

The landlord cast a glance off across the pub, halting over a group of particularly revelous Friday night office workers. One of them was precariously balancing his pint — still about two-thirds full — on top of his head. I wondered if I wasn't keeping the landlord from his work on the busiest night of the week ... but, then again, he was the one who had approached me. He shifted in his seat to face me once more. "Yeah," he said. "Been looking out for him though."

"Really?"

"Mm, you know we share stuff between us?"

"Sort of like a pub landlord social network?"

The landlord gave me the sort of smile that could easily twist itself into a snarl and be followed up with a deft right hook at half a second's notice.

I knew it would be an extremely bad idea to get on the wrong side of that smile.

"Yeah," he said. "Sorta."

I glanced at my own pint, and then to my plate of fish and chips again.

I wondered if there wasn't something within me that secretly savoured the flavour and texture of cold fish and chips. Perhaps that was why I kept ending up consuming my fish and chips in this particular way. I returned to meet the landlord's gaze, feeling the heat coming off his glare and knowing that the time for joshing was over.

"He's on what we call a 'watch list'," the landlord went on. "It's for patrons who have ... you know, not done anything wrong ..."

"Not enough to get barred?"

A slight smile tweaked the corner of the landlord's mouth. "That's right. Nothing to get barred ... just, you know ... someone you should keep an eye on."

I sat up straighter in my seat, leaned slightly over the table, propping one elbow beside my plate of fish and chips. I had to admit that I was somewhat intrigued to learn just what Lucas had done to get himself on this "watch list".

"What was ... uh, worth watching about him?" I asked.

The landlord puffed out his cheeks, glanced down at my plate of fish and chips. "That must be stone-cold now, huh?"

"Hmm?" I replied, and then glanced down at my food — somehow having forgotten about it in the fractions of a second that'd elapsed after asking the question. "Uh, yeah ..."

"I'll get the kitchen to warm it up for you," he replied, and then, meeting my eye once more, "I dunno. There's just something ... *funny* about him, you know?"

I had to admit that Lucas was lots of things ... "funny" wasn't one of them, though.

"Uh huh?" I replied.

The landlord jerked his thumb over his shoulder. "Over at the Bridges" — I guess he meant The Three Bridges, about a fifteen-minute walk in the direction of the town centre from the Sermon — "Langley, the landlord there, said he was seeing him in the place with a different girl every night. And, well, it wasn't like your standard thing of a ladies' man, you know? Different girl every Friday, or Saturday, something like that? He was in there every day of the week. Different girl every day."

"I see," I replied, having no idea at all what this meant ... and more intrigued than ever.

"Things like that .... they don't go unnoticed, you know? Gotta be careful getting caught up in things like that." He dropped his voice and leaned over the table. "Soliciting. Drugs. That sort of stuff can get an establishment into bother." He waved his hand around us. "Got cameras all over the place. Bouncers on the doors. Not noticing ain't ever gonna wash as an excuse with the licensors — let alone the police."

My mind spun with the revelation.

I had to admit that I had pinned Lucas for many things, but I had never thought that he was anything of a "ladies' man" ... although from what the landlord was saying it added up to something different.

"Anyway, couple of weeks back," the landlord continued, "Langley got one of his door boys to have a chat with him, you know, down the alley?"

My stomach dropped with the suggestion of just what he meant. I couldn't stretch my imagination to believe that anything pleasant happened "down the alley".

"You know, didn't want him hanging around anymore. Not like he was, anyway. Seemed to do the trick from what Langley said. Didn't see him since then. And nobody else did, although we've been keeping an eye out. Nope, nothing till he showed up here last Friday — that's when I saw him talking to you, then I saw you sitting here tonight and thought I might have a word." The landlord settled back in his chair, breathing out a heavy exhale, flaring his nostrils like an inadequately tethered bull. "So, question is, I suppose, what can you tell me about him?"

It felt as though the Sermon was steadily spinning around me.

I sank my teeth into my lip and unfocused my gaze, allowing everything to go blurry.

I reminded myself that *I* wasn't in any trouble.

And that the thing I was wrestling with most of all was just how much I was to tell him ... just how much the landlord needed to know. I decided that I needed to buy some time — feel things out just a little more. It was kind of like a customer-service rep call when you're trying to get a read on the customer. On their mood ... their *patience* ... while you're attempting to build rapport. ... Jesus, I guess that some of those LifeWare training courses have sunk in on a deeper level than I want to believe possible.

"He wasn't barred?" I asked.

The landlord stuck out his bottom lip, shook his head. "Nah, not from here. Nor from the Bridges. Didn't do anything wrong. Gotta have a reason to stick someone on a list like that. Proof ... bringing different ladies along night after night is suspicious, sure, but not enough to justify barring anybody." He gave a shrug. "He was paying good money for drink, anyhow ... that's kinda why I want to find out just who he is and what he's up to ..." The landlord gave a sheepish grin. "If the explanation turns out innocent could turn out to be a good customer for the Sermon, huh?" His features darkened once more. "Twenty years in the trade, though, doesn't make it seem that way ... I can feel something wrong about this one in my knees, that's sort of where I always get my intuitions from." He stared me down in that unnerving, slightly threatening way. "So, who is he, and how'd you know him?"

Not seeing any reason not to tell the truth, I told the landlord the story.

That Lucas was my boss at work. That I knew next to nothing about his life outside work ... I even told him about his cycling habit, as if that might be at all relevant. What I didn't tell him was that the girl on that particular Friday night had been my ex, Olivia.

After about ten minutes of me blathering, it appeared that the landlord had heard enough. He rose from the chair, reaching for my plate as he did so. "Name's Henry," he said. "You ever need me for something — you hear something more about this — just ask at the bar." He pointed to the ceiling. "Live upstairs so I'm always around about. That's right, I get to live in the pub, and it's just like it sounds — both blessing and a curse." He nodded to my plate of fish and chips he now held. "I'll get this warmed up for you quick, okay? What is it you're drinking?"

My mind went blank.

But then I remembered.

"Harvest," I replied.

The landlord — Henry — nodded back at me. "I'll get Jeanette to bring you over another pint of Harvest." And with that Henry the Landlord bulldozed his way through the Friday night drinkers in the direction of the kitchen behind the bar, barking for people to mind their elbows and let him through.

As I sat back with what remained of my current pint, and the empty table where my fish and chips had been standing, I glanced down at the tablet in my lap.

The screen was blank and yet I was certain it was laughing at me.

# A SUIT FOR ALL OCCASIONS

O n the day of the funeral, golden sunshine flickered through the elm and beech trees on the road leading up to the church. The shadows from the leaves made psychedelic monochrome patterns on the newly tarmacked road surface. It was late September and probably one of the last good days of weather in the year. I could hear a lawn mower humming to itself from behind some pensioner's garden fence and birds still chirping away merrily as if winter would never come. I could also feel the sun across the back of my suit jacket. And the sweat prickling out. Despite the unpleasant sensation of being overheated and sweaty while wearing a suit, I quickened my pace, knowing that getting to the service on time would be a Very Close Thing Indeed.

How had I ended up running so late?

Like lots of questions, the answer was the same:

Riko.

I had had plenty of time to get ready. Plenty of time to get out of the house and to the church in an unflustered manner ... but it just hadn't happened. It hadn't happened because Riko had barricaded himself in the bathroom for a full forty-five minutes earlier that morning, apparently in the belief that since I hadn't been up at the crack of dawn to go to work I wasn't planning on going anywhere all day. Because that was the sort of thing I might do on a whim ...

If I felt like giving him the benefit of the doubt then I suppose I could stretch to allowing that he had thought it was a weekend.

Whatever the explanation, by the time I finally got into the bathroom it was extremely steamy ... and smelly ... and it was a good twenty minutes after I should really have been leaving the house.

I glanced at my watch and broke into a jog, deciding that since I had already sweated so much already, and I was going to have to get my suit dry cleaned anyway, I might as well get my money's worth from the cleaning bill.

A lot like my bed sheets, I only have one suit. I use it for weddings, baptisms, and, of course, job interviews. The good thing about men is that — for the most part — nobody ever gives what you're wearing a second thought ... unless you make the effort to stand out.

Like Lucas.

I trotted on a couple of paces then doubled over myself, panting.

My face felt extremely hot.

For someone who has often been described as skinny, I'm actually in pretty poor physical condition. I have the sort of physique that a zephyr wouldn't have to struggle to knock over.

Up ahead, the church spire stuck straight up at the sky.

A slate-grey Gothic tower with a twisted metal weathervane.

A sobering beacon on an otherwise beautiful day.

I carried on, my shoes crunching the gravel pathway.

I admired the stone wall which encircled the graveyard, thinking about the skilled hands that had placed the stones there. People actually doing something *productive* with their lives ... instead of something as nightmarishly existential-crisis inducing as staring at a computer screen trying to help other people make sense of the computer screen they themselves were staring at.

I could see people up ahead — people in formal wear.

The good news was that the schedule seemed behind.

Maybe the coffin was running late ...

The funeral started at ten and although it was a work day there had been no obligation to go into the office that morning. That had given me time to think through my outfit ... or I'd mistakenly thought I'd had time to think through my outfit before Riko put the bathroom out of commission. Maybe if I was a touch more daring — and a little less

OCD — I would've just left the house, forgoing my ablutions for one day only ... although it did seem a mite disrespectful to turn up at a funeral unwashed whatever my thoughts on the existence, or non-existence, of the afterlife. In the end, after my hurried washing, I had knotted on a tie my mum had got me for a birthday years ago. It was the colour and texture of amethyst.

I liked the way it shimmered in the light.

Why I had thought this might be an appropriate dedication to John Horsham's memory, I couldn't recall but the reason had seemed compelling at the time. Maybe it had something to do with aesthetically pleasing patterns? Wasn't that all computer programming really was? Patterns?

It's never too late for that master's in computer science ...

It was oddly unsettling to arrive somewhere and find that Fil had got there before me but it had happened today. I guessed the whole business with the bus timetables, and dropping his sister off at school, was made much neater by the late start.

I caught sight of him hanging off a group of other suits ... or, more accurately, he caught sight of me, wildly waving in my direction.

Fil was immaculately turned out — as always — his hair slicked back with wax, the collar of his white shirt starched within an inch of its life, and he smelled lightly of elderberries. He clearly wasn't sure how we were supposed to interact — that much was apparent from the wild waving. To tell the truth, it's near impossible to tell what the tone is supposed to be these days. Sometimes people like their funerals to be a "celebration of life", or whatever, and as I hadn't known John Horsham at all, let alone his family, I couldn't anticipate what his wishes might actually have been. And weren't the rules different if the death was premature?

... Or was I just overthinking it a tad?

I spotted Kelly among the others standing with Fil.

We still hadn't spoken since our awkward chat a week or so back where I had sort of invited her for a drink ... asked her out? I had even said I'd be happy to go to a yoga café.

... I did my best to purge the thought from my brain.

Too much cringe.

I also noticed Lucas was part of the group, and that this was who the focus was centred upon. I thought about what Henry the Landlord had said about Lucas and couldn't help but wonder why he hadn't brought a woman along to the funeral today. Perhaps even for Lucas — the sub-human that he was — it was a stretch to bring a date along to a funeral.

Fil muttered a greeting under his breath before shifting his attention back onto Lucas. I did my best to blot out Lucas's words and succeeded seeing as he was murmuring so quietly that he clearly hoped we'd be straining to hear the pearls of wisdom dribbling from his lips. While he droned on, I took stock of the rest of my surroundings.

In another group, arranged in a shabby half-moon outside the oak church doors, I recognised the Horshams, mainly because Toby was standing among them.

There were half a dozen of them, in all.

I thought about Toby wielding the stun gun a week or so back, coming across all menacing, and it was difficult to reconcile with his skinny-as-a-rake physique ... not that I'd be much use in a fight given my current physical condition.

He met my eye briefly but either didn't notice me or decided not to acknowledge me before shifting his attention onto someone else.

There was an older couple, too.

John Horsham's parents, I supposed.

Then there was a female version of John Horsham — equal to if not exceeding John's body weight — who I supposed had to be his sister.

Or half-sister.

Daymian was there, also, dressed in a bizarre all-black getup:

Black shirt, suit and tie.

He was wearing the same mirror shades as the day we'd met.

Like Toby, he made no sign of having recognised me.

Then again, I supposed that if Simple Sun indulged itself in anything it was mystery.

The last person standing with them was odd... out of place.

132

A black man in about his late thirties, early forties, a toothy smile fixed upon his mouth. He was wearing chunky, square-framed sunglasses, and had a thick blue-black afro beard with a full head of matching hair.

Another half-brother?

Adopted, perhaps?

What set him apart, above all else — the obvious physical differences between him and the rest of the Horsham family aside — was the way he carried himself, how he squared his shoulders and stood with his hands clasped at his belt buckle, a perma-grin smeared all across his face as if he was the Most Confident Man in the Universe.

"Marc? Marcus?"

I turned, realising Fil was trying to catch my attention.

It was then that I saw everybody had started to filter into the church.

I gave Fil what I hoped was a resilient smile and the two of us shuffled to the back of the queue.

I've never been all that keen on churches, although I guess that anyone who's not a fully paid-up Godsquadder is the same. But even for atheists like me there's something undeniably weighty about a church. Maybe it's being surrounded by all that limestone, the stained-glass of ecstatic religious types all shone through with gleaming sunlight. When I'm in a church if I close my eyes and block out all my thoughts I can almost manage to convince myself that there is ... *something* ...

What, exactly, I don't really know.

On our way to the pews, there was a collection in lieu of flowers; a charity with the brain-scratching name "Kidz What Code" where the family had requested any donations be made in John Horsham's memory.

I dug out my wallet and scrounged together a few pound coins.

Like any good Millennial it's beneath me to carry cash ...

As we filed into the pews, the speakers around the church hissed and clicked with a techno beat. I was surprised the vicar allowed it.

Then again, they seem to be on a constant recruitment drive these days so maybe they're willing to make certain allowances in service to the continued worship of the Lord. That said, I always thought techno was somewhat Pagan for Christian tastes ...

Throughout the service, Fil sat beside me with his mouth slightly latched open, eyes empty, fixated upon the vicar as if he was witnessing some sort of avant garde theatre. His head bobbed and arced as he shifted his attention to John's father, his sister, and Toby as they all went up in turn to the parapet to speak to his memory. Just as I thought the ceremony was winding down, and the vicar was about to rise for the final time to lead us all in the inevitable parting prayer — sort of like church's version of the credits rolling at the end of a film — the black man I had seen at the entrance with the Horshams took up the mike. As he stood over us, I noticed the badge pinned to the lapel of his suit. Even from some distance — dozens of rows back — I could tell what it depicted:

Simple Sun

I couldn't help thinking that a badge was a safer statement of allegiance to a cause than a tattoo ... you can get tattoos removed, of course, but it's not exactly a painless procedure from what I've heard.

The man had removed his sunglasses when he had come into the church, tucking them into the breast pocket of his suit. His smile was unwavering — his teeth so evenly spaced and blocky that they looked like they had been set with an ice cube tray. Or else he had dabbled in some form of Hollywood dental treatment. When he spoke, I noted right away he had an American accent. I couldn't pin it down any more specifically than that because I have always had a tin ear for pretty much anything ... accents, music, social cues ...

"Most of you won't know who I am," the man began.

This seemed pretty much redundant, given that half of the congregation was made up of John Horsham's ex-work colleagues from LifeWare. The most any of us knew about John Horsham was his famous odour matched only by his acerbic approach to human interaction.

"My name," the man continued, "is Emmerson Ray." He paused for a long moment, allowing the final syllable of his surname to rebound off the church walls. "John and I were going to change the world. That was our aim. Nothing less. And while his untimely demise means John shall no longer be with us in body, he shall remain with us in spirit." Here the man — Emmerson Ray — clenched his fist and held it before him.

This was all starting to come across a little Shakespearean.

I just hoped nobody was going to attempt to pry open the coffin lid and waltz about before us with John Horsham's stiff, and bulky, corpse à la a certain Danish prince.

As I swept the room with my gaze, doing my best not to look at the coffin, I found myself settling upon Daymian and Toby in the front row. There was something in the way they looked at Emmerson Ray. It took me a moment or two to figure it out:

*Dim-witted devotion.*

That same glazed-over vaguely smug look that fanatical political supporters wear.

That look smeared over cultists' expressions.

Was that what Simple Sun was?

A cult?

Emmerson Ray brought his fist down upon the parapet lectern. The thump resounded about the church, magnified and slightly distorted by the tinny echo of the speakers.

Emmerson Ray's eyes shot wide open.

His nostrils flared.

"Because continue we must! Even when we lose our greatest warriors we shall overcome! Now and forever more!"

He halted, as if awaiting a round of applause.

But it didn't materialise.

Just stunned awe ... was it even really "awe" or just ... confusion?

There was a dead body among us and if society tells us nothing else then it is that dead bodies must be respected ... which usually means — if in any doubt — with silence.

Without another word, and only taking his eyes off the congregation at the very last possible moment, Emmerson Ray backed away from the lectern, stepping down from the parapet and returning to the pew.

Daymian and Toby exchanged open-mouthed glances.

What was going on here?

Did I *want* to know what was going on?

Finally, the vicar put us all out of our misery.

A rambling prayer with a horribly wrenched-in introduction to make it seem somehow entirely appropriate to the occasion. And to John Horsham.

Religion is such bullshit.

It was hard to believe I had a pint in my hand before midday on a Tuesday.

And it wasn't even a bank holiday.

Neither had I taken the day off.

Outside the church, following the service, Lucas had announced that LifeWare had decided to shut the office for the remainder of the day out of respect for our fallen comrade. He had made some comment about "emotions running high" and couldn't resist firing a glance in my direction. It was on the condition that we attended the wake which was to take place at a community centre around the corner.

The best feature of the community centre was the bar. Oh, sure, it wasn't much more than a cheap chunk of wood nailed into a gap in the wall, but they had beer, wine and spirits. I guess the local rotary club had a gay old time on weekday evenings when they met here.

I can only speak for myself but I'm very much looking forward to my descent into alcoholism once I've got my grubby hands on my pension … Only forty years to go …

The rest of the community centre was fairly standard.

It wasn't a large building.

There was the entrance, some toilets, and then the main hall.

Dozens of plastic chairs were stacked in neat columns, shoved up against the walls.

Someone had set up a few collapsible tables and scattered a few sausage rolls and other picnicking detritus across them. The air smelled of dust and cheap furniture polish. The floors were scuffed wooden boards covered in a plethora of rubber marks from generations of shoe soles; the legacy of thousands of Cubs and Brownies meetings, amateur gymnastic evenings and tango classes for the over sixties. Every couple of seconds a floorboard creaked under somebody's foot.

Even though it was sunny outside, a conclave of towering oak trees threw persistent shadow over the community centre which made it surprisingly draughty inside. I had to admit that I was glad to be wearing a woollen suit jacket despite the unpleasant, overheated journey to the church earlier. From the goose pimples on their exposed flesh, the way they crossed their arms protectively over their chests to cover what I could only imagine were bullet-hard nipples, I could tell that the female attendees were feeling the chill thanks to the delicate dresses and blouses they wore. Late-September is always a difficult time of year to get your wardrobe right.

As with all wakes, it was an awkward affair.

Two distinct groups emerged:

On one side, John Horsham's close family, along with a scattering of friends and relations.

On the other, his ex-colleagues from LifeWare.

Things were made more awkward still by the fact that absolutely everybody from LifeWare was present. Hayden Shepherd — LifeWare CEO — was even here. She was the only one who had dared breach the invisible line separating the two sides of the room. She clasped a lime and tonic water while making conversation with John's bereaved parents.

Meanwhile, on LifeWare's side of the room, everybody was doing their level best to stay out of their line manager's reach. God knows, I was doing my best not to end up standing next to Lucas, although I had to admit that I was ever so slightly intrigued to garner something else regarding these mysterious appearances at pubs with numerous women.

"So, what'd you make of it?" Fil asked, appearing next to me, a half-pint glass of something black and fizzy in his hand.

I glanced about, making sure I wouldn't be overheard. I settled on a shrug as I sipped at the pint the barman had poured into a glass for me from a bottle.

Already, the glass was half empty.

"I dunno," I said. "I've been to weirder ones."

Fil nodded to himself, and then glanced around. I saw his eyes had come to rest upon Emmerson Ray. And why not? He was certainly doing little to prevent drawing attention to himself. Every minute or so, he erupted into booming laughter and everyone would stop and stare. It was uncomfortable and — to tell the truth — I'd never felt more British in my entire life than right then. After the latest of these outbursts of laughter, my gaze fell upon the Simple Sun brooch still pinned to his lapel.

It was weird.

*Definitely* weird.

But this — hopefully — signalled my last involvement with the weird-ness.

John was dead and although I had to take care with Daymian and Toby following that incident with the stun gun, I was fairly certain that they really hadn't a clue about the tablet.

Anyway, it soon wouldn't be in my possession at all.

It was then that I realised Kelly was standing nearby.

She was with a bunch of others from IT.

With an aspiring alcoholic's eye, I saw she was already on her second pint.

That was all the justification I needed to go get a refill myself.

Kelly caught me looking.

I blushed, smiled briefly and abruptly shifted my attention back down into my own glass of beer. From somewhere, I summoned more con-versation with Fil. "Any plans for the rest of today?" I asked.

Fil was staring into his drink, too, which he hadn't yet touched. His focus appeared to have drifted elsewhere. "Hmm?"

"Any plans?" I repeated.

"Oh, I dunno," he said. "Do some studying or something."

Seeing my opening, I went for it. "What're you studying for?"

"Uh ... actually, it's not really studying."

I pouted. "What'd you mean?"

"I mean, I'm doing ... it's drawing."

Great.

Now I had made him blush.

"I've been taking some classes." He looked at me for about a millisecond. "It's a hobby. That's all."

"I see," I replied, and thought about my own secret art ... I wasn't about to get into a discussion with myself, or anyone else, about whether or not stand-up comedy is an art.

Of *course* it's an art.

It's performance.

A performing art ...

I thought about all those self-help books I'd read.

The keys to personal fulfilment ... *happiness*.

The ones which told you about how to make friends with those who had similar goals and ambitions. In the chapters where they taught you how to come across as relatable they would highlight the importance of showing "vulnerability" ... this could either be read as telling people your deepest darkest desires — i.e. being genuine — or it could also be read as a sort of social "hack" in that you could make something up that you thought would chime with that particular person. A sort of way to short circuit the process of making friends. The greatest fear which had dawned on me from reading all those books was that everyone around me had read those same books and they were just faking their behaviour.

I cut off that train of thought, deciding to be optimistic.

This *was* the moment to open up.

To confide in *someone* about my dreams.

My *real* dreams.

"I ... uh," I began, unconvincingly.

And then I noticed Lucas standing at my elbow.

"Sorry for interrupting," he said. "Hayden has asked to speak with you."

My chest tightened and my stomach dropped.

"She ... what?" I said.

Lightly, Lucas took me by the elbow and guided me across the room.

"This way," he said.

I'd never said so much as a single word to Hayden Shepherd.

There had never been any need to.

If someone was to draw up a LifeWare org chart — and I was certain someone in HR had — there would probably be about ten or eleven reporting levels between our positions. Even if I did manage to somehow slice through all those levels of hierarchy, I was fairly certain her personal assistant would head me off before I got so much as a finger on the doorknob to Hayden's office.

What did I — a grunt customer service rep — have to offer of value?

Hayden had silver-white hair, an angular face and one of those healthy glows that spoke of tennis holidays in the Canary Islands or mountain-walking in the Alps. She could've been in her early fifties or late seventies. She had a slender frame and was tall.

Taller than me, even.

Today, she had opted for a smart navy-blue trouser suit with a no-nonsense white blouse underneath. She wore a necklace of flattened pearls. Her earrings were two small grey-blue feathers. She had the penetrating green eyes of an apex predator.

Annoyingly, Lucas remained standing at my elbow as if he was my dad or something.

Ready to step in if things got too much for me to handle.

Or maybe he thought of himself as a kind of courtier having brought a peasant before his Royal Highness's throne, and now he was to stand by, waiting for the eventual order to come that the peasant's presence was no longer required and that he was to be frogmarched on his way.

Also present were John Horsham's parents.

Although John's mother was smiling, her cheeks were doughy, reddened.

And there were black bags under her eyes.

John's father's eyes, meanwhile, were watery. He had the gaunt, saggy look of someone who has shed a lot of weight in a short amount of time.

Hayden, Lucas, John Horsham's parents ... were all staring at me.

Somehow I had ended up being the centre of attention.

Hayden broke the silence in that effortless wrecking-ball manner all executives possess. Maybe it's part of initiation. "This is Marcus. The one I was telling you about."

John Horsham's parents' focus fixed upon me.

And I felt a lump in my throat.

My eyes darted about their sockets and I wondered if I was supposed to say something. I wasn't sure I could even if I'd wanted to ... at the same time I prayed Lucas would stay silent. There's nothing more humiliating than having someone speak for you.

Mercifully, Hayden carried on talking. "As I was saying, I was out on that ... that ... *awful* day. At a conference. It was my PA, Charlotte, who gave me the news as I was driving back home. And it was Marcus's name that kept coming up." She beamed at me.

That made me feel uneasy.

I'm well-versed enough in corporate to know that there is a training course somewhere out there which tells you the right way to smile ... the *professional* way to smile.

Hayden went on. "He did just the right thing. I have ... well, no idea how *I* might have reacted to such a traumatic situation. But Marcus kept his wits about him. He did everything right, and in keeping with company measures."

To *my* best recollection I had acted wholly upon instinct.

Complete with stealing a recently deceased person's property ...

Or maybe I just wasn't familiar with this particular part of LifeWare's policy.

There was a pause in the conversation and I realised I was supposed to speak now.

I sensed Lucas standing in the wings waiting for his chance to pounce.

"Mr and Mrs Horsham," I said, keeping my tone of voice measured, "I'm really sorry for your loss."

I caught Lucas's eye momentarily.

He wasn't smiling but that wasn't necessarily a bad thing.

"Although I didn't know John all that well," I continued, feeling as though I was actually doing okay, "in all of my interactions with him I can say — hand on heart" — I winced internally as I uttered the phrase, trying desperately not to commit a completely bold-faced lie — "that he was excellent at his job. He was ... he was ... *irreplaceable*."

My throat squeezed slightly at the final word but I realised that I hadn't said anything — technically — untrue.

Hayden clasped her hands to her chest.

Where I suppose a heart would be traditionally found.

"It's utterly devastating for the whole LifeWare family," she said. "I like to think that not a single one of us will ever, wholly, be replaced. It is bringing our own personal skills and experience to our roles which makes our work so unique. I can assure you both on one matter, John's good work shall go on — the organisation has been forever elevated by his efforts in life."

There was a long beat of silence and I hoped that I might be able to skulk away.

However, it seemed Mr Horsham had something to say.

He took a stride forward.

And clasped my shoulder.

As he looked me in the eye, a tear rolled down his cheek.

My stomach dropped to the floor and I did my best to stand my ground even though every instinct within me was telling me to run. That old "fight or flight" response is still live and well in all of my social interactions.

After the initial reaction, I had a deeply weird urge to reach out and wipe away his tear. I wasn't too sure what Mrs Horsham or — indeed — my two superiors would have made of such a gesture. Thankfully I hadn't drunk enough so that I was unable to restrain myself.

When he spoke, his voice was raspy, like he was about to completely lose control. It was only as he started speaking that I realised he was making his best effort to whisper.

To keep his voice down as far as possible.

However, unfortunately for Mr Horsham, and everybody who happened to be in the vicinity, it seemed he was slightly deaf ... and he overcompensated with his own raised tone. "I just want to know one thing, Marcus, as you were the last one to see him. I never got to speak with any of the paramedics, the doctors who attended to his ... his body. Until now, I have spoken with nobody who ... who saw him last."

He paused and I couldn't help but feel that if someone had been passing by outside the community centre they would have stopped dead in their tracks to hear what Mr Horsham was going to say next. And he didn't disappoint.

"I just have to know, and promise you'll tell me the truth, won't you?" He exchanged glances with his wife who appeared to be just as uncertain about what he was going to say next as everyone else. Mr Horsham continued, "Had he been ... uh, I'm not quite sure how to say this ... *pleasuring* himself when you found him?"

Right then the whole world went silent.

It felt as though Mr Horsham was clasping my shoulder so tightly that he was driving me into the ground. After a second or so of assuring myself that I *had* heard just what I had, I pictured in my mind's eye a crater the two of us had sunk into.

Just me and him.

But we most definitely were not alone.

I looked to Hayden, and then to Mrs Horsham.

I even managed to sneak a glance at Lucas.

They were all dumbfounded.

So were the partially blurred faces now all looking in our direction.

When I inevitably focused my attention back onto Mr Horsham, my mouth felt impossibly dry, and my chest was so tight I thought I was in danger of running out of air.

But I managed to keep myself calm enough to get the words out.

To buy myself a little more time.

"Uh ... 'pleasuring himself' ?" I asked, just to make sure I'd got it right.

Mr Horsham's eyes bulged slightly in their sockets and his cheeks became a little pudgier. He made me think of someone squeezing a bullfrog in their fist. "Yes," he said. "You know, uh ... how else to put it? *Wanking?*"

That sent a fresh hush over the community centre.

But, strangely, it also focused my mind.

I assessed my memories. Sure, John Horsham had been perving at those pictures of my ex-girlfriend when he had died but I had been fairly certain that his trousers had been very much pulled up to his waist ... or had I suffered some form of PTSD and ended up blanking out an even more unpleasant memory?

I looked Mr Horsham back in the eye. "No, Mr Horsham. Definitely not. He died ... uh ... *honourably* ..." I wasn't sure that was quite the right word but I had gone and said it now.

Mr Horsham continued to stare at me, waiting for more.

So was everyone else.

I scrabbled at the basement of my mind for something.

"You know, like they say ... he, uh, ... 'died in his boots' ?"

Still, Mr Horsham wouldn't release me from his gaze. "Not wanking?" he replied, his voice raspy, much quieter than it had been before.

"No," I said, shaking my head and doing my best to press on a smile. "Not wanking."

# HALLOWEEN

I decided this was the single most ridiculous thing I had ever done.

The single most ridiculous thing I had ever allowed Riko to talk me into.

And yet ... here I was ... doing it all the same.

Maybe I'm just a ridiculous person.

Or maybe I'm just an idiot.

I looked myself over in the mirror.

My whole face was covered in golden concealer.

It was one that had belonged to Olivia; the kind that glossy magazines tell women to use to "extend" their holiday tan. I guess Olivia might've used it once before deciding that following the advice had been a mistake. When Riko had uncovered it from the depths of my bathroom, he had told me that it would help give me a "bit of colour"; to make it look like I spend my days outside rather than in a cubicle farm.

A garden gnome rather than an office drone.

I wondered if garden gnomes spend all day itching, because that was the prevailing sensation I was getting from being one.

The red hat I wore was the shape of a cone. The cheap felt material made my scalp itch. My nose and lips also itched, because of the fake white beard I wore. It was secured courtesy of criss-crossing elasticated bands which pressed uncomfortably into the skin around the back of my head. This had the added bonus of pressurising my skull, basically begging my brain for the migraine it had so dutifully produced. Or maybe the migraine was in part down to the rum and cokes me and

Riko had been throwing back for the past two hours in service of getting ready for tonight's grand celebrations of all things "Hallo" and "ween".

As if the hat and beard weren't enough, there was the racing-green tunic I also wore.

It was made of wool, which I've always been borderline allergic to, and the belt squeezed on around my gut was so tight that I was certain that at some stage of the night I was going to have to spend a solid quarter of an hour evacuating my bowels.

Finally, there was the matter of the skin-tight corduroy brown trousers. These were applying a little too much pressure around my testicles for comfort.

As well as being — a theme was starting to emerge — itchy as fuck.

The trouser cuffs had been lovingly rolled up by Riko and — in a strangely paternal way — he had helped me jam my feet into a pair of black boots that were about a big toe too small. They were the sort of boots that people on construction sites wear. The steel toes made walking almost entirely unfeasible ... let alone *running* ... which I was hesitant to rule out given that it seemed almost inevitable that we would have a run-in some time later in the evening with some of the local yobs dressed in black hoodies and tracksuit bottoms out to egg and flour people who had actually put some effort into dressing up and enjoying the day on some kind of level.

The boots itched the soles of my feet, too.

I wondered if the previous owner of the boots hadn't been a carpenter. That would go some way to explaining why the insides were saturated with sawdust.

As I re-examined myself in the mirror and looked deep — *really deep* — into my own eyes, I came to the conclusion that my facial expression was as close to perfect for the Illustrated Dictionary's picture definition of "Suicidal Depression" as was feasibly possible.

I had always thought gnomes were supposed to be happy-go-lucky types.

"I'm not gonna do this," I said.

"Don't be such a drama queen, Spark," Riko said. "Nobody's gonna know it's you. Not with all that make-up on."

I shifted my attention away from myself and onto Riko.

There was no way in hell that anyone who dressed up as a gnome could manage to make themselves look anything other than a complete and utter tit.

No one except Riko, of course.

To start with, Riko had foregone the bronze concealer, deciding he was going for a different effect. He had instead used some rouge we had uncovered — again from the depths of the bathroom; this had also belonged to Olivia — and daubed it on his cheeks. And while it would've made me look like the typical deckchair Brit with sunburn if I'd used it, the rouge actually accentuated Riko's natural complexion, bringing attention to his handsome, protruding cheekbones. From the same charity shop we had raided for my costume, Riko had come across a vermillion waistcoat, suit jacket and shirt combination in which he looked more like Prince Charming than Jack the Garden Gnome ... or whatever gnomish names get bandied about these day. He had, of course, also sourced a matching coloured sheet of felt which he had used to create his own conical hat. Somehow it didn't look as itchy as mine.

Riko had produced the boots he wore from the bottom of his sports bag, which apparently miraculously contained his entire wardrobe. He had claimed he had bought them years ago but never worn them until tonight.

They fit him perfectly.

That much was obvious.

I didn't want to get into the logic of him lugging around those boots with him without so much as putting them on all these years when his wardrobe was as limited as he claimed it to be.

"Tell me why I'm doing this again?" I asked.

"Because it'll be *fun*," Riko replied, as if it was the most obvious thing in the world.

It was also just about the most unconvincing argument anyone in recorded history could ever make. But I didn't do anything about it.

Riko had used guerrilla tactics to get me to this point, that was impossible to deny.

When I'd woken up that morning — Saturday morning — and blearily chewed my way through some soggy cereal, he had told me we were invited to a Halloween party that evening.

It was at Julie's house.

Julie from Frothy Cups.

"And," Riko continued, "we might even find someone to get you over Olivia." He grinned. "You might even be able to get your own back. Go for a roll in the hay with one of Julie's mates in Julie's bed, huh?"

I grimaced, wishing that he hadn't reminded me of the "romancing" which'd taken place on the sofa bed ... where I slept *every* night.

Riko went on, "It's not good for self-esteem to mope about babes for days on end."

"First of all," I said, "I don't think anybody over the age of fourteen or under the age of sixty uses the word 'babe'. And it's singular. As in just the *one* babe that needs to be got over. And it's been well over a month that I've been 'moping'. Not a few days. We *were* together for quite a while, you know? This wasn't just some bloody holiday romance."

Riko held my eye for the longest time.

I dared him to shrug.

He didn't.

"Come on, Sparky, it'll cheer you up — promise."

And that should've been all the warning that I needed.

A promise from Riko.

Outside it was dark.

Night, actually.

I struggled to keep pace with Riko as he marched us up the street. We had taken the bus across town and the asphalt was slick with rain water.

A steady drizzle was still falling.

It was pretty much stereotypical late-October weather which meant it was ugly, damp and dark as the clocks had gone back a few days previously.

En route, another thing I had learned about my gnome costume was that it was the opposite of waterproof. Even though it was at best a ten-minute walk from the bus stop, by the time we reached Julie's I felt like a sopping-wet sponge wrapped in a fake beard.

Riko took pity on me, and my shitty boots, and my shitty drenched, miserable outfit, agreeing to carry the plastic bag filled with tinkling glass bottles of assorted alcohols we had purchased from some dodgy corner shop. I've always wondered why anybody bothers to bring drink along to a house party. A house party is generally so chaotic that nobody can ever tell what's going on at the time ... let alone what people did or didn't contribute to the communal stash of booze when they reflect on the party a day or so later.

It's a question of conscience, I guess.

Always good for peace of mind to know you've done your bit for the cause.

The cause of getting pissed.

Or maybe I'm just a sucker ...

Once we got to the right street, it wasn't difficult to tell where the party was taking place.

It was the only one where the curtains hadn't been drawn.

And had the windows wide open.

Bright golden light shone out.

Writhing bass seeped into the street.

The first neighbour would complain at any given moment. There they would be in their dressing gowns, fingers poised to speed dial the police the minute their kitchen clocks ticked past ten o'clock. It was a street of terraced houses, small front gardens enclosed behind brick walls in various states of repair. Most of the gardens we walked past had paving slabs thrown down across them, plastic wheelie bins parked on top. Others had bushes which'd grown wildly for maybe decades and in some cases appeared to be threatening to force their way into the houses themselves. I counted on one hand houses with gardens that looked like they'd had any sort of care tossed their way in the past year.

For some reason, Riko nodded to me in a conspiratorial manner as he led the way through a beaten-out-of-shape, rusted-up, wrought-iron garden gate. The gate had once been painted white or so I gathered from the few flecks of white gloss still clinging to the rust. It had buckled on its hinges and was no longer fit for purpose. It had either been left where it was for ornamental value or because nobody could be bothered to replace or remove it.

The cynic in me had me leaning towards the latter as the most likely explanation.

"I'm guessing this is a house share?" I asked.

Riko answered me in that unnervingly factual way he sometimes does.

That tone he uses where I'm unsure whether he's joking or not.

"I've only been here a couple of times," he said. "I haven't asked about the ownership situation. Can do, though, if you like?"

"I wouldn't worry about it," I replied. "I was just curious."

Riko knocked thirteen times, as he always does. He does it in a weirdly specific pattern which is strange too because he's really not someone I would describe as obsessive compulsive. The rhythm is something like three-four-three-three, getting louder with every knock until it reaches a crescendo which sounds loud enough to split wood.

Or split his knuckle.

I have warned him that out in public this insistent knocking might be mistaken for something other than quirky high spirits. Not that he ever pays attention to me.

Probably rightly ...

Julie — who I instantly remembered from that fateful afternoon at Frothy Cups and the silhouette I had seen lying on my sofa bed — answered the door herself. Her hair was no longer purple. She had dyed it jet-black. I gathered from the crooked pointed hat and the skimpy, lacy black dress she wore that she had dressed up as a witch for the evening.

Oh, and she was wearing green face paint, too.

That was probably the giveaway.

"Ricky-Rick!" she cried out, her eyeballs nearly exploding as she threw her arms about Riko's neck and gave him an awkwardly long smooch.

As they embraced post-smooch, Riko eyed me over her shoulder.

I arched an eyebrow.

"Ricky-Rick" was certainly a new one to me.

They prised themselves apart at last.

"This is, Sparkly Mark," Riko said, his hand firmly gripping Julie's left buttock. "Remember?"

"Of course," she said, smiling politely at me, head tilted to one side in what could only be a ditsy fashion. "He was there when we met."

There was a tense moment where nobody was quite sure what to say.

Other than the fact that Riko had got Julie's number, I couldn't think of anything else that had made the trip to Frothy Cups memorable. All staff members had worn burgundy polo shirts, I remembered that much useless detail.

Riko took it upon himself to break the silence, as he always does. "Sparkly here got dumped so he's feeling a little low."

Julie clasped her hands at her chest, tilted her head to the other side and made an "oh" shape with her lips — an expression that a soap-opera star might've been proud of.

Riko pouted. "He could do with some love. That's all I'm saying."

Now I was truly starting to regret having let Riko talk me into this. The initial warming alcoholic hum of those rum and cokes that had made this seem like any kind of a good idea was starting to wear off. I was reverting to my gut reaction now. "I'm fine, really. It's just — "

But before I could get any further, Riko launched Julie at me.

To begin with, I was utterly confused.

Afraid that she might tumble to the ground, I caught her in my arms.

And that was when she suckered her lips onto mine.

She thrust my teeth apart with her tongue.

I went through a few emotions:

Shock.

Disbelief.

... A sad sort of acceptance.

Like a good dancer saddled with a poor partner, I allowed her to expertly manipulate my tongue about my mouth. The kiss — if that was what it could be described as — came to an end after one of the longest five-second periods in my life. As she drew back, her eyelids got all droopy and her lips were slightly parted, exposing a gossamer of saliva coating her tongue. I told myself that some of that saliva was mine. And some was Julie's.

And some was Riko's ...

I'm not sure I have the right make-up to ever be involved in any sort of a threesome.

Too much bacteria in play.

Julie gave a strangely high-pitched girly giggle as she stepped away from me, nearly stumbling into the doorframe. She would've struck the wood if Riko hadn't been there to stop her. "Easy there!" he said, steadying her with his arm.

I suspected she wasn't completely sober.

And, all being well, in about twenty minutes' time I wouldn't be either.

Soon this gnome idiocy would be lost in an alcoholic fog ...

I was sitting in an incredibly comfortable armchair.

And the whole room was spinning.

Some kind of witchy EDM blasted out of the speakers.

Every minute or so, it felt like someone was bumping up the volume a notch.

Everybody in the room seemed to be laughing.

Everybody except me.

My mistake had been the bottle of vodka.

I had spotted it in the kitchen.

I wasn't sure why the idea had appealed to me ... but it had.

For some reason, whenever I find myself in a situation with people I don't know, I immediately reach for the most efficient source of alcohol. I'd run the numbers and decided that if cool-headed efficiency was the name of the game then vodka was my best bet.

Across the room, there was a game of Jenga happening on a coffee table. There was an improvised bong — an adapted two-litre soft drink bottle — filled with dirty grey water cast off to one side. There were three Jenga players: one guy and two girls. The guy was dressed as Count Dracula and the girls were dressed as sexy cats.

I wondered if the girls had chosen the same costume by accident or by design.

Not that I was in any state to be able to verbalise my query.

Or to be criticising others' costumes.

One of the sexy cats yanked free one of the wooden blocks from the tower and the whole thing came crashing down with an anticlimactic, disappointingly dainty, tinkle of MDF.

The three of them howled in laughter and I observed with a weary eye as Count Dracula inched his hand just a little closer to one of the sexy cat's waistlines.

"... Excuse me ... excuse me ..."

It was only when someone started to tap away at my bicep that I realised the words were directed at me. I shifted my focus upwards.

This time it was a girl whose skin was covered in grey-blue paint. Her hair was cropped short and the same grey-blue colour of her skin, although I guessed it was usually blond. She wore a tattered brown loincloth and matching top wrapped about her chest. At first I wondered if she was some sort of a zombie alien ... but then it clicked.

My brain successfully operated my tongue.

"You're a ... *ghoul?*" I found myself saying.

"Uh-huh ... and you're a ... a *pixie?*"

"Gnome," I blurted out, managing to suppress a burp — or something worse — threatening to escape.

I noticed that the girl was now perched on the arm of the chair.

I could feel the heat from her body up against my skin.

It seemed a long time since I'd been this close to another human being — at least in some kind of relaxed state. What had occurred with Julie out on the front doorstep had been so frantic I still wasn't quite sure it had happened at all ... having any sort of chance to enjoy it had simply been out of the question.

"... And just who are you?" she asked.

I realised I could feel her fingers kneading the back of my neck, weaving in and out of the fuzzy hair sprouting there. I was probably due a trip to the barber's.

"Marc ... Marcus ..." I began, feeling as though I was learning to speak again after a long and painful illness. Or at least that was how I was making it sound.

Despite the fact she was sitting down, she was swaying back and forth, in danger of toppling to one side or the other at any moment.

"Who invited you here?" she asked.

There was a slight edge to her question, although I convinced myself that it was just my drunken state that made it seemed more pointed than it was in reality.

"... Ruh ... Riko," I managed, and then, "Julie."

I hope she would connect the dots.

I was in luck.

"Ah, you must be ... must be ... Riko's flatmate?"

I tried to gain control over my lips again, but struggled this time.

They felt about as substantial as soggy cardboard.

I wanted to tell her that, no, Riko wasn't my *official* flatmate, that he was only staying with me on a *temporary* basis ... admittedly the end point of this "temporary basis" seemed to be extending further and further into the murkiness of infinity.

But I couldn't express that.

Not right now.

Her hand had now made its way from my neck, all the way around to my chest, where it came to rest. And then she clawed at my ribs. Her grasp was strong and her nails dug into my skin through my unsubstantial tunic. She dropped her voice to a near-whisper and I felt her damp, hot breath in my inner-ear. "I never *fucked* a gnome before."

For some reason, my smart aleck logical mind wanted to explain that I wasn't a real gnome. That this was all pretend. That I was a gnome for tonight — and tonight only ... and that I had no intention of ever dressing up as one again.

But I was still having brain-mouth connectivity issues.

Maybe this was a "feature" rather than a "bug", as Simple Sun might've put it, because speaking would surely have stopped the girl from slurping away at my earlobe, working her way around the side of my face to my mouth. When she came up for air, her eye lids were droopy in the way that I remembered Julie's had been. "I live close — *very close*. Just upstairs, in fact."

She wobbled back up onto her feet, yanked me up from the armchair.

It was then that my brain reconnected itself to my mouth ... and spoiled everything.

"I want to go home," I said.

However, despite my brain's best efforts, this somehow didn't deter her.

"Don't worry. I'll let you go home ... *Eventually.*"

And she yanked me towards the staircase.

Sunlight filtered in through the slatted blinds.

Even through my throbbing head, the dryness in my mouth, and the profound warm weight lying across my chest, my brain told me it was about seven in the morning.

I was in bed.

Still fully dressed in my gnome costume.

I was lying on top of the sheets, the duvet scrunched up at my feet.

I took stock of the scene.

Saw — almost immediately — that I had at least discarded my fake beard and conical hat on the carpet. I had removed my boots, too, before getting into bed. There're not many ways to make a worse impression on a stranger than by getting into their bed with your shoes on.

I wondered whether vodka actually *improved* Marcus Raisin.

Elevated him to a level which was impossible to attain while sober.

I realised the weight across my chest related to the girl from the night before. As I listened to her heavy, hungover breathing, I tuned into the pins-and-needles sensation of the cramp taking hold of my left arm. Breathing in gently, not wanting to aggravate my already-grumbling stomach and cause a scene — to put it mildly — I pulled lightly on my arm, trying to extricate it from beneath her weight. The girl grumbled something in her sleep before shrugging her shoulders and rolling on her side, turning her back to me. I saw that she was still fully dressed too ... in the ghoul outfit from the night before. That was a relief.

... Wasn't it?

At first I thought it was my own pulse ticking at my temples, but I soon noticed the alarm clock sitting on the bedside table. One of those vintage ones with miniature bells.

And an unnecessarily loud second hand.

I thrust myself up with my elbow and perched on the edge of the mattress.

I thought through my footwear options — realised I didn't have any — and so set about the task of jamming the ill-fitting boots back onto my feet. It was made more of a mission due to the fact that I didn't have Riko to help me out.

Feeling that if I tried to walk I would stagger from one side to the other, when I finally stood up, I allowed myself a moment to stabilise. I felt like a pine tree with a lumberjack's notch worked in halfway through its trunk.

It could fall in any direction.

I knew this morning — indeed, the rest of the day — was going to be a struggle.

If I even made it out of the house alive ...

When I reached the bedroom door, I glanced back over my shoulder to the girl, and wondered whether I was doing the right thing. Although it seemed somewhat measly reasoning, I convinced myself that she would only be embarrassed to find a gnome in bed with her. And it wasn't like anything had happened. Yep, the most painless option was for the both of us to go our separate ways ... *silently* ... do our best to pretend we had never met in the first place. That we were just strangers — as we were — and would go on being.

You know, like the majority of the planet's population ...

I was glad to make it down the stairs without breaking my neck and doubly glad to see that I wasn't the only visitor left in the house.

In actual fact, I counted, hunched against the wall in the corridor, a Frankenstein's monster, a mermaid, three skeletons — they looked much younger, teenagers who had crashed the party. As I picked my way past the sitting room, I peeped in to see a polar bear sprawled across the sofa with one of the sexy cats perched at his feet, doubled over propping her head up with her arm resting on her knee — a position which couldn't have been at all comfortable ... but, then again, if there's anything I've learned about people's sleeping habits it's that everyone is different; what's weird for one person is second nature for the next.

Whatever works for you, I suppose.

To tell the truth, I thought it was a touch unfair to dress up as a polar bear for Halloween, that subtle yet offensive implication that they are somehow monstrous. As far as apex predators go, polar bears are having a tough time of it, environment-wise, and they could do without any further negative press.

Also in the sitting room — as was to be expected of any house party worth its salt — there were empty, or half-empty, bottles and glasses scattered to all parts. The carpet had several new, still-damp, stains and a general sense of debauchery clung to the very air.

Or maybe it was just flatulence and spilled beer.

Speaking of smells, there was a strong odour of warm cooking oil which I supposed signalled that someone had had the bright idea of making chips in the early hours.

Being the dedicated friend I am, it was only when I reached the front door that I remembered Riko. He would still be upstairs with Julie.

And there was no chance of me barging in on *that* scene.

I considered my options.

True, I was going to look like a complete tit doing the walk of shame in my gnome costume (although I had thankfully had the presence of mind to ditch the beard and hat with Sleeping Beauty upstairs) but I was going to have to do it at some point today and it might as well be while there was still a respectable amount of alcohol shredding its way through my veins. Even if I did wait for Riko to ...*finish* ... there wasn't much that being accompanied by him would do to improve my situation.

Mind made up, I pushed down on the front door handle and readied to be on my way.

A draught of cool morning air rushed out through the slight gap I had opened.

After the stilted air of the last twelve hours it wouldn't be an exaggeration to say that it was restorative, like setting a bare foot in the suckling tide of a pleasantly warm sea.

It was then that I heard a toilet flush over my shoulder.

For some reason — *intuition?* — a scurry of terror ran up my spine.

I knew this was my chance to run ... and yet ... I also knew there was precisely zero chance of me being able to make it more than five strides without tripping over the ill-fitting boots I was wearing.

Footfall beat the staircase.

This was my last chance, I had to bolt now if I was —

"Off, are you?"

My stomach squeezed and I felt the acidic bite of bile at the back of my throat.

Against my better judgement, I turned around, my nose leaving the promise of the fresh-smelling outside world, once more turning inwards to the putrid stench of "after-party".

Julie was standing there. Her hair was messed up, sticking up all over. She had changed out of her witch's costume and now wore a pair of faux-silk, crimson pyjamas with a golden trim. She had also clearly spent a good amount of time scrubbing the face paint off her skin, given her rash-red complexion. Despite her best efforts a green tinge remained.

I also noted her eyes were red — damp in a way that could only mean one thing ...

"Yes," I replied, and then stupidly added, "Thanks for having me."

Julie blinked several times, apparently processing this remark.

To be fair to her, it was an utterly ridiculous thing to say.

"Thought you would've skulked off in the night with *him*."

The words passed my lips before I fully thought them through. "... With who?"

This elicited a flash of anger.

Rightly so, really ...

"Who the *fuck* do you think?"

"... Riko?"

Julie breathed out heavily, threw up her arms. She called up the stairs. "Frankie? Frankie! Come down now!"

The front door was still open. Cool air still wafted through the gap.

Should I close the door now my escape had been rumbled or open it up completely ... leaving me the option to break for it? In the end, I did neither, staying right where I was.

In no-man's land.

Upstairs, I heard a groan which could only have been my dearly beloved stirring from her slumber. The groan was followed by creaking floorboards, a few phlegmy coughs. A fresh wave of nausea swilled through me as the ghoul joined the ex-witch at the bottom of the staircase.

So "Frankie" was her name, apparently.

Frankie eyed me dizzily through those same droopy eyes.

She hadn't had the chance to get as lucid as Julie yet.

"Whatsa ... you?" Frankie said, barely making sense.

"... Uh, Marcus ... Marcus," and then because I'd already gone and repeated my name twice I knew there was no option but to add the surname. In the fraction of a second I had to respond to the request, I wondered if I should give a false one ... but it was too late, I was out of time. And my fate was sealed. "... Raisin," I added, in defeat.

Frankie gripped the banister so tightly she might as well have been aboard a ship being thrown about in rough seas.

I decided Julie was the key to escaping this encounter.

From somewhere, I summoned something resembling a smile.

"Nothing happened," I said, palms open, down at my waist, a defensive, open posture, doing my best to phrase this in a tone that suggested everything was okay.

Julie remained stone-faced.

"Last night, I mean." I flipped my attention onto Frankie, looking for her support. "We just slept on the bed ... you know ... and I just woke up ... and I was just letting myself —"

Julie cut me off. "Don't fucking tell me what you were doing. I'm not an *idiot*. We're not *idiots*." She shifted back onto Frankie. "He wake you up? Tell you he was going?"

Frankie's sleepy, droopy expression was giving way to something firmer, sharper.

More unpredictable.

More *dangerous*.

I've always been amazed at the way that female emotion can be transmitted from one woman to another like a kind of air-borne virus.

"No?" Frankie said, and then shaking her head as if clearing a delusion before adding, a touch more definitely, "No, he didn't."

If I'd been half the opportunist Riko was, this was my opening.

That there was a seed of doubt in Frankie's tone that I could mercilessly exploit.

I had only to claim we'd said goodbye to one another — perhaps shared a peck goodbye — and then I'd take my leave. She was still clearly too drunk to know much different. But I was too gallant for my own good ... Or maybe the other word ... what is it? ... Oh, yes, *chickenshit*.

And so I did what only Marcus Raisin would do in such a situation.

I started apologising.

"I'm sorry," I said, doing my best to imitate Frankie's expression, hoping for empathy. "It wasn't the right thing to do. I wasn't, uh ... feeling well" — that was still the truth although I was still on shaky ground — "and I thought the best thing was for me to go home." I risked a quick grin. "The last thing you want is gnome vomit in your bed, right?"

Both girls remained unmoved by this explanation.

And then, finally, Julie put me out of my misery.

"Get the fuck out," she said, crossing her arms over her chest. "I don't want to see you or that *scumbag* ever again."

My heart beat hard in my eardrums for a few moments as I felt a blush filling my cheeks. My stupid mind wanted me to point out that while I of course would not come around to her house again, there might be some vague chance of us, I don't know, "bumping into one another" on public transportation, or maybe through some kind of weird circumstance where I needed to interact with her through work ... I told myself that such clarifications were unnecessary and perhaps even symptomatic of a psychopath ... or is it a sociopath?

And so, my cheeks shining as brightly as a smacked arse, I turned on my undersized boot heel and clumped out of the house.

Maybe I made a better gnome than a human after all.

# HOLDING TOGETHER

It was almost December by the time I managed to suck up the guts to confront Riko about his living situation. Or — as it was rapidly turning into — *our* living situation.

Perhaps it was the pragmatist in me but I saw Christmas, and the implied time spent with family — *birth* family, to avoid any misunderstandings — as the perfect opportunity to propose that Riko move onto the next step of his "plan".

Because he would surely be headed back home over the festive period.

Wouldn't he?

I chose a particularly damp Sunday, at the arse-end of November, for us to have our little chat. It was almost a month since that fateful Halloween party, and consequently the termination of his relationship with Julie from Frothy Cups. And whatever it was that had happened between me and Frankie ... let's settle for calling it "one-sided heavy petting".

Of course, Riko being Riko, he had explained away the situation he had landed me in as "unfortunate" but then justified himself by saying that he had believed, with I guess good reason, that me and Frankie were "getting along famously" and that he didn't want to "kill the mood". The only conclusion I could draw from this conversation was that he didn't know me well at all. When had I ever gone through successfully with anything as straight-forward as a one-night stand?

As was the case pretty much every day, I had been first up in the flat. And I had taken the opportunity to rouse Riko from his sleeping place on the camping mat on the kitchen floor. I had recently realised that it gave me a strange power buzz whenever I nudged him awake with my foot in the morning so I could get to the fridge. I wondered if I was turning into my dad or something.

Being the responsible one and all.

I made a note to myself to nip in the bud any indicators of surrogate fatherhood such as this before they had time to blossom into something more ... complicated. One thing I was determined not to do at age thirty was become responsible for someone the same age as me.

I made a point of being especially nice to Riko that morning, as if I had already started apologising to him for what I had committed myself to doing. I'd made him a bowl of breakfast cereal and clutched a cafetière in my fist, readying to serve him a refill of coffee. This behaviour was nothing if not naïve, however, as Riko has always been highly adept at sensing incoming trouble and slipping away unscathed ... kind of like Halloween at Julie's house ...

As part of his sabbatical Riko had decided to take up vaping. This gave him an extremely convenient out whenever he needed one. Whenever he felt that he needed to get away from what showed all the signs of brewing into an Unpleasant Scene. And so, stooped over his coffee cup, he pulled on that same slightly vexed expression, padded his pockets and then ventured over to his sports bag where he produced his vaping kit. When he slipped out past the front door I knew that he might be fifteen, twenty minutes. When he returned it would be with the hope that whatever storm had been brewing had blown itself out.

Once when I'd grown curious as to exactly what he was doing, I had peered out of the window down into the street, seeing that he was deep in conversation with my neighbour Mildreth in the basement flat. I had pulled away from the scene knowing that absolutely nothing good could come of *that* interaction ... I wondered if Riko's habit-changing was a conscious thing, calculated so that he would forever remain an enigma. Because I found that just as I grew used to Riko's other quirks, he started some new, completely off-the-wall and perplexing habit which didn't square with anything else that had come before. Now, however, I had become accustomed to him disappearing at random times during the day only to return smelling faintly of a chemist's idea of apricots and whipped cream. Whatever curveball was coming next I had no idea.

But I knew it would get me going cross-eyed before long.

I guess I should've just been glad that he was courteous enough not to vape in the flat ... or at least I hadn't *caught* him vaping inside yet.

While Riko was gone, I busied myself tidying up the flat in a manner that befitted the serious talk we were about to have. This involved folding up the sofa bed, rinsing out the cereal bowls and setting them to drip dry beside the sink (I had run out of washing-up liquid two or three days earlier and for some reason, despite multiple trips to the shop for beer, bread and other essentials, the thought of stocking back up simply hadn't occurred to me).

I also cracked open one of the skylights a little.

Fresh air could surely only help discourse ...

I perched on the edge of the folded-up sofa bed, and then, rethinking my position, deciding that I should aim for a more dominant physical presence, I settled for standing with my arms crossed tightly over my chest, glaring at the door.

This was one situation Riko wasn't going to wriggle out of ... I was sure of it.

I listened to the creaking floorboards as Riko climbed his way back up to the flat, apparently having had his fill of vaping chemicals.

I swallowed hard.

That week LifeWare had sent me on a course on "Negotiation Strategy" and although I felt a tinge of embarrassment to be thinking about work on a weekend I couldn't help but allow my mind to skim back over the summary points that the instructor had delivered.

Perhaps the training would come in handy after all.

The front door opened.

And I sucked in a deep breath.

Waited for Riko's gaze to drift onto mine.

For the two of us to understand what was about to happen.

... However, Riko's eyes were elsewhere.

More specifically on the jet-black object he held in his hand.

He glanced up at me, a faint smile on his lips.

I caught a faint whiff of apricots and cream ... and reminded myself I was breathing in noxious chemicals. I guess it's better to know than not ...

"This came through the door," Riko said. "It's addressed to you."

I realised I had shifted away from the straight-backed, chest-thrust-out, shoulders-square posture the instructor on the Negotiation Strategy course had recommended. There had been a particularly painful episode when the instructor had spent ten minutes — longer? — demonstrating the right way to walk through a door ... you know, so the *whole* room respected you from the off?

I screwed up my eyes, trying my best to stop thinking about goddamn *work*.

While I was somewhat successful in achieving this aim, I also noticed that I had slipped back into my trademarked slouched pose.

"You okay?" Riko asked. "Got a headache or something?"

I rubbed my temple, admitting to myself that I did feel the tingle of something coming along. I did my best to put it to the back of my mind for the time being.

"Who's it from?" I asked.

"Dunno," Riko replied. "It's got a crappy logo of a sun on the front."

My stomach dropped through my waistline.

Riko held up the envelope.

I took it from him.

He wrinkled his brow. "I swear I've seen that sun somewhere before."

"Yeah," I replied, my stomach realigning itself with its normal position, the aftershock of the reaction sending dread creeping through my blood. "On the tablet."

"Oh yeah," Riko replied, in a completely unconvincing manner. "Crappy Sun?"

"Simple Sun," I replied, tearing the envelope open with my finger and prying the contents free.

The folded-up paper was weighty, had a sort of glossy surface with a fuzzy signature at the bottom which had clearly been scanned or copied a dozen or more times than it could handle. My initial forensic work done with, I saw the name printed beneath the signature:

*Emmerson Ray*

And his title:

*Simple Sun Enabler*

"What does an 'enabler' mean?" Riko said.

I realised he had silently manoeuvred himself to stand behind my shoulder.

"I ... think it's just a fancy way of saying CEO?"

I really hoped Riko wasn't going to ask me what a CEO was.

If he did then I knew that I was all too right to despair for his future career ... and to banish the idea of me *ever* getting my flat back for myself.

And it was right then I realised that Riko had done it again.

He had successfully distracted me from the conversation I was determined that we were going to have. Or was it just fate?

... Some outside force conspiring to keep Riko in my flat forever more.

I shifted my focus back onto the letter.

My address was printed up in the top right-hand corner.

And the letter was addressed to me by name:

*Dear Marcus ...*

There it was, in black and white.

Simple Sun knew where I lived.

I gave Riko a glance out of the corner of my eye. "Do you want me to read it aloud or would you prefer to keep on snooping over my shoulder?"

Riko gave me one of his vacant expressions, throwing in a shrug for good measure.

I sighed. "Why don't you get cosy on the sofa bed and I'll tell you a nice story."

Riko didn't pick up on my ironic tone, or chose to ignore it — I was never entirely sure which it was with him — and he promptly made himself comfortable — *too comfortable*, really — on the sofa, folding his arms back behind his head and staring up at the ceiling.

Somehow, he had a knack of switching around any given situation so that he ended up being the one in total control. Maybe I should recommend that he get into teaching corporate courses ... if what he does can even be taught and it's not just some fluke of natural selection.

Some dumb talent.

"'Dear Marcus,'" I began, already feeling as though I was embarking on a career as a primary school teacher, "'It is with great pleasure that I extend an official invitation to Simple Sun Conclave 20—. During the event, you can expect to hear from a range of speakers on a variety of hot topics surrounding the theme of activism in technology. This is not only a chance to further your own understanding of these topics but to put questions to expert panels, and to network with fellow tech enthusiasts.'"

"I didn't realise you were a tech enthusiast," Riko put in.

"I'm not," I replied.

"Then how come they're inviting you?"

I sifted speedily through my memories.

I hadn't actually ever filled Riko in about my kidnapping by Daymian with a "y" and John Horsham's half-brother Toby let alone about what had gone on at John Horsham's funeral; that was where I had met Emmerson Ray, Simple Sun Enabler.

Perhaps it had been tactical or maybe Riko had distracted me with some other bullshit that particular day or maybe I had just decided that Riko wouldn't care so I hadn't even made the effort to try to explain ... a more and more frequent occurrence these days.

I decided that while I was reading him the letter that I might as well tell Riko the whole story. After all, he was the only person I ever seemed to interact with outside of work these days. And it might even give him more context surrounding the tablet, and perhaps — this was surely a wild dream — have him treat it with more respect. Then again, I suppose I could hardly talk myself given that I had taken to virtually breaking into pub wifi networks and perusing their barred lists.

Once I had spilled the beans on all of the above events, Riko descended into what I have always considered his most dangerous state:

Silent thought.

More than anything, I wanted to speak up, to break the silence, and to get him off whatever train of thought he was wildly running along ... ready to slip from the tracks at any given moment.

But I was conflicted.

Because at the same time I was interested in what he might make of all this.

Finally, he glanced up.

And I braced myself for anything.

*Absolutely* anything.

"Where's the tablet now?" Riko asked.

The question took me off guard because it was so obvious.

And yet I realised I had given it almost no thought for weeks.

"Here," I said. "In the flat."

I waited for Riko to pin me down to a more exact location.

But he merely clasped his hands together and nodded to himself, gnawing gently on one of his knuckles. "And they know about it?" He met my gaze. "They know that there's something out there — that's for sure. And they're pretty sure you're the one that took it?"

"I don't think they know exactly *what* it is ... when I met ... was *kidnapped* by Toby and Daymian, with a 'y', they just said they knew that John had been working on something. And that he most likely had it with him at work."

"What's with the 'y' thing?"

"I dunno. Some kind of affectation."

"You know, his parents doing that to him, adding in that extra letter, has probably cost him like a whole pen's worth of ink up to his life right now."

I puzzled over this for a few moments and then wondered if accountancy might not be where Riko's true passion lay. They could use a mind like his.

He'd probably make a very good *creative* accountant, in any case ...

"You think they're watching?" Riko asked, surprisingly.

Returning to the topic at hand seamlessly was unusual for him.

"They know where I live," I said. "They brought me back here after their, uh ... *meeting* with me."

"And you said that was their HQ? And it was sort of ..."

"*Crappy* ... I mean, like just some desks. No windows. Computers. That's it. Out in the middle of nowhere."

168

Riko held the letter at an arm's length — I had handed it to him after I had finished scrutinising it myself. He squinted at the text. "Do you think it's some sort of trap?"

"Well, given that I know next to nothing about the topic of this conference, or whatever the hell a 'conclave' is, then I would say so, yes."

"You think there might be anything online about it?"

"Maybe."

"Do you want to search?"

After about ten minutes of the two of us on the sofa, sitting in front of my laptop, flipping through various pages that seemed to have little or nothing to do with this "Simple Sun Conclave", we stumbled across something that looked official.

Unfortunately, it wasn't especially informative.

More specifically, the webpage in question featured the now all-too-familiar Simple Sun logo painted on against a black background with a cryptic phrase — or perhaps not so cryptic now that I had received the letter:

*Your invitation awaits*

"Do you think there's any other info on the page?" Riko asked.

I gave him a blank look.

And that was all he needed from me.

"We can always check the page source," he said.

Another blank look.

With a sigh I would've been proud of, Riko gave me a nudge in the ribs and I reluctantly gave up the laptop, allowing him to take hold. As he tapped away with practised ability, Riko went on, "From one tech enthusiast to another, you can find the code for any page up here, in the menu on your web browser."

"Oh, I see," I replied. "'Web browser'. That's what you download with, right?"

Riko gave me a smirk as he perused the page of what looked to me like indecipherable code now filling the screen. I had to admit I would never have credited Riko with having any interest in computers whatsoever. And it made me wonder what other special abilities I might have overlooked ... mostly for reasons of self-preservation.

I didn't want to find myself caught unawares.

*Ambushed*.

"See here," Riko said, pointing at a line of code as if it was a dead giveaway.

It wasn't.

At least not to me.

He went on. "You can see that this leads to another page. But someone has disabled the link. They've made it invisible when you look at the page itself but the code is still here in the background."

I really resisted the urge to mumble something along the lines of "Hold on, Bill Gates", but said nothing further. I had already shown enough ignorance for one day ... and I should leave some for the rest of my monthly quota.

Riko selected the line of text he'd identified. Even to my inexpert eye, I could tell that it was a hyperlink. He dropped it back into the address bar on the web browser.

Hit the Enter key.

I squared my shoulders, leaned back from the screen as if something might leap out at me suddenly. After the usual three-, four-second wait courtesy of my crappy internet connection, the page loaded.

It was a blank white page.

Except for a single feature.

Something I actually knew the name of.

"A QR code," I said. "Shall I scan it with my mobile phone?"

Riko gave me a look that said, *Who're you trying to impress?* before shifting his attention back onto the screen. "Marcus?"

My guard shot up, as if someone had thrown cold water at my face.

Riko almost *never* referred to me by my first name.

And I decided that it was a distinctly uncomfortable experience.

Like he was telling me off or something.

Or, worse, he was my girlfriend ...

"Yeah?" I replied, my tone cautious.

"You still have the tablet here, right?"

I paused, still unsure whether I should show my whole hand ... but just what was I trying to pull here? Riko lived in the flat *with* me — anything that I had cherished as some sort of secret had been dashed after about a fortnight of sharing the same living space.

"It's at the back of that cupboard — above the oven."

Riko met my gaze.

We exchanged the kind of look that made it clear Riko was in no doubt about where I had "hidden" the tablet. Riko, of course, had promised he wouldn't go looking for it ... and he had given me no reason to believe that he had. If he had broken his promise about using it then he remained as straight-faced as any hand-to-heart loyal soul.

"Shall I get it?" I asked.

Riko nodded, turning his attention back to the screen. "Yeah, let's see ..."

I fetched the tablet from where I had left it above the oven.

For some reason, I had decided to wrap it in sheets of old newspaper. It was the sort of thing my grandmother would've done if she were still alive. Then again, when my level of tech savvy was compared with others in my generation, I couldn't deny that I gave off the distinct impression that I was from another age.

It was powered up as I had left it when I had stored it in its hiding place.

When I switched it on, the familiar screen appeared before me.

The Simple Sun logo.

I tapped through several menus, finding and selecting an option for "QR Scanner".

The screen filled to show its inbuilt viewfinder fed through the pin-hole camera on the other side of the casing. I aimed the camera at the QR code.

Then waited.

And waited.

"This is stupid," I said. "It doesn't make any — "

The tablet gave a happy bleep.

And its screen went completely black.

"Ah, crap," I said. "It looks like we've wiped it ... or something."

Riko's eyes, however, remained locked on the screen. "Look."

I shifted my attention back.

Sure enough, something had appeared on the screen.

More specifically, it was a virtual-reality figure standing against a stark white background.

Uncomfortably, it put me in mind of some sort of purgatory — some kind of void.

My heart rose up to my throat and beat hard.

It wasn't too big of a jump to realise it was a virtual-reality rendering of the late John Horsham ... although I couldn't help noticing that John — or whoever was responsible for creating the virtual-reality model — had shaved off a few pounds.

John Horsham's virtual-reality self wore a white shirt, the top button undone, tucked into a pair of simple black work trousers. His hair was neatly tucked back into a pony tail and his beard looked as though it had recently been trimmed. Or maybe it was because the three-dimensional modelling software didn't have the requisite texture packs — or whatever the hell they're called — to do justice to the reality of the dishevelment. John Horsham pushed his black thick-framed glasses up his nose in an endearingly geeky way. And then he did something which I hadn't ever seen him do in real life.

He smiled.

I wondered if I — or indeed *everybody* he had encountered in life — might not have got on better with him if he hadn't been more like his virtual-reality self.

It also puzzled me that he presented himself in a mildly businesslike manner.

I would've thought that if John Horsham had the option he would've dressed like his half-brother Toby and Daymian ... all in black. I would've believed that he would've wanted to portray himself as Technomancer — like the nameplate on his office door.

"If you're watching this," John Horsham's virtual-reality self began, "then I am dead."

I couldn't help a sly glance at Riko.

Perhaps under other circumstances, we might have cracked up.

It was like that line had been pilfered from some crappy film.

Maybe it had.

Corny or not, I couldn't bring myself to raise so much as a smile. I had gone to this guy's family, and I had looked his father in the eye, answered his ... *question* ... That just about sucked any humour out of the situation that might have been present. Was this why I hadn't ever put the pieces together and launched my fledgling comedy career? Don't they say that comedians are supposed to be able to find the lighter side to everything?

I didn't seem to be able to find a lighter side to this one ...

John Horsham continued, his smile becoming wider, "And you know enough to have accessed this message. That means that you have been directly nominated in my will. And this device has been passed to you by the lawyer for my estate. If for some reason this is not the case then, please, say so now. This device utilises voice recognition so please speak clearly."

There was an awkward pause.

I exchanged glances with Riko.

I was afraid to so much as breathe.

That the tablet might recognise it as speech.

I told myself this was the first time I had so brazenly disobeyed the will of the dead.

And yet staying silent seemed the right thing to do.

All that had happened to me ... I had to know more ... I was *entitled* to know what I was caught up in.

I flushed when John Horsham spoke again, as if he might implausibly be hiding somewhere in my tiny flat, observing us, ready to leap out and catch us red-handed.

Had he made some provision in the device to catch unwanted viewers out?

Facial recognition?

I guess we were about to see ...

The screen narrowed to focus in close on John Horsham's virtual-reality features.

Any trace of a smile had disintegrated.

He wore a sombre expression now.

"I hope that all is well with you, and that this message is not too difficult for you to view, given my recent demise. It's important that you hear what I have to say. And that you understand the implications." He bowed his head for a moment.

I felt a stabbing sensation in my chest.

I guessed that this was the moment where John had decided to give his family a chance to absorb the gravity of viewing his digital ghost.

The moment up, John raised his head once more.

"Because if you are viewing this then I have been murdered."

There was such a long silence — and as John Horsham's virtual figure didn't appear to move — I was certain one of us had hit Pause somehow. But I was also sure that neither of us had put our fingers anywhere near the screen. Or moved so much as a muscle. This was the longest I had ever seen Riko sit still for *anything*. The longest he had ever been *quiet*, too.

Just me and Riko.

John Horsham staring out at us from a screen.

I half expected the whole room to start shaking.

The lights to flash on and off ...

But that was such an *analogue* poltergeist thing to do.

And this was a digital poltergeist.

Again, John Horsham's expression shifted out of neutral and into a slightly sheepish smile. "If it's any consolation, I shall always remain alive, in a way, for as long as this device is in service." He spread his hands, indicating the void he was standing in. "I have created an interactive model of my personality that has just downloaded onto the device. You will find the icon on the central menu. You can ask me questions as

174

if I was still here. You *will* definitely have questions. Especially regarding what I am about to say."

Downstairs, someone slammed their front door.

Riko flinched at the sudden sound and I nearly threw the tablet across the room.

Somehow, though, I clung onto it.

A tingling sensation continued to run across the surface of my skin.

"What I have to say is difficult to hear. But it must be followed without question."

I exchanged glances with Riko.

"It is imperative that my murder is *not* investigated. Any investigation would serve only to destroy the work that I contributed to throughout my life — work that must be kept confidential until such a time as it is ready to be revealed. I must also ask, although this is perhaps more obvious, that you do not share this tablet, or its contents, with anyone but yourself. I imagine that you have already seen some of this device's capabilities. I can instruct you on many others that might help you further achieve my desires."

I really wasn't sure I wanted to help Technomancer "achieve his desires".

John Horsham's expression shifted into an irked frown — an expression much more in keeping with my recollections of him. "There will be those who will come looking. But they must be resisted. If I have made my selection appropriately, and I believe I have, then there should not be any suspicion. And neither should there be suspicion regarding the circumstances of my murder. *You* hold the key."

It was there that John Horsham stopped speaking.

He seemed to be standing still.

Well, actually, he was swaying ever so gently from side to side.

Me and Riko must've sat there, in stunned silence, staring at what amounted to a virtual-reality statue of John Horsham for about five minutes. Perhaps longer.

In the end, deciding there was nothing else for us to see, I took the initiative and jabbed the Standby button. The screen faded to black.

"Bloody hell," I said.

That was maybe the first time in my life I could be certain that I was speaking for both me and Riko.

Inaction was what John Horsham had wanted regarding his murder investigation. But never had I been more certain that I should hand the tablet over to the police without delay. And yet, I couldn't help but think about the devices capabilities. And how I had already become so wrapped up in the world of Simple Sun.

What might happen if I went to the police?

They'd ask me why I'd taken so long to hand over a piece of property belonging to a deceased person, of course. But then any reasonable-thinking person would've asked the same question. And I wasn't certain that I had a ready answer to that. Then there was the question of what might happen once the police's IT guys figured out just what the tablet was capable of ... then it would become more obvious to them why I hadn't turned over the tablet straight away.

There would be more questions.

... And with a cold sensation up my spine I couldn't help but feel that the police might make me a suspect in John Horsham's murder. I had motive, after all. I was the one holding the tablet — and not only that but making *use* of the thing.

Another option might be to brick the tablet.

To wipe everything off.

And then go to the police.

But I had no faith that either me or Riko had the skills to scrub the thing so clean that the police wouldn't be able to find *something* incriminating.

We could always dump it in a ditch?

... But then whose hands might it fall into then?

Burn it with fire?

"So," Riko said, breaking the constant stream of thoughts flying through my head, "you gonna take it to the police now? I mean, now that it's a murder, or something?"

I looked him in the eye, studied the cogs turning in his skull.

"I ... don't think that's the best thing to do," I said.

Riko parted his lips ever so slightly.

176

Then nodded his head in agreement.

I thought about what would happen if I didn't go to the police right now.

It might buy me time.

Or get me into a whole load more trouble down the line.

As I sat on the fence, swaying back and forth, I recalled Daymian's not-quite-so-veiled threat. About how I'd better not go to the police "for my sake" ... and then I thought about the letter, the invitation I had received to the Simple Sun "conclave" ... another veiled threat if ever I knew one. They knew where I lived.

If me and Riko spent some more time with the tablet we might learn more about what we were dealing with. And just why Simple Sun were so adamant about getting their hands on it once again. With time we might even find a way to use the tablet to get us out of the hole we were dug into. I wasn't quite sure why I was using "we" because it was pretty clear that the only one in any kind of trouble was *me* ... Riko was merely tagging along for the ride.

All the same, I decided right there and then that if "inaction" was what John Horsham wanted surrounding his murder investigation then inaction was what he was going to get.

I could always just tell the police I had picked up the tablet on a whim and forgotten about it. Yeah, playing dumb would definitely work ...

# SUSPICION &
# SURVEILLANCE

I might not have been the correct recipient for John Horsham's farewell message but I decided to carry out his intentions as best I could.

Following my meeting with Toby and Daymian, I was fairly certain he hadn't intended for the tablet to fall into their hands; even though Toby was ostensibly family ... if only half-related. I decided to read his comment of "those who will come looking" as a perfect description of them both. It also meant I had to find somewhere better to hide the tablet than in the cupboard above my oven. Toby and Daymian knew where I lived, after all.

One day while I was at my desk — phones ringing, keyboards clacking — an idea presented itself. I recalled that during my LifeWare cooperate induction — worryingly close to becoming too hazy to make out in my past — Lucas had given me a tour of the premises, showing off all the wonder the company had to offer.

And one of these "wonders" had been the changing rooms.

"Changing rooms" was almost too grand a term to describe it.

"Broom cupboard conversion" would've been far more accurate.

The changing rooms were windowless and had just about enough space to accommodate a stack of a dozen or so battered lockers. The lockers looked as though they were in their second or third life ... and at least one of those had been at a school.

Only a couple of lockers had been claimed, padlocks fixed upon them. And even these had probably been long abandoned by employees who had come and gone, leaving their padlocks behind. As we had flown past the changing rooms on my induction, Lucas had smirked as he had casually told me that I was welcome to take one of the vacant lockers.

As long as I brought in my own padlock.

Well ... I *had* brought a padlock today.

And I had something I was hoping to keep safe.

My mind had spun as I had considered where the best place to stash the tablet might be. From now on I had to assume that Toby and Daymian — and Emmerson Ray — were watching. I had even thought about leaving the tablet with my parents ... before deciding it was too risky. It would be too obvious if I suddenly started "popping" to the other side of the country every other weekend. And not only to outside observers but to my parents too.

Riko's parents were out of the question because ... well, he was doing his level best not to have any sort of contact with them at the present time.

Considering that I wasn't likely to either quit or get fired in the near future, I had decided work was the safest place to leave the tablet whenever I wasn't intending to use it.

In a way, I felt weirdly anti-authoritarian.

I was piggybacking on LifeWare's security.

Of course, Toby and Daymian might well draw the conclusion that I had concealed the tablet at my place of work. They had revealed as much in my meeting with them that they wanted me to search the office for any trace of the device. But as long as I was careful — as long as I didn't let them pick me up off the street corner again when I was packing the tablet — everything would be fine. For all their bravado out there at Harper's Lake — that stun gun Toby had brandished — I couldn't help but believe that they were more bark than bite.

Whether the same could be said for Emmerson Ray, I really couldn't tell.

He was the wildcard.

The unknown quantity.

I picked out an empty locker three from the top of the stack.

I chose it because it had the least dents in its door.

I hoped that meant it was resilient.

I had only just snapped the padlock into place, given it a tug to make sure it was secure, when I heard a familiar voice.

"Making use of the facilities, I see."

I nearly leaped clean out of my skin.

My heart did a tap dance on my tongue.

Finally, when I got myself under control, my eyes told my brain that it was Kelly.

Blue eyes.

*Check.*

Jagged blond hair.

*Check.*

Delicate pink mouth ... *check.*

"You'd make a rubbish poker player, you know? You look guilty — as if I've caught you red-handed."

I regained my composure. "I don't like gambling anyway."

"Good thing. You'd only spaff your *measly* wages."

Because I was on edge, it took me a couple of seconds to realise she was joking — and she actually had to crack a smile before I caught onto her tone completely.

I moved away from the lockers, wondering how long she had been standing there.

I was pretty sure I had secured the padlock in place ... but now I was starting to doubt it ... I wondered if I shouldn't double check before returning to my desk.

But I'd have to wait until Kelly was gone.

Kelly raised her arm and placed it against the doorframe. She then pressed her head against her forearm. She had dark circles under her eyes and even I could tell — as someone who never notices these things at all — that she seemed to be wearing more makeup than usual. Or maybe I was just seeing things. "I'm sorry," she said, "that comment, even in jest, wasn't in keeping with LifeWare's Guiding Principles, was it?"

It was then that I caught a whiff of tangerine, at odds with her usual lemony scent.

What had prompted this change in her choice of citric perfume?

"It's okay," I said. "It's ages till I have my next review with Lucas so you're safe until he asks me whether there's anyone senior to me that's been causing me grief."

"Lucas seems to have been distant from you recently."

I felt myself blushing slightly. "You noticed?"

I was a bit taken aback that anyone noticed anything about my day-to-day work life.

An unrelenting borefest.

And I have a front-row seat.

"Did you have a falling-out?" she asked.

I couldn't help but sneak another glance to the lockers, to where I had concealed the tablet.

Was it going to be safe there?

I had to hope so ...

"No," I said. "I mean, nothing that I can think of ..."

"There's been some gossip," Kelly said. "Something that I thought you should hear — before you hear it from anyone else?"

I felt a coolness drip through my blood. "What?"

"Someone saw Lucas out with a ... uh ... *his* new woman."

My stomach dropped but I managed to keep my expression straight.

Maybe my poker face is better than Kelly gives me credit for.

"What ... do you mean?" I asked, wanting to get this over with.

"Well, the *someone* I heard this from said that the woman they saw with Lucas carried a certain resemblance to those pictures you used to keep pinned up beside your desk."

More blushing.

I did my best to play innocent.

"Really?" I said, a prepubescent hop in my voice.

Kelly nodded.

I took a moment to stare into mid-air. "It could be a coincidence," I said, deciding against a shrug, thinking it would be too obvious. "She's my *ex*, anyway," I added, taking no awkwardness out of the situation

8

RAYMOND S FLEX

whatsoever. I went on, "It's likely that ... whoever this *someone* was who you've got your information from is misinformed." I allowed a dramatic pause. Dared to flash a grin, even through my blushes. "Let's level. It's Adriana, isn't it?"

Kelly smirked. "Maybe ..."

And because I always have to make things as awkward as possible, I asked, "Where?"

"The ladies' toilets."

Again with the blushing.

"Anyone there at that time would've overheard them talking." She swept her gaze upwards in a faux expression of innocence. "I might just have spent a *little* longer in the cubicle than I really needed. But only because Adriana was coming to the really juicy part."

"I see," I replied, unable to stop myself sounding like a punctured tyre now. It must've been the first time in my entire career that I realised I was actually looking forward to getting back to my desk. I couldn't wait to pick up a ringing phone and chat to some customer about a problem with a piece of software I couldn't care less about.

Only Kelly was still blocking the doorway.

My stomach did a flip all of a sudden.

And I wondered why ... until ...

"I was ... *thinking*," Kelly began, "about your proposal."

"My proposal?" I replied, and then, managing to contain myself suffi-ciently to wrinkle my brow, I added, "I think I'd remember if I asked you to marry me ... ?"

There was a frozen silence as I watched a thousand HR sexual harass-ment recovery workshops flash before my very eyes.

Finally, though, Kelly gave a throaty laugh and the skin around her eyes wrinkled in a way I decided on the spot was borderline adorable. Then again, anything that saves you from the clutches of HR has to be positive. "No, no," she said, smiling widely, "I think I'd remember you getting down on one knee." She cast a glance behind her into the corridor as if she was afraid someone might be coming and then turned back to me, dropping her voice. "Were you serious about the yoga café idea?"

182

That caught me off-guard.

My heart stopped working ... just for a second.

And somehow I caught up with sense.

"I ... uh ... maybe not the yoga café exactly I — "

"Too late!" Kelly replied. "You already said it — it's out there in the world." The corner of her mouth tweaked in a smile. "You really should watch the sounds that squeeze out between those lips, you know?" She started to turn away.

"Wait ..." I said, not even realising why I'd said it after I'd said it.

As if the very concept of her walking away from me was impossible to bear. My dumb brain on some level suggested that never seeing her again might be a distinct possibility.

Kelly glanced back.

There was a beat of silence.

And then she spoke, "Mondays don't generally work for me. Shall we say a Friday night? Whenever you're next free? That's usually a pretty good day. Everyone seems to be either out drinking or eating fish and chips in front of the telly on Friday nights. But we'll be doing yoga and drinking lemon-infused white tea." She gave me a beaming smile.

When I replied, it felt as though I was doing active battle with my teeth to get the words out. But I managed it in the end. "Sounds great."

As Kelly left, she gave a disbelieving shake of the head.

The truth of the matter was that it *did* sound great.

My only — potentially large — concern was that boyfriend of hers.

Was he still in play?

... Jesus, just what was I sounding like?

All the same, I knew I had a long evening's "research" ahead of me when I got home.

After an especially epic telephone call with a neurotic young woman from Dorchester, I finally replaced my phone in its cradle. It was one of those calls which I dubbed a "Greek tragedy" because there were so many distinct dramatic and emotionally-galling phases. But most of all it was because the calls were always *so bloody long* and seemed to have next to no logic underpinning them. Whenever I got them over with it was always a little like emerging from a dream world ... a nightmare vision ... actually, I'm probably just being melodramatic; the best way to describe them would be more akin to a purgatorial landscape.

I realised most of the office had emptied out while I had been dealing with the customer.

Indeed, looking at the clock, I could see that it had gone five.

It was easy to lose track of time at this part of the year as daylight faded at around four in the afternoon. At this time of the year I have issues even remembering which day it is ... I swear I never have the same problem in summer. I seem to be all too aware just which nice, long, sunny day of the week I happen to be missing out on. Winter is basically just one big black hole we all sink into before clawing our way out some time around March, like moles popping up and squinting in the bright sunlight.

I did a quick glance around the office, saw Lucas was safe and snug in his office, tapping away at something or other. I grabbed my bag from under my desk and fled for the door.

"Wait up, Marcus!"

I halted my escape, seeing Fil rising from his desk, shrugging his jacket over his shoulders.

I checked the clock.

Sure enough, it had just struck five thirteen.

Outside, it was brutally cold.

I was certain we were going to wake up the next day with icy pavements and reports on the local news about motorists being "caught out" during their daily commutes. That usually meant they had to spend thirty seconds squirting de-icer across their windscreens before gunning their motors ... providing their batteries hadn't gone flat. All the same, I would smugly enjoy my brief moment of glory at not being one of those fabled "motorists" ... having to do nothing more onerous than stagger onto a bus, flash my pass and take my seat with the rest of my fellow working-age full-timers.

I turned the collar of my jacket up to guard against the chill as Fil paced alongside me. He was talking about the drawing classes he was taking and I was a touch ashamed when I realised that I had tuned out. I only noticed I'd done so when he fell into silence and gave me a glance out of the corner of his eye. We were approaching the gate when I realised I had almost forgotten what I had promised myself to do earlier in the day.

I wished Fil a good evening and he did the same back.

On my right, in the guard booth, Geoff sat wrapped up in a scarf, rubbing his gloved hands together. A steaming cup of something hot stood on top of the magazine spread in front of him. From the salty, meaty smell in the air, I guessed he was drinking some kind of gross meat-based beverage. Maybe it was just a class thing. I knew that my parents would've turned their noses up at it just as quickly. Geoff rested his head on his fist and it was only from looking at him closely that I realised his eyes were almost closed; that he was on the brink of falling asleep.

Well, now I *had* to talk to him.

I didn't want Geoff to get into trouble for sleeping on the job, after all

...

"Uh, I wanted to ... ?"

Geoff startled, immediately straightening bolt upright. Like a stunned wild beast — working out whether fight or flight was on the cards — he shifted his attention onto me.

Blinked.

And gave a heavy exhale, holding his hand to his breast out of relief.

"Oh, it's only you," he said. With a yawn and a shake of his head, he added, "Thought you might be that bleeding bastard Lucas."

I couldn't help but smile at this and feel myself warming to Geoff all the more.

Nothing united two people as much as shared opinions.

Geoff leaned forward on his seat. It was the same footstool he always perched on, in a kind of squatting posture. He peered into his hot drink and wrapped his gloved hands about the mug. He made no motion to take a sip and I wondered if he had prepared the drink just so he'd have something warm to hold onto.

Feeling like I was some sort of a crappy secret agent, I glanced around.

The coast was clear.

Fil had disappeared from view.

"You remember that conversation we had ... a while back?" I asked.

Geoff yawned widely, belatedly concealing his mouth with a gloved fist. "Excuse me ...?" he said, blinked a few more times, apparently to clear the last of his daydream, and then eyed me above his half-moon glasses. "You mean the only conversation we've ever had?"

I felt a slight burn off that remark ... another blush for the diary.

I pressed on a smile. "That's the one."

"About the bird?" He nodded past me, as if some phantasmal recreation of that not-so-fateful scene was still playing out kerbside for anyone to observe for posterity.

I couldn't help but think there was a whole page in the LifeWare handbook dedicated to detailing the policy on discrimination among staff and the severe consequences resulting. The right terms of reference to use, and so forth ... I supposed it wasn't exactly in line with the Guiding Principles to call fellow colleagues "bastards", either. Somehow, though, I imagined that particular handbook had never made it out here to the frontier lands that Geoff's booth occupied.

Geoff snorted some phlegm and swallowed, his Adam's apple bobbing as he did so.

It made me want to vomit ... just a little.

"You wanna know what I've seen?" Geoff asked.

I gave a sheepish grin, a stupid half-shrug as if I couldn't care less ... I really did care — *quite a lot* ...

Geoff gave me an earnest look. "It'll cost ya."

My heart played my ribs like a xylophone.

I hadn't been prepared for this.

But then a sneaky smile crossed his lips. "Just joking," he replied, setting his steaming mug down and then rising up off his footstool, stretching his chubby arms upwards.

He closed his eyes.

Breathed in deeply.

And then out again.

He opened one eye.

Smirked.

"Yoga," he said.

I flushed once more.

Of course he had been there to overhear the conversation.

He returned to his footstool, perched over the steaming hot drink. "I've given it a go, you know, for my back, like all the other stuff they say helps. Didn't do me no good, though. Just like everything else. Still " — a sly smile — "they say that yoga helps keep you flexible. *Limber*. And there're certain benefits to a woman who possesses such qualities. Know what I mean?"

"I think we're on the same page," I replied, my cheeks now so full of blood that there was none left for my brain.

"That girl," Geoff continued. "*Kelly* ..." He flashed his eyebrows as he said her name then narrowed his eyes as if he was a mystic staring into a crystal ball. "Yeah, yeah. Think there was something — something which sticks in the brain." He focused on me again. "Something to do with a ... uh, what's the politically correct way to say it nowadays ... ?"

"Partner?" I suggested.

Geoff snapped his fingers.

Gave me a wink.

"That's it, pal. Thought there was a reason why you're sat in there all nice and warm with a computering box and I'm out here in this booth so damp and draughty it might as well be carved outta Swiss cheese."

Somehow, I was certain that wasn't the only reason ...

"'Boyfriend' is what I was gonna come out and say." Geoff held his hands up as if surrendering to an invisible group of armed policemen surrounding him. "But I didn't want to upset someone." He shook his head and stared into the murky depths of his hot meat drink. "Political correctness, huh? Everyone's so touchy these days — a bloody snowflake."

I made a murmur that could have been interpreted as agreement ... even though I was fairly certain that this potted critique of twenty-first century times was squarely aimed as much at me as "everyone".

A breeze blew in around the collar of my coat and all the way down my back.

I hopped from one foot to the other, gritting my teeth, hoping Geoff was going to get on with it. I might've believed Geoff's protestations at his draughty guard booth if it hadn't been for the portable electric heater blazing away at his feet ... perhaps the situation wasn't quite as Dickensian as he was trying to make out.

"Yeah, yeah," Geoff continued without any further prompting from me, but insinuating that I was hurrying him along, "she used to get picked up by that boyfriend, only one day — about two, three weeks ago ... when was it now?"

I did my best impression of looking disinterested.

I don't think I was at all successful.

"Some time not too long ago," Geoff continued, "I remember I was sitting in here, you know, minding my business as I always do" — I wasn't sure whether this was self-satire or a misplaced sincere belief — "I hear some shouting coming from up the road." Geoff sat more upright on his footstool, holding court. "Well, in my duties, I'm meant to stay aware not only of the buildings themselves but the public pathways around. Secure-the-perimeter sort of thing ... know what I'm saying?"

"Yes," I replied.

"Yeah, well, hearing that shouting I decided I better go investigate. So I got up off my backside, hobbled off up the road. Saw a woman standing on the curb — that bird, you know? — had a car parked up alongside her. She was crying, hands covering her face. From what I could tell the man was trying to get her into the car. Although I've seen them arguing before this was much worse than those other times — thought I'd better go see if I could do anything. Keep everyone safe, see? Soon as I get there, though, on the scene, the guy wound his window up, gunned the motor and took off. Left me there with ... uh ..."

"Kelly," I put in.

Another snap of the fingers. "Kelly. She was crying, obviously." He crossed his arms, shook his head and pressed his lips together so they resembled a miniature water mattress being folded over itself. "Anyway, I gets her back to the booth. Gave her some tissues. Waited with her till she'd called a taxi."

I felt my chest tightening. "Did she say anything?"

"Oh … not really, no. She just got in the taxi when it came and disappeared. I wanted to be sure she was all right but she didn't have anything else to say to me."

It was hard to believe she hadn't taken full advantage of Geoff's sympathetic ear …

"One thing I've got for sure, though," Geoff said.

"Oh?" I replied.

"Yeah, that boyfriend … uh, *partner* … ain't never shown up since then."

It was as if someone had fed a stream of warm brandy directly into my veins.

She had ditched her boyfriend.

Even though I am a man and I clearly never stop thinking about … well, let's call it the "female allure" … I wasn't completely convinced I'd ever thought about Kelly that way.

At least not consciously.

Still, looking back on the scene between us earlier that day there was little doubt that it could've been anything other than flirting.

Objectively speaking.

And then something occurred to me.

"How's she been getting home, then?" I asked.

"Huh?" Geoff replied, as if I had thrown in a comment that was completely wild, totally unexpected. "Oh," he continued, apparently catching my drift, "dunno. Bus, I guess."

I did some mental piecing-together.

It was strange that I hadn't seen her at the bus stop at all … but, then again, I suppose she had been working much longer hours as she was covering John Horsham's role.

Was that the explanation?

Even though IT professionals no doubt receive far better compensation than customer service representatives, I don't suppose even their salaries are sufficient to stretch to a helicopter, or some other mode of transport that would negate needing to pass by Geoff's booth.

I realised I'd been staring into space — into the rapidly approaching night — when I heard Geoff's voice again. "That help?" he asked. "That what you were after?"

I blushed again. "Uh, yes — yes it was. Thanks a lot. Have a good night."

"Evening."

"Huh?"

"It's still evening," Geoff said. "For a little while."

"All right," I replied.

As I trudged my way up the road to catch my bus, I wondered at the wisdom of this pedantry. Was it something I could work into a stand-up routine? Something along the lines of "Zen Optimism for Security Professionals" or "Warm Thoughts for Draughty Booths"?

Both seemed a touch sneering.

People would see right through it.

And hate me.

# WE ARE SIMPLE SUN

"**I** look like a prize prick," I said, half to the mirror and half to Riko. It was difficult to believe I had allowed Riko to convince me there might be anything good to come from letting him dress me up again. It was as if I hadn't learned from Halloween. It was a new year ... it was supposed to be a fresh start ... and yet with hardly two weeks of January gone, I was already slipping into old habits.

Clearly about to commit the same mistakes all over again.

Riko was still living with me, for example.

Maybe I just needed to reframe things.

Look at them a different way.

It might be that they weren't mistakes at all.

Perhaps it was just my life ...

"Nah," Riko said, standing beside me, eyeing me up in the mirror. "You'll blend right in with everyone else."

I looked at my getup.

Just like with Halloween, we had resigned ourselves to scouring charity shops, turning up whatever might accommodate my outfit. This had resulted in the purchase of a tight-fitting sable suit jacket — which I secretly quite liked the cut of — and a brilliant-blue turtleneck jumper, which I was violently opposed to. Riko had allowed me to use a pair of my own jeans, although he had insisted that I tucked my turtleneck into my waistband. I was in the middle of drawing a line on this issue when he decided to up the ante, tucking the jumper into my waistband with his own hands. I jerked away from him.

"For fuck's sake, Riko! You really don't need to do that, okay?"

191

He gave me that puppy-dog look which instantly made me feel as if I was about to deal him a smart blow across the snout with a rolled-up newspaper.

I sighed long and hard. "It's fine," I said. "Just give me space. I'll do it."

Once I had completed tucking in the jumper for myself, I realised I was sort of like a puppet that's broken free of its strings and — confused by its newfound freedom — ends up doing whatever its past master would have wanted it to do ... or something.

Talk about Stockholm Syndrome.

Again, I looked at myself in the mirror.

I told myself there was still time.

"I am *not* going out like this."

"Come on, Spark, you'll be fine."

I shook my head, pinching at the collar of the turtleneck, feeling it squeezing my oesophagus shut. With a flicker of rage, I peeled the turtleneck up and off over my head and dumped it at my feet. "Look," I said, examining my bare torso in the mirror. "I'm on-board with the jacket and jeans, but *please* just let me put on a normal t-shirt, okay?"

Riko threw up his hands as if he was dealing with some prima donna.

Someone who was utterly reckless and had no sense of situation.

Out of my cupboard, I pulled out one of the white t-shirts I used under the work shirts I wore to the office every day. I put it on, slipping the jacket around my shoulders. I glanced at myself in the mirror, instantly feeling about a hundred times closer to looking like a normal human being. "See?" I said. "Don't you think this looks better?"

Riko cupped his chin in his hand. "You're definitely going with un-tucked?"

I breathed in deeply, told myself to hold things together.

This *was* a weekend, after all.

I was *supposed* to be relaxed.

And yet ... and yet ... I was about to go attend some bloody conference for some tech cult. I wondered whether this whole John Horsham thing wasn't just some giant practical joke that was being played on me. As if today was designed to lead up to some ultimate humiliation. Perhaps someone had been filming the whole time. Maybe when I finally got to see the film I would laugh along with everyone else. Or at least pretend to laugh before slipping away to cry in secret afterwards ...

"Okay," I said, looking my reflection in the eye. "I'm ready."

Riko walked away from me, shaking his head. "If you really want to blend in then take the turtleneck with you." He sighed as if he washed his hands of this all. "It's your funeral."

When Riko was out of earshot, pulling open drawers in the kitchen, seemingly intent on removing every single piece of cutlery I owned, I replied to his remark, addressing only my own reflection.

"I hope not."

I met Kelly at the train station.

The invitation I had got through the post had specified a plus-one so I had sucked up all the courage I possessed and asked if she wanted to go. On paper it made sense. She was a natural fit for this event. She had the tech expertise to save me from making too much of a fool of myself and hopefully to keep me out of any trouble I might mix myself up in. If I had been any sort of a believer in fate then maybe I would've thought that us going to the Simple Sun Conclave together was written in the stars. Not only that, but it had saved us ... *me* ... from a trip to a yoga café.

It also meant I wouldn't have to endure dragging Riko around.

Me and Kelly hadn't spoken at all since the day in the changing room at LifeWare when I had stashed the tablet in the locker. As the weeks had trundled by I had started to second guess that the meeting had taken place at all. That she had provisionally accepted my offer for us to go on a "date" together — if that was really what the proposition had been. Whenever we happened to bump into one another in the corridor at work, we didn't exchange more than a greeting.

It never seemed the right time. Lucas always seemed to be prowling nearby or else Kelly was in a hurry to go and save the day for someone who was having "IT issues" threatening to trample all over their "urgent" deadline.

I hadn't gone back for the tablet since that day. It was still safely — I hoped — secured in the forgotten work locker at LifeWare. To tell the truth, the tablet had become something akin to some kind of Ring of Power ... only that it ran off a battery and had a spooky virtual-reality rendering of a deceased system administrator saved on it ...

The point was that it seemed to possess — of itself — some sort of evil intent. And it attracted those with evil intent towards it. If there's anything I've learned about "evil intent" from my years of life upon this Earth, it's that you're usually better off not messing with it.

So not mess with it, I surely would.

After all the messing around with my outfit, I was running five minutes late.

In fact, I saw the train we had agreed to catch together pulling into the platform just as I was jogging along the bridge which crossed the railway tracks.

Thankfully, it was easy to spot Kelly.

Today she had combed and slicked her blond hair back and she was wearing a short black leather jacket over a pair of tight blue jeans. She was also wearing sunglasses. As I jogged my way onto the platform, I caught her eye and gesticulated for her not to wait for me and to get onto the train. The train guard was already peering along the yellow line which marked the platform edge, looking for anyone who might be inclined to slip into the gap between train and platform. Just as he put his whistle to his lips, readying to give the train the all-clear to depart, I hopped onto the nearest carriage and bundled my way along the aisle, heading through the carriages stuffed with families and children and older couples heading into the city for a cultural day out. Or — who was I to judge? — maybe they were intending to attend the Simple Sun Conclave as well.

I eventually found Kelly sitting at a group of four seats — two facing forwards, two facing backwards — with a table in between. She had a disposable coffee cup in front of her and steam wafted out through the drink-hole cut in the plastic lid. I couldn't help noticing that there was a matching cup sitting on the table in front of the seat opposite. As I stood over the seats, grinning inanely, I found myself saying, "Is anybody sitting here?"

"Yes," Kelly replied, straight-faced.

My smile slackened a little bit.

She broke into a grin.

Stretched her neck out, indicating the seat, urging me to take my place.

I started to blush and told myself that it was the outfit Riko had dressed me in that had put me in such an oblivious mood. *Blame it on the clothes, Marcus ...*

Kelly lifted her coffee cup to her lips and took a swig. "Didn't think you were coming — thought you were going to leave me standing on the platform." She nodded. "Nice suit."

I blushed a little deeper. "Thanks," I said. "I wasn't really sure what I was supposed to wear ... so ... uh ..."

"Let me guess, your housemate helped you get dressed?"

I decided that this was close enough to the truth. "Yeah, flatmate. That's right."

As the train rocked into motion, and more people filed into the seats surrounding us, I was aware of a man in about his seventies, dressed in a long tweed coat, swaying his way along the aisle, grabbing hold of a seat headrest every half dozen steps to steady himself and taking a nip from the hip flask he was carrying. Before I had a chance to catch myself, he saw me looking and fixed me in his glare. I busied myself looking out the window at the scenery blurring past but I knew that it was already too late. I had just got myself caught up in an uncomfortable situation.

A situation which would require great delicacy to extract myself from.

A subtle skillset I didn't possess.

Even as I stared out of the window, I was aware of the man standing over me.

He was blocking me in.

There was no way of avoiding what was about to happen.

"You!" he began, his tone more than slightly accusatory.

I glanced to Kelly, as if she was going to be able to save me from my fate, but from her look of surprise I could tell that she had only just clocked this man for the first time.

"You!" the man repeated.

"Yes?" I replied, turning in my seat, and sounding as though I was answering a reasonable request for my attention. That it wasn't one so clearly steeped in aggression.

The man glowered at me, resting his weight upon the headrest. He leaned over, his breath stinking of a heady mix of whisky, halitosis and fish. "What you ... what you ..." He lost his focus for several moments, seemed to sway on the spot ... and then, turning puce and his cheeks puffing out, he vomited on me.

I yanked the towel down from where I had thrown it over the shower cubicle door and set about drying myself. I was surprised at how easily Kelly had taken what had occurred in her stride. Once the man had stumbled away from us, leaving me — and the two seats — covered in his vomit, we had sat in near silence for the remaining ten minutes of the journey to our station. As I had sort of aimlessly wandered my way along the platform, heading for the bright EXIT signs pointing the way out of the station — and the immediate aftermath of this nightmare — Kelly had come up with a plan. I guess that kind of outside-the-box, quick-thinking is why she's "got on" so well in the working world, as they say.

She had pulled a card from her purse and told me that she was a member of a gym franchise, one of which was located just around the corner. They had showers there. Kelly had told me to take the card and go get myself cleaned up while she went and got me a replacement outfit in the meantime. There wasn't time for me to voice what seemed the most obvious resolution for this situation, which was for me to flag down as many taxis as it took to find one which wouldn't mind having a passenger covered in vomit.

And so here I was, drying myself off ... my vomit-covered clothes in a heap in the corner of the shower cubicle.

As I stepped out of the cubicle, and into the changing room which smelled of sweat and talcum powder, I was confronted with an eyeful.

It was a stocky man, perhaps a head and shoulders shorter than me, but his entire body — and I was in a good position to judge as he was entirely naked right now — was covered in ripped muscle. It also appeared that he was so proud of his genitalia that he had taken the time to wax off all his pubic hair. I've always believed that bad things come in threes, and if I was counting the man vomiting on me on the train as one — and I saw no reason why I shouldn't — then I guessed that the image of this man's bronzed, flaccid penis now scarred upon my grey matter was the second. Just what did the world have in store for my third thing?

I could hardly wait to find out ...

Thankfully this particular man hadn't noticed me watching or he had caught me looking but been nonplussed or — *potentially* — glad that I had done so.

I suppose that all totems need their worshipers.

Towel wrapped protectively about my much more modest take on the Male Body, I tiptoed my way past some more muscly men getting changed, in the direction of the changing room entrance and exit. There I was happier than I ever might've imagined to find Kelly with two plastic bags from nearby clothes shops dangling from her fingers. She gave me a smile of what I chose to interpret as mild amusement rather than nervous sympathy. There's nothing to make a situation like this worse than having someone feeling sorry for you ... especially if you are *into* that said someone. "Here you go, Marcus," she said, handing me the bags. "I think I got your size — I just went with medium."

"That's fine, thanks," I replied, with a smile, taking the bags from her, and for once praising my average, stock-in-trade body type.

Once I got back into the changing rooms, I fished through the bags, finding that Kelly had picked out a scarlet polo shirt and a pair of dark blue jeans. She had also got me a blue-and-white striped jumper to pull on over the top if it got chilly. There was also a pair of socks and some clean underwear. I couldn't help but feel just a touch embarrassed that something like this had occurred on our first date. But I could address that later.

Right now I just needed to get out of this as best I could.

Dressed up once more, I left the changing room behind — and the stocky, brazen man still stalking about completely naked — and vowed never to return.

Not to this gym, or to any other.

It was only when I was back out on the street, striding alongside Kelly in my fresh, newly-bought clothes, that I realised I had left my soiled outfit behind on the floor of the shower cubicle. I knew that Riko would be suspicious when I told him what had happened later. He would much more readily believe that I'd second-guessed his fashion decisions than been vomited on by some strange man on the train.

"It's just up here," Kelly said, pointing the way along the narrow cobbled street. "Vincent Circus Theatre."

Sure enough, we crested the hill and over the top I saw the spread above the theatre:

*WE ARE SIMPLE SUN*

It was the same design that had become so familiar to me from the tablet and the tattoos ... if not quite succeeding in occupying a place close to my heart.

The colour scheme was indeed simple.

Golden lettering with black outline.

As we got closer, I saw that they had used a special sort of reflective material so that it twinkled in the sunlight. I guess these were the sorts of promotional gimmicks that made these organisations so attractive in the first place.

"So," Kelly said, in a casual tone, "I've been meaning to ask, although I have to admit that now I'm afraid what the response might be ... what is Simple Sun?"

"It's a good question," I replied, doing my best to keep my attention fixed upon the road ahead of me, and not distract myself by looking Kelly in the eye as I walked beside her. "And one that I was hoping you'd be able to help me answer."

"A mystery?" she asked.

"You could call it that."

In the lead up to this day, I had toyed with the idea of telling Kelly everything.

After all, if I was expecting her to help me out then the least I could do was level with her.

Tell her about the tablet.

How I had discovered it ... what it was capable of ...

And yet, I just hadn't been able to find the right moment.

At least that was my excuse and I was going to stick with it.

"I got an invitation, in the post," I said. "I just thought I'd check out what it is."

"And because it's software you thought I might know something about it?"

"Yeah," I replied. "Right."

A guy with what could only be described as a laptop affixed to his chest with a harness hustled by us, his fingers flurrying across his keyboard as he went. I caught a glance at his screen and saw line-upon-line of code seemingly scrawling back and forth of its own volition.

It made me think about back when I had started writing The Routine.

The stuff just bursting out of me like a kind of automatic writing.

Maybe there wasn't so much different between me and programmers.

Except maybe knowledge of higher maths ...

Kelly flashed her eyebrows at the guy who had passed us by. "He's making me feel like a slacker."

I pouted. "Why? It's a weekend?"

Kelly gave a dry laugh and rested her hand on my shoulder — just for a second — "Oh, Marcus, just wait until you bump up the chain. You don't know what a privilege it is to be restrained by standard office hours — to have a clear start and end point to your day." She drew in a deep breath. "The day that they give you a laptop and mobile phone so you can work at home seems like a privilege at the time but it's just a trick. The dream of any organisation is to so badly blur the line between work and leisure that they eventually become impossible to untangle."

"So you start living to work rather than working to live?"

Kelly exhaled sharply, gave a wry smile and shook her head. "You want to be careful with that brain of yours — my tip is that you don't let anybody at work know you've got one ... before you know it you'll end up like me."

"We can be drinking buddies."

"Except I'm not much of a drinker, remember?"

We had reached the box office of the Vincent Circus Theatre.

Behind the plastic glass there was a woman about my age with horn-rimmed glasses and tangled blond hair. She was wearing a cardigan and looked for all the world like someone had summoned up the exact stereotypical image of a librarian and placed it in reality. From the glare she served me and Kelly, I guessed she wasn't exactly down with the idea that the Vincent had "lowered" itself to offering this sort of an event when — if the posters on the foyer walls were anything to go by — its hallowed premises was much more accustomed to giving Shakespearian performances. Still, everybody's got the pay the bills, I guess.

That's just how the world works.

We got in thanks to surprisingly low-tech credentials:

The letter I'd been sent in the post.

"This your plus-one?" the girl had asked me, apparently referring to Kelly.

I hadn't a chance to respond before she chucked a pair of laminated passes, each with a lanyard affixed to it, beneath the window, crying out, "Next!" as if this was some form of government office rather than a leisure-time arena.

The inside of the theatre was decked out in faded purple wallpaper with black swirling stencilled designs all over. There were several glass chandeliers, although none appeared to offer more than the dimmest glimmer of orange light and we were rendered in near-darkness as we navigated the ... well, there was no other way to describe them really, computer nerds streaming through the hallway.

"So," Kelly said, holding her badge up to get a proper look. "I guess we're Simple Sun now? Whatever that is."

I looked at my own badge, seeing that it was a copy of the billboard above the theatre:

WE ARE SIMPLE SUN

Kelly spoke up again. "I guess this is something to add to my CPD record."

"What's that?"

"Never mind," Kelly replied. "You don't want to know — trust me."

There were several stalls set up in the hallways. They bore leaflets and other hand-outs mostly with young people staffing them. I'd define "young people" as anybody in their early-twenties ... I'm not quite sure when I decided I was no longer a young person but it happened sometime around when I turned thirty.

"Good afternoon, friends!"

The voice was so chirpy, so upbeat that I nearly leaped straight out of my skin.

There's something about positivity ... at least in people rather than, say, a dog, which has always got my hackles up. When I turned I saw that it was a girl in her early twenties — about the same age as the other "young people". She had long, smooth blond hair. Her skin was either flawless or the foundation she had picked out was a perfect match for her complexion. She was wearing an orange t-shirt with the black monogram of Simple Sun splashed across the breast pocket. "Can I ask you what you expect to get out of today?" she asked.

Her smile looked computer-designed — beyond pearly-white.

"Uh," I replied, catching Kelly's eye. I guess it was up to me to answer this question seeing as I was the one responsible for bringing us both here. "I ... *we* were interested in finding out exactly what Simple Sun is."

The girl's smile widened.

She was wearing one of those red-and-white "My Name Is ..." labels which had become so corny that they had become cool ... before becoming corny again.

I guessed they were rising on a fresh wave of popularity.

Or maybe computer people didn't really care about stuff like that ... although the sheen I had witnessed so far surrounding Simple Sun appeared to contradict this.

The name scribbled in permanent marker on her label was "Susan". I wasn't quite sure that she looked like a Susan and wondered if it might not be some sort of pseudonym.

"Well, you're in the right place — Emmerson Ray will be giving the Keynote in about fifteen minutes."

I exchanged glances with Kelly again.

"Emmerson Ray from the funeral?" Kelly asked, and then something appeared to twig with her. "So that was what that whole ... *talk* was all about ... I'm loath to call it a dedication. It sounded more like a sales pitch."

Here Susan broke in.

For the first time, her smile faltered.

"No, Simple Sun's nothing to do with selling. As you'll see everything here is free. Everybody who was invited here today was specially selected."

Kelly wasn't happy to let this one go. "Then where does your funding come from?"

"Emmerson," she said.

"I see," Kelly replied, catching my eye.

"Well," Susan continued, clearly catching a slightly uncomfortable vibe off the two of us, "I'll let you go find your seats!"

We watched Susan go.

A couple of guys in their late teens walked past us with tote bags, the Simple Sun emblem emblazoned across them.

I spoke up. "If you're getting a bad feeling about this then we can leave."

Kelly stayed quiet for a long few moments.

I was fairly sure I could hear the cogs in her mind whirring away — that sound I'm always fairly certain I can hear whenever I'm with someone operating on a higher intellectual level than I'm capable of.

Finally Kelly replied. "Nah, my interest is kind of piqued." She touched my shoulder again. "Let's see what it's all about."

Another young person dressed in an orange Simple Sun t-shirt nodded to us with an inane grin, mentioning that we were free to take a seat anywhere in the theatre.

The theatre itself was just like the one I could recall from a school trip half a lifetime ago. Our English class had all piled onto a coach and we'd proceeded to drive about three hours to some provincial location where the production was taking place.

I can't remember exactly what the play was about — let alone what it was called — but from what I could recall, the theatre had been very similar to the interior of the Vincent. This was to say that the seats were a faded fabric which looked as though it had originally been the colour of red wine, that I could see a clear dip in the wooden floorboards of the stage from decades of accumulated Thespian footfall, and then there was the definite scent of dust and wood which cut through the air and attempted to ram itself down my throat if I breathed in deeply enough.

We took our seats three rows from the front.

Not many others had entered the theatre yet and I started to feel uneasy for the first time. I was wondering what course an interaction with Emmerson Ray might take ... what if he recognised me from John Horsham's funeral when I had spoken with him and John's parents? ... I reminded myself that I was the one who had received the invitation so surely Emmerson Ray would've been aware of the possibility that I might be there today. As he was the head honcho, or whatever the hierarchy of Simple Sun was in reality, and given what appeared to be its fairly modest size — at least at the present time — I was fairly certain he would have a decent idea of who was on the guest list and who wasn't. Perhaps even on a names-to-faces basis.

Then, with a chill in my chest, I caught sight of a familiar face, half-hidden in the darkness on the right-hand side of the stage.

Daymian, with a "y".

"So what's your conclusion so far?" Kelly asked.

"Hmm?" I replied, glancing to Kelly briefly.

When I looked to the stage once more I saw that Daymian had disappeared into the darkness entirely. I wondered if he had seen me at all.

If he had noticed that I had seen *him*.

"What do you reckon?" Kelly repeated, and then because I was clearly such a poor conversational partner took it upon herself to grab the initiative. "I mean, there's lots of kids — looks like it's a pretty classic cult trick. Go after the young minds. Easily malleable. Then once you have control, weaponise them."

I glanced around the theatre, seeing the young adults dressed in the orange t-shirts, all with the Simple Sun logo. "Do you think it's that bad?" I asked.

"'That bad' how?"

"You know, a cult?"

Kelly shrugged. "I wouldn't rule anything out at this point. What you've got to remember is that I'm a computer scientist. I spent three years at university , four years including my masters, plus ten years in industry with these people." She cracked a smile which made me wonder if she wasn't taking the piss. "I *am* these people."

I looked back to the stage, seeing the curtain rustling about.

I knew that Emmerson Ray was behind there somewhere.

And that he would soon start his talk.

We would get a better idea of what was going on.

I decided I was going to take the risk of hurting Kelly's feelings, although from what she had already said I was fairly convinced I was on reasonably secure ground.

"I have noticed that IT people tend to have a high opinion of themselves." Immediately it felt as though I had gone a little far so I tried to walk it back a bit. "I mean, from the people I've talked to ... they seem to think you're a moron if you don't know what a RAM is, for example?"

Kelly sniffed a laugh, turning her attention to the stage. The corners of her mouth tweaked upwards in a smile and I felt her fingertips brush my forearm — resting on the armrest — for just a fraction of a second.

It *had* to be intentional.

... And yet I still had my doubts.

Better to play it cool.

From somewhere a bell started to ring.

I noticed an increased amount of activity.

The young Simple Sunners — I bet they had a much catchier name than that — became more animated, more vigorously ushering people into their seats.

The curtains swept open.

The house lights dimmed into darkness.

My eyes focused upon the stage backdrop.

The same as the billboard on the theatre outside.

The familiar logo. And the words:

WE ARE SIMPLE SUN

As the last of the audience took their seats, I realised that the theatre had filled up almost so that there wasn't a spare seat in the house. Emmerson Ray appeared from the right-hand side of the stage, all grinning white teeth, waving his arm over his head. It appeared he had toned down his dress style significantly for the occasion of John Horsham's wedding because the bright orange suit he wore today matched the t-shirts his young followers were wearing.

There were whoops.

And wolf whistles.

Clapping — but that went without saying ... some people were stamping their feet.

At the back of my brain I wondered just how much of this vibration assault the Vincent Theatre could take. I didn't imagine the architect had designed the place with this sort of audience in mind.

Kelly spoke at last. "Guess we'll see just what kind of an opinion Emmerson Ray has of himself, huh?"

# EMMERSON RAY

E mmerson Ray arrived at the middle of the stage, stepping up onto the podium with the microphone before him. Still grinning, he held his hands aloft, like an evangelical preacher. After about a minute, when the applause and general commotion showed no sign of dying down, he waved his hands and called over everyone. Finally, the rejoicing masses decided they'd had enough and descended into a mere smattering, with only the true die-hards carrying on their show of appreciation. He began his opening monologue.

"Friends, members, brothers and sisters."

Kelly nudged me in the ribs with her elbow and I gave her a glance. She was already smiling wide.

There was something within me that wanted to tell her to play it cool, to pretend that we were just like anybody else in the audience here which was to say that we were ... what exactly? Sort of willing to be brain washed by whatever Emmerson Ray was intending on doing with this crowd. I reminded myself that I had come here out of a sense of wanting to get a handle upon exactly what Simple Sun was ... that on some level I had to remain open-minded. And that ostensibly was what Kelly had agreed to also.

Yet, I wasn't naïve enough to let my guard down.

... Or at least that nudge in the ribs had reminded me as much.

"We have assembled here for the very first Simple Sun Conclave. Before I begin, I thought that I would introduce just what a conclave is and how it might be referred to in the context of Simple Sun." He brought his hands together with a smack and for a terrible moment

I was sure he was going to drop to his knees and tell us all to start praying. However, instead, a filthy smirk twisted his mouth. "You were all probably expecting me to start talking about a higher power — about giving yourselves over to a greater being, weren't you?"

Nobody said anything.

The jubilation which had previously racked the theatre appeared to have disintegrated completely now.

"Well that's not what Simple Sun is about." He separated his hands, placing them in a classic power posture upon the lectern before him. "Let me say it as simply as I can, Simple Sun is not a cult."

Once more, Kelly tapped me on the arm.

"Simple Sun is a *movement* ... a time for change. A nascent point in history from which *everything* shall expand outwards. And the conclave — a *conclave* — is nothing more than a privileged group sharing their knowledge with others similarly privileged. To be part of this conclave is in itself an achievement ... an admission of your potential ... of nothing less than your personal *importance* to the continuation of the human race."

I had to admit that Emmerson Ray had a knack for grabbing attention.

He held up a remote control and clicked it.

The visual behind him, showing the *WE ARE SIMPLE SUN* slogan disintegrated and was replaced by a three-dimensional model of the world.

A blue-and-green globe spinning about its axis.

"The world," Emmerson Ray said, unnecessarily and smiling more widely still. "Where we make our home. Where humans have developed and progressed throughout countless years of history."

"Actually," Kelly said, mumbling under her breath, "I'm pretty sure people have had a go at counting ... and if peer-reviewed process has any value whatsoever then I think they've had a pretty good go at it too."

One of the young people in an orange Simple Sun shirt turned in their seat and scowled at us. It made me feel as though I was back at school and that was one place where I certainly didn't want to go.

Emmerson Ray clicked the remote another time and the globe disappeared from the screen. It was replaced with what I believed to be —

from my dim recollections of biology classes at school — a strand of DNA.

"We are all code," Emmerson said.

I thought I was beginning to see where this might be going.

Or what John Horsham's involvement might be ...

The visual swooped into a close-up of the strand of DNA before blending once again into complete darkness.

"For centuries man has attempted to decode his own structure — and so learn the secrets of which being or force it was that originally programmed him." He smiled to himself in a more than slightly self-satisfied way. "Our own Lead Coder."

This elicited a few chuckles throughout the crowd and I couldn't help thinking that several of these were not people laughing along with Emmerson Ray but laughing *at* him.

Just where had all these people come from?

A nearby university, perhaps?

That would be the perfect place to find volunteers willing to spend the best part of a day helping out in exchange for something as frivolous as a snazzy t-shirt.

The visual faded to black.

Now it was replaced with an image of an enormous hall.

Seats stretching rows and rows back.

The seats themselves appeared to be populated entirely by shadows ... sort of faceless phantasmal beings. They were all dressed in suits.

Emmerson Ray continued. "Our world has advanced ahead of our own bodies. Our own perception. The human mind was designed, created ..." he paused "... has *evolved*, however you wish to phrase it, to deal with a village of people. Nothing more than a village. A couple dozen. Fifty people. Maybe a hundred at a stretch." Holding out the remote and gesticulating pointedly with it at the audience, he emphasised each word with a beat of his hand. "Let me ask you a question. When was the last time you realised you couldn't picture someone's face?" He poked at his temple with his index finger. "Inside your mind." He continued to stare at the audience, as if he was willing someone up out of their seat to oppose him ... to somehow challenge this fairly innocuous question.

209

"I want to see a show of hands," he added, finally. "Come on ... who struggles to conjure faces in their mind's eye?"

Nearly everybody's hands rose into the air.

When I slipped Kelly a sidelong glance, she shrugged at me and raised her hand.

I justified with myself that if I was indeed attempting to infiltrate this "conclave" in any meaningful way then I had better go with whatever the group-think was.

Besides, it wasn't like this was something that had never happened to me.

In fact, it had happened a hell of a lot ...

"Uh-huh, uh-huh," Emmerson Ray said, nodding to himself as he surveyed the audience as if he was counting every single vote and storing it away somewhere in his brain. He waved his hand as if he was wiping away ink on an invisible white board.

Everyone in the audience put their hands down.

"So what would you say if there was some way you could see — I mean *really* see — faces in your mind?"

Nobody said anything.

Emmerson Ray's expression was smouldering, serious for maybe ten, fifteen seconds.

It would've been possible to hear a pin drop.

But then, with a winning smile, a flash of blindingly bright white teeth, he let all the hot air out of the room with this mere tweaking of some minor muscles.

"Of course you all want that — *I* want that — *everybody* wants that. We want to be more than mere human beings. We want to *evolve*. We want to *catch up* to the complexity of our world — the complexity of the world we have built around ourselves." Here he stepped off his lectern, standing upon the stage. I realised that he must have been wired up with a wireless mike as his voice continued to carry around the theatre speakers as he strode along. "The governance systems," he went on, gesturing to the hall filled with shadowlike figures dressed up in suits. "Who can truly tell me that they are satisfied with our politicians?"

Nobody said anything.

And I couldn't help but thinking that this was a fairly safe thing for Emmerson Ray to be saying. Because he could be fairly certain — to maybe near one-hundred-per-cent probability — that he knew exactly what every member of the audience was thinking.

Kelly leaned into me, held up her finger and thumb with the slenderest of gaps between them, and whispered, "He's about this close to saying, 'Wake up, Sheeple!' I reckon."

I couldn't help a smile sneaking across my lips.

"You there!"

My gut dropped.

And I looked up.

There's something in the tone of an authority figure's voice — whether they be teacher, or parent, or cult leader (like Emmerson Ray) — which cuts right to the very wick of that human fight-or-flight response. And I could feel it tingling those senses right now.

Sure enough, when I looked up, it was to see Emmerson Ray staring without question directly at me. "Yes, you! Would you mind coming up here?"

I waited a second blindly hoping that my subconscious might throw up a witty remark that would get me out of this horribly sticky situation.

But, of course, my brain gave me nothing.

As I turned side on, leaving the safety of Kelly's company, and shuffled my way past the seated members of the audience on our row, I guessed that after getting thrown up on, seeing that bronzed man's flaccid penis, this was the third bad thing the universe had in store for me today.

It was sort of like being on train tracks. As if once I had taken the decision — subconscious or not — that I was going to do exactly what Emmerson Ray wanted — there was a kind of weight lifted up off my shoulders.

No more did I bear the burden of decision making.

I had only to face my fate.

And — no doubt — let it kick me in the face.

As I stood up on the stage, with the spotlight shining upon me, setting dazzling stars twinkling before my eyes, I couldn't help but turn my thoughts to that horrible aborted night when I had believed that I had it in me to be some sort of stand-up comic.

Thankfully — on some level — because what was occurring to me right now was approximately a thousand times more traumatic, as there was someone in the audience who I actually wanted to impress, I didn't dwell on thoughts surrounding that particularly unpleasant night. I looked Emmerson Ray in the eye, waiting for him to inevitably recognise me from John Horsham's funeral.

I stood before him, marvelling at the manly, musky scent emanating off him.

He was also much more muscular than I had initially recalled.

If I was a woman then there was no doubt I would've felt protected. *Attracted*.

But I wasn't a woman, I was a man ... or I was supposed to be.

"What's your name, sir?"

Standing beside Emmerson Ray, looking him in the eye, there didn't appear to be so much as a shred of recognition. My initial reaction was one of relief ... but this was soon replaced by the much more depressing realisation that I was eminently forgettable. That Emmerson Ray might have talked to me all night and still wouldn't have realised who I was.

Or was I just sticking the knife into my own heart?

"Marcus," I replied, thankfully omitting my surname this time and this time only ... who says that I'm a complete idiot twenty-four hours a day?

"So, Marcus," Emmerson Ray continued, unabated wearing a broad, everyman smile that told me without question he was thinking of just about anything else in the world right now except who I might be. "Do you honestly feel that in the modern world you have true represen-tation? Do you believe that this whole *system* of putting things to a vote, seeing which person is the most *popular*, is really the best way of deciding decisions? From which nights you put your bins out to be collected by the council to whether or not we should invade a foreign country?"

Even though I could barely see the audience in the theatre for the bright light shining down upon us, I could *feel* their eyes upon us.

Upon me.

I had been fairly certain it was a rhetorical question but Emmerson Ray continued to stare at me, waiting for me to say something.

"Um," I said, "it works, I suppose."

Emmerson leaped away from me as if I might've revealed that I had some horribly contagious deadly disease. "'Works!' It *works*!"

I looked out into the blaze of light and thought I caught sight of Kelly's face amongst the audience. But even if it was Kelly then it was impossible to read her expression. And even if I could read her expression — if we managed to communicate some sort of a silent message between the two of us — did I really *want* her to save me?

I guess it would be another layer of humiliation that I could stack upon the pile.

Kind of like how geological formations come into being.

One heap at a time.

"Marcus, please. You've come here today — to the Simple Sun Conclave — by *invitation* because you have the right sort of mind."

"The 'right sort of mind' ?" I said, feeling the unpleasant swell of my own words echoing back at me through the theatre speakers. I guess that when Emmerson Ray had greeted me on stage he had somehow clipped a mike onto the front of my jumper. When I looked down I saw that — sure enough — he had done exactly that. Sleight of hand was part of his charisma arsenal.

"Yes," Emmerson replied, beaming. "You have been chosen to come here *because* you are inquisitive. Because you are unwilling to bow to the 'way things are.'" He actually made bunny ears with his fingers to mimic quote marks. "Because you are the sort of person who wants to change the world."

"... Am I?" I asked, my voice barely making it to my mike.

"Yes you are!" Emmerson Ray boomed back at me.

Someone in the audience cried out something I didn't catch.

Then someone started clapping.

Soon enough an applause broke out.

There was more whooping.

After about a minute of this, Emmerson Ray did that whole wav-ing-his-hand-in-the-air thing to bring everyone back to silence. He dropped his voice to almost a conspiratorial tone. As if it was just me and him and he was about to relay something top-secret. He gestured at the screen featuring the faceless hall of people. "Look there, Marcus," he said.

Looking at the screen was better than looking at the audience so I did what he told me.

I could see the blurred faces — the shadows stuffed into suits.

"Don't you think there's a better way? A more *satisfying* way for the human race to organise itself?"

Again, there was a long pause and I wasn't quite sure what was expect-ed from me. Finally, because even I'm not so much of a moron to stand in a spotlight and say absolutely nothing at all, I ventured a response. "...Yes?"

Emmerson Ray's smile stretched from one cheekbone to the other. He reached out and clasped my shoulder. There was something reas-suring about his touch — almost paternal. He covered his microphone with his mouth, reached out for mine and unclipped it from my jumper and then said — this time in a husky whisper nobody else would be able to overhear — "Come see me backstage, after the show."

Back in my seat, and the flush on my face so hot that I felt as though I was holding molten lava in my cheeks, Kelly nudged me in the ribs again. When I looked at her she was grinning.

At least someone had enjoyed the spectacle.

"You were great, Marcus," she said, in a whisper.

As she turned her attention back to the stage, and I did the same, I scanned her tone of voice for signs of sarcasm. And yet, slipping another — what I hoped was — casual glance in her direction, she appeared to be enjoying herself.

In my company.

Or maybe I was just making projections.

Perhaps she was trying to put on a poker face while we were among these cultists, only later to let her mask slip and let me know how she really felt.

I wondered if — inside — she might actually be livid with me.

I know I would've been if someone had brought me to an event like this.

Emmerson Ray went on talking. The screen behind him had shifted away from the endless hall filled with shadows stuffed into suits and now showed an extremely and very extensive circuit board. What it was exactly, I had no idea. Guess I'm not such a computer whizz after all.

"Mankind's development has outgrown its mind," Emmerson Ray said, and then poked his finger into the audience, broadly in my direction. "As you saw so well illustrated by my friend Marcus. But then the question moves from the merely philosophical — into the practical." He had been pacing back and forth but he came to a sudden halt now. "What do we do next?"

Once again, there was no trace of the previous jubilation which had racked the theatre. Everyone was glued to their seats, fixated upon Emmerson Ray ... hanging on his every breath.

To tell the truth, I was no different.

I guess that Emmerson Ray was right about me having the right kind of mind.

Maybe he just meant that I'm easily bamboozled ... and yet Kelly, too, was similarly enthralled. But she had forgotten more about computers than I had ever known.

"Well, my friends, if we look to the last century, we will find our answer. It has been lurking there, in the background, forever. It is just up to us to seize the opportunity ... to seize control of our destiny." He glanced to the screen behind him briefly, almost derisory of the image. "Computers."

The screen shifted again.

It showed a video sequence of various natural disasters.

Chunks breaking off icebergs and tumbling into the sea.

Forest fires.

And then a close-up of an antelope staggering and then falling onto a cracked plain dried-up by drought.

"Climate change," Emmerson Ray said, as if he needed to say what we were all seeing. "A problem which man, and his priorities, his prejudices, his very *nature*, is incapable of solving."

I didn't see anybody in the audience protesting against this assertion, although I would've said that he was being a mite melodramatic. It wasn't like *no* progress had been made towards solving climate change, although admittedly more and more it was looking as though time would run out sooner rather than later.

Now Emmerson Ray showed on the screen a picture of what I assumed was an African village. Starving children. Babies covered in flies. Animals nothing more than skin and bone. "Injustice," Emmerson Ray said — apparently to fire home his point. "Humans have passed centuries without resolving this. The need for there to be winners and losers is built into the human condition — our global politics is merely a reflection of our own basest natures. Because, for all their faults, politicians most certainly *are* humans, just like ourselves."

There were a few chuckles around me at this comment.

I couldn't but think that politics was always pretty low-hanging fruit when it came to comedy ... then again I was under no illusions that Emmerson Ray had any aspirations of taking a career as a comic any further than the odd off-the-cuff remark here and there.

Finally, Emmerson Ray showed a close-up of a face ... a face a *lot* like mine.

As the image zoomed outwards, it showed a man dressed in a shirt, tie knotted about the throat, hand on his computer mouse, the other splayed across the desk, thumb on the spacebar as he gazed into the middle distance. I wondered briefly just what the man might be thinking about but then told myself that I *was* that man.

And his thoughts were my own.

"Dissatisfaction," Emmerson Ray said. "An internal conflict, but one which is just as perverse as the other two I have mentioned." He looked up to the heavens as if imploring the aid of a higher power ... but thankfully he kept his next comments to the here and now — to the innate ridiculousness of our own world rather than the imaginary ones endorsed by religion. "A man, or a woman, may go their entire life, nodding along in their daily routine. Never questioning the wider impact of what they do — accomplishing their dreams. What they *believe* are their dreams. What society has *trained* their dreams to be." He paused his pacing and counted out the next items on his fingers. "House. Car. Two kids. Holidays ... maybe twice a year." He puffed out his mouth in a pout, his lips forming a tight circle. "And the rest of the time ..." He stood where he was until the audience realised he was waiting for their contribution before continuing.

Someone in one of the front rows — perhaps one of the volunteers in an orange shirt — eventually called out.

"Work!"

Emmerson Ray's gaze slowly came to rest on the person who had spoken — unseen from the vantage point where I was sitting. "*Work*. Numbing. Monotonous. Dull ... but insidious, also. It creeps into every-thing." He tapped his temple. "It creeps into our minds, gets its hooks there. Keeps our brains busy so we don't get to put them to any other use." A slight smile caught the corner of his mouth. "Is it any wonder governments worldwide want to see their citizens employed in some activity or other?"

I couldn't help but think of a stream of reasons why governments might "want to see their citizens employed" beyond the reason that Emmerson Ray had pointed out ... but I wasn't about to raise my hand. From the glance that I exchanged with Kelly in the gloom, I saw that she had come up with other reasons herself.

"Civil obedience. *Compliance*," Emmerson Ray continued, almost spitting the word. "You do what they say so you can live the way they want." He jabbed his finger at the floor now, as if the lava lakes of hell were bubbling right beneath his feet. "They make the rich richer ... and they give everyone else ... *just enough.* And do you know why?"

Nobody said anything.

Emmerson Ray clicked over to the next slide on his presentation.

This time it was a cartoon of a fat man dressed in a suit, perhaps in his fifties, sixties, holding tight to a bag of money, bills spilling freely in his wake.

"We talked insidious," Emmerson Ray said. "Ain't nothing more insidious than greed ... ain't nothing more *human* than greed."

He clicked the control another time and the original backdrop returned:

*WE ARE SIMPLE SUN*

For a long few seconds there was total silence in the hall.

Clearly Emmerson Ray wanted to allow everything he had said to seep into our skulls.

When he spoke again, his voice was low, almost a drawl, as if his energy was running low ... as if he had used up all his enthusiasm on his opening pitch and now he had little remaining. "What we lay out here, today, is the start of a new world. A fairer world. One in which everyone attains contentment. Where nobody goes hungry. And where we make our planet safe to live on for uncountable generations of our grandchildren to come".

Now Emmerson Ray removed something from his pocket.

I realised, fairly quickly, that it was a smart phone.

"You've all got one of these, I reckon."

Since just about everybody in the audience was copying Emmerson Ray — slipping their smartphones out of their pockets and holding them up in the air — it appeared that he was correct.

"We've got an app," Emmerson Ray said. "I can't tell you to download it, and anyway that wouldn't be what this movement is all about. But I would encourage you to ask questions through the course of today — ask *me* questions — see if it might broaden your mind. The app is to unite us ... wherever we are. You'll never be alone now." He paused for a long moment and then about three-quarters of the audience spoke the words with him.

"We. Are. Simple. Sun."

Emmerson Ray straightened up, fired off a parting blinding grin to the audience, and under the blanket of rampant applause, he paced off the stage and into the darkness of the wings.

I looked to Kelly sitting beside me and — like me — clapping Emmerson Ray off the stage. She was wearing a wry smile as she met my eye. "So," she said, "what'd you think? Are you gonna wake up, Marcus? Are you going to download the app?"

For a terrible second, I thought she was being serious. And that she had somehow contrived this whole episode ... that there was some kind of a conspiracy going on to bring me here, to this time, right now ... but then she gave me another smile.

One which told me that this was just about the most ridiculous pile of horseshit she had ever been witness to ... which happened to be pretty much along the lines of what I was thinking.

"Emmerson Ray asked me backstage," I said. "Do you want to come?"

I only realised that I was still trembling — reeling from my trip up to the stage — when Kelly took a light hold of my arm just above the elbow. Her touch sent a fresh shudder through my whole body, and a warm feeling through my gut. Even someone like me — who was certified blind to any kind of flirtatious body language, or just body language in general — could tell that this was a good sign. It was almost enough to make everything else melt away.

But I told myself I needed to remain aware.

If there was anything I had taken away from the talk Emmerson Ray had given it was that I was dealing with committed, passionate people.

And those types of people aren't always the most logical thinkers.

In fact — more often than not — they're impossible to predict.

There wasn't any security to get to the backstage area except for the stick-thin blond boy in his late-teens dressed in one of the orange Simple Sun t-shirts. He recognised me from the stage and insisted I give him a high-five. That made me feel about eighty years old.

Back when I'd been young, the high-five had long been out of fashion ... but I guess as with all things in human culture, it worked in waves and the high-five was well and truly back.

Whether it was ironic or authentic was beside the point.

Because it *was* back.

There was a series of doors which all had varying sizes of chunks of wood which'd been knocked out of them. Despite the fresh coat of glossy black paint which'd been applied to them they were beginning to look somewhat dilapidated. I guess that's sort of par for the course if you happen to be a dressing-room door ... frantic people coming and going all the time and a theatre's budget tends to be tied up in things front-of-house rather than what goes on in the back rooms.

With Kelly on my heels, using a primitive process of elimination — looking under the doors to see which had lights on — I located which was Emmerson Ray's dressing room.

After knocking and getting the go-ahead to walk right in, I heard over my shoulder that the next speaker was being announced back on stage in the theatre.

At the back of my mind, I wondered if Toby or Daymian (with a "y") might be speaking. It boggled my brain to think of them standing up in front of an audience and making any sort of sense. They just didn't seem to be that sort of person.

But, then again, who was I to judge? I would just as soon die a thousand deaths than stand up in front of an audience and say anything. *Do* anything.

The dressing room itself was about as stripped down as the state of the dressing room doors had promised it would be. The paint was flaking off the walls, and the only furniture besides the makeup tables and polished-up mirrors was a freestanding hanging rail with an assortment of coats arranged on it. I wondered if other revolutions had started this way.

I wondered if any *successful* revolutions had ever started this way.

Emmerson Ray swivelled around in his chair to face me and Kelly.

He rocked up onto his feet, his smile just as blinding as it had been back on stage. Perhaps his persona wasn't just for show ... or maybe — more likely — this was still part of the show.

"Marcus!" Emmerson Ray said, lurching forward and clasping my hand with his, as if we were long lost friends. "I knew I recognised that name when you got up to speak on stage."

I glanced to Kelly who was smiling cautiously.

When I had gone on stage it had seemed that Emmerson Ray didn't know who I was — that he hadn't seen me before in his whole life ... but now, with this greeting, I wasn't so sure any longer. Maybe his selecting me from the whole audience sitting in front of him hadn't been as much of a matter of chance as I had believed.

I reminded myself that *someone* had sent me the invitation in the post.

Emmerson Ray was clearly operating on two or three social interaction levels above my own, because he seemed able to read my thoughts. "Toby and Daymian brought you to my attention," he said. "They thought you would make a grand addition to Simple Sun."

I shifted Kelly another look.

She remained thin-lipped.

I turned back to Emmerson Ray. "Uh, did they?"

"Mm-hmm," Emmerson Ray said, flattening his palms one against the other and pointing his fingertips at the two of us as if he was a beggar ... or a yoga teacher. "May I ask you a personal question?"

His tone of voice was such that I knew this was a rhetorical question.

We *were* on his turf after all.

He could ask whatever question he wished and if we didn't abide by his desires I was certain he could get one of those orange t-shirt wearing volunteers to toss us out on our ears ... metaphorically speaking, of course ... because I was fairly certain that even with my modest set of muscles I would present most of the lanky students with a challenge. And I was also fairly sure Kelly was the type of woman who'd taken a self-defence class or two in her time.

"Are you two together?" Emmerson Ray asked, still pointing his fingers at us.

I decided that his pose was more like an Olympic swimmer readying to leap into the pool and set a new world record.

This time Kelly spoke up. "What'd you mean?"

A smile flicked the corner of his mouth. "Romantically?"

I felt my cheeks flushing ... not for the first time today ... and I wondered if the universe wasn't going to break its unspoken promise and hit me with an unprecedented fourth Bad Thing in one day. I guess even the universe wants to keep things fresh from time to time.

"No," Kelly replied, answering for both of us before I had a chance to put my clumsy foot in it.

"Ah," Emmerson Ray replied. "I see."

When Kelly spoke again her tone was harder and I could see by the look on her face that Emmerson Ray was starting to test her patience. It was surprising for me because I couldn't remember any time when Kelly had been anything but cool-headed. Then again, I guess the truth of it was that we really didn't know one another all that well.

That's the whole point of "dating", I suppose ... if this even qualified as a "date".

Which from the sound of Kelly's emphatic answer, it was not ...

"What does it matter?" Kelly said.

Instead of backing up, getting all apologetic at having made Kelly cross, Emmerson Ray shifted his head to one side as if by physically viewing us from another angle he might find the answers he was searching for. "It was a leading question, as I imagine it sounded." He pursed his lips, stared at the ground for several seconds, and then looked up at us once more. "I wanted to invite you to my island."

A stony silence settled over the room.

"But before doing so, I wanted to establish the dynamics." He widened his smile and his eyes flickered between the two of us. "I didn't want to make anybody *uncomfortable* — it's my intention that the island is a safe space for everybody."

Kelly butted in, shaking her head. "You're out of your mind," she said, and then becoming more animated, jabbing her finger in the direction of the stage. "You do realise how many other people have stood up before crowds and run through a monologue on pretty much the same topics, don't you? Or are you so far up your arsehole there's no longer any light to see your reflection?"

I had to admit that I was just as impressed by Kelly's sudden anger as her turn of phrase.

"No, no," Emmerson Ray replied. "You're taking this the wrong way. It's entirely up to you." He looked at me. "It's up to you both." He pouted again. "If one of you wants to come, fine. See what it's all about. An adventure, if nothing else."

I could tell that Kelly was on the verge of bursting from the room so I knew I had to ask the questions that mattered while I still could. "Sorry," I said. "It's just sudden, and, well, you know, kind of ... weird?"

"What's weird about it?" Emmerson Ray said. "As you yourself admitted before the audience, this is all logical. What we're working towards is logical. And you can be a part of it."

I could tell that Kelly had something more to say but I spoke up again, keen to say my own piece before I lost my chance. "But ... why me? What skills do I have? What could I possibly offer Simple Sun?" I shifted Kelly a glance and risked turning her ire upon me. "I mean, I can understand that you'd want her, she's a computer whizz ... a tech person ... but I'm just a ... a customer support rep ... I know how to answer a phone and right-click a mouse but that's about it."

Another silence followed.

And then Emmerson Ray erupted into bellows of laughter.

He doubled over himself and slapped his thighs.

When I caught Kelly's eye again, I saw her mouthing, "Let's go", and jerking her head in the direction of the exit. But I felt rooted to the spot.

I wanted my answer.

I wanted to hear from Emmerson Ray's own lips what he had to say.

Finally, Emmerson Ray got control of himself. He straightened up, tears of laughter sparkling in his eyes.

"What's so funny?" Kelly asked.

Emmerson Ray reached out and clasped me by the shoulder. His grip was powerful and I could feel the beat of my pulse against his fingers. The way he peered into my eyes was unnerving. Like staring into twin barrels of a rifle ... not that I had ever found myself in such a perilous situation as that. "Marcus," he said, shaking his head, apparently in disbelief, "why're you doing this to yourself?"

"Doing what?" I replied.

"Knocking yourself down all the time — belittling your accomplishments."

I was about to respond, outlining the pathetic nature of my "accomplishments" when I caught myself, realising that I was only falling into the trap he had set.

Emmerson Ray's smile widened. "Now, Marcus, a recommendation to join Simple Sun must come from a trusted member — one of those closest to me. This is not an open-membership organisation and shall never aspire to be. We are a close-knit group."

"And not a cult," Kelly put in, tongue firmly in cheek.

This comment didn't throw Emmerson Ray off balance — his smile unaffected — "And definitely *not* a cult." Emmerson Ray poked me in the ribs a couple of times with his index finger. "What you've got to do is look where that stuff has come from. Your parents? Your teachers? Someone's told you you have to fit into this iddy, biddy box and you've fallen for it hook, line and sinker. But you can still break out. Simple Sun is your chance to break out." He furrowed his brow, the first sign of any crack in the otherwise unabashed positivity being emitted from Emmerson Ray's very being. "Didn't you feel identified by one of those slides I showed in particular?"

I thought of the man in the suit, working in an office.

And the monotonous melancholy the image had presented.

Sometime years back — at another job, potentially in school — I had been asked to outline where I expected to be in five years' time. I don't think that the five-year plan is anything particularly revolutionary but I can clearly remember sitting by myself, for hours, with a blank sheet of paper, and seeing only fog. Through the fog — perhaps on the horizon — I could see ... something ... but I had no idea what it was. Once when I had really tried, I had waded forward into the fog and found it damp, unyielding, disorientating, and it soon surrounded me so that I could no longer see. Did Emmerson Ray really have the answers?

Did anyone?

Emmerson Ray released his grip on me a few notches. "Here, Marcus, let me put this a little more plain, huh? How much do you make in your current place? At your current job?"

I flipped Kelly a glance.

At some point when Emmerson Ray had seized hold of me she had started to back away, getting closer to the door.

Even though I was certain that Kelly was well-versed enough in corporate structure, corporate pay scales, to know precisely where my salary sat, it felt weird to be sharing the information with her in the same room.

Then again, who in polite society asks how much you get paid?

... Unless they're offering you a job.

That was when the penny — *literally* — dropped.

Deciding I had nothing to lose, and equally curious and terrified as to where this was all leading, I gave Emmerson Ray the information he wanted. His eyes never left mine the whole time and I wondered if I wasn't being put under some sort of hypnotic spell. "I'll double it if you come partner with us." He snapped his fingers. "Just like that — *done.*"

I glanced at Kelly.

She was shaking her head and backing away to the door quite openly now.

Everything seemed so far away now.

Our journey here this morning.

The presentation we had been subjected to ... the jokey way we'd taken it ... all those jokes about it being a "cult" ... This was different now, though. Emmerson Ray was offering me a job. A job which paid twice as much as my current job which — by the way if you haven't already caught onto the hints — I abhorred ... True, I had no idea what the job entailed, or what dangers I might be opening myself up to, but the island Emmerson Ray had mentioned sounded intriguing.

Water gushed through a pipe over Emmerson Ray's shoulder.

Someone passing by in the corridor coughed.

And it felt as though the stasis in the room had been broken.

"Marcus?" Kelly said. "Let's go."

Emmerson Ray remained fixed upon me, his hand on my shoulder. I felt a strange tingling energy ebbing out from his fingertips, seemingly humming directly into my blood. "Think about it, Marcus," he said. "You don't need to give me an answer today."

Finally, he released me ...

However, rather than feeling a sense of relief to be getting away from Emmerson Ray's irrepressible intensity, I felt something else — something akin to sadness ... as if I had come close to reaching the answer to some deep-felt psychological, perhaps philosophical need, and I had pulled back at the very last moment. Maybe losing the chance to know the truth forever.

I found myself backing away.

Going after Kelly.

Some part of it was fear — that much I was sure of — but another was the desire to slip back inside myself. To peer through my mind's eye once more.

Might I peel back those layers of fog now?

# THINKING IT OVER

It was a long old week after the Simple Sun Conclave.

I only realised once I had got home that despite Emmerson Ray's offer, he had given me no means of contacting him. No number, nothing like that. The only way I could think of for getting through to him would be via Toby or Daymian. Despite the shudder of resistance I felt through my chest to think about either of those guys, I knew it would be equally problematic to get hold of them. Or maybe not ... perhaps I just needed to expose myself a little. Walk around outside LifeWare and wait for them to come kidnap me again.

The truth of the matter was that following the meeting with Emmerson Ray everything felt duller than it ever had before. However, the worst part of it was not due to this innate "dullness" but more my attitude to said dullness. Whereas previously I'd always been fairly adept at seeming happy while at work, I was finding it harder and harder to stop the mask from slipping. There were a couple of calls when I'd nearly lost my temper with customers ... coming only a word or two from openly swearing at them or calling them a name. If Lucas hadn't happened to be passing by when those conversations had reached their zenith, I wondered whether I might've just followed through. Said what was truly inside me.

I knew this grumpy attitude was because of what Emmerson Ray had planted in my mind.

An alternative. A better, brighter alternative.

The more I thought about what he'd said to me, the more I realised I couldn't believe I had left the Simple Sun Conclave without verbally accepting his offer.

Just what the fuck had I been thinking?

Whatever he was offering, surely it was better than this?

It was strange. The meeting with Emmerson Ray had been so impactful upon me that I barely noticed I hadn't spoken a word to Kelly since the Conclave. If Emmerson Ray's objective had been to occupy my every waking moment with his offer then he had been successful. Who wouldn't be tempted by a mysterious job which paid double your current salary? And then there was the fact that I — *me* — had been cherry picked for the role ... and although I knew that it was most likely a mistake, or that Toby and/or Daymian had had ulterior motives in recommending me, it made me feel special all the same. And although I would've been loath to admit it — I've never wanted to appear arrogant or big up my accomplishments — there was something magnetic about having someone interested in me.

Maybe because it hadn't happened before.

Or at least not for a *long* time.

It wasn't until Thursday that I spoke to Kelly.

The conversation happened out of the blue.

I had been tapping away at some customer feedback surveys, making sure the data had all been collated correctly. It was the sort of task that was more befitting of a Friday afternoon or a Monday morning than a Thursday afternoon ... but the mental toil of turning over Emmerson Ray's offer throughout the week had got me pretty much worn out even with a day to go before the weekend. I was half listening to Fil speaking into his phone. It was always an entertaining proposition because he had to be the most patient, most empathetic person who had ever worked at LifeWare. No matter how scattered or stressed the person on the other line was he was nothing but calm and collected, going through the steps in the logical, "this-and-then-this" way that came so naturally to him. Like a robot with high-level AI.

Wow, is that a backhanded compliment ...

When Kelly spoke she startled me.

I hadn't noticed her standing at my shoulder.

"Marcus," she said. "We need to talk — have you got a sec?"

My heart fluttering up in my throat, and my palms quickly having become clammy, I turned in my chair to face her. There was a serious expression fixed upon her face — it hadn't changed since we had met with Emmerson Ray at the weekend.

Perhaps he had affected her as much as he had affected me.

I glanced back at my computer screen, seeing that my finger had drifted onto the "A" key and that I'd continued to press it. The cursor was blinking away, clearly distressed at my treatment of it and maybe in its binary way wondering just when I was going to stop. Acting on instinct more than anything else, I looked over my computer monitor, seeing that Lucas was in his office, chatting away on the phone. I couldn't help thinking that he looked more vexed than usual.

Not that that was a bad thing ...

"Sure," I said, sounding far more casual and carefree than I felt.

It was the first time I'd been in the sysadmin office since Technomancer had kicked the bucket. It was kind of funny given that me and Kelly were ... well, whatever we were ... a bit like work colleagues ... a bit like friends ... and maybe just a smudge like ...

Oh, come on, who was I kidding?

That whole *date* idea had been a complete wash-out.

Just what had I been thinking?

... But, then again, I couldn't help coming back to the idea that the meeting with Emmerson Ray had been the start of something.

His offer certainly still rang in my ears.

In the office, I noticed straightaway the lack of stacks of pizza boxes, the absence of flatulence and body odour and the return of natural light. The window was even open a crack letting frigid air in. "Wow," I said, because I couldn't think of anything else. "It looks twice the size I remember it."

This comment drew a smirk from Kelly, the closest thing I'd seen resembling a smile from her since we had met Emmerson Ray. "It's amazing the difference a woman's touch makes."

"Don't let HR hear you saying that."

And then, as if it was written in the stars, Fabrice the HR officer walked past the open doorway, glancing in briefly before carrying on.

When me and Kelly looked at one another we couldn't help smiling.

Besides the lack of greasy flammable material and unpleasant odours, there was now a fresh scent of peaches wafting about the room and I also noticed one of those Chinese kitties that bats its paw. Are they lucky charms or something? The servers even seemed to be whirring away more tunefully than they ever had done for John Horsham. The desk, too, was spotless, the only items upon it besides the computer mouse and keyboard was an empty reusable coffee mug which — judging by the tag — had a few minutes ago contained herbal tea. I'd be willing to take a wild stab in the dark and guess that John Horsham hadn't been the type to indulge in herbal tea. Not unless it was heavily saturated with sugar of some sort. Don't they say you actually burn more calories drinking herbal tea than you do ingesting it? Biology's never been my strong point so I have no intention of looking it up to see whether it's true. I'm willing to believe any old wives' tale to steer clear of having to think too hard about stuff.

A slightly uncomfortable silence fell upon Kelly's office.

I knew it was because of how things had ended at Simple Sun Conclave.

We had travelled back together, of course, but it had been a pretty much silent journey. My mind had been boggling over everything Emmerson Ray had said to me. And I had told myself over and over that it couldn't have been true.

That it was a trick of some sort.

The only thing Kelly had said to me — when we had parted — had remained equally as scarred upon my mind:

"Be careful."

I looked at the computer monitors, the code scrawling back and forth. "What did you want to see me about?" I asked. And then, deciding that I might as well address the elephant in the room before it had a chance to spook the both of us, I added, "Contrary to what Emmerson Ray thinks, I'm not all that much of a computer whizz so if it's some coding thing you want my opinion on — "

Kelly's eyes flashed fire. And my survival instincts told me unambiguously and unequivocally that this had *not* been the right thing to say.

"There's something you're not telling me, Marcus."

She might as well have given me a hard shove in the chest.

For a second or so I was winded.

"... What'd you mean?" I jabbered out.

Kelly sighed hard, threw up her hands, then appeared to freeze for a few moments, as if she was uncertain how to address this situation.

I knew this reaction pretty well.

It was the common crisis that tech people find themselves in when they need to explain themselves to mere mortals. When they need to bring things down to a level normal people can understand. With another sigh — one which racked her whole body — Kelly finally allowed her arms to fall back beside her sides. Her eyes sunk back in their sockets as if she was thinking.

*Calculating.*

No doubt trying to work out just how much pain she would need to put herself through to get the results she required.

"We're under attack," Kelly said, finally.

Because I'm an idiot, I looked past her, out of the window, and into the company car park.

Everything looked normal out there.

Geoff the Security Man was in his booth, perched on his footstool, staring into mid-air ... I guess there's not a huge amount going on throughout the day when employees are neither arriving or leaving — just deliveries to deal with for the most part.

"No," Kelly replied, managing to hold in her sigh this time.

I wondered if she was using her yoga practice to flex her patience.

"I mean it's a cyber-attack."

"Ah," I replied. "I see."

I turned my attention to the computer monitors, furrowing my brow in expectation.

Kelly shifted past me and sat in her desk chair.

Her fingers flurried across the keyboard and I watched multi-coloured lines of code fly across the screen. She might as well have been writing in runes for all it meant to me.

"On the log we've had non-stop attempts at DoS attacks every minute for the past hour."

"Ah," I said, feeling like I had to say something.

Kelly continued to tap away at the keyboard, shaking her head every so often and sighing some more. Once she looked into her reusable coffee cup and tutted.

"Do you want me to freshen your cup?"

"Huh?" Kelly replied, glancing over her shoulder, apparently having forgotten that I was even there. Turning back around, she replied, "Uh, no ... don't worry about it."

After another minute or so had passed, I started to wonder if she was expecting me to leave. I wasn't any closer to having an answer as to why she had asked me to come to her office. Maybe she just wanted to show how much of a noob I was ... or something. Well, I could certainly show her a thing or two about following conversational flowcharts for managing customer complaints and recommendations. I could show her the *shit* out of one of those flowcharts ... maybe because it was the only thing I did forty hours a week ...

"Kelly?" I said, finally speaking up.

"Yeah?"

"What'd you want me here for?"

She gave the Return key half a dozen hostile jabs with her index finger.

I started to get worried that she might be about to erupt again.

They didn't teach hand-to-hand combat in yoga classes, did they? Maybe the joke was going to be on me for never having gone to one to find out what it's actually like.

Kelly spun around in her chair, glaring. "It's Simple Sun," she said. "I know it is ..." She shook her head. "An attack this persistent, this sustained. It's not some passing chance. It's Emmerson Ray ... he's behind this."

I felt strangely scorched by this remark, as if it was something that I'd done which'd made me responsible for this DoS attack ... whatever that was.

"What did you say to him?" Kelly asked.

"Nothing," I replied. "You were there, remember? For the whole conversation."

"After, I mean," Kelly said.

"After?"

"Yeah, he said that you were going to be in touch with him, you know, about that 'job' he offered you."

I had to admit I was glad that I could tell the truth here.

Even if it did make me sound like an idiot.

"I ... uh, he didn't give me any way to contact him."

Kelly continued to stare at me. "You're telling the truth?"

"Why would I lie?"

She had no intention of breaking eye contact. "I don't know," she said. "Why would you?"

I was beginning to get a little tired of this conversation. Lucas would be on my case sooner rather than later, wanting to know where his gimp had got to ...

"Marcus," she said, her tone of voice shifting, giving way slightly, "if there is something then you can tell me. Anything at all." She jerked her thumb at the screen and dropped her voice to a whisper. "This stuff's serious. If you're involved, in any way at all, you could get into serious trouble."

"I ... don't know what else to say," I replied. "I can only tell you the truth."

Something softened in her expression and I hoped I was getting through to her finally. Her gaze slipped out of focus and she nodded at something that was passing through her brain. "Okay," she said. "Maybe I'm just being paranoid ... it's just ... I don't trust him, or anything that's going on." She looked up at me again. "And I don't like the connection between Emmerson Ray and John Horsham. It means that I'm in the middle of anything that might've been going on. That there could be something I should be seeing — something that I'm responsible for."

I thought I was beginning to see the reason for Kelly's panic.

I was certain to listen carefully to anybody that might be passing in the corridor.

It seemed that the coast was clear.

"You mean, you might lose your job. Something like that?"

Kelly met my eye.

Nodded.

"Yeah, something like that." She paused, poking her tongue between her lips as if to stopper the words she was about to speak next. In any case, she decided to speak. "It could bring the company down — potentially."

I resisted the urge to do a mock celebration — throw my arms in the air and let out a silent cheer, that sort of thing. I had only just got back on Kelly's good side so I didn't want to instantly burn the good will I had earned. I also knew that this was the right moment to tell Kelly my true secret. The one that would hopefully help her to see that I could be trusted.

That she *should* trust me.

"Kelly?" I asked.

"Uh huh," she replied, shaking her head, having returned her attention to the computer screen.

"Have you got five minutes, before you go home tonight, to take a look at something?"

I waited until thirteen minutes past five — and Fil had left the office — before venturing into the changing rooms of LifeWare, where I had told Kelly to meet me.

She had given me a weird look when I had told her to meet me there and I had wondered if she wasn't going to think that I was a massive perve of some description.

And whether she shouldn't call the police, let alone HR ...

But I was clear myself that my intentions were sincere.

I worked away at the padlock on the locker where I had stashed the tablet, getting it out from inside. I had to put it down to my mind being elsewhere — that was the only explanation for my carelessness — because I heard a horrifyingly familiar voice on my heels.

"Thought you'd be long gone, Marcus."

I turned around to find myself nose-to-nose with Lucas.

Even despite my panic, at holding the tablet in my hands, I couldn't help noticing his pallid complexion. The slightly withered quality to his skin. He looked as though he hadn't been sleeping as well as he usually did ... perhaps he wasn't able to find his favourite moisturiser and so was unable to put his mind at rest.

"What've you got there?" he asked.

"Uh," I replied, turning the tablet over in my hands like an idiot — as if it had just materialised out of dark matter.

"That's not LifeWare property, is it?"

Before I could stop him, Lucas reached out and gripped the tablet lightly. He shifted it up so he could see the back plate. I realised after a second or two what he was looking for. All of LifeWare company hardware was branded with a security label. It was magnetic, or something, and I supposed some clever scanner could scan it and tell you exactly who that piece of hardware was assigned to ... or something.

Seeing that there was no security label — as it most definitely wasn't LifeWare property — Lucas released the tablet, frowning to himself. He flashed his eyebrows and nodded at the lockers. "I'd be careful leaving something like that in one of these — you know it's a LifeWare policy not to accept responsibility for any loss or damage to private property."

On another occasion the cutting edge of Lucas's officious response might've affected me negatively ... but today it felt as though a pair of angel's wings were lifting me a few centimetres above the ground. I had to remind myself not to smile.

"Okay," I replied, "I'll keep that in mind."

Making to leave, Lucas half turned away from me in that annoying way of his. He always likes to make you think that the conversation is over — that the tension's off — only to give you a fresh stab with his tongue. I'm sure he'd learned the strategy on one of the many less ethical management courses he'd been on.

A way to get your employee's guard down.

And get them to spill everything.

"Remember that your access card will only work for half an hour past your specified office hours." Lucas rolled back his suit sleeve to examine his expensive wristwatch. "So as you work nine-to-five, with no stipulation for overtime, and it's five twenty now, you have ten minutes to leave the premises."

With Emmerson Ray's voice resounding in my ears, I had the urge to follow up his provocation with a childish retort along the lines of, *And what if I don't?* ...

However, mercifully, I managed to keep myself reined in.

With the same disappointment Lucas always experiences when someone doesn't rise to the bait he's laid down, he bid me a good evening and set off out of the office.

I guess that Lucas had oversight from his own bosses. And that he'd have to explain being on company property after hours in the same way I did.

Thankfully, Kelly showed her face soon after. She looked bleary-eyed and was holding her reusable coffee cup in her hand. It was steaming away now and the odour was without a doubt coffee this time. Her eyes lingered briefly on the tablet I was holding. "Can you make this quick, Marcus? I've got a shit-ton to get done before I get out of the office tonight."

"Want to take a quick walk outside?" I asked.

Kelly yawned and then rubbed the side of her face. "I'd rather not," she said. "I like to save stepping out into freedom as the ultimate reward for my work day done."

I felt an uncomfortable squirming sensation in my stomach. I decided that I might as well be open about my feelings of discomfort. Kelly would be just as keen as I was to prevent Lucas from having so much as a moment of joy. "It's just ... my access expires in ten minutes."

Despite her tired eyes, she raised a slight smile. "And who'd you think controls the computer system that tracks employee comings and goings?"

Because I couldn't help myself, I found myself saying, "Is that ethical?"

Kelly glared at me, finally giving me an intense shrug.

"Okay," I replied. "Point taken."

And so in the LifeWare changing rooms I told her everything.

Just how it had happened.

From top to bottom.

Leaving absolutely nothing out.

From Technomancer's untimely — although perhaps not entirely *unexpected* — demise to the gnomic pornography me and Riko had stumbled across on my neighbour's computer, to the list of barred patrons at the Street Sermon.

Kelly listened patiently, clearly forgetting about her own work with each passing sentence of the story I was relaying to her. After all that, I felt a sense of relief, as if I had squeezed a troublesome spot that had been bugging me for weeks.

Kelly was staring at the tablet I held in my hands.

Finally, she spoke.

"What do you think it's for?" she asked.

The question sideswiped me. "What'd you mean?"

Her eyes met mine again. "Why does this thing exist?"

I was still stumped. "... To make hacking easy?"

"Uh huh," Kelly replied. "And why would someone like John Horsham, who had all the coding knowledge in the world, need to make hacking easy?"

"He was lazy?"

"I don't doubt that," Kelly replied. "Especially when it comes to documentation, but to create what you have just described is such an enormous piece of work that it just defies belief unless there's a root cause — a *belief* really."

"A belief like Simple Sun?" I replied.

Kelly met my eye. "Do you think this is why Emmerson Ray made you that offer? Does he know that you've got the tablet? He must do," she added, answering her own question, seeing that my mouth was flapping open and shut like a banked fish.

Despite sounding logical through and through, something deep within me fought to resist Kelly's suggestion. I guess I wanted to think that I was special.

That Emmerson Ray *had* truly seen some sort of potential in me.

That it wasn't just because this thing had fallen into my lap.

But who was I kidding?

I had told Kelly about Toby and Daymian (with a "y") harassing me for the tablet so I knew that she had fed all of that into her conclusion. And I knew — unless I chose to lie to myself — that this was the most reasonable version of the truth.

"What should I do?" I asked.

Kelly met my eye once more. "Give it up."

"What?"

"To me, I mean," she replied. "Let me take a proper look at the thing."

I thought through this proposal.

The tablet felt a little like what I supposed the weight of a baby might feel like to its mother. In my mind, I imagined myself as a female orangutan, baby clinging onto her hairy chest, as she swung about her enclosure at the zoo, out of reach of the other primates trying to steal away her precious cargo. I knew I needed to stop being ridiculous. This tablet had nothing to do with me beyond me being the one who had happened to come across it when John Horsham had died.

There *was* one thing which still bothered me, however.

"Uh," I started, "do you think that when this thing breaks into other systems it might ... you know ... keep some sort of trace of what it has seen?"

"What do you mean?" Kelly asked.

"Sort of like a browsing history on a computer?"

Kelly remained straight-faced a few seconds before breaking out into a smile for the first time in our interaction. "You're worried about those gnomes!"

Feeling as though an invisible person who'd previously been pressing down upon my shoulders had given up all of a sudden, I decided to play along. "Yeah, you know ..." I scratched the back of my neck. "It just doesn't look good?"

Kelly sniffed a laugh and then reached out to take the tablet. "Really Marcus, it's fine. You can trust me to be discrete. I promise I won't judge you unfavourably for anything I happen to find on that tablet. Even if it does happen to save stuff."

I kept the tablet close to me and my eyes fixed on it at all times as if — of its own will — it might grow legs, leap out of my arms and go scuttling out the door.

Finally, I relinquished, allowing Kelly to take the tablet from me.

I noticed that she was examining it with a kind of reverence ... the kind of respect that an art dealer might give an especially intriguing antique.

"Hmm," she said, "how interesting."

She elaborate for the less technically minded among us.

As I bid her goodbye, and headed off out of the office, I was well aware that there was one thing I had left out when I had told her "everything". I hadn't told her anything about the photos of my ex-girlfriend, Olivia, that had been present upon the screen when I had discovered the tablet, in front of Technomancer's corpse. Then again, what damage could it do?

I had been the victim, after all.

Technomancer had been hacking into *my* phone.

Why was it my fault what I might have there?

Try as I might, though, I couldn't quite shake the feeling that I was about to open myself up for a whole world of pain. And there I'd been thinking that me and Kelly were getting along famously.

There was something ... *off* when I climbed the stairs to my flat.

One of those feelings you get when you feel the hairs prickling up at the back of your neck. If it had been a scene out of a movie then it would've been the time that the protagonist is about to discover that someone has broken into their home and is lying in wait.

What was lying in wait for me?

I paused at the front door.

Listened.

I could hear voices on the other side.

Cackles of laughter.

I shut my eyes for a moment, telling myself that I needed to have the conversation with Riko sooner rather than later. Things just couldn't go on like this.

I wondered if I should just sit this one out down at the Sermon, but it was a Thursday and — from experience — I always felt a sense of anti-climax at going down to the pub on a Thursday night. As if I was jumping the gun on the weekend ... making it less special than it needed to be.

And this was *my* flat.

*My* home.

Riko was just a guest.

... Or so went the theory.

And so I took a deep breath and decided to be a man, letting myself in through the front door. As I looked out upon the scene, I noticed that at least the sofa bed was still in its upright position — no sign of any bedding ... I guessed that I had been particularly focused that morning when it came to keeping things tidy.

Sitting on the sofa bed, however, were two girls.

I recognised them instantly ... from the Halloween party.

Julie.

Her hair now the shade of multi-coloured sherbet.

And her friend Frankie.

Whose bed I had slept in.

It turned out that Frankie's hair was a natural rusty-red colour ... not the ghoulish grey-blue as I had correctly assumed way back then.

Standing before them, his back to me, was Riko.

I processed the scene, trying to work out just how this fit in with where everything had been left at Halloween. Hadn't Riko broken up with Julie and left me to fumble about in the smouldering rubble? Admittedly social skills have never been a strength of mine.

Everybody turned to look at me and I realised I could smell the thick scent of marijuana wafting through the air. It appeared that they'd been having a good time while I had been squashed into an overcrowded bus on the commute back home. Then again, I suppose that it's more or less taken for granted that any given person on the planet is having a better time than me at pretty much any time of day or night.

Because I have a knack with words, I found myself saying, "Uh, what's all ..." And then my eyes fell upon Riko, who had turned to me, his mouth slightly parted, showing off a very black hole within his head. In his hands I saw that he held a few pages of A4.

Given how many hours I had spent during the course of my life staring at those very pages, it didn't take me long to recognise what they were.

It was The Routine.

Everybody's face was stone right then.

Smiles frozen in time.

Eyes just starting to betray the sense of shock.

I couldn't help thinking that the fact that they were all stoned couldn't be helping the time it was taking them to process things.

Maybe I'd give them a nudge.

I channelled all my ire upon Riko. "What the *fuck*, Riko?"

It felt as though this was becoming something of a catchphrase.

Riko looked at me, then down at the pages he held in his hands, and then he shot a worried glance at Julie and Frankie, lounging on the sofa, their eyes glazed over as if I was some kind of a vision ... like a particularly dirgy unicorn materialising out of smoggy air.

Even despite the numbing effect of the drugs, Riko started into his whole damage-limitation routine. "It's okay, Spark, really, I can explain. You see — "

But standing there in my suit and tie, I felt as though I was already in Dad Mode, and there was no chance of walking it back. And so with my finger thrust out behind me, indicating the open door to my flat, I simply said, "Get the fuck out, Riko."

Riko looked dumbstruck for maybe the first time in his life.

That was little wonder.

My cold, measured tone had surprised even myself.

There was some throat clearing over on the sofa, some rustling about.

Out of the corner of my eye, I watched Julie drop what remained of the smoking spliff in a near-empty glass of water which was sitting on the carpet beside the sofa.

As Riko stood his ground before me — for the time being — gripping the pages down at his thigh, Julie and Frankie made their exit without speaking so much as a word.

We listened to their footsteps creaking upon the staircase as they headed down and out of the building. It seemed as if we had agreed to wait until the heavy front door of the building swung shut with its distinctive *thump* before breaking the silence between us.

Riko attempted a smile but aborted it after only a few seconds when he recognised the severity in my eye. He held the pages out to me as if they were something I had lost which he had helpfully found. "We didn't mean to go looking," Riko started. "It's just ... they came over and ... Julie just happened to pull out those pages ... from a notebook. We're ... *I'm* sorry, Spark. It was a mistake. I — "

But I shook my head. My voice was quiet but firm. Like the fabled not-angry-but-disappointed parent. "I don't think you heard me, Riko. I want you out. And I want you out right now."

Riko's mouth latched open again but the sheer force of my own mind seemed to will it shut once more. His eyes left mine and he sauntered across the room, placing the pages of The Routine down on the sofa. Then he went about the room, recovering the clothes he'd left strewn about the place. He dropped everything into the sports bag he had arrived with on his first day here. Finally, with a last glance at me, wearing an expression like a brow-beaten dog, he disappeared out the front door, bringing it shut with a gentle *click*.

I realised I'd been holding my breath and I exhaled hard.

It felt as though a huge weight had lifted off my shoulders.

I had my flat back again.

As I wandered over to the sofa, to the pages of The Routine, I heard a knock at the door. I sighed long and hard. I should have known it wouldn't be so easy to get shot of Riko from my life.

Sure enough, when I opened the door, sports bag slung over his shoulder, Riko was standing there. And he was looking doleful indeed. I expected him to launch into one of his trademark sob stories, rake up the embers of whatever sympathy I might still feel towards him — somehow contrive his way back into my good books.

"I forgot my toothbrush," was all he said, however.

I didn't speak, only nodded, stood back from the door and allowed him to pass.

I scolded myself the second I allowed him to set foot back in the flat once more because I convinced myself he would say or do something any second that would make it impossible for me to throw him out on his ear. However, he merely returned from the bathroom — surprisingly actually only with his toothbrush and not even a tube of the toothpaste which *I* owned — and headed back out the front door. As he passed me by it was that same stray-dog look of hurt. This time when he got to the doorway, his back to me, he lingered.

"... They were laughing," Riko said. "That's a good thing, isn't it?"

I drew a sharp breath, wanting to hear precisely zero more on the subject.

"You were laughing *at* me, Riko."

I expected him to launch the standard Riko defence; that old traditional baffle-them-with-bullshit strategy. But he just nodded vaguely and disappeared once more.

Standing in the open doorway to my flat, I listened to his footsteps sound on the staircase, and then the front door to the building thunk shut.

For about a minute I just absorbed the quiet and the calm.

The background buzzing of my fridge.

Water gurgling through pipes.

The throbbing of my own heart.

# THE BIG BAD WORLD

The day you leave your job is supposed to be a joyous event. All of that pressure, all of that expectation, is all of a sudden lifted right off your shoulders. You can breathe again. You can cut your mind loose of all that ... *crap* that you didn't even know it was mired in.

I had decided on Riko Kicking Out Day that it was also the point for me to make other dramatic changes in my life. And so with Riko not even ten minutes gone I had started typing on my letter of resignation to LifeWare. I thought I might've been nervous about it, that there might've been some trembling on my part, a sort of fear, but I felt curiously detached from the whole act. Even when I forwarded the draft to my work email — so I could think it over in the morning before finally pressing send to Lucas — it didn't seem real.

... Or, perhaps, more precisely, it felt like the only logical action to take.

Later that evening, after I had "cooked" a frozen ready-meal lasagne which I'd liberated from the back of my freezer, I set about figuring out just how in hell I was supposed to get in contact with Emmerson Ray. As far as I had any plan at all about what to do next — now that I was about to sever my one and only income stream — I had been banking on the offer still remaining open. After an hour or so of bouncing around various websites, following the ever more enigmatic trail of Simple Sun in cyberspace, an idea finally occurred to me.

I did have one piece of information.

I knew Toby's full name, or I thought I did ... they were only half-brothers, after all.

Still, it was better than nothing.

So I did a search for "Toby Horsham" and then sat back to take in the results.

I scrolled through them, weeding out faces smeared with fake tan, the muscular Tobys pouting into mirrors as they took selfies, the Tobys dressed up to go to elegant restaurants or to the club ... those weren't the Tobys I was looking for.

Finally, though, I found him.

Or what I thought was him.

Buried in the search, about four pages back, there was a simple web-site for a "freelance programmer" called Toby Horsham with a contact form attached. The website itself — to my inexpert eye — looked as though it hadn't been touched for the best part of half a decade but it was the best lead I had to go on. Maybe Toby still picked up email from the site even if it was no longer his online marketing hub.

So I tapped out an email, refreshing Toby's memory as to who I was — I guess my self-esteem was so low that I didn't think he'd remember someone he'd kidnapped — and asking how I might get in touch with Emmerson Ray.

About ten minutes later my phone started to buzz.

It was only as I viewed the unrecognised number showing up on the Caller ID that I realised I'd never knowingly given Toby or Daymian (with a "y") my number.

"Hello?" I said, my stomach for the first time feeling tight ... that primordial sense that you're either making a massive mistake or you're about to do something completely life-changing — or even a bit of both ...

"Marcus?"

It was Emmerson Ray.

"Yes?" I replied.

"You ready for some truth?"

I couldn't help but think that this sounded like something directly out of the mouth of a sixties folk singer. Still, I was the one who had called him. I was the one who was pinning short-to-medium term hopes on Simple Sun.

245

With a smile, I said, "Yes. Yes I am."

The next day at work, armed with the knowledge that my draft letter of resignation was sitting in my inbox, my mind spun with what Emmerson Ray had said to me over the phone. He had asked me a sequence of perplexing questions ... following the one about wanting to know some truth. He had asked me whether I had resigned from my job yet, to which I had told him that I was in the process of doing so.

He had just responded, "Good, that's good."

Minutes later a job offer from Simple Sun had arrived in my inbox.

Emmerson Ray's handwritten signature scoring the bottom of the letter.

I couldn't help thinking, as the letter laid out the basic terms, that Emmerson Ray had an excellent memory. Because he had exactly doubled my salary. When I paused to think about it I realised that he'd even factored in the — all too slight — pay increase I had received less than a week earlier. That got me thinking about what Kelly had said, about LifeWare being under cyber-attack. I told myself that it was probably just a coincidence, although I knew I'd be foolish to shake Kelly's concerns clear from my mind.

She was a computer geek, after all.

As I had walked past Geoff on the way into the office, he greeted me as usual before adding an extra comment which he had never had cause to utter before.

That I was looking particularly happy that morning.

"What makes you say that?" I asked, turning side on to let one of my unfortunate soon-to-be ex-colleagues in through the gate.

"Well," Geoff said, leaning forward on the footstool he perched on and lowering his voice, "I could hear you humming all the way down the road and you're wearing the biggest shit-eating grin I've ever seen on anybody around this place. Haven't won the lottery, have you?"

Belatedly realising that a smile was responsible for the fact that my cheeks were aching I did my best to return to what I thought of as my regular hangdog poker face.

It wasn't all that successful.

Geoff dropped his voice another notch. "Or better ... you're quitting?"

I glanced around and then tapped the side of my nose.

Geoff gave me a smirk. "Good on you, son. Get out while you still can, huh? Already got something else lined up?"

"Yes," I replied. "Yes, I do."

The office itself was a deeply strange experience that morning. It was like having a bomb sitting under my desk to know that my resignation letter was waiting in my inbox, primed and ready to be sent out. I was beginning to have a few doubts but I told myself it was only natural. When you've been doing something — *anything* — for long enough it becomes habit. More natural than nature itself. I once read somewhere that the brain is kind of like a plastic storage medium. Whatever you do actually affects its physical shape.

Who you are.

I've always wondered why people answer the question, *What do you do?* with the non-linear response, I *am* a ...

The night before I had toyed with all sorts of resignations. And while I had considered going with a Riko-style nuclear option, in the end I decided that I didn't want to reach that level of bridge-burning. Well, that and I didn't have the guts to do the same. There was still a strand of caution underlying the decision to take the Simple Sun job — the healthy pessimism that it might not all work out in the end.

... Not that I ever contemplated returning to LifeWare.

I was resilient on that point.

As I sat at my desk, all the other emails in my inbox faded into a blur around the one I had forwarded from my personal address. I had given it a cryptic title, "MR-R" on the basis that if it was somehow intercepted by LifeWare security agents — which I knew for a fact didn't exist — then they might pass over this extremely important and confidential document. I had also given thought to pompously marching into Lucas's office and announcing my decision ... just to see the look on his face. But in the end I decided that I'd just keep a low profile.

Get out quietly.

And so, after the briefest of re-readings, I pinged the email off to Lucas and then sat back at my desk to await the fall-out.

To tell the truth, it was a lot less dramatic than I had been building it up in my mind to be. Which was to say that I was going about my work as normal when ten o'clock rolled around and I noticed Lucas standing at my elbow. That wasn't unusual, however, he was often to be found lurking nearby ... apparently looking for something to ding me for.

"All right, Marcus," Lucas said. "Shall we step into my office?"

I was aware of everyone's eyes upon me — but none more so than Fil — as the two of us weaved between the desks to Lucas's office.

Lucas brought his office door shut behind him with a gentle click and waved for me to take a seat in the chair before him. Once the two of us were sat down, Lucas tapped something into his computer quickly then punched the Enter key. Next, he sat up in his chair, resting his elbows on the table, bridging his knuckles and peering at me over the knobbly joints. "I read your letter," he said.

A silence opened up between us.

I hadn't been expecting to have to elaborate.

The letter was fairly self-evident ... or so I had thought.

Lucas unclasped his hands. "I just wanted to have a quick chat to make sure this is really what you want."

There was an odd tone to Lucas's voice. It was a deeper shade of something that I had picked up on previously. That weird paternal vibe I had always thought that he contrived.

Maybe I'd been somewhat wrong.

248

"Listen, Marcus," Lucas said, becoming oddly unfocused now, not meeting my eye. "If this is about ... *her*" — he met my eye for the briefest moment before looking out the window — "then there's nothing for you to be worried about."

My ribs squeezed my heart and lungs.

I followed Lucas's gaze, seeing that he was looking out over the company car park to where Geoff was perched on his footstool, leafing through a newspaper, resting his elbow on his leg, and the side of his head against his fist. A couple of times he appeared to drift off for a second or so before suddenly snapping back awake.

Lucas opened his mouth to speak again.

But I cut him off.

I guess the words of Emmerson Ray continued to flow through me.

That sense of raw power — of firm belief — whatever it was that he had imparted to me there was no doubt that I couldn't do this.

"It's not about that," I said, although in truth I knew that it was most certainly something which had flashed through my mind as I had been working on my resignation letter ... there was something more than a little depressing at having to see your boss every day knowing that they were now going out with your ex-girlfriend.

Lucas raised his eyebrows slightly.

I went on, "I've got another offer."

Lucas's eyebrows rose higher still.

I wondered if I should've been more offended by this reaction. As Lucas found it a borderline ridiculous idea that there might be any other employer that would want me.

Finally, Lucas blinked away his daze. "Oh," he said, and then leaning forward a little in his chair. "Congratulations." He glanced at his computer screen and then back at me. "Can I ask you a personal question ... about the opportunity?"

I couldn't help but feel bolstered by this chance to gloat.

I wasn't an especially gloaty person but after the years of putting up with Lucas's regime — the shedload of hours of my life I would never get back — it felt only right that I should get at least one moment to wallow in glory.

"Yes, fine," I replied.

"Is it ... Simple Sun?"

The serious expression I had worn throughout the meeting so far threatened to collapse in upon itself like a poorly supported mineshaft. I managed to catch myself at the final moment before giving it away. "Uh, yeah?" I replied, unable to keep the surprise out of my voice. "It is."

Lucas got fidgety again, nodded to himself a couple of times without meeting my eye, and turned his attention out the window.

It appeared that Geoff had completely dozed off now.

Then again if I'd been in his position I most likely would've done the same.

There can't be many more boring jobs than sitting on your arse all day watching people coming and going. Other than my job, of course.

"Did they invite you to the Conclave?" Lucas asked.

I felt a shudder pass up my spine. "Yes ... they did."

Lucas nodded to himself again. "And you met Emmerson Ray? He was the one who made you the job offer?"

"Uh-huh."

"Okay," Lucas replied, and then eyeing his computer screen again. "Okay, okay ..."

Lucas had a large white plastic clock on his wall. It was the type of clock that was one-hundred-percent utilitarian. Made for functionality and nothing else like one you would find in a school classroom. Usually it was unobtrusive — fading into the background of whatever was playing out in Lucas's office — but now as the silence stretched out before us, its second hand seemed to tick by so loudly that I could feel the sensation throbbing in my eardrums.

I decided that I might as well press Lucas for the truth.

Most likely I wouldn't get another opportunity.

"Did he make you an offer?" I asked.

His mind appearing to be somewhere else entirely, Lucas returned to the room briefly. "Yes," he said. "Yes, he did."

Although I told myself I was being ridiculous, I couldn't help but feel as if my elation was a touch tainted. The fact that Lucas had been offered a role with Simple Sun made me feel less special. I decided to keep pushing.

"But you didn't accept?"

A little of Lucas's old swagger returned. "Obviously not."

"Do you ... do you mind me asking why not?"

Lucas pressed his lips together, squeezing the blood out of them. He had picked up a paperclip a few seconds earlier and started to unravel it — straightening it out. "I ... didn't quite ... *believe* it," he replied.

I wasn't sure what to say to this.

Lucas continued, tentatively meeting my eye, "I've always thought that if something sounds too good to be true then that's most likely the case." He cast a glance around him, slid a drawer open, closed it again, and then sighed. "I'm comfortable at the moment — in my life — and I didn't want to jeopardise that."

Now I sensed something else coming through in Lucas's tone of voice.

It took me a second to properly identify it.

And then another second to truly *believe* it.

*Regret ... ?*

Peering down at something in his drawer, Lucas forced a smile. "You'll have to tell me what it's like, Marcus. If it really does live up to all that Emmerson Ray promises." His eyes rose from the drawer and met mine. "If the offer does fall through for any reason then there will always be a place for you here. At LifeWare."

I was almost willing to believe that there was some sentiment behind Lucas's statement — that he was genuinely emotionally affected by my potential departure from the company.

But then he elaborated.

"We're always looking to cut costs wherever we can and — between you and me — recruitment and training are a real money pit."

I looked out across the car park to Geoff again. He had stirred once more and was blearily looking over his newspaper, holding it at arm's length and squinting.

"Don't be too proud to come back," Lucas said. "That's all I'm saying."

"Okay," I replied, getting out of my seat. "Thanks."

As I ventured over to the door, I felt the thickness in the air.

That near-indescribable sensation of words still to be spoken.

And then he went there.

"About Olivia," Lucas said. "It's not what you think it is ... I've been running a sort of hobby business for a few years now and, well ... it's a modelling agency."

"Oh?" I replied.

"Yes," he said. "In actual fact, it's a bit more than a *hobby*. I have a member of staff working full-time. They answer phones, emails, that sort of thing."

"I see."

"Anyway," Lucas continued, "I hear the stories. In an office it's impossible to pass the gossip by completely, even if you've got an ivory tower."

I decided he must be referring to his own office.

He rose from his chair. "Everyone talks about my ... *me* being seen with lots of different ... *women*." There was something distinctly awkward about his tone of voice now as if he was ashamed at having to admit what he was currently saying. "That's all it is," he finished with, appearing to return to reality with a perceptible bump. Finally, his mouth curled into that most unnatural of forms ... at least for Lucas ... at least when Lucas was around *me* ... a smile.

"Okay," I replied, looking out across the office and realising this must be the first time ever I was looking forward to getting back to my desk — back to my phone calls and emails.

I reached for the door handle.

"There was one other thing," Lucas said.

Increasingly wary, I turned back to him.

Now that he had admitted to his modelling agency — whatever it was — I wondered if he was going to use me as a confidant for something else. To tell the truth I have never been much of one for gossip ... it just happens to *find* me occasionally ... and I had little to no interest in holding onto any information I didn't have any reason to.

"I saw you get into the car that day," he continued.

My mind spun.

I fumbled the pieces together.

Did he mean Toby and Daymian?

"The two from Simple Sun," he went on. He sniffed a laugh, shook his head lightly. "Don't worry, I wasn't stalking you, or anything. I was just on my way out of the office on my bike when I noticed you speaking to the two of them in the car ... you'd notice that old tin can anywhere if you'd seen it before. Always got its sunroof open. Sticks out like a sore thumb."

I couldn't rightly deny this comment.

Lucas went on, "I ... had a bad feeling about it ... so I gave you a call, a bit later on. You didn't answer, though, obviously ... but ... now that you're telling me this, now that you're leaving, I thought you should know it was me."

When I spoke again, something stuck in my throat.

My voice was raspy.

"What did you want to say?"

Lucas met my eye. "I just wanted to check you were all right."

Another long silence lingered.

I looked out through the glass walls to the office beyond, seeing that Fil was looking especially flustered at the moment. He had his phone in one hand and my phone in the other, one pressed to each ear. I wasn't quite sure how to leave all this ... wasn't quite sure what to say to what Lucas had just told me. So I settled on a neutral, say-nothing, "*Thanks.*"

As I prepared to leave Lucas's office, he offered a final piece of advice.

"Be careful," he said.

# NIGHT-TIME VISITOR

Everything that comprised my possessions was contained in the half a dozen cardboard boxes surrounding me. To tell the truth, I hadn't realised I had such a small amount of stuff. I wasn't sure whether it was a good or bad thing after thirty-odd years of life.

Tomorrow morning my dad was going to drop by in his car, picking up the boxes before dropping me off at the airport so I could catch my flight out to the Caribbean where I would rendezvous with Emmerson Ray. My parents had been surprised when I'd told them that I was leaving LifeWare, but then intrigued when I had told them about the new job offer.

I had of course left out the culty sounding bits.

It was approaching midnight as I lay down on the sofa bed for the last night in my attic flat, allowing myself a cleansing exhale following my day of moving preparations. My mind still flurried with everything I had to do. The mental checklists flipping by non-stop.

It seemed weird to be leaving my flat — I had been living here for three years now ... the first place that I'd had to myself after years of sharing houses. At least until Riko had moved in. And now that I'd sampled the wonders of having my own space I knew it would be deeply uncomfortable if I ever had to go back. Hopefully I never would need to go back.

I *had* just doubled my salary, after all.

Perhaps I might even aspire to that one goal which to any millennial of sound mind and body is as distant and lofty as climbing Everest ...

or maybe something altogether more fanciful, like discovering Atlantis: owning my own home.

I could still smell the faint odour of smoke clinging to my clothes.

As I had been packing I had fully thrown myself into the idea that this was a good opportunity to reinvent myself totally.

New job.

New country.

New *life*.

And so I had taken those pages of The Routine which Riko, Julie and Frankie had so thoroughly ridiculed, crumpled them into neat balls and then stepped out of the attic window and set fire to them on the roof tiles. It hadn't been quite the spectacle I had been hoping for. I had been sensible enough to check whether there was a breeze this evening before starting my flaming but I needn't have worried about starting a blaze. When I put the cigarette lighter to the balls of paper they merely shrivelled up into disappointing flaky bundles of ash. There was something about the way they burned which reminded me of rose petals. I had also been slightly disturbed to note that my burning hadn't made the words completely illegible upon the pages. If someone squinted just the right way, and assembled the torched pieces into the correct order, then they might be able to read my pitiful comedy routine.

That dream I had once had.

But the time for dreaming was over.

The world was waiting for me.

Jesus, I was definitely starting to get melodramatic if nothing else ...

The point was that The Routine was no longer. If Riko wanted to go poking around my personal possessions it was one thing he would never find again.

A piece of my soul that was gone forever.

Now I was definitely being melodramatic, no two ways about it.

There was a knock at the door.

My heart struck the back of my throat.

And my tongue pounded with my pulse.

Who was knocking on my door at this time?

... It surely couldn't be good news.

I wondered if it was Riko. Maybe he'd come to make the peace. I'd been waiting for him to come back with his tail between his legs — *expected* it actually ... and I'd run several imaginary scenarios as to just what I would say to him ... because I knew that if he turned up on my doorstep he would find *some* way to finagle his way back in.

I probably wouldn't even feel that bad about it.

That was the sort of power he held over me.

There might've been something reassuring about Riko's development — that he had taken it upon himself to distance himself from me.

I thought about just lying where I was and waiting for the person to go.

I even almost convinced myself that nothing could come from such an interaction.

Maybe it was someone looking to talk me out of what I had already decided to do.

In the end, I rocked to my feet, deciding that in this new life I wouldn't simply lie back and allow things to happen to me. I would face them head on. And maybe I needed to start with laying some part of my past life to rest forever.

At the front door, I paused for a few seconds.

Listening.

On the other side I thought I heard heavy breathing.

*Strange* ...

My chest tightened and a tingling sensation passed through my lungs.

I wondered if it was a warning.

Soon I was going to find out.

A dozen different ideas flashed through my mind but in the end only one was the right answer. The one which was rooted in reality. My neighbour from the basement flat — the one whose patio I had thrown up on, and who had an affection for gnomes which bordered on obsession — stood on my doorstep.

Mildreth Loaves.

"Oh, hi," I said, scratching the back of my neck, feeling awkward like you do whenever you're confronted by a neighbour without warning.

I saw that she was holding a parcel in her hands.

She was wearing a fluffy pink dressing gown. There was a fishing gnome embroidered on the breast pocket. "I heard you were leaving tomorrow," she said, with a smile. "I thought I should bring this to you before you went — someone left it for you earlier this week. I was just drifting off to sleep when I suddenly remembered. Does that ever happen to you?"

"Hmm?" I replied, realising I had drifted away, staring at the parcel. "Oh," I said, "yeah, except I probably have it worse. I spend my whole time trying to remember what I'm supposed to be doing ... only to forget again."

She laughed at this and passed over the parcel.

It had a steady weight to it ... a *familiar* weight.

I was already pretty sure what it was.

And who it was from.

I tried my best to sound casual. "The person who left it with you ... were they ..."

"A girl," Mildreth Loaves said. "A *woman*, really, I suppose."

I guess concepts like girl/boy, woman/man are all relative.

"Did she have ...?" I started again.

"Blond hair," Mildreth Loaves said, and then wrinkled her brow. "And very odd sort of rectangular shoes ... trainers, really, I suppose."

It was all adding up to what I expected.

The parcel was wrapped in brown paper, a little squashy in a way that I thought had to mean the contents were covered in bubble wrap.

"Do you know who I mean?" Mildreth Loaves asked.

I returned to the present. "Uh, yeah ... yeah I know her."

"A girlfriend?"

The question was odd. A little bit invasive, sure ... but then again this was an older woman and I imagined she spent a large amount of time on her own. She probably wasn't used to thinking about how she sounded when speaking to someone else — just glad to have the company at all.

As if I was some sort of social butterfly.

"No," I replied, reddening. "Just a friend — a friend from work."

"A colleague?"

I nodded. "Yes, that's right." I shifted my attention downward onto the parcel once again. I thought about all the times over the past couple of weeks I had attempted to speak with Kelly — to tell her about my decision to leave. But it had been impossible to get her alone. In the end, I had got the message plain and clear. She didn't *want* to speak with me.

I had made my decision and now I was on my own.

I wondered just what she had against Emmerson Ray in particular. That whole scene at the Simple Sun Conclave had been so *aggressive*, or defensive, or something.

I glanced up, expecting to see Mildreth Loaves had stepped out of the doorway, and was descending to her basement flat. However, she was still standing there.

I couldn't help noticing that she had allowed the hem of her dressing gown to billow open ever so slightly. I caught a glimpse of the pyjamas she wore underneath.

A gnome covered the entire design, a beaming smile, plump rosy-red cheeks, a long, tangled red beard.

She stepped over the threshold.

"Um," I said.

Her eyes were sapphire blue and they still had a youthful twinkle to them.

When she spoke again, it was as if her voice wasn't her own — it was throaty, raspy.

As if there was something deeper, impossible to tame within her.

"Do you still have the costume?" she asked, still approaching me.

I backed up another few steps, all too aware that before long I would end up bumping into the sofa bed behind me. "What costume?" I asked.

And then the penny dropped.

The gnome outfit.

The one Riko had forced me to wear for Halloween.

"I've ... I've ..." I began. "I've already ... uh ... packed it?"

Her eyes remained fixed upon mine.

Lips parted slightly.

And her dressing gown billowed open to reveal the complete picture of the gnome impressed upon the front of her pyjamas.

Although I'm not much of one for fashion, I was fairly sure that they were *silk* pyjamas ... which — if I'm reliably informed — are the finer kind.

When I felt the backs of my calves come into contact with the sofa bed behind me, I managed to stir up some sort of resistance. I held up my hand, as if I was a member of the transport police directing traffic.

Mildreth Loaves came to a halt although her eyes remained hungrily fixed upon me.

A strong smell of lavender and talcum powder emanated from her.

Her hand rose to my cheek and not really knowing what to do — or anyway to stop it — I allowed her fingertips to brush my skin.

"So delicate," she said, her voice wispy now. "So ... *precious*."

A chill ran up my spine.

And for the first time since he'd been gone I missed not having Riko around the flat.

It would've negated this whole situation.

I cleared my throat and then — in the most awkward movement possible — I ducked under her reach, sidestepped her and ventured back towards the door.

Because when I'm nervous I always become overpolite, I couldn't help but smile widely, standing by the open door. Somehow words tumbled out of me in more or less the right order. "Well, thanks very much for bringing me that parcel! I wouldn't have wanted to leave without having picked it up ..." I grinned wider still and shook the parcel beside my ear. "I wonder what it could be — a leaving present no doubt!"

Mildreth Loaves remained standing by the sofa, the pyjama top showing off the gnome still very much in my line of vision. She appeared struck by a daze, as if she'd been sleepwalking or something. And then she seemed to snap back to reality.

To realise where she was.

*Who* she was.

"Oh," she said, with a slight smile. "I am glad I got it to you." She looked about her once more as if she might've left something behind but she had brought nothing with her save the parcel and a sense of utter confusion. When she reached the open doorway I had to restrain the urge to slam the door shut to put a definite end to the latest bizarre episode of my life.

*Damn my well-mannered upbringing ...*

"You are leaving," she said, a statement rather than a question.

I answered it as if it had been a question anyway. "Yes," I said.

"You're not coming back?" she asked.

Even though this sounded just a little too final I decided I might as well err on the side of caution. I didn't want a septuagenarian stalker on my case ... although perhaps she already was. "No," I replied. "I'm leaving for good."

"Oh," she said. "Oh, I see ..."

She still lingered in the doorway.

Maybe I should slam the door shut and live with the consequences.

What was the latest on whether or not you could kill people trespassing on your property?

I never do keep up with the latest legal wranglings.

There was a slightly doleful look in her eye.

Actually, it was *extremely* doleful ...

And I was already starting to feel bad, even though I knew that I had only hours left before I would leave this flat for good. The country.

Searching for something to say, I added, "It's been a pleasure living with you." I paused an uncomfortably long time, and then kept going because I'm an idiot. "That time when you found me on your patio ... thanks for not ... uh ... complaining ... you know, to my landlord?"

From the distant look in Mildreth's eye I thought she had stopped paying attention to me completely. That she was thinking about something else entirely.

But then a slight smile tugged at the corner of her mouth.

"Really," she said. "As I said at the time, that was nothing. I have children. And ... well, if I'm completely honest, I have been through such ... *unfortunate* episodes myself."

I thought about when I'd been at the Street Sermon browsing the list of punters who had been barred. And finding Mildreth Loaves's name

260

among them. I guess that there was no other time when I'd get the chance to ask and if I ever did decide to dip my toe in the comedy pond it might give me a few more scraps to use for material. "I did want to ask," I began, already regretting keeping this conversation going when she was clearly giving me an easy out. "I heard rumours ... one night at the ... pub."

Her gaze became unfocused once more.

But she was still smiling slightly.

As if remembering a not-entirely-unpleasant event.

I went on. "I was speaking to the manager, at the pub, and he said, uh, just by-the-by when I told him where I lived that he had to bar a lady who lived there. That, uh, wasn't you, was it?"

Mildreth met my eye once more.

And then she nodded.

"Yes, yes it was."

Again, there was no sense of shame to her tone, not so much as a note of regret. Unless I was inventing it in my own head I was pretty sure that there was even a hint of happiness as if recalling a fond memory.

"What happened?" I asked.

She breathed out a heavy sigh. She cast her gaze around the room — what had been my living quarters for the past three years. "I'd been awfully *lonely*," she said.

Now I was starting to regret my curiosity. And my ridiculous half-arsed notion that this might make appropriate comedy material.

"When you're alone," she continued, "you get caught up in your thoughts. The things you *like* — the objects that you remember with joy — they seem to reach out of the past and take hold of you. Their warmth, although it is only a secondary, inadequate warmth, is what draws you in." She met my eye again. "And if you let it it will turn you crazy."

"I see," I replied, not really following at all.

Maybe it was something that older people were afflicted by. And although some days there was no doubt I felt like a pensioner, I was fairly certain that I wasn't quite there yet.

Not quite.

She pressed on a smile this time, huffed out a sigh. She leaned against the doorframe and I wondered if I wasn't being a heartless bastard for not inviting her in to take a seat on the sofa.

I could've made her a cup of tea if I hadn't already packed my kettle and all my mugs.

"It wasn't just one night, Marcus," she said.

It sent a slight tingle through my stomach to realise that she knew my name.

"It was a long drawn-out period that led to my permanent ban at the Street Sermon."

"Okay," I said.

She gave a couple of birdlike blinks. "It started out innocently enough, every night I would go down to the pub with one of my gnomes or two and sit down at a table in the corner where I would arrange myself for the evening. I would always order myself a gin and tonic, with a slice of lime. Nothing particularly exciting, I know, but it started as a means for me to get out of the house. That's the reason I started going there, I think."

"And then what happened?"

"Well," Mildreth continued, "at first it was wonderful. I would sit down at my table at about half past four and different people would just come over and ask questions about my gnomes. Sometimes silly things ... like what their names were ... and other times there were more sincere, direct ones ... asking me if I was okay, what I was doing there night after night. The thing you learn from going to the pub every day is that no two days are the same. There's the empty pathos of Monday evening — the scattering of resigned drinkers looking to preserve the afterglow of the weekend as long as possible. Tuesdays and Wednesdays are defeated days, unless there happens to be a football match on. Then there would be a few middle-aged men deposed from their houses by their long-suffering wives to go and watch the game down the local. Thursdays were almost as rapacious as Fridays — Saturdays were for friendly laughter shared amongst friends and family while Sunday was an introspective day mostly populated by older drinkers. Like myself. I became a fixture in the corner, during all of that. Everyone knew my name. I became what

I had never thought that I would become, which was a pub personality. Not that I minded being viewed in black-and-white terms. Thought of always with reference to my gnomes. After such a long time on my own I finally had someone to speak to on a regular basis. Oh, my children are good about calling me up every once in a while, and we get together three, four times a year ... birthdays, Christmas, those sorts of occasions ... but sometimes I would go — *do go* — days at a time without ever speaking to another person."

My heart sunk in my chest. If the aim of this conversation was to make me feel like a totally self-centred prick then it was a roaring success. I'd only been living here three years ... and then I'd gone off and dressed up as a gnome, potentially antagonising this poor, lonely woman.

What a twat.

It must've been past one in the morning by then and I still couldn't quite get my head around everything that had occurred ... was still occurring. I knew I had a ready-made excuse if ever I needed one. I could legitimately say that I had to get up early the next morning — I was moving out, after all.

*Forever.*

I couldn't even remember how we had got onto this conversation and decided that a gentle nudge to get her back on track wouldn't hurt.

"What went wrong?" I asked.

She straightened up once again, as if she had noticed that she was leaning on the doorframe and decided that it was inappropriate or impolite or something. She had dark bags tugging at the bottoms of her eyes and I wondered if I shouldn't just apologise and let her go. She *had* been the one to bring me the parcel, after all ... albeit with a strange unwanted entrance into my flat.

But she had seen the error of her ways now.

I wasn't the gnome she was looking for.

"Well," Mildreth continued, "to begin with I would spend forty minutes, an hour there, of an evening. But that soon stretched to an hour and a half, two hours. And before I knew it I was there all evening, in the company of others. Every day of the week."

I shrugged. "What's so bad about that? I mean, I'm sure there are loads of people who go to the pub every day of the week for a drink ..."

Mildreth went on in a tone which left me in doubt as to whether she had heard me at all or if she was simply stuck in her flow. "I was drinking more, too. That just went with the territory. I was spending more time there and a pub is a pub; it's a business, not a library or a community centre. And so I suppose I thought I was doing the right thing. Two, three gin and tonics. Four or five some days when I got to chatting with someone. I wasn't out of pocket all that often. People would willingly buy me drinks to talk to me about my gnomes. I became quite a local celebrity."

I still couldn't see what the issue might be, aside from creeping alcoholism, but isn't that what we all aspire to in our later years? What else is there to look forward to?

Listening to Mildreth, I had to admit I didn't feel as though my view had changed at all.

"Then one night ... it was ... *unfortunate* ..."

I could hear my blood thundering through my eardrums.

My heart rattled my ribcage.

I knew this could only be spectacular.

What else would lead to being barred for life?

"It was a group of students. They had all dressed up for the evening. And they were doing a *pub crawl* ... is that right?"

I nodded in response, confirming her suspicions.

Mildreth went on, "Only they were all dressed up as gnomes." She sighed out and stared at a spot on the carpet. "At the bar, the landlord or the barman or one of the punters must've said something, because before I knew it they were swarming about my table in the corner, fawning over the half dozen gnomes I'd brought with me that particular evening. I ... I ..." Tears glistened across the surface of her eyes and I wondered if I should try to go dig out some tissues or — more likely — a roll of toilet paper to offer her. But she sucked up the courage to continue and no tears spilled their way down onto her cheeks. "They were picking them up ... playing *games* with them ... I ... I'd had a few drinks. More than a few. Six, seven ... more than that probably. And I ...

I ... don't know ... there's always been something — something about gnomes ... ever since I was a little girl. This kind of ... uh ... *sexual* curiosity about them."

My whole body felt as though it was physically attempting to make itself smaller.

There's something about sex and old people which seems to be the ultimate taboo.

"And so there were two things on my mind. One that I wanted to ... to *touch* the one nearest me ... and the other that ... that I was worried that some damage would come to one of my gnomes. They were treating them quite ... quite roughly."

Here she brought her hand up to cover her eyes and breathed out hard.

"You don't have to tell me anymore," I said.

She remained still for several moments as if thinking over my offer.

I couldn't help but wonder if our conversation was being overheard by any of my insomniac neighbours. Thankfully I was moving out the next day so I wouldn't have to suffer any awkward looks out in the hallway.

Mildreth Victoria Loaves continued. "I ... everything was hazy. Because of the alcohol. It was kind of like a waking dream."

I nodded as if I understood exactly what she was saying.

"One of them was waving Mr Huntsman — one of my *dearest* gnomes — through the air as if he had some kind of magical power. As if he was able to fly. And ... I just got scared. I made a grab for him, but ... in the end I scratched the man's arm. My nails sunk into his skin. I remember smelling the blood on the air almost instantly." She closed her eyes now, massaged the backs of her eyelids with her fingertips. "I can still recall the sound ... the *shatter* of the porcelain as Mr Huntsman broke apart on the floor."

She remained still for a long time.

Although it would've been difficult to bear — being a man by its definition makes you suspicious of emotions — I almost would've preferred her to start crying. My brain kept launching at me all the possibilities of what might happen next.

Kind of like a horror film when there's a jump-scare of some kind.

Something leaping out of nowhere.

Finally, she carried on.

"Everything went black," Mildreth said, opening her eyes and allowing her arm to drop back down by her side. "When I came around ... when sense returned to me there was a lady with a severe voice. I remember trying to move my arm, and finding it was impossible. I realised I was being held — that the woman was gripping tightly to me. I had a horrible headache, the worst I think I've ever had. Around me everything was a blur. It took me a few seconds to realise just where I was ... and even then when it came back to me — and I knew I was still at the Street Sermon — my surroundings just kept spinning around. The pub was deserted. I remember seeing someone standing on the other side of the bar — the landlord? Glowering. And then, across the other side of the room, three men dressed as gnomes, one of them sat on the floor being attended to by paramedics. I was just ... so confused about the whole episode ... until I saw what remained of Mr Huntsman, the shattered pieces of porcelain. And then it all sort of came back." She shook her head. "I don't know what possessed me. I didn't know I was capable of such ... such violent acts."

My pulse was pounding in my temples and I was doing my best to figure out just what my exit strategy was for this conversation. I decided that I should just do my best to express empathy — which wasn't too difficult since I more or less felt sympathetic to her situation anyway. "It's okay," I said. "From the sounds of it you were in a bad place. And ... you weren't in control of your actions. Alcohol, it's a, uh ..." I allowed myself a moment's pause just to think through whether I was actually going to commit to speaking the next line; it was going to make me feel like an "educational" video for school kids "... it's a *hell* of a drug."

There, I'd said it.

She didn't respond right away. But when she did she started nodding vaguely, as if she was a marionette and hidden just out of view her operator was delicately tweaking her strings. "I was never allowed back, of course. And I stopped drinking ever since that ... *incident*."

"Sounds reasonable," I replied, feeling my stomach squeeze in upon itself as I wondered if I ever would escape this conversation.

"Reading the police reports. That was what did it. That was what sharpened my focus to how far I had fallen. And I knew that I needed to make some changes."

There was a lull.

It was my opportunity to end this.

And yet ... I was still curious.

"What did the police reports say?" I asked, my soul filling up with equal parts grim fascination and dread.

Once more, her focus was distant as if she was peering into her mind's eye, reliving the memories within her imagination. When she spoke it was in the tone of voice that someone might use when channelling a spirit at a séance. "It was all such a clinical, factual account. That was what made it seem all the more absurd. The barman, the man who I later found out to be the landlord, had provided the central witness statement — he had watched the whole scene open up and the action play out." She sighed. "As I said, all that I remembered was striking one of the men ... the one who was treating Mr Huntsman roughly. That was where my memory gave way. According to the landlord's statement the man I struck lost his balance — it turns out that he was not entirely sober either — and I landed on top of him." She pursed her lips as if the next thing she had to say was difficult to express in words. "As the landlord described it, I ... well, some kind of a carnal urge must have possessed me ... because I commenced to writhe upon the ... the poor boy ... it must have been the costume he was wearing."

"And the alcohol," I numbly put in.

"And the alcohol," Mildreth Loaves agreed. "Apparently the boy was stunned, unable to help himself. To get me off him. His two friends did their best but ..." She stopped speaking and shook her head and I worried that she might be about to burst out into uncontrollable sobbing.

There wasn't an awful lot of good I could do in a situation like that.

She went on, "When they tried to get me off, I apparently turned violent. I wonder if I wasn't half-mad with grief at Mr Huntsman's demise. That was when the police were called. An ambulance, too." She made a throaty sound — something between a laugh and a hacking

267

cough. "When I heard the full story I'm not sure that I've ever been as embarrassed in all my life." Her eyes perked up somewhat and settled upon me.

I hoped with all the spirit that possessed me that she wasn't going to proposition me again.

"I've never told anybody else this whole story, you know. And I would ... well, I know that you're moving away from here, but all the same I would appreciate you keeping this to yourself."

"I will," I replied, not needing to even think about it.

"Thank you," she said, sighing again, her eyes wandering behind me, into what was soon to be my ex-flat. "I do hope that you settle into your new place nicely."

"Thanks," I replied.

Her eyes returned to me. "Are you going far?"

I told her I was going to the Caribbean.

She flashed her eyebrows, pursed her lips and whistled faintly. "Well, I can't say I'm not envious. I think, somewhere in my personal history, there was a chance for me to end up on a tropical island but that time has long since passed. Something that never happened. What is it they're always saying about regretting most what we don't do rather than what we do?"

"I don't know," I replied, thinking without hesitation about the episode at university when the universe had proved its point to me that I was never destined to become a comedian.

If that was even what I had wanted to be.

"I think some things are best left undone."

"Perhaps so, Marcus," she said. "Perhaps so." She pressed on a wide smile, cocked her head to one side and said, "Do *enjoy* the rest of your life, wherever you plan to live it. And if there's any advice I have to offer you — anything to take from that little episode I recounted for you just now — it's that it's impossible to repress that which we truly, deeply long for. Eventually our deepest urges take on a life of their own and force themselves into the world."

"Point taken," I replied, with a nod.

"Good," she said, giving me another smile as she backed away from the door, heading back downstairs in the direction of her own flat. Her final words to me as she disappeared from view were, "Live your life. And don't forget to have fun."

"Thanks," I said, my voice surely too quiet for her to hear.

I finally brought the front door of my flat shut.

# A NEW LIFE – A NEW WORLD

I dug my feet into the fine sand. The strong sunlight sent prickling sensations through the hairs on my legs and heat through the centre of my bare chest.

It was difficult to believe that it was a Tuesday afternoon.

Random recollections of LifeWare needled their way into my brain from time to time but they never lingered. Almost as if my subconscious was still scrapping around in the background working on all of those problems that were no longer my problem. Just because that was what it had been trained to do for such a significant amount of time.

I was wearing only a pair of sunglasses and some swimming shorts. I could still feel the coolness as the water evaporated off my skin following my dip in the Caribbean sea five minutes earlier. When I breathed in, the air was heavy with moisture — fruity and full ... there were some banana trees a little way up the beach and the novelty of their scent on the breeze still hadn't worn off — even though I'd been here, on the island, for almost three weeks now. It was difficult to believe that my life had changed so rapidly and so dramatically in such a short space of time. It just went to show how effective dramatic reaction could be.

I wondered why *everyone* didn't do this.

Then again, I supposed that most other people are well entrenched in their lives. Hooked into their families, attached to their jobs out of unshakeable habit if not out of a need to put food on the table. Most people *aren't* able to accept the kind of offer which Emmerson Ray had presented to me. Money wasn't the only consideration.

Or even the most important.

In truth, I was waiting for the punchline.

Just waiting to see when this would all end. When the rug would be unceremoniously tugged from beneath my feet, sending me reeling backwards, falling flat upon my back with a slap of flesh and a stinging rash creeping its way up my spine. Perhaps it would be today.

Or even tomorrow.

But I'd made a deal with myself.

I was going to take Mildreth Victoria Loaves's advice.

I was going to enjoy my life just as long as I was able.

"Marcus?"

I turned my head to look, although the tone of voice would've been unmistakable even if I hadn't had the chance to get used to it after hearing it every day for the last few weeks.

Emmerson Ray strode his way towards me, down the beach. He was wearing a Hawaiian shirt with psychedelic flowers printed across the fabric. He wore khaki shorts and a pair of leather sandals strapped around his ankles. He also had on a pair of sunglasses — green lenses which flashed in the sun with each of his loping strides.

I eased myself up onto my feet, reaching for the t-shirt I had discarded close by. It was a grey-white t-shirt with the Simple Sun logo etched onto the chest. I had soon learned after a brief time of living on the island that there wasn't much point in bringing a towel to the beach. The sun was so strong that it would get you dry within a couple of minutes.

I brought the t-shirt on over my head, tugged it down into place.

I felt a slight lurch in my gut.

Although Emmerson Ray had never shown himself as being anything other than supportive towards me, clearly wanting me to be a part of ... well, whatever it was that I was a part of ... there was a certain unease that I had never quite been able to shake. Perhaps it's that same mechanism the brain has when you're dreaming a good dream. And it has to remind you of the fact that you could wake up at any moment of its choosing.

Emmerson Ray clapped me on the shoulder and grinned. "Missing having a tie lassoed on about your throat?"

I smiled back at him.

Shook my head.

"The air-conditioning? The buzz of the watercooler gossip? Office *politics*?"

My smile widened. "No — definitely not."

Emmerson Ray gave me another clap on the shoulder, as if congratulating me on these observations. As if I was perfectly assuming the form of the mould he had prepared for me.

That I had taken the shape he aspired for me.

To tell the truth, I was happy enough to assume whatever shape he wanted me to assume if it meant that I got to go on living here, where there was twelve hours of sunlight a day and pleasantly warm swimming waters and deliciously fresh fish dishes in abundance.

Did I mention my beach-side shack?

... Although "shack" is doing it more than a minor disservice.

"Good. Good," Emmerson Ray continued, guiding me back up the beach, to what he and everyone else on the island referred to as the Main Lodge.

The Main Lodge wasn't much more than a roof of woven rushes propped up over the sand to provide some shade and protection from monsoons. The Main Lodge would've been comfortably large enough to accommodate three storeys, although there was only a ground-level. Within the Main Lodge there were half a dozen long tables with benches pulled up alongside them. It was enough to accommodate the fifty or sixty of us living on the island. At meal times, the area would fill with the pleasant mewling of conversation and the clicking sound of cutlery on plates. More often than not tucking into a plate of sea bass, or even swordfish, drenched with garlic butter, a side of fragrant rice. The gentle lilt of the locally born-and-raised head chef — Zachary — grinning from ear to ear wandering about seeing that everybody was chowing down in a satisfactory manner.

Right now, the Main Lodge was near-deserted.

Everyone was carrying out their tasks on the island.

The only other person in the Main Lodge was a "Scripter" — as they were known — busily working away, frown lines sketched upon her forehead as her fingers flurried across the keyboard, multi-coloured lines of code snaking their way across the screen.

Code that was incomprehensible to me.

She was wearing an ankle-length summer dress and had on a pair of thick-framed glasses. She had heaped her blond hair upon her scalp and pinned it into place. As me and Emmerson Ray passed her by she smiled at both of us, her mouth forming the shape of a silent hello before she returned to her serious expression and the work before her eyes.

Emmerson Ray picked a spot at one of the vacated benches and signalled for me to sit down opposite. It was as if the staff here had some kind of a sixth sense for when Emmerson Ray was around because one of them appeared from the kitchen area to the side of the Main Lodge.

Emmerson Ray requested two glasses of fresh-made lemonade — or whatever you call the version that's made from limes ... limeade doesn't sound right to me ... He was straight-faced for a moment, clasping his hands together on the table in front of him and staring at his own skin.

Then, a moment later, his familiar easy smile returned.

He prodded his sunglasses up the ridge of his nose and onto the top of his head. "How're you finding everything?" he asked.

I glanced about, still not quite used to this actually being reality — still expecting to wake up at any moment, in a cold sweat, in my old familiar flat, stretched out on the sofa bed, hearing Riko snoring away from his place on the kitchen floor.

But, no ... I had escaped.

"It's, uh ... been great," I replied.

Emmerson Ray nodded to himself as if this was the response he had expected. There was a note of disappointment there, too, as if he had wanted me to surprise him somehow.

I glanced over my shoulder, to the tropical sands along the beach, to the sea shushing into shore. The odd tropical bird from the jungle in the centre of the island cawing or trilling. I settled briefly upon the Scripter, hard at work, at her laptop. When I returned my attention to Emmerson

Ray, he was grinning from ear to ear. "Still trying to figure it out, huh? Where you fit in?"

To begin with I thought it was more of a philosophical, meaning-of-life question, but after another second of thinking I realised he was referring to the literal situation.

It might've been the first time I'd sighed since I arrived.

"Yeah," I said. "I mean, this is all great. I ... can't really believe this is all real — that this has happened to me." I met his eye. "But ... it feels like it's just been a holiday so far ... I mean, I've got my cabin, and there's the beach, and all I have to do is just ..." I shrugged my shoulders, another gesture more closely associated with the previous Marcus Raisin. "Get up, eat, sleep ... and that's it really."

Emmerson Ray chuckled at this. He crossed his arms over his chest. "You say it like it's a bad thing."

"Yeah," I replied, eyeing the server bearing the chilled glasses of lemonade ... made from limes. "I guess what I'm trying to say is ... I'd like to know what you saw in me ... or what you want me to actually *do* here?"

"Mm," Emmerson Ray replied, still smiling, the sound he made like a cat purring.

The server deposited the glasses of lemonade before us. As it was made from limes, the contents of each were a vibrant green. In the kitchen they'd mixed it up so about a third was crushed ice. The glass was perspiring as the server retreated from where we sat, returning to the kitchen and Zachary's dominion.

"So," I said, curling my fingers around the pleasant coolness of my glass. "What is it that you want me to do?"

Emmerson Ray's smile faltered slightly. His gaze became unfocused.

I followed the direction of where he was looking.

There was a pair of motorboats — about a hundred metres out to sea.

They had stopped and were bobbing about in the gentle Caribbean waves.

The sea never really got rough out here except when there was a storm in full flow.

I've never paid all that much attention to boats but these ones looked as though they probably each had a crew of seven or eight. They were about the size of the lifeboats I would occasionally see launching whenever my parents took me down to the beach during the school holidays. Both boats had blue-and-red lights perched on top although they were not currently illuminated.

"Police?" I asked, not recalling ever having seen police on the island here.

There weren't really enough people to merit a police force.

"Coast Guard," Emmerson Ray replied, his smile completely gone now. As he continued to stare them down — who knew exactly where they were looking themselves — I took a slurp of my lemonade ... it was delicious, refreshing, the elixir I needed following the baking in the sun.

"What do they want?" I asked.

Emmerson Ray wrestled his focus off the boats and down into the lemonade sitting on the table before him, eyeing it as if it had materialised out of nowhere. "They want to keep an eye on us." His voice was as quiet as I could remember ever hearing it.

I wondered at this.

Was it fear?

Or ... something else?

As if our conversation had triggered a change in circumstance, one of the boat's engines roared into life, and the other followed soon after. Half-turned in my seat, I watched the boats bob over the small waves, heading away from the island, apparently back to wherever they'd come from.

"We bought this place fair and square," Emmerson Ray said. "All on paper — all completely legal." He shook his head. "But somehow I knew it wouldn't be that simple. Whenever you get yourself tangled up with anything to do with a government it's never simple."

He caught my eye.

RAYMOND S FLEX

I wondered if I was supposed to draw some kind of wisdom from this statement.

But if I was then I wasn't sure what it might be.

"I guess they're just curious," I said. "I mean ... I guess that if anyone buys up an island, starts bringing people in from abroad, it's bound to raise questions."

"Hmm, I guess," Emmerson Ray replied, in a way which told me that he wasn't really listening to what I was saying.

For a few minutes we sat there in silence, the two of us sipping away at our lemonades, both lost in our own tumbling thoughts. I noticed the Scripter had stopped working away at her laptop and she too was watching the Coast Guard closely as they left the bay and slipped away out of view. Finally, Emmerson Ray appeared to remember himself.

His smile reappeared.

And he looked me over.

"You want to know where you fit in," he said, pouting. "Only natural. I'd be asking the same questions. This guy comes up to me, tells me he'll double my salary, flies me off to some exotic locale, has me sunning myself on the beach, eating fresh-caught fish, getting plenty of rest. What's the catch, right?"

"Right," I replied, feeling my stomach a little hollow as I wondered just what the catch might turn out to be. There weren't many mornings I didn't wake up with Kelly's words in my ears urging caution. I'd been careful, keeping an eye out for anything that seemed weird, an ear pricked for anything unusual. Maybe I'm just not that observant, or perhaps I'm an extreme kind of naïve, but I hadn't yet noticed anything that seemed out-and-out suspicious.

Nothing more suspicious than the original offer, of course.

I couldn't help thinking that my nerves had been calmed greatly when I'd checked my phone one morning and found that my first month's salary had been deposited in my bank account. There's something dependable about money. Something about it which makes everything else seem somehow more real.

"Well, Marcus," Emmerson Ray said, stretching his arms up above his head, "Simple Sun isn't like most other organisations. We don't see

276

recruitment the same way as other places. We don't have a bunch of square holes that we attempt to fill with circular pegs. We take people — people we think have potential — and we let them fill up their own mould, contribute to the organisation in the way that they see best."

"Ah," I replied, pretty sure this was about what I had expected. "I see."

I waited for the next question I was sure was coming ... the reason that Emmerson Ray had hoiked me off the beach to have this chat ... he was going to ask me how it was that I was going to contribute. Only I didn't have anything to say. Because the truth of the matter was that — even after spending weeks on the island — I hadn't come any closer to understanding just what Simple Sun was. Just what I had let myself in for.

Emmerson Ray looked off over my shoulder again and I wondered if the boats had returned. However when I took a glance, I saw he was focusing upon the bright blue line of the horizon. "There's no time limit, Marcus. We don't rush people. This isn't a business. It's a lifestyle."

It was here that I was sure Kelly would've called out, "Cult!" but I managed to block the word from my brain. At least for the time being.

"If you haven't already noticed, Marcus," Emmerson Ray continued, "Simple Sun has a cellular structure."

There was a pause while he apparently wanted to note the confusion or understanding sketched upon my face. In this particular case it was the former rather than the latter.

His smile widened.

"Everybody knows bits and pieces — nobody knows the whole picture. That's what makes it strong — that's what's going to make it last forever. The human brain" — he tapped his temple — "like you saw in that presentation I gave at the Simple Sun Conclave, it's just not capable of handling all the information we throw at it — it can't think in terms of much beyond a village, let alone a country, let alone a *planet* ..."

I had to admit that my thoughts were swimming now.

It was more than a little like those times at school — usually on sunny afternoons in spring — when the teacher was droning on about something or other and I was only taking in the most superficial layer of the information. No wonder I hadn't done as well in my exams as my parents would've liked. No wonder I ended up going to a sub-par university and working somewhere like LifeWare ... that's what happens when you stop paying attention.

Life just happens.

"Simple Sun," Emmerson Ray continued, "accepts this fact. It embraces the truth. Only within these cells, these *bubbles*, can we progress our individual work to the collective good."

I took another sip of my lemonade, thinking that I was starting to understand, but cautious lest I make a total fool of myself. "So, what you're saying is that I need to find some others to sort of ... uh ... 'club together' with?"

I winced internally at that turn of phrase.

It was the sort of thing that my dad might say.

Emmerson Ray held his palms out flat to me. "Maybe, maybe not ... like I said, everyone is different. We all find different ways to contribute to the cause."

I narrowed my eyes, wondering if I was starting to see the whole scope of this now. "You mean that if I ... I dunno, wanted to go work in the kitchens ... I could go do that?"

Emmerson Ray widened his eyes and pouted. "Sure."

I tried to get a read on him — whether he saw this as a stupid question or if he was answering me in a genuine fashion.

"Or ..." I continued, eyeing the Scripter, in the process of slapping her laptop shut and shoving off someplace else.

Maybe she could overhear my chatter and I was throwing off her concentration. I wouldn't have blamed her. There are few things more distracting than hearing someone chatting unadulterated bollocks when you're trying to get some Serious Work done.

"... I could do some ... programming?"

"You know how to code?" Emmerson Ray asked, arching an eyebrow.

I flushed slightly. "Uh, no ..."

"Is it something you're interested in?"

I shook my head, flushing deeper ... although I wasn't sure why.

I was only telling the truth.

Emmerson Ray reached over the table and clapped me on the shoulder a couple of times, chuntering laughter that in any other context might've seemed slightly cloying but here — on the beach, on this specific day, under the banner of Simple Sun — seemed to fit just fine and wasn't offensive at all. "My-my-my," he said, at the top of his voice. "We've some work to do on you. That's the problem with jobs, you know?" Again, he pointed to his temple, rolled his wrist so his finger seemed like some kind of biological screwdriver. "Mess with your head. Get you on rails. Make you think that *you* have to fit them when it should be the other way around."

I sat there, staring at my not-lemonade for several moments, losing myself in its greenness.

There was something that needed saying and it needed saying now.

But I didn't want to think about the implications ... that it might cause all of this to come to an abrupt halt. "You see," I began, "I don't really ... *know* ... if there's anything that I'm good at?"

The whole sentence was a complete abortion.

But there didn't seem any other way to get the meaning out.

Emmerson Ray sat back on his seat, swilling the last of the lemonade about the bottom of his glass, peering at it in the same way that someone might read tea leaves or coffee grounds. "Everybody's good at something," he said, for the first time striking a level, reasonable tone. There was none of the rampant enthusiasm present any longer.

It was more like a chat between one man and another.

A "heart-to-heart", if that wasn't too twee.

He went on.

"You've just got to look inside yourself — *deep* inside yourself ... and you'll find it ... I'll bet you do."

Another long pause.

And then ...

"If you don't mind saying," I replied. "What was it you saw in me?"

Emmerson Ray placed his now-empty glass down. "Oh," he said, "I saw a lost soul — that was what I saw ... that was what Toby and Daymian saw ... and that was why they brought you to me." He flashed another smile. "I ain't got regrets, I can promise you of that ... it'll just take time. And trust. It takes a while to undo a lifetime of habits."

I weighed up the situation.

I knew that if I was going to ask the question then this was the perfect time to do it.

I might not get another chance.

Emmerson Ray looked so at ease in the tropical sunlight. I couldn't recall having ever seen anybody look so seemingly at peace with themselves and their place within the world.

Could I end up like that too?

I averted his gaze, shifting my attention onto the departing Scripter, laptop tucked under her arm, shifting off across the sand apparently in the direction of her beach shack.

It was probably time for a siesta.

"So," I said, turning to Emmerson Ray. "It's not all about the tablet?"

"The tablet," Emmerson Ray echoed — not a question.

There was no doubt in his voice as to what I meant, and neither was there any sense of triumph that this was something he had been hoping I might bring up eventually.

It was just confirmation of a stated fact.

Emmerson Ray shrugged and shook his wrist at me, making the links of the loose gold bracelet he wore jangle. "Just a trinket," he said. "What we're building is much, much bigger. What we're building is the *future*."

# A VIRTUAL
# COMPANION

I t was that point of night when everything sunk into pitch blackness. Despite the tropical humidity, the thick, sweet smells of the jungle all around me, I couldn't help but be reminded of those long, dark winter days back in the UK ... when the nights sometimes seemed never-ending. And whereas it was a kind of trade-off — short winter days for long summer evenings — here I knew that there wasn't as much variation.

There was a dry season and there was a wet season.

That was about all that changed throughout the year.

I was lying on the straw mattress upon my bamboo bed in the beach shack which had been assigned to me on my arrival to the island. There was a door and a single, large window — unglazed — which had a thick piece of sack fabric pulled across the opening for privacy. The beach shack didn't have much by way of luxury, but it fulfilled all the basic human survival requirements. I had been pleasantly surprised that during the handful of downpours I had experienced while being here on the island I had remained dry as a bone as I lay in bed listening to the hammer of raindrops on the woven rushes.

The person who had shown me around on the first day had told me the beach shacks — and the Main Lodge and all the other buildings — were entirely built from materials found on the island. The log building blocks and the rush roofs had been harvested from the palm trees.

However, it wasn't a complete eco existence.

Like the other shacks, mine was wired up to mains electricity (a central battery which was fed from the solar energy panels scattered about the island — making use of the ample supply of sunlight). I had a laptop assigned to me and the option to plug in up to four other electrical appliances. One was, of course, reserved right away for my mobile phone (even though I was thousands of miles away from anything that I might've once called home, I still couldn't shake the strange trembling I'd get if I didn't touch my phone at least once every ten, fifteen minutes ... like I was down a limb or something ... I was under no illusions, it was completely pathetic, and yet — like a lot of pathetic things — also the truth). That left me with two spare plug sockets, one of which powered the small lamp I had in the cabin — the only artificial light source. The final plug socket seemed as though it was destined to recharge the tablet.

I dug about in my rucksack, finding the tablet right at the bottom, beneath a couple of jumpers I had packed just to be on the cautious side. As it happened, however, there were moments when I felt as though I was baking myself alive just wearing cotton t-shirts, let alone anything with a woolly make-up. The jumpers did, however, serve as decent protection for the tablet. I laid the tablet down upon my bed, plugging it into the mains socket and then tapping the power button.

I cast my mind back to those final hours in my flat — bidding my farewell to what, for want of a better word, had been my "home". That conversation with my neighbour Mildreth Victoria Loaves that had seemed like it would never end. And the package she had brought to me. It was as I had suspected — as Mildreth had hinted — Kelly had brought the parcel by for me bearing the tablet. Once Mildreth had gone, I had slipped the tablet out from within.

There had been a folded-up note inside.

Handwritten.

My heart had pounded as I had turned the note over, putting off the moment that I would open it to read. When I finally did unfold it, the lettering within was written in a florid, surprisingly cursive style. I guess that my prejudices about IT people are still showing even in paradise because I'd always assumed that an IT professional's handwriting would be about on par with doctors':

*Marcus*, the note had begun, *I hope your prep for the journey is going well. I thought you should have this back. I have spent some time looking it over, running diagnostics, etc., and it is my professional opinion that this diabolical device should be destroyed immediately. However, I don't believe it's my place to destroy it — it is someone's private property, after all, and as you are the one who has "inherited" it I thought you would be best placed to make the final decision around its fate. I don't want anything more to do with it. ...*

As I had read the note, I hadn't been able to help the quiver passing through my stomach. I wondered about the reaction and decided it was something which afflicted me whenever my name and "responsibility" were mentioned in the same sentence.

*... I have no interest in what John Horsham was working on before his death, and don't want to get involved — hence the paper note and nothing digital. Without incriminating myself by looking I believe that he was tapping into LifeWare's systems to do ... whatever it was that he was doing. What I have done is wipe any record of this access to Life-Ware's systems, and added as a security measure a block on any future LifeWare access through this device or any like it. Somehow, though, I'm not convinced it will be enough. I am still working on determining the exact source of the cyber-attacks we have been experiencing.*

*I know you don't want to read what I'm going to write next, that I've told you before, but I'm going to write it anyway.*

*Be careful.*

*You have no idea who you're getting mixed up with. They don't have your best interests at heart. They have some kind of angle. Those sorts of people always do. Believe me, I've met enough of them to know. There's just one thing left to say. On the tablet I installed a new feature. Something that you can use in an emergency (assuming you don't destroy the tablet like I'm asking you to and that they don't snatch it off you the second you end up wherever it is they want to send you). It's not particularly subtle — you'll do well not to notice it's there.*

*Ok. I think that's everything. I already told you to be careful, didn't I?*

*I guess there's only one other thing to say:*
*Good luck.*
*Kelly X*

The amount of times I scanned through the handwritten letter it was a wonder the type hadn't embossed itself upon my irises. Of course I'd gone through stages, just as anybody reading a letter written in that sort of a tone would. I thought Kelly's caution was melodramatic but I realised she had my best interests at heart. And, well, I had to admit she had a point.

It was only now as I looked at the piece of paper — the blue ink blotted from when it had been caught outside in a heavy shower — that I realised Kelly had probably wanted me to destroy the piece of paper after I had read it. That was the whole point of her writing it and not sending any sort of digital communication, as she had mentioned, after all.

Then again, what harm could it do?

Simple Sun, Emmerson Ray, they all knew about the tablet.

They knew I had it with me.

If they wanted they didn't have to so much as sneak into my shack to get it, they could overwhelm me with physical force and take it from me any second they wanted.

They had had weeks to do so.

And yet they hadn't.

What did that say about them?

What did that say about me?

The tablet hummed gently as it started up.

Outside I could hear the rain lightly beginning to fall, rustling the palm fronds of the shack roof. The rain smelled different here. Sweeter. The pleasantly warm drops brushed your skin soaking you and yet not making you cold. It certainly made British rain seem outright nasty.

For several seconds I just listened to the rain, and the sea lapping at the shore.

This was a peaceful place indeed.

Kelly hadn't been joking when she had said the app was impossible to miss. There it was — right in the centre of the screen — all the other icons clustered around it in a deferent circle.

A bright red button with a word written in white block capitals:

*PANIC*

I couldn't help but smile at the affectation.

In some ways it was the most touching thing anybody had ever done for me.

Even if the button did nothing at all, I at least had the knowledge that someone had bothered to do something which they hoped would make me feel better.

More comfortable.

And it went without saying that I had analysed — on a very deep level indeed — as to exactly what this meant in terms of Kelly's opinion towards me. Perhaps there was a future there ... even if it was a particularly distant and hopeful one.

There was something else about the tablet which made me feel more at ease.

And who ever would have thought it ... it was John Horsham.

As I skirted the PANIC button, deciding today was not the day when I was going to need to give it a jab, I instead followed the icon which led to John Horsham's post-mortem avatar materialising upon the screen. Each time I did this I couldn't help but think of that spiel he had unwound when I had watched him for the first time with Riko.

That whole thing about only the person who's *supposed* to see this actually watching.

It was only as I spent more and more time with the tablet that I managed to convince myself that I was actually the one who John Horsham was talking about. I mean, it was just like Riko had said. This was hacking for idiots ... he hadn't been intending to share the device with Toby and Daymian, or anybody who knew their way around anything beyond rudimental coding.

The rain had let off over the past few minutes, but I could feel the air getting thicker. Having been here long enough now to understand what old people mean by "feeling the weather in their joints" I knew what was coming next. Sure enough, with an almighty crash, and a flash of lightning which stabbed in around the corners of the curtain, illuminating the whole shack momentarily in white light, rain began to come down in buckets. For the first time during my stay on the island, I felt a few of the drops splatter through the roof, wetting my cheek. I huddled closer to the wall of the shack as if by supporting my back a little better I might be better protected from the ensuing storm. I guess there's a little kid in all of us — one who never truly goes away.

I focused back upon the tablet, plugging my headphones into the audio jack.

And there he was, on the screen:

John Horsham.

In all his smart-white-shirted, black-trousered, much-trimmer, glory.

As always, his avatar wore a smirk.

Still even with that expression John Horsham looked jollier than I could ever remember seeing him in life. But then again, I suppose I had never really known the "real" John Horsham.

"How may I serve you today?" John Horsham asked.

It was difficult to tell whether he spoke sincerely or if he was taking the piss.

John Horsham was certainly as deadpan as I could remember him.

I glanced up as if there might be someone standing out there in the pouring rain, sneaking a peak in from behind the curtain. Waiting to catch me out.

I thought about the questions I had asked John Horsham since I had arrived here. They had ranged from simple yet important ones such as, "What is Simple Sun?" to "Tell me more about Emmerson Ray." John Horsham had sometimes been brief, sometimes he had gone off at length on these topics. Any info was good info in my book.

"I want to get in touch with someone," I said.

John Horsham cocked his head to one side like an abiding genie or an especially well-trained spaniel.

I glanced at my phone and dropped my voice. "But I want a secure connection — I want to make sure that nobody hears what I'm saying."

John Horsham bowed his head slightly. "Please give me the name and form of communication."

Diligently, I gave him the details he requested.

And then John Horsham announced in my earphones, "Calling Riko Hitachi."

The phone line purred in my ear.

My heart jostled my throat.

I wondered if I was thinking straight.

Or if I had maybe bumped my head at some point.

But there was no denying the truth.

I was ... *worried* about Riko.

He was my best friend, after all. And until recently he had been the person I had been closest too. We had shared the same living space for a significant amount of time. I hadn't spoken to him since the day ... well, since the day that I had kicked him out.

The phone line stopped its chirping and I heard the rustling of what I decided were bedsheets. A groan which undeniably belonged to Riko.

"Hello?" he said.

"Riko?"

"Who is this?" Riko replied, through a yawn. "It must be bloody ... four, five in the morning?"

"It's me, Riko. Marcus."

There was a pause.

I waited for Riko to come back with a bright response.

"Sparky" ... or "Mark Sparks" ... something equally as braindead.

But he remained circumspect.

Apparently feeling out the lay of the land.

And why wouldn't he?

Our final meeting had hardly been jovial.

"Is everything okay, Marcus?" he asked. "How, uh ... have you been? What's that sound?"

I realised he was referring to the drumming of the rain on the beach shack roof.

My smile took me off guard. I never would have believed I'd be so pleased to be speaking with Riko. It sent a warming glow through my chest.

"It's a tropical storm," I said.

"Oh," Riko replied. "It ... must have missed me."

I counted the seconds, feeling as though I could actually hear the penny drop.

"*Where* are you?" he asked.

"In the Caribbean," I replied, and then waited for the expression of shock.

Of course, though, if there's one thing about Riko it's that he's almost impossible to shock.

"What're you doing there?" Riko asked, as if I had just told him I had popped to the corner shop.

"It's a long story," I said.

"Are you on holiday?"

The muscles around my mouth squeezed and I realised I was smiling without being able to help it. "No, Riko, I'm not on holiday." I looked up at the sturdy palm beams within my shack. "I got rid of my flat — I'm here for good, well ... for the time being, anyway."

"That's, uh ... *dramatic*," Riko said.

I took some satisfaction from his tone of voice.

It sounded as though I had actually succeeded in *surprising* him.

Albeit he was taking it in his stride, as he did everything.

"Hey," Riko said, "actually, I'm glad you called. You see, there was something I wanted to talk to you about. I tried calling you up. Last week, I think?"

I glanced over to my mobile phone, realising I didn't get any signal for my network out here. He hadn't thought to call me via an app or to send me an email. I felt a slight chill pass through my blood to think of it. To realise he was probably *afraid* of getting in touch with me in case I was still angry. "Listen, Riko," I said, wanting to get this out of the way, "about how things ended. You know, with the whole ..."

Riko was breathing heavily on the other end.

And then I wondered whether there might be someone else in the bed.

Presuming Riko was in bed alone was never a safe assumption to make.

It was as if Riko read my mind.

"It's okay," Riko said. "I'm at my parents' house. In my old bedroom. They sleep at the other side of the house. Convenient."

I could hear the smile in his voice.

And it made me smile too.

"Yeah," I said. "Okay. I just wanted to say that, you know, I'm sorry for how I reacted. It was completely out of context — I exploded ... it's just that was something ... it was ..." I tried to think of a simple way to encapsulate The Routine in its entirety — my final answer was deeply unsatisfactory "... it was something I was working on."

"It's okay, Sparky," Riko replied.

I felt a jolt up my spine to hear my pet name again.

It had a much greater impact on me than I would've expected ...

"It's not good to get laughed at," Riko went on, "I can appreciate that. And we shouldn't have gone skulking around the place. It was your flat, after all."

I couldn't quite believe that Riko was being as reasonable as this.

Perhaps it was time for me to change my opinion of him entirely ...

"Look on the bright side, though."

I felt my stomach sink. This was more like the Riko I remembered. "What 'bright side' ?"

"I mean, at least you found out it doesn't work — that it's, I dunno, not funny?"

It felt as if he had ploughed an ice axe directly into my heart. Even though I had mentally prepared myself for it ... nothing quite prepares you for ... *that*.

"Spark? Sparky?" Riko said.

"I'm still here," I replied, and wondered if I shouldn't just hang up.

I'd got what I'd needed.

All I'd wanted was to make my peace with Riko.

To make sure there were no hard feelings ... and now I realised hard feelings weren't such a big deal as I'd built them up to be. Actually, I was happy to leave them be.

Now I was reliving the old Marcus Raisin.

And I had made a pledge with myself to leave the old Marcus behind.

It was time to front up and be a man.

I traced the curtained window, still hearing the drumming rain outside.

"What did you want to call me about? Last week?" I asked.

I heard the rustling of sheets and I imagined Riko sitting up in bed, propping himself up against the headboard with some pillows. "Well, it started out with Julie," Riko began.

Already I held in a groan.

It brought back memories of that scene.

Somehow I'd hoped never to see Julie or Frankie ever again.

That would help me blot the image from my mind.

Once again, I told myself to be a man.

To *confront* what had happened.

And move on.

"No, no," Riko said, "it's not what you think. Julie got arrested."

"Oh?"

"Yeah. She phoned me up a week or so ago. Said she needed to speak with you."

"Me?" I replied. "Why?"

Riko sucked at his teeth. "Well, one of those days, you know ..."

"When I was working?"

"Yeah, one of the days you were working, and Julie was off, she came over ... you know?"

I reached up and massaged my temple. I felt as though I had gone some way to undoing all of the aches and pains I had eliminated while I had been living here on the island. "And what happened?"

"It was after you'd got the tablet ..."

I couldn't help myself this time. "Riko? Really? You promised you wouldn't touch it!"

"Nah, nah," Riko went on. "This was before I said that."

I racked my brains trying to remember.

I couldn't exactly recall the order of events.

Damn him ... but I was certain he was lying ... and it infuriated me even more to think that he was knowingly taking advantage of my sieve-like memory.

"Anyway," Riko said, "we were playing around with the tablet — I was showing what it could do ... and that was when, uh ... I guess that's when things got bad."

"'Bad' how?"

"Well" — I could hear Riko scratching the back of his neck — "you see, Julie got a plan in her head. She decided on doing something ... *bad*."

"What?" I replied, already regretting asking the question.

"She wanted to rip off Frothy Cups."

"'Rip off'?" I echoed. "What is she, a gangster, or something?"

"Kind of ... I mean, she was serious about it. There was nothing I could do to stop her."

"You didn't give her the tablet, did you?"

"No, of course not ..." A long pause, then, "She took it -"

"Riko!" I spoke so loudly I was afraid I might bring unwanted attention to my beach shack.

I breathed in deep, calming myself as best as I was able.

Riko went on. "It was just a few days. You didn't even notice it was gone."

"That doesn't make it okay! What did she do with it? Are you telling me she 'ripped off' Frothy Cups with it? Whatever the hell that means."

"You see," Riko said, "Julie studied accountancy and finance at university. Most of the first year, anyway, before she dropped out. She kind of ... you know, gets this stuff ... she understands the systems. What you need to do to ... you know?"

I stared long and hard at the tablet, trying to allow the revelation to settle within my skull. "And ... did she?" I asked. "From the sounds of it she did ... was that why she was arrested?"

"You know, Sparky, what I've missed so much about you is how quickly you cotton onto things. I never have to spell things out." He snapped his fingers. "You just *get* it."

I was well-versed in this particular Riko technique.

The old "flattery as distraction".

And yet just because I could identify it didn't mean I could combat it. I guess I'm going to be a complete walkover as a parent ... if I ever do manage to successfully procreate ...

"And now she's in trouble with the police?" I asked.

"Uh-huh," Riko said.

I screwed up my eyes, rubbed harder still at my temple. "Just one thing, I suppose, that sticks out. Why does Julie want to speak to me?"

"Well, she knew the tablet was yours."

"Why didn't you offer to help her? You're the one who showed it to her?"

"I ... it didn't occur to me ... anyway," Riko went on, "the police want to speak to me too."

"And what did you say?"

"Uh," Riko said, "I'm ... supposed to go tomorrow."

I exhaled. "Well, then it's sorted. You can just go and tell the police what happened. You can own up to it. Or not. If it was Julie's idea then I don't see how you're to blame?"

A long uncomfortable silence followed.

I tried my hardest not to be the one to break it but I realised there was no other way.

"What's the matter?" I asked. "Just tell the truth."

"Julie told them about you, about the tablet," Riko said. "They want to bring you in for questioning too ... I don't know ... it's all getting pretty serious."

My heart started thumping in my ears.

But I felt strangely calm and collected.

"Do they know where I am?"

"Nobody knows, Spark, you took off without telling anyone ... without telling me, anyway."

I got up off the bed and started to pace back and forth, thinking aloud as I did so. "My parents know roughly where I am — in the Caribbean — but I didn't reveal the exact location. Nobody at LifeWare knows anything at all ... except that I just sort of upped and left."

I could hear Riko breathing on the other end of the phone.

I waited for him to say it.

I *dared* him to say it.

... And he didn't disappoint.

"What about me, though?"

I felt a twisting sensation in my gut. All through my life, whenever I've felt truly and deeply angry I have always done my best to push it down ... but for some reason, on this particular occasion, it proved impossible.

I just exploded.

"What about you! Who *gives* a fuck! This hasn't anything to do with me, Riko! The only thing I've got to be sorry for is walking in on some IT creep a few seconds after he died!"

As I listened to the blood tick through the veins at my temples, I forced myself to breathe steadily. To try and calm down. But that was all the invitation Riko needed.

"You took the tablet, Marcus," he said, his voice frustratingly measured and reasonable ... how the hell did he always manage to do that?

More deep breathing.

And then the realisation.

Riko was only telling the truth.

I *had* taken the tablet.

That had without a doubt been my responsibility.

And not only had I taken the tablet but I had failed — on multiple occasions and across a period of time — to hand it in to the relevant authorities. I said the only thing that came into my head, "I need some time to think."

And then I hung up.

☼

Dawn had just crested the bay outside my beach shack when I shuffled out through the doorway. I was still shaking following the conversation I'd had with Riko hours earlier. I hadn't slept, of course, and although the humidity was often to blame for sleepless nights on the island, this time there had been the additional factor of Riko's revelations buzzing around my brain.

I knew which beach shack belonged to Emmerson Ray. There wasn't much distinctive about Emmerson Ray's beach shack. It was pretty much a carbon copy of mine.

In lieu of a door, I knocked on one of the support beams.

The wood was harder than I thought. It stung my knuckles.

I waited to hear stirring within.

Emmerson Ray emerging from his slumber.

But there was nothing.

When I heard Emmerson Ray's voice over my shoulder I nearly jumped clean out of my skin. I turned on my heel to find him standing a few paces away, a chilled glass of what looked like purple juice clutched in his fist. His voice was soft, perhaps wary of waking anyone who was still asleep. "I always believe in being first up," Emmerson Ray said, coming closer. "It gives you an edge — a head start."

I sidestepped this piece of life advice, sticking to the reason why I had come here in the first place. "I need to tell you something."

He flashed his eyebrows — more out of intrigue than surprise ... he gave off a definite sense that it was impossible for anything to surprise him.

I relayed exactly what I had heard from Riko on the phone. I expected him to look around as if being pursued by someone, or at the very least widen his eyes slightly ... but he only took another sip of his drink and gestured in the direction of the beach.

As we strolled along the shore, the morning tide crept its way up before dragging back into the murky depths. A couple of birds squawked in the palm trees and I caught the sharp scent of lemon on the air. With each step, Emmerson Ray outlined the plan of action ... how we would go about resolving the situation.

First, he explained, there was the question of getting Riko to safety. Here I had maybe laid it on a little thickly, referring to him as a "life-long friend" but it had done the trick sufficiently to convince Emmerson Ray that drastic action needed to take place. He explained that he would arrange for Riko to be put on a charter flight and for him to travel out to the island at once. He would be allowed into Simple Sun and assigned a beach shack all of his own. Although it felt a little like I was looking a gift horse in the mouth, the pragmatist in me had to ask whether he would be compensated, you know, in the same way that I had been compensated.

When I had revealed that Riko was in fact currently jobless and living with his parents, I expected Emmerson Ray to give a sharp grin and shake his head ... however, instead, he seemed to give this piece of information serious consideration before finally declaring that he would be "compensated appropriately" and that "some of the best people [he] knew had been living with their parents well into their thirties".

It was another way of spinning that old refrain about everyone coming good eventually.

A refrain I was personally invested in seeing come true.

The biggest reason why I was here, on this island, and not still stuck in some stuffy office.

Well, that and the money ... and the paradise ...

Emmerson Ray certainly knew how to sweeten the pot.

And so that was how it happened.

That was how Riko got to the island.

# ESCAPE TO PARADISE

I looked up from my glass of cool pineapple juice to Riko, sitting on the bench opposite, his own drink — a banana smoothie — in front of him. We'd been sitting there for about half an hour, neither of us saying anything, just gazing out at the placid Caribbean sea lapping at the shore.

"So," Riko began, finally breaking the silence, "what's there to do around here? When do we get put to work?"

"That's not really what Simple Sun is about," I replied.

"Then what *is* Simple Sun about?"

Now he was really testing me.

"It's a ... philosophy," I said. "The idea is that you have to ... find yourself" — I winced as I said it thinking just how much I hated the phrase — "you get all the time you need and you just ... just *decide* what you want to do."

I realised I was doing a terrible job of convincing Riko. If that was indeed what I was attempting to do. Was I trying to make him feel better about having thrown his lot in with this place of refuge?

Riko pouted. "And what if I just want to do nothing?"

"Uh," I replied, "I think the idea is that you'll have to do something eventually."

When the familiar laugh sounded behind me I nearly spat my tongue out of my mouth.

Emmerson Ray took a seat on the bench alongside us. Today he was wearing a more sedate pastel blue shirt over a pair of white shorts — at least it was more sedate than the Hawaiian shirts he usually wore. He didn't have a drink with him and it appeared that he'd just been passing by. "Listen," he said, resting his elbows on the table. He appeared to be meeting Riko's eye although it was impossible to tell for certain because he was wearing sunglasses. "You're part of Simple Sun now," he said. "You're part of a larger ... *thing* ... you've got to know that this community has your back, no matter what. Just the fact that you're here is enough. Believe me, it's not anybody who gets into this situation. There has to be something about you — something *deep* ..."

"So," Riko said, looking at me in that unnerving way of his, "what you're saying is that I'm ... *special?*" He risked a glance back at Emmerson Ray.

"Yes, sure, if you like."

Riko went on — I could already hear the cogs turning in his mind. "And say I did just want to sit around and do nothing all day ... or maybe for the rest of my life ... you'd just pick up the bill? You'd, uh ... keep paying the salary, compensation, whatever, like we agreed?"

Emmerson Ray tilted his head to one side. "Why not?"

"Why not?" Riko replied, turning his attention upon the banana smoothie in front of him. "Well, it just, I don't know ... sounds *insane?*"

I knew from experience that Emmerson Ray was on familiar ground here.

He was used to shifting around the non-believers.

Getting them to see things from his perspective.

But, then again, he was only just becoming acquainted with Riko.

Perhaps Riko would be the one who finally broke Emmerson Ray ...

Emmerson Ray propped himself upright in his seat. "You're thinking about things from the way you've always seen them. And that's okay. It's a starting point. But what I hope Simple Sun will teach you — being *part* of Simple Sun will teach you — is that it's all about the larger picture ..."

"Ah," Riko said, with a faint smile, "then it is a guilt-trip kind of thing?"

"In what way?" Emmerson Ray replied, his tone still cool and clearly in control of the conversation. But for how much longer?

"Well, you know," Riko said, "you say all this good stuff about being able to sit around and leech if that's what I really want but the subtext is that I'll eventually feel bad for doing what I'm doing. That I'll eventually snap out of that mentality and start to, you know, make myself useful?"

Emmerson Ray remained steeped in silence for a long few seconds.

And then he burst out laughing.

He kept on laughing until tears rolled down his cheeks.

Finally, he propped his head on the table and banged his fist a couple of times, making the juice in our glasses bounce around — spilling a little of Riko's banana concoction.

In the end, Emmerson Ray got himself together. He wagged a finger at Riko. "You know, you're a good thinker. You consider the angles. I like that *a lot*."

"Really?" me and Riko said at the same time.

"Uh huh," Emmerson Ray replied. "And to tell the truth, that's what I'm always banking on. It's just human nature, huh? I mean, maybe with all the good thinking in the world Simple Sun still can't make that much of a dent in man's make-up." He dropped his voice. "But that's where you'd be wrong. We've got plans. We've got *developments* that'll change the world. All we need is a small, committed group. We'll change the world." He stared Riko down, his eyeballs like the holes in a double-barrelled shotgun. "I select those who join." He jerked his thumb at his chest to emphasise this point. All sense of joviality had evaporated now. The intensity had jacked up a notch. "That should be enough of a plan for anyone."

I looked at Riko, with no idea whatsoever as to how he might take this. As it happened, he brought the conversation to an anticlimactic close with a shrug and a sheepish smile. It was the closest I'd ever seen Riko to admitting someone had won a victory against him.

I couldn't blame him really.

I would've admitted the same.

It was later in the evening and me and Riko were in my beach shack, chatting things over. We'd managed to locate a couple of beers and we were each nursing one, enjoying the chilly tickle of the bubbles down our throats, the coolness emanating from the glass bottles. I was lying on my back on my bunk, staring at the ceiling while Riko slumped up against the wall, feet stretching out along the floor. "The day I left," Riko said, "Julie called me up again."

"Oh?" I replied, feeling as though the conversation we'd had several days ago over the tablet was separated by a whole other world — a world we didn't need to pay attention to any longer. Because, now, We Were Simple Sun ...

"What did she say?"

"Just the same, really," Riko replied. "She said the police wanted to talk to me. That she was going to get a letter."

"A court summons?"

"Something like that."

"What did she actually do?" I asked.

"What'd you mean?" Riko replied.

"You know, with Frothy Cups?"

"Well, the way she sold it to me was that she was just gonna go in there, use the tablet, and empty the place's bank account into hers."

"I see," I replied. "Was that it, then? The extent of the plan?"

Riko gave a wide yawn. "That was what she said to me."

I couldn't help thinking that Julie might well have simplified it for Riko's sake.

"How was she planning on getting away with it?" I asked.

Riko shrugged. "Dunno. She had ideas ..."

"But she got caught."

"Yeah, guess they should've thought it over more."

My ears pricked up. "*They*? Who else was involved?"

"Oh," Riko replied, clearly hoping he could bat this away as if it was nothing. "Frankie."

"*Frankie?*"

"Uh-huh."

"Are the police speaking to her?"

"Think so," Riko replied, wiggling his toes and staring at them. "I'd be surprised if she didn't come up during their enquiries."

I breathed in deeply.

Sighed out long and hard.

"Who else knows, Riko?"

"Just them — just those two. And me and you, obviously."

Somehow I wished I didn't know anything.

That way if the police did one day pick me up I could truthfully claim I was naïve.

"It's messy," I said, shaking my head, as if I had any sort of experience of this sort of thing in my past. As if I knew what a *tidy* criminal operation looked like.

Riko yawned again and made to get up from his spot. He reminded me of a dog which has been dozing for a few hours and — all baggy eyes and weary limbs — was making the gargantuan effort to hoik itself off to its nightly sleeping spot. He trudged over to the door of my beach shack. "Emmerson'll look after us," he said.

I felt a faint whine at the back of my brain as if there was the voice of some nearly dead thing trying to tell me something. Maybe it was another of those deeply imbedded parental dictums that go along the lines of being cautious of anybody in the adult world who claims that they will "look after you" ... because they most likely will ... "look after" their best interests, that is ...

My resilience for an elongated conversation with Riko was however at a low ebb and I was ready for a long, dreamless sleep. And so I opted out of any further dialogue in the swiftest manner possible. "Yeah," I said. "You're probably right."

A day or so later I was sat on a bench at the Main Lodge, a few Scripters around me to go with the girl with glasses from the other day. While I had the tablet in front of me, all of them were tapping away at their laptop keyboards, eyes glued to their screens. I couldn't help thinking that it was more than a mite pathetic that after a full decade of office-droning

I still needed to snatch a glance at my computer keyboard from time to time when typing.

Perhaps the Scripters were some higher form of human being.

The next rung on the evolutionary ladder.

Or maybe I was just on a lower rung than the norm.

It's just a matter of perspective I guess.

As usual, the heat was bordering on oppressive, the breeze had dropped away completely, and I could feel the sweat seeping out of every pore. If it hadn't been for the glass of freshly squeezed natural lemonade before me then I might've rolled over on my back, my up-turned limbs pointing skyward.

Riko had left me a few minutes earlier, gone off for a "walk on the beach", which in Riko's language meant he was off looking for attractive women to speak to and possibly fornicate with. Already Riko had some-thing of a reputation, which was remarkable given the short amount of time he had spent here. Yes, all things considered, it was quite incredible how quickly he had adapted to island living — but then again I suppose there hadn't been all that much to uproot him from.

He had been jobless, back at his parents' house. And then Simple Sun had flown in on golden wings and saved him from a police investigation.

I had to admit that despite Emmerson Ray's confidence that there was nothing to worry about, the matter had been on my mind for several days. Although I hadn't been involved in the digital robbery — or whatever the correct legal term is for what Julie had pulled — I was in possession of the item which had been used to commit the crime.

Whenever I spoke with Emmerson Ray, he would give me a broad smile, clap me on the shoulder, and tell me that I had a "worried" face ... he had assured me that everything was "taken care of" ... that didn't completely assuage my fears. Although I couldn't see the prospect appealing to me in the immediate future, I knew that at some stage I might like to return to the UK without ending up in handcuffs and a custodial sentence to look forward to.

What if one of my parents died?

I'd need to go back for their funeral(s).

During these days, while I had been making my best attempts at "finding myself" or however Emmerson Ray and Simple Sun preferred the term, I had mostly spent my time tapping through the tablet's various options and settings, trying to find an answer ... as time marched on, however, I was becoming all too aware that I was likely looking in completely the wrong place.

I had taken to checking my email more regularly on the tablet via — what John Horsham's avatar had assured and guided me through was — an encrypted connection. Whatever I did here, on the island, was likely being monitored. But, then again, even if it was, Emmerson Ray had told me that he was on my side. So why should I have anything to worry about?

I convinced myself that I could explain away almost anything.

And that Emmerson Ray would most likely accept the explanation.

Jesus, it really did seem as though this was getting more and more culty by the day.

On that particular day — feeling at a particularly low ebb in terms of the whole making-myself-useful thing — I was flipping through my emails when I found one with a subject written in block capitals. My eyes scanned across the screen.

It was from Kelly.

My heart leaped up to my throat.

I had to swallow it back down.

With a trembling finger, I jabbed the subject of the email: "PLEASE READ THIS".

In retrospect, the subject was more than a little spammy.

But I guess having spent several weeks on the island by that point, I was having weird sort of withdrawal symptoms surrounding emails, even despite all the pain they had caused me over the years. Maybe that was some deep secret to my psyche ... I actively went out and searched for pain:

*Marcus there's some stuff you've got to know. And we need your help.*

Right away the "we" clanged in my mind.

Who was this "we"?

I read on:

302

*I think my life is in danger. Filseek, too.*

My heart started hammering again.

What did Filseek, Fil, have to do with this?

... Whatever *this* was ...

*It began a few weeks ago. I noticed someone following me in a car. Two men inside. I checked over my shoulder quickly but didn't stop. I turned down an alleyway too narrow for traffic. They pulled up at the opening and just waited there. Staring after me.*

There was little doubt in my mind as to who these two men could be. Daymian with a "y".

And Toby Horsham ... or whatever his surname happened to be.

My mind whirred. I tried to get things together. That, of course, was one of my big questions while I had been here, on the island ... where did Daymian and Toby fit in? They seemed chummy enough with Emmerson Ray back at the Simple Sun Conclave, but I had never seen them on the island. I thought back to Simple Sun HQ as they had described it. That worn-out unit on an industrial estate outside town. They had claimed they had started Simple Sun ... that it had started out as them and John Horsham as some sort of a gaming clan ... I had since stopped being so curious as to where Emmerson Ray exactly fit in with all of this.

I carried on reading:

*Then a few days ago it happened again. This time it was a Saturday. I was leaving my home — I live in a block of flats — when I noticed their car parked across the street. I was taking out the rubbish. I saw the two of them sat in the car, the two of them with their eyes fixed upon me the whole time. They looked familiar but I don't quite know from where. I'd almost say one of them looked like he might be related to John ... that's when it hit me. The reason why they might be looking. The tablet. And so I decided the best way to sort things out was for me to confront them. To clear up the confusion. When I approached the car I half expected them to speed off. But one of them wound down the window. The one which didn't look like John.*

Daymian with a "y", I thought with a frown as I read the text.

*I asked him simply why he was following me. And he confirmed my suspicions. He just asked me where the tablet was. I told him I didn't know. He said he didn't believe me and then he threatened me. He had one of those electric stun guns, a Taser. Even though it sounds stupid thinking back on it, I froze. It was clear daylight — certainly not the time to shock someone with a Taser, especially right in the middle of the street. I should've called their bluff. They said I could go get it for them right now or they would pay me a visit later that evening. I just sort of backed away from the car. Some sort of response kicked in. I went back up to my flat. It was only after I'd been sat by the window for about twenty minutes, staring at where their car had been parked up, that I realised what I had to do. That I needed to call the police.*

I thought about my own brush with Toby and Daymian with a "y" and wondered why I ultimately hadn't gone to the police. And then I remembered the tablet. If I had gone to the police then I would've had to tell them everything — including the tablet I had taken from John Horsham soon after he had passed away …

*An officer spoke to me. I gave her a description of the vehicle, stuff like that. When she asked me about why they might be following me — stalking me — I told her I might have something they were looking for. I stayed as vague as possible but the officer asked lots of questions. Where I worked, what I did. Stuff like that. I felt as if I was the one committing a crime rather than those two.*

I glanced up from the tablet, across the Main Lodge.

The Scripters' fingers continued to flurry across their keyboards.

On the beach, I eyed Riko. He was dressed only in a pair of scarlet swimming shorts with puffy white flowers on them. I noticed his chest and abs had got a fair bit more muscular since he had arrived and I wondered if he had taken to doing sit-ups or press-ups or maybe both.

He wasn't alone.

The female Scripter with the glasses from the other day had left her laptop behind, having stripped down to a bikini top and denim cut-offs, as she picked her way along the shore at Riko's side. Already, I could see those trademark little flourishes of Riko's flirting armoury.

It wouldn't be long before she succumbed.

Like so many before her.

If only she knew what she was getting herself in for ...

After so many years, after witnessing the same thing play itself out countless times, I had reached the point where I started to believe that they *all* knew — on some level — what they were getting themselves in for. I returned to Kelly's email on the tablet in front of me:

*The police didn't reassure me at all. She said she probably wouldn't be able to do much. I told her about the stun gun — that seemed to get the officer's attention but in the end she just told me to give her a call if they came back. The day after Filseek came to see me in my office.*

*He looked pale, shaken. I don't think we'd ever said more than "hello" and "goodbye" to one another before but he started talking and I struggled to make sense of what he was saying. Finally, when I got him to slow down, he told me from the top. He said about how it all happened. The day John Horsham died. He says he was on his way out when he saw you in the doorway to his office, he said the cleaner had just started vacuuming. He said he didn't want to interrupt because he had had run-ins with John Horsham before and didn't want to end up in a conversation, get you into trouble when you were trying to get something fixed.*

I felt a warmth through my gut.

It's always nice to know you have someone looking out for you.

And especially when it's a soul as genuine and good-natured as Fil.

*So he headed out. When he got through the gate he noticed the car — it was pretty distinctive, green and with a purple bonnet cannibalised from another car. It stuck in his mind. Just as, it seems, Fil stuck in the occupants' minds. Because after they had paid me a visit, they decided to pick on Fil. Only they managed to get him in the car. I know what you're thinking but please don't be too quick to judge. He was probably panicked. Maybe they were nice to him, or something. Anyway, however it happened, he got in.*

I felt myself blushing. I was glad Kelly wasn't able to see my face herself right then. Maybe men don't have as much of a reason to be afraid of getting into strangers' cars? Or perhaps me and Fil shared the same idiot lemming gene that has mostly been weeded out of the pool after generations of evolution. For some reason I felt a little better about having got in that car.

At least I wasn't the only one ...

When I read on any sense of glee dissipated:

*They took him to a place they call Simple Sun HQ. They shot him with the stun gun, asking them to tell them about the tablet. Of course, he didn't know anything about it. But they didn't believe him. When I asked him why he didn't go to the police, instead of to me, he told me they were watching him, and that if he went to the police they wouldn't be able to help. He came to me because he knew I had spoken to you — because I was taking over John Horsham's old job. He asked me about the tablet, what they had been asking him for. I was surprised, obviously, that those two had spilled what they were looking for. A bit amateur, maybe. But it confirmed what I had suspected. What they were looking for. Why they were following me. Strangely it made me feel more secure for a while. And then when I thought it through I felt even more afraid. I've never liked blatant displays of power. Someone so arrogant as to think they are untouchable. Fil showed me some of the marks. No doubt we have the evidence if we wanted it.*

I straightened up on the bench.

Looked out over the beach.

Riko and the Scripter with glasses were splashing in the shallows. Cackling at one another, their laughter lazily carrying to where I was sitting.

I shifted in my seat, unable to quite get comfortable.

Now I was thinking about Kelly, and Fil.

About how I had somehow put them in danger.

How by being loosely associated with me they had fallen into danger.

*Look, Marcus. I know you made up your mind — that you made the decision to go with them. But surely you can speak with someone. Emmerson Ray? Tell them about what these two are doing. They're all part of it, part of Simple Sun, aren't they?*

I felt my ribcage squeeze my heart and lungs.

It was as if some well-intentioned poltergeist wanted me to do the right thing.

... Whatever the "right thing" was.

I read the final part of the email.

*I just want to live a normal life, Marcus. Is that too much to ask? If I don't hear back from you in the next day or two I'm going to have to go back to the police. I'm going to have to tell them everything. My fear is that there's no way back. But I have to try. Until I'm sure it's too late.*

*Speak soon, I hope.*

*Kelly*

My head was spinning by the time I finished reading the email and it wasn't just because of the blazing heat. It was a racking sense of guilt.

Just who the hell did I think I was?

Here, on an island in the middle of paradise, leaving all my problems behind.

Leaving my problems for others to deal with.

There was a simple solution.

And — like all the other problems — it was the same one:

Emmerson Ray.

There was a slight breeze weaving through the palm fronds, sending them bobbing like nodding heads. I took it as a sign that I was doing the right thing. That there was an audience somewhere — *somehow* — goading me on.

Emmerson Ray was in his beach shack this time. As I peered in through the uncovered window I saw he was cross-legged on his bed, hunched over his laptop. He was focused upon the screen, jabbing at the keyboard every five, ten seconds.

"Can I ask you something?" I said.

I couldn't help but think that Emmerson Ray was surely growing weary of me popping around to ask him for favours. I wondered just how long it would take to wear out his good will ... I did have my salary to justify, after all. However, if Emmerson Ray was growing tired of my presence, then he didn't show it. Once more he greeted me with that winning smile of his. The one which was like a golden ray of sunlight. It felt as though whenever he smiled he set flames kindling in my stomach. A definite sense of confidence rippled through me.

"Take a seat," he said, indicating a bamboo chair with its seat woven out of reeds.

I did as he said, at the same time savouring the coolness in the beach shack.

One thing I had learned during my time on the island was that hot weather all the time can make your life just as miserable as cold. Well, actually, thinking about it properly, at least in paradise the sun is always shining ... I wasn't missing the dismal grey days back in Blighty.

The chair was firm and didn't wobble, as I had expected it might.

Grinning wide, Emmerson Ray said, "You're not going to ask me to bring someone else to the island, are you?"

"No," I replied. "I ... wanted to ask you about Daymian ... and Toby."

Emmerson Ray glanced to his laptop and then, gently, pawed it closed. He clasped his hands and brought them up to his clavicle, in a sort of prayer position.

It was a pose that said that he was listening completely.

And yet I wasn't convinced I would get the answers I sought.

But I could only try.

I had promised that to myself.

"What would you like to know?" Emmerson Ray said, his tone of voice measured, reasonable, as it always was even when speaking about lofty, worldwide matters. He had a rare combination of earthliness and power. I wondered if this was what demi-gods were like ...

"I ..." I thought about Kelly's email, and could see no other way around it — I just needed to come out and tell the truth, "... Toby and Daymian are ... uh, following some of my friends. They're ... making them feel uncomfortable." I recalled what Kelly had said about them shooting Fil with the stun gun. A flash of heat passed through my veins.

I knew I had to do justice to those I considered my friends.

"They're getting violent."

Emmerson Ray's mouth formed an "oh" shape. His clasped hands gradually fell away to his abdomen. He was staring into empty air now.

I wondered if he was genuinely caught off guard or if he was just calculating the next move. "What have they done?" he asked finally.

I told him about the stun gun.

And about Fil.

"They want the tablet," I said. "They don't seem to realise I have it ..."

"Mm," Emmerson Ray replied, having brought his clasped hands up to his mouth now. He stared over the ridges of his steepled knuckles. I thought I could hear the machinations of his brain ticking away ... thinking through the angles.

"Can you," I started, "you know, tell them to leave them alone? Tell them that — "

Emmerson Ray raised his hand. For some reason this gesture had a more powerful effect on me than if he had roared a reprimand. It's what people call "presence", I suppose.

His eyes focused upon me.

Although he had what I would term an "arresting gaze", this was the first time I detected anything like anger brewing just beneath the surfaces of his irises.

Or maybe it was just determination.

"You recall our conversation surrounding 'purpose', and each person finding theirs?"

I didn't really see what this had to do with what I was asking.

But I replied.

"Yes."

"And that within Simple Sun, everyone functions within their cell, their own personal bubble. A protected place which the organisation strives to preserve."

I couldn't help but think that this was the first time I could remember him referring to Simple Sun as an "organisation", or anything else for that matter ...

"Yes," I replied.

"Then," Emmerson Ray said, leaning slightly forward, over his closed laptop, "you know Simple Sun *depends* on the autonomy of its members. One of its guiding principles, if you will."

That sent my nostril hair tingling. My heart thumped a couple of times.

I had heard *that* particular term before.

Several times, actually.

All of those HR comms, all of those "performance review" meetings, etcetera, etcetera ...

Yes, LifeWare's Guiding Principles were firmly bruised into the soft tissue of my brain. I wondered vaguely if someone might be able to read them off the surface of my mind with a CAT scanner. It was then that I started to wonder if I had really escaped at all.

Or if I had just ended up somewhere exactly like LifeWare.

Maybe even worse.

They *were* paying me more ... and there are certain schools of thought that say the amount of bullshit you have to put up with is proportional to the amount of pay you receive.

Was this the long-awaited bullshit?

I pushed everything down. Told myself I needed to stand my ground for my friends. They were depending on me. I pictured Fil, Toby and Daymian looming over him, him smiling back at them as Daymian — for some reason I could only imagine that it would be Daymian — shot him.

Fil's smile faded.

And he crumpled to the ground.

I arched my shoulders and tried to project my voice ... I only realised I was on the verge of shouting when a soreness afflicted my throat. "But I have the tablet!" I said. "Can't you get a message to them? Tell them I have it?"

Emmerson Ray continued to stare at me.

To say it was unnerving was an understatement.

I didn't need his lips to form the words to know what he was going to say.

It was then that the realisation struck me.

Like someone tipping a bucket of ice water over my head.

"Jesus," I said, standing on the spot, unable to shift for the time being due to shock, "what the hell is this? Where the hell am I?"

Emmerson Ray remained still. So still I thought he might have quietly suffered an aneurism. Passed away right in front of my eyes. But then he said, "You're part of the future, Marcus. You're part of Simple Sun."

I felt angry, sure.

But my behaviour was more like that of a stroppy teenager.

I returned to my beach shack and promptly turned over my mattress and then started on my bed. Once I had thoroughly turned my little world upside down, I paused to take breath.

I guess all the good tropical island living had taken its toll on my physical form ... not that I had ever been anything like a prime specimen — there's only so much of a work out you get from lifting a phone up from its cradle to your ear.

As I towered above my wrecked lodgings, I tried to slow down my thoughts, to get myself to concentrate on what I was going to do next. All I could think about was Kelly and Fil, and the idiotic principles which made up Simple Sun ... funny that they seemed idiotic now that they weren't working in my favour ...

I forced myself to breathe.

To take honking breaths.

And that was when I heard his voice outside.

Riko.

My heart ticked in my eardrums as I heard his voice and the voice of the girl he had been "courting" earlier. I knew Riko well enough to know he would be guiding the two of them back to his beach shack for an evening of love-making. I clenched my teeth, sank my fingernails into the fleshy parts of my palms, and stormed out of my beach shack.

Outside, the air was thick and moist and warm.

Across the ocean stretching out into the distance I could make out banks of cloud rolling towards the island through the pitch-black night. The slightest of cool breezes in the air told me that in about half an hour the heavens would open and everything would be soaked. I pivoted on the spot and caught sight of the backs of Riko and the girl with the glasses — the "Scripter" I thought with a pathetic sneer at the corner of my mouth as if I was someone superior who had any sort of right to criticise anyone else on this island.

What was *I* doing there?

What had *I* done to deserve being there?

Still, I stalked onwards, eyes fixed upon Riko's bare calves. I couldn't believe someone as lazy as him could manage to keep his muscles looking so tight and pert ... perhaps he had a routine he did on the sly. He was wearing a Hawaiian shirt Emmerson Ray wouldn't have been ashamed to swan about in. He had on a pair of khaki shorts. The girl — the Scripter — had on a loose-fitting summer dress, a turquoise colour with twisting, weaving yellow and green patterns.

I'm not sure I've ever laid hands on another human in anger — not that I can remember anyway — but an otherworldly strength took hold of me as I snatched for Riko's shoulder and spun him around to face me.

His eyes were wide in surprise and the girl with him let out a shriek.

Blood ran hot through my veins.

I felt it well in my brain.

And send a ripple down my spine.

My fingers dug into Riko's shoulder.

"Come with me," I said, through gnashed teeth.

He glanced to the girl. "It's okay," he said, and then, submitting to my hold as I attempted to drag him back towards the shore, he added, "I'll see you around, okay?"

Crickets, or whatever they were, croaked out of sight in the foliage on the fringes of the sandy beach. I kept on looking around, all too aware I was being conspicuous.

I let go of Riko once we were out of sight of the Main Lodge and the last of the beach shacks. I half expected Riko to turn on me with his own rage ... I had got in the way of him and that Scripter. I should've known better, however, because as always he looked entirely unfazed.

"What's this about?" Riko finally said.

I dropped my voice to a near whisper hoping he would cotton onto the seriousness of the whole situation. "Kelly and Fil are in trouble."

"Who? And who?" Riko asked, pouting.

I gave him a potted explanation of who they were and what their relation was to me.

"Work colleagues?" Riko said, and then, apparently to clarify, "*Ex--work colleagues?*"

"Yes," I replied, feeling as though the seriousness of what I was going to say next was already being undermined by his reaction.

His brow furrowed. "How're you in contact with them?"

I coloured slightly although there was no need to feel embarrassed about anything.

Didn't work colleagues often exchange personal email addresses, that sort of thing?

I filled in the details as requested. This didn't clear up his confusion ... although he hadn't yet given me the chance to explain the issue. "Look," I said, holding up my hands, in surrender. "It's about the tablet. It's causing issues. You remember what I told you about Toby, about Daymian ..."

"Daymian with a 'y'?" Riko replied.

"That's the one. Well, they attacked Fil."

Riko said nothing.

I just hoped he'd keep his mouth shut long enough that I could get through with everything I had to say. Whether or not he appreciated the peril of the situation was all by-the-by at this point.

"And they've been threatening Kelly ... wanting to know where the tablet is."

"Why don't they tell them the truth?" Riko said. "That you've got it?"

I shrugged. "I ... I was going to suggest that."

"Well, suggest it, then."

It was at this point I caught the whiff of something. One of those smells which'd become so familiar during my commutes on the bus every morning.

Male cologne ... if there is in fact a female or gender-neutral equivalent ...

"You're not to tell anyone anything."

Both of us looked along the beach.

To where we saw Emmerson Ray.

His silhouette was stark and imposing against the night-time sky. Over his shoulder, raindrops began to spatter upon the surface of the ocean. For just a moment, the moon emerged from behind a bank of cloud and struck him with a ray of light as bright and powerful as a sunbeam. An actor lit up by a spotlight. Centre stage. "You two understood the conditions," he said, his voice possessing an oddly grave quality now. "You took on Simple Sun's help. And so you must begin to pay Simple Sun back for all you have received." He broke out in a smile but it didn't move past his cheekbones.

It was eerie ... like looking at an oil painting.

"Everything happens for a reason. We all exist in our own small circle. We cannot affect others. Only as one can we affect everything."

I had to admit I was beginning to get lost in all these philosophical musings ... if I had ever truly had any sense of being on level ground before.

Emmerson Ray added, "The situation shall resolve itself — there is no question ..."

This was the time for me to speak up.

I wasn't going to fade into the background, walk off into the night like I had done when I'd been all set to perform the Routine. This time I was going to be the protagonist.

"You wouldn't care if they got *killed*, would you?"

Emmerson Ray remained unmoved.

His eyes stared through the gloom.

Pinning me and Riko to the spot.

Wordlessly answering my question.

I expected Riko to chime in but even he appeared to acknowledge the gravity of the situation. He seemed to realise what was at stake.

As Emmerson Ray spoke, his mouth was all teeth.

Showing us some fang.

"Whatever happens, it happens for a reason."

# A NEW DAWN

I woke up early the next morning — not that I had got anything like a decent night's sleep.

I cast my blanket into a heap at the foot of my bunk.

My mouth felt dry, as though I had been drinking. I hadn't had any alcohol since I arrived on the island or even felt the urge. I hadn't noticed anybody else partaking either and I wondered whether it might've been prohibited. The strongest thing on offer seemed to be fresh fruit juice. I swung my legs out over the side of the mattress and sat there, my head pounding from the day before ... from the conversation with Emmerson Ray.

For the first time I knew I had to acknowledge my naivety.

I scolded myself for not having paid more attention to Kelly's warning.

It seemed like one of those times in your life that those Bible stories are always trying to steer you clear of ... you know, the type about accepting worldly riches at some sort of spiritual cost. I wondered whether I'd ever end up being any kind of worldly or if I'd be stuck this way for the rest of my life. Just sort of flitting about at the whim and will of the world.

Another office drone in an ambling procession of office drones.

I focused on the wooden logs of my beach hut — the ones dead ahead of me that were placed in vertical patterns so as to make up the walls. I rubbed at my scalp, massaging my brain into a more positive outlook. Last night in my semi-sleepless state I had experienced those kinds of half-dreams when your conscious brain is still very much awake while your subconscious is blurring the edges of whatever's flitting through your mind's eye.

In my head, I had saved Kelly and Fil from innumerable perilous situations involving Toby and Daymian with a "y". There had been the obvious ones, the showdowns on cliff-edges, driving rain, storming seas far below when I had nobly entered — *stage-left* — and started swinging punches and kicking with a force I did not possess in the real world.

And there had been more surrealist takes. The time when I had imagined a kind of cloud kingdom. I was there in the throne room saving Queen Kelly and Fil the Courtier from the pair of knaves who had invaded and were threatening to strike both down with neon-glowing nunchucks. As that particular dream had progressed, Toby and Daymian had nobly withdrawn following their defeat, and Fil too, had slipped off the scene. That had left me alone with Kelly ... and, well, let's just say that my passion had ended up being directed elsewhere.

Finally, as the early morning light had seeped into my beach shack, a more realistic rendering of how things might play out had taken the place of the earlier fanciful imaginings. We had found ourselves at the place which Toby and Daymian dubbed "Simple Sun HQ", that abandoned business park outside town, in that dingy little steel-shuttered unit.

Unlike the preceding episodes, the fight had been much closer.

My physical prowess had been altogether more realistic.

My fists more like skinless, raw chicken drumsticks than the granite mallets they had resembled in other realities. And I had taken some blows, too. Even getting stuck with those electrical needles from the stun gun. But after a bit of pain, and not a little angst, I had yanked them free of my skin and eventually persevered ... albeit with a respectable amount of blood seeping from various orifices and the odd bruise swelling up across the landscape of my body. If the universe was trying to tell me anything at all, I decided that it was that I'd be able to take Toby and Daymian in a fight. In the cold light of day, however ... although point taken the that light of day here was anything but "cold" ... I felt I had no choice but to acknowledge reality.

I was powerless.

And there was nothing I could do to fix it.

Or was there?

My eyes fell upon the tablet.

I huffed out a heavy sigh.

And thought back to that fateful day when I had walked in on the corpse of John Horsham.

With those scandalous photos of my ex-girlfriend upon the screen.

What if I'd just handed the tablet into the police?

Would Daymian and Toby have turned their ire upon me for having given it over to the authorities? Would Kelly and Fil have been spared? Or perhaps Toby and Daymian would've continued to seek out answers. Not trusting me ... such was their desire to get hold of the tablet.

I picked up the tablet, feeling its steady weight in my hands — much heavier than it appeared. I guessed that it was because these things needed a substantial battery to keep their apps all powered up. I pictured the battery — as if rolled over by a ten-tonne lorry ... flat as a pancake.

I tapped the Standby button and watched the familiar Simple Sun logo come up.

Why did Daymian and Toby want this tablet so badly?

And why was Emmerson Ray so completely blasé about me having it?

I had always believed at the back of my mind that Daymian and Toby were stooges, doing Emmerson Ray's bidding ... and yet, the more I thought of it, the more I considered the many words which'd spilled forth from Emmerson Ray's mouth throughout our acquaintance. I had started to wonder whether he was actually telling the truth when he spoke about everyone within Simple Sun existing in a kind of isolation. Everyone going about their own goals and desires.

Was it possible to have an organisation like that?

And if not what might it be called?

... A "movement", I suppose ...

I channelled back into the tablet sat on my lap before me. Already I could feel my thighs beginning to sweat from the heat of the device, coupled with the warm atmospheric temperature.

I might just turn what Emmerson Ray had said on its head.

If he wanted everyone to go about seeking their own desires, to indulge themselves in self-discovery, I reasoned that I wouldn't be acting outside of Simple Sun's mission by getting Kelly and Fil to safety.

... Whatever that meant.

But then there had been that conversation with Emmerson Ray the night before, on the beach, with Riko as my witness ... albeit not a particularly reliable or useful witness, but a witness nonetheless ... Emmerson Ray hadn't wanted me to interfere.

That suggested there was more to this than he was letting on.

And yet he knew I had the tablet.

... It just went around and around in circles ...

I tapped my way through all the menus, trying my best to find something that might help my situation. Last time when one of my friends had been in peril, I had gone to Emmerson Ray, but I knew this time that would not be an option.

The very nature of what I was doing was against his wishes.

I would have to do this particular deed myself.

And so I set to work.

I knew I needed to get Kelly and Fil to safety.

Did that mean they needed to leave the country?

... If possible.

That might be the best way to throw Toby and Daymian off the scent.

I knew that me and Riko needed to get back together with them.

That only with the four of us together could we plot properly.

Put our minds to work.

Calculate the exact nature of the mess we had got ourselves into.

The mess *I* had got everyone into.

Bringing Kelly and Fil to the island was of course not an option. That would be to corner all four of us exactly where Simple Sun ... whoever that truly was, whatever that truly was ... would want us. I knew I had to get me and Riko away from the island. Get some distance between us and Emmerson Ray ... But where would we go?

I flipped through the screens on the tablet hoping for inspiration.

I stumbled across a map app and gave it a tap.

Immediately, the surrounding area was shown upon the screen.

RAYMOND S FLEX

I had attempted to see where we were located previously using my mobile phone but had found that that particular functionality had been blocked. I suppose that even despite all those affirmations about freedom from Simple Sun, they still held secrecy as an important tenet.

I swept about the screen, watching for an viable place for Kelly and Fil to fly into.

To the closest large island to our position.

I did a quick search on the tablet browser — completely anonymised, of course — and checked out the possibilities for flights. They would have to change in Puerto Rico and catch another, smaller flight into the island but that was a minor detail.

It would get them closer.

Nearer to safety.

Now for me and Riko.

How were we supposed to get to the island to meet them?

I did some searching around and saw that if we could find an appropriate boat then it would take us about three, four hours to reach the island. There was of course the minor detail that I had no expertise in navigating a boat and — as far as I knew — neither did Riko. Another option would've been a plane, of course, but we would need Emmerson Ray's blessing — and not to mention a *pilot* ...

Then what?

For some reason, the thought of seeing Kelly arrive at the island airport sent a flutter through my heart. My pulse throbbed in my ears. I was excited about possibly seeing Fil, of course, just not in quite the same way. My logical mind put a dampener on all this fancifulness.

What was I doing?

What was I thinking?

Had I been away from the real world so long as to forget the rules Kelly and Fil still had to play by? They were contracted to LifeWare. And as such were bound by various company policies. Not least designed precisely to stop employees up and leaving at the drop of a hat. There was certainly the feeling that getting them to safety was far more important than any company policy ... and yet I started to feel the old world creeping up on me.

Its cold, clammy breath on the back of my neck.

I thought it through some more.

I could only ask the question.

That was all I could do.

And so I opened up Kelly's email and glanced over her text another time.

My brain chewed through it again.

Onto the memorable line right at the end.

I started typing:

*Hi Kelly*

*Have you gone to the police yet?*

*Marcus*

I set the tablet aside as if I had just completed some emotionally-draining task.

About five minutes later, as I was staring at the ceiling of my beach shack, Kelly replied:

*Call me Marcus*

*Kelly*

It took me a couple of taps on the tablet screen to locate the phone application. I used the number I had saved in my phone for Kelly. For a long few moments, I sat perched on the edge of my bunk just staring at the number, wondering what I was going to say.

Deciding the words would come to me, I tapped to put the call through.

The phone chirped a few times in my ear.

And then Kelly answered.

"Marcus?"

I breathed in deeply and then sighed out long and hard. "Yes," I replied. "It's me."

"Thanks for calling."

In the background there was a shuffling sound and background chatter. People talking amongst themselves animatedly. With a smart few heavy footsteps, the slam of what sounded like a door, the background noise on Kelly's line hushed.

"Where are you?" I asked. "Are you safe?"

Kelly didn't reply right away. I pictured her distracted by something — *someone* ... finally, she returned her attention to me. "It's over, Marcus."

My stomach dropped. "What do you mean?"

"LifeWare," she said. "We just had a talk from Hayden Shepherd. Everyone's been put on notice. We're to leave the office within the next hour. Leave the premises."

My head was spinning. "I don't understand ..."

When Kelly spoke again, there was a note of hysteria in her voice.

Someone who had just experienced a big shock and was dealing with the fall-out.

Kelly breathed heavily. Clothing rustled. I realised she was manoeuvring her mobile so it sat between her ear and shoulder, so she could speak with me and keep her hands free. "I've ... got to pack up my stuff," she said. "Make sure I don't forget anything."

Still feeling numb to what was going on, I said, "You don't have too much stuff, though?"

On her end of the line, I could hear the sliding of drawers, the clunk of wood-on-wood. "You'd be surprised about all the crap you accumulate while on the job ... it all just sort of blends into the background until you have to move it someplace else. Today's that day."

I listened to more sounds of movement — mostly thudding and thumping with the odd swearword spoken under her breath.

"There must be something else," I said. "I mean ... wasn't there a sign this was going to happen? Budget cuts, that sort of thing? You mingle in those management circles, surely it's something you heard about?"

"Nope," Kelly replied. "This one was a bolt from the blue."

"What're you ... going to do now?"

"Get my stuff. And get out," she said.

"And after that?"

Another pause. "I've had an offer, Marcus."

I reached up and combed my fingers through my hair, raking my scalp. "Right?"

"I ... don't know ... it's something I wouldn't have even given a second's thought a few weeks ago ... but ... I don't know ... now it seems like it's just come along at the right time."

"What is it?" I asked.

"I was speaking with Lucas," she said.

A tingling sensation passed through my blood.

Like walking across a grave.

"He's, uh, had an offer. Another company. He told me about it a few weeks back. Asked me to think about it. And I said I'd consider."

My brain felt as though it was operating on autopilot at that particular moment. "What's the name of the company?"

"Black Pine."

"Black Pine," I replied, as if that name meant anything at all to me.

"A start-up," Kelly continued, "although from what Lucas was saying they're maturing at a rapid rate. Only growing, it seems."

It felt as though the beach shack was spinning all around me. "What about LifeWare?"

"What *about* LifeWare?" Kelly said. "It's just a job, Marcus. They come and go. Companies come and go. I've got to keep on eating."

"Yeah," I said. "Suppose so."

It sounded as though someone was shouting in the hallway, outside Kelly's office.

"What's going on?" I asked.

"Someone's shouting at one of the managers. I don't know who. They're clearly not happy." She gave a nervous laugh. "I guess no one's particularly happy."

I needed to get back on topic.

Back to the reason why I had called Kelly up in the first place.

"Toby and Daymian," I said. "Did you go back to the police? When you spoke to them did you tell them about the tablet?"

"I ... didn't see the point. I thought telling the police about a pair of weirdos stalking me would be enough ... it seems weirdos stalking women is something fairly run-of-the-mill."

"But what about Fil?"

"He didn't want to say anything. I didn't want to get him involved without his say-so."

I allowed this revelation to drift about my skull.

The thoughts twirling about my mind ... finding somewhere to settle.

"Okay," I said, finally. "Where does this leave us, then?"

The shuffling of drawers and the thumping of boxes, or whatever storage medium she was employing, ceased momentarily. "What do you mean?"

My chest tightened and I felt my heart give a half dozen thick beats. "I mean," I started, feeling a bead of sweat trickle down the side of my face, "I thought you needed my help — Simple Sun's help with those guys ... they're after the tablet. And I've got it."

I could hear Kelly's breathing on the other end for maybe five, ten seconds before she spoke again. "I need to go, Marcus. I need to get out of here."

The sun was beating down on the beach. I was sat crossed-legged, feeling the soothing sensation of the rough sand up against my shins. It was early afternoon and I could feel my pale skin burning in the fierce tropical sunlight. Riko sat beside me, his feet stretched out, his hand thrown back over his forehead like an overwrought Renaissance woman, his chest rising and falling gently in the heat. He had a film of sweat across his face but his naturally darker complexion wasn't taking the same beating.

I had filled him in on the latest re: Kelly and Fil ... namely that it didn't appear that they would require "saving" imminently, which sort of kicked my plans into the shade for the time being. And, to tell the truth, left me at a bit of a loose end. I had never thought someone telling me that they didn't need me to act the hero might cut so deep.

The sparkling sea was gently sweeping into the shore, suckling at the golden sands. Blue sky stretched all the way to the horizon. Not so much as a wisp of cloud in sight. Further out, I could make out a yacht bobbing upon the calm ocean. I wondered what the people on that boat might make of the island ... of the blurred blobs that were me and Riko lying on the beach.

Did they think we were holidaymakers?

Millionaires with our own private island?

Or just some castaway beach bums?

They certainly couldn't believe that we were part of a "movement".

That this was the Headquarters of Simple Sun.

Helmed by Emmerson Ray.

An organisation set on nothing less than global revolution.

Or maybe if they knew the details they would see us for what we clearly were.

Just a bunch of marooned delusionals.

Riko straightened up, like a dozing cow suddenly bitten by a horsefly. He blinked away the sun-soaked daze he had slipped into and stared at me with an intensity I couldn't quite believe.

"I just had a thought, Spark."

This was not necessarily a good thing.

But it wasn't like we had anything else planned.

"Okay," I said.

Folding his legs up to his chest, wrapping his arms about his shins, and peering at me over his kneecaps like a bashful nine-year-old, he elaborated. "You know that thing that me and the girls found in your flat."

"The tablet?"

"No," Riko replied. "Not that — you know, the piece of paper, with those words on it."

Even despite the time and distance — the *forgiveness* — that had taken place following that particular scene, I could do nothing to prevent the blush filling my cheeks.

I settled on an unflustered, "Yeah," in response.

"Well," he said, in that tone of voice which always suggests he feels on somewhat unsteady ground — that he might end up invoking my ire, "why don't you try doing that?"

I breathed the hot air into my lungs, feeling it puff me up, roll my shoulders back.

It felt as though I might lift off into the air.

Just sort of float away.

That might be quite nice actually.

It would solve some of my immediate problems ... if I just floated away ... landed on some other island ... and stayed there.

"I don't think that's the sort of thing Simple Sun is about."

"Why'd you say that?" Riko replied.

"It's just a hunch."

"Why don't you ask Emmerson Ray about it?"

"I ... don't think that would be appropriate."

Riko stretched out his legs into the sand again and gave me a wide smile. "'Don't think it would be appropriate'? You're sounding like my dad now. Bloody hell! Come on Marcus you might never get this opportunity again. Think about it. If it's something you really want to do then this is the time. Just speak up."

"I'll ... think about it," I replied.

Riko stared long and hard at me. "You've gotta think about what you really want, Sparky. Otherwise other people will get you to do what they want you to do." He gave a pout and a shrug. "You can always find someone to pay you to do what they want you to do — when're you gonna get another opportunity to get paid to do what *you* want to do?"

I had to admit Riko was doing a good job of sounding profound, if not full-blown philosophical ... but I had to guard myself against such statements. I reminded myself that for all Riko had just said he was someone who most definitely did not live in the real world.

"What was it, anyway, Spark. Some sort of poem?"

I exhaled long and hard staring at a point on the horizon as if it was the focus of my wrath. "It was a comedy routine," I said. "Look, I haven't told anybody this *ever* but you remember university — "

"Bits and pieces."

" — yeah, well, one night I saw they had one of those open-mike kind of things, and I thought I'd give it a go ..."

I paused.

"And how'd it go?"

A smirk tweaked the corner of my mouth. "Not well," I replied.

Riko shrugged. "It probably didn't go as badly as you think."

"I sort of chickened out before I'd even started."

This only made Riko more determined. "Don't worry about it, Spark. Most likely you'll never see anybody who was there that night ever again. I mean, probability-wise. How many people were there, fifty, sixty ...?"

"Maybe more like twenty, thirty."

This enthused Riko. "See!" he said. "Just forget about it — everybody, those twenty, thirty people who were there, probably have. A long time ago. They're getting on with their lives, you know?"

I could see what Riko was saying. What he was trying to tell me ... but I wasn't altogether sure I could shake off such a deep psychological wound. Maybe I had to try. Was it the only way to exorcise the indifference I felt about the world around me?

That old cliché of "living the dream" ...

"I'll think about it," I replied, feeling the sunrays wash over me.

It was hard to believe LifeWare had been brought to an abrupt halt. That it would soon cease to exist in the real world as well as in my memory.

Perhaps that meant other dreams of mine had a chance of coming true.

Or was it just wishful thinking?

# A NIGHT-TIME WANDER

"What're you writing there?"
I flinched.

It was as if someone had pinched me on the fleshy underside of my upper arm.

I looked up, saw Emmerson Ray was standing at my shoulder, head tilted to one side, examining what I was scrawling away at.

I was at the Main Lodge. The beach was spread out ahead of me, those golden sands. As was the case most days, the sun was beaming down upon the world, making the dainty waves in the Caribbean sea twinkle. I could smell a faint scent of banana, and there was a tropical bird trilling off in the thick jungle further inland. There was also the mashing sound of keyboards from the Scripters pulled up at the surrounding benches.

I was the only person utilising ink and paper.

Sometimes it's genius to be different.

And sometimes it's the height of idiocy.

I decided that my best hope was that I might come to rest somewhere in between.

As with every day on the island, the heat was borderline oppressive. I could feel the sweat seeping out of every pore. I was constantly brushing beads of sweat off my forehead, making the hairs on the backs of my hands tingle as I did so.

My heart stopped beating for a few seconds.

At first I thought Emmerson Ray was frowning — then I realised it was a smirk.

"Uh," I started, unconvincingly, "it's something I'm ... working on?"

I realised as I spoke that I shouldn't have phrased my response as a question.

But it was too late.

"Hmm, yeah," Emmerson Ray replied, clutching his chin and leaning in closer. "I can see that."

My muscles drew tighter still.

I swallowed hard, hoping to drop my heart back into my ribcage where it belonged.

He caught my eye. "Sorry, shouldn't be snooping." His smirk widened into a fully-fledged smile. "Not good for the creative process." He glanced at the seat opposite. "Mind if I sit?"

"It's your island," I replied.

Emmerson Ray's smile faltered for perhaps half a second, then re-claimed its former glory. He sat, gesturing to Zachary, casually smoking a cigarette in the kitchen doorway ... was it something stronger than tobacco? With a heavy nod, Zachary wetted his thumb with his tongue and stubbed out whatever he was smoking, replacing it behind his ear. He disappeared into the kitchens. "Do you know what the key to human advancement is, Marcus?"

As casually as I could manage, I rested my wrists on top of the piece of paper I had been scrawling on. The immediate sense of panic had gone — replaced by the more subtle but not less pervasive sense of shame. What was I doing? What was I writing? How could I ever fool myself into thinking that it would ever be ready to show to the world?

"No," I replied. "I don't."

"Mm," he said, "I don't think that anybody rightly does, although if we study history I do believe that it reveals patterns. Can you think of any of them?"

I didn't want to admit I had studied history at university and yet didn't really have any proper knowledge of it ... education imparted is a distant secondary effect of university, but it's something that nobody is ever actually supposed to say out loud.

"I'm sure there are some," I replied.

Emmerson Ray grinned. "And you would be correct in that assumption."

Out of the corner of my eye, I spied the lanky frame of Zachary emerging from the kitchens. He was bearing a pair of perspiring glasses of tropical fruit juice. I wondered what flavour it would be today. I couldn't help thinking it would be impossible for me to ever go back to drinking cartons of fruit juice from concentrate when I returned to the UK.

It just wasn't the same as the real thing.

"Thanks, Zach," Emmerson Ray said as Zachary wordlessly placed the glasses upon the table between us and then withdrew, removing the stub of whatever he was smoking from behind his ear and easing it back between his lips as he returned to stand upon the fine sands of the beach.

Emmerson Ray gestured to those surrounding us.

The Scripters.

All with their laptops cracked open before them.

Tapping away at their keyboards.

Brows furrowed.

Among them I noticed the girl with glasses that I had last seen with Riko. I caught her looking at me and Emmerson Ray. She swiftly averted my gaze, returning to her work.

"Group-think," Emmerson Ray said. "What'd you know about group-think?"

At first there was nothing. And then there was something.

One of those fated LifeWare "training" sessions.

I sighed out long and hard, hating myself for having the information stored in my brain somewhere I didn't even know about. "It's when everyone approaches the problem from the same angle. When everybody thinks about doing things in the same way."

Emmerson Ray snapped his fingers.

I couldn't help thinking he was currently inhabiting his charismatic stage persona.

I wondered why he was trying so hard to convince me of what he had to sell.

Did he see me as some sort of challenge?

"Exactly," Emmerson Ray said. "*Group-think*. You say something because you think it's what the group wants to hear. And what's worse, everybody else in the group will agree with you because they want the same ... they want to feel *included*." He propped himself up on his elbows and leaned closer. "Do you know how you break through that?"

I shrugged. "By not having groups in the first place?"

"Hmm," Emmerson Ray said. "Sure, that's something you can do." He widened his eyes. "That's a strategy Simple Sun employs, as you are aware."

I thought of Toby and Daymian with a "y" and how they apparently had Emmerson Ray's complete and total blessing to be a pair of loose cannons ... in the way that a pair of computer nerds can ever be loose cannons.

"Another way," Emmerson Ray continued, "is to get different people involved. Different backgrounds." He dropped his voice to a husky whisper so there was no chance of anybody around us being able to overhear. "See, these Scripters, they'll all have gone through a similar set of circumstances, experiences, you know?"

A slight breeze blew through the Main Lodge and I pressed my paper tighter to the table, afraid it might fly away ... or, worse, that it might flutter beneath the table and Emmerson Ray might stoop to retrieve it — and *read* it.

"Uh huh," I replied.

"They've got all those *academic* subjects — those *sciences* — well covered. They've gone to college, they've got their computer science degrees, and they've gone to work in IT departments in whichever organisation paid them the most."

"Until Simple Sun came along."

Emmerson Ray beamed. "Until Simple Sun Came along. The point is whenever these people are presented with a problem they solve it quickly, efficiently, and as a group. But" — he held his finger up in the air as if he was proposing a point of law in a TV courtroom — "they'll often stay on their rails. Never break down the issue. They see the light and run towards it."

"Like they're dying?" I asked.

Still smiling, Emmerson Ray shook his finger at me like I was some devilish rascal. "Similarly as unavoidable — it's always the same with ingrained habits. People need to be shaken out of them to be truly effective."

I decided I should push the boat out. "And that's what Simple Sun's doing?"

"Precisely," Emmerson Ray replied, and his eyes shifted down. "So, what is it you're working on there?"

My chest felt tight. A single bead of sweat rolled down the side of my face. Although the warmth was oppressive it wasn't entirely the fault of the climate. I felt the heat off Emmerson Ray's examining gaze. I decided there wasn't much point in hiding. Riko was likely to spill the beans at some point so Emmerson Ray might as well hear my ambitions from my own two lips while I still had the chance. "Uh," I started, unconvincingly, "some time ago, when I was younger, I mean, I wrote this ... *thing* ... and, I dunno, I thought it might be a good idea to, uh ... *revisit* it? You know, as like a way of benefiting Simple Sun?"

"Hmm," Emmerson Ray said, before adding a slightly more committed, "I see." His eyes never left the paper I held concealed beneath my wrists. Finally, he lifted his gaze to mine. "Comedy?" he asked.

I was too surprised to be embarrassed. "Yeah," I said, "that's right."

He bobbed his head, looking at my notes beneath my wrist again. "They say comedy is a great tool for getting your mind into a creative state — into a receptive state."

"Do they?" I replied.

"They do," he said. "Comedy is all about holding up contrasting ideas — playing with them ... seeing what you can shake out."

"Okay," I replied, glancing off down the beach, to the sea sweeping into the shore, and wondering whether Emmerson Ray wasn't over-cooking the value of comedy.

At least *my* comedy.

"Marcus," he said. "How would you feel about taking on an advisory role?"

It felt as if someone had shoved me in the chest.

For a few seconds I was completely winded.

"Uh ... what would that involve?" I asked.

Emmerson Ray's smile dialled up a couple of notches. "Well, we're close to leaving the current phase of operations."

I looked about me as if there might be someone — Kelly? — to share my disbelieving reaction to the madness radiating from Emmerson Ray's words.

But who was the real mad man?

I was the one who'd accepted his offer and come to this paradise island ...

"And what ... *phase* are we about to enter?"

Emmerson Ray looked away from me, for the first time a wistful expression struck his eyes as he moved his focus to the horizon. "This isn't something you get to deliberate over, Marcus. You're either in, or you're not."

I thought again about Kelly.

About Fil.

And then I thought about their response.

That everything was under control.

That they were ... *safe* ... at least as far as I knew.

Now that had been established wasn't it important to get myself safe too?

... Or was I just being a selfish bastard?

Perhaps both were true.

As I shifted back to Emmerson Ray, seeing the intensity burning behind his eyeballs, I wondered about leaders throughout history. Those who had brought about sweeping change.

Had they been similar characters?

Had they drawn in, captivated those around them?

... Tangled them in their webs?

My mind made up, turning back to Emmerson Ray, I decided it was time for me to find out.

☀

I wasn't entirely sure what to expect when I heard the throaty voice from outside my beach shack in the middle of the night. I hadn't really been sleeping, the temperature was still sweltering. I hadn't had a decent night's sleep since I had arrived on the island. Maybe I've got Nordic blood.

I shifted off my mattress and trudged bare foot across my shack and peeled open the curtain covering the entrance. Standing there I saw Zachary, the head chef who was so attentive to Emmerson Ray's beverage requirements. He was wearing a kind of dressing gown made of a thin material with colourful, swirling patterns dancing across it over a pair of low-slung board shorts — the kind that you might use for surfing, if that's your sort of thing. He also had on flip-flops, the standard choice of footwear for everybody on the island.

"Emmerson is ready for you now," Zachary said, in his easy, Caribbean lilt.

I peered out past him, seeing the slick lemony reflection of the moon splashing across the placid ocean beyond. Everything seemed so still. There was no sound even of the animals in the forest. As if the whole world was keeping quiet just for a little while. Some evenings I could hear the clacking of computer keyboards floating in on the breeze from the Main Lodge but there was no sound at all today. I made to step out through the doorway but Zachary remained standing in my path. I smiled as if this was a simple matter of a misunderstanding.

"Bring it with you," Zachary said, simply, before turning his back and treading away.

There was no need for me to clarify just what "it" was.

I returned to my backpack, and to where I had stashed the computer tablet.

When I held it in my grasp, the weight was more than I could remember.

It almost slipped through my fingers.

As I reminded myself that this would be the second time I had dropped the tablet, my eyes slipped across the screen. And that was when I noticed ... there was no crack.

It had completely disappeared.

For a few seconds, my mind was racked by confusion. I tried to figure out what was going on ... maybe I'd imagined the damage in the first place, or perhaps I didn't have a bright enough light to be able to see the damage properly. I ventured out into the moonlight, held it up, catching a moonbeam sheening across the surface of the screen. There definitely wasn't a crack there.

Which meant this was a different tablet altogether.

Zachary clearly hadn't believed in waiting for me to tag along on his heels. He was already a good fifty, sixty metres away, pacing along the beach in a way that seemed at odds with the island people. They always seemed so laid-back, so unwilling to get caught up in the hustle and bustle of life ... never in a rush.

That was when I felt a thrill through my blood.

Because if Zachary was on edge about something then there had to be a good reason.

For what must've been the hundredth, or perhaps thousandth time, I wondered quietly just what I had got myself in for.

I was about to find out.

It went without saying that I was almost always perspiring owing to the island heat but when I broke into a steady jog — in order to keep up with Zachary — I began to sweat profusely.

I could feel the heat filling my cheeks.

My heart throbbing in my throat.

My lungs were too large for my ribcage ... a pair of ever-expanding rubber balloons.

Between fetching the tablet and returning to the doorway where Zachary had awaited I hadn't taken the time to jab my feet into a pair of flip-flops, so I was barefooted as I arrived upon the fine sand. I felt a few sharper, harder rocks lurking just beneath the sugary surface and I wondered whether I shouldn't have taken just a couple of seconds longer to consider my get-up.

It was a part of the beach I had never previously visited ... I don't know why ... I guess I've never had a particularly inquisitive mind and it was showing here ...

At first it seemed as though the sand was going to continue forever, that it was going to wrap all the way around the entirety of the coast. However, after about five minutes of sweaty trundling along, I caught sight of Zachary scrabbling his way up some rocks which emerged from the coast and stuck out into the calm sea. I shifted the tablet over to my other hand, held it down at my side. My mind wasn't entirely preoccupied with my physical exhilarations, I was wondering just what Emmerson Ray would want with the tablet I was bringing him. And I couldn't help wondering what he might say if he discovered it wasn't the original one.

In a way it was good that I had Zachary to focus on — a point in the near-distance drawing me onwards one heavy step at a time. When I reached the rock, I steeled myself. It was a clear night and the moon was full so visibility wasn't an issue. It was almost as easy to see the details of everything as it was at midday. I sank my teeth into my lower lip as I anticipated the first step up, immediately feeling the scrub of the igneous rock against the bare sole of my foot. It reminded me of those times when I had gone on holiday to British beaches and I had gone rock pooling. For whatever burly reasoning that all kids seem to be consumed by, I had eschewed any offer of footwear then just as I had done this evening. Back when I'd been a child, the soles of my feet had become accustomed to rough surfaces following hour-after-hour of conditioning ... lots of time spent going barefoot over gravel driveways and other similarly uncomfortable surfaces. A decade or so of wearing socks and shoes had had the effect of making the soles of my feet much more delicate than they had once been. I felt every single jagged point of the rocks I clambered over. And all this was of course made more difficult by the fact that I had to carry the tablet in one hand. One misstep would be all it would take to send me tottering over to one side, landing unceremoniously — and painfully — upon the hard, uneven surface.

Zachary was up about ten, fifteen metres above me now, and I could see the rocky surface was evening out. Beyond, I could make out trees ... although that wasn't out of the ordinary for this island ... just about anything that wasn't beach or rock was trees ...

My big toe stubbed a chunk of rock and I pushed myself on harder, attempting to keep up with Zachary before he slipped out of sight. My pride stopped me from calling out to him and asking him to wait ... neither did he look back over his shoulder to check whether I was following. With a giddy chuckle I wondered whether this was another of Emmerson Ray's tests — if he was checking to see how resilient I was ... and I'd been thinking my days of being tested were over.

Not quite yet, it seemed.

Finally, and sure I had inflicted more than one wound upon my poor, beaten-up office-worker's feet on the way up the rock, my toes sank into an altogether softer, claylike soil. I felt my toe throbbing from where I had stubbed it earlier and the mud was a little like a salve.

Zachary had disappeared between a cleft in the rock.

A dark space.

I held back for a moment, unsure whether I should continue.

Zachary had told me to come with him — *true* — but what might be awaiting me up ahead? I decided as I was already in this far that I might as well see what else fate had in store for me.

In any case, Emmerson Ray not only knew where I slept every night, I was on an island which I was unable to escape without his assistance.

And so I trod into the shadows of the cave.

At first the pitch blackness was unsettling. I had got used to how the sun would set at about half past six in the evening here — and that the darkness would descend like a sudden death before the moon would rise a little later to soften the obsidian surroundings.

I felt claustrophobic, as if the walls were pressing in on me on all sides.

A couple of times, I grazed my bare elbows — I was wearing a short-sleeved t-shirt. The touch felt as though it had come from some bony spectre rather than rock.

The soft ground beneath my feet gave way to a firmer surface, and then to rock itself. I felt the rock scratch the soles of my bare feet and wondered why I hadn't hesitated for about a second longer to think whether my choice — or non-choice — of footwear was really a sensible idea. Then again, I suppose many would argue that following strangers, or near-strangers, off into the night wasn't a sensible idea in the first place ...

I thought it was getting lighter up ahead. I wondered if it was the passive, lazy aspect of my personality which always looked for the simplest, and most conflict-free, means of escaping my problems. Because if it was truly getting light up ahead then all I needed to do was continue placing one foot in front of the other. I didn't need to, say, go back on myself, and abseil down the rock face I had scrambled up after Zachary. However, with the next series of footsteps further forward, there was no denying that it *was* getting lighter. It wasn't just the hopeful cortex in my brain — or whatever it's called — chiming into my interior monologue.

It was a neon-blue kind of light. It reminded me of those lights I would often see in butchers' shops. The ones which were used to zap flies ... great, now that had me conjuring imaginary flies buzzing around my head ...

My eyes must've got accustomed to the gloom, because as I crept closer to the light, I could feel a strain at the backs of my eyeballs from the glare. I brought up my forearm to guard against the unpleasant sensation, eyeing my feet as I continued on my way.

Finally, the whole cave was lit up in the otherworldly blue glow.

It was like being in a night club when they had UV lighting ... although thankfully there weren't any grubby stains to show up on the upholstery and floors.

The light bulb loomed above me, seemingly screwed into the ceiling of the cave, about eight or nine metres above my head. I sniffed a quick breath, and then shifted my attention to the path ahead. That was when I saw Zachary. In an opening, a steel door swung wide.

"Thought I'd lost you," he said. "You are a bit of a sluggish one."

If his tone of voice hadn't been so cool and the remark seemingly so off the cuff, I might've taken more offence. But as it happened the charm was too much for me to resist. I just ended up grinning like an idiot ... as if it was the greatest joke in the whole damn world.

"Sorry," I said. "Guess the sun got to me today."

With a flick of his beaded dreadlocks, he gestured for me to follow him inside.

Once I'd passed by, I heard the steel door swing shut with an ominous *clang*.

Whatever I'd just done — I'd definitely gone and done it now.

"Ah, Marcus."

It was Emmerson Ray.

But I didn't pay attention to his voice right away.

There was a lot to be distracted by.

The whole room was brightly lit — not like the blue light on the way here, but a golden, mock sort of sunlight. The space reminded me of one of those control rooms for television programmes. It was a hollowed-out portion of the cave and there were TV screens stretching across the length and breadth of the rock face. My heart thumped at the base of my tongue ... one of those primordial warning signals that any living organism avoids at its peril.

Perhaps I was about to learn the meaning of the word "peril".

There were about half a dozen people in the cave.

Everybody seemed to be wearing headsets except Emmerson Ray who wore his dangling about his neck.

There was a faint smell of sulphur clinging to everything mixed up with a sweeter scent of pineapple juice. I guessed there was some sort of ventilation system at work and that Emmerson Ray had commissioned some kind of odour-neutralising device to spare everyone from the unpleasant olfactory experience of body odour and flatulence.

My eyes were drawn to the TV screens on the walls. They showed various video feeds — what appeared to be surveillance footage. I tried to work out whether I recognised any of the locations from the island. I guess I was scanning to see whether my beach shack was one of the places Emmerson Ray was keeping an eye on ... but I didn't have time to draw any decisive conclusions. Emmerson Ray approached me, blocking off most of my view. He stood a half dozen paces from me. Zachary was standing almost on my heels.

"Sorry about all this," Emmerson Ray said.

I looked about me again, not really sure what he had to be sorry for ... or for what reason he was apologising. It appeared Emmerson Ray recognised my confusion.

"I mean, for getting you up in the middle of the night."

"Oh," I said, and then, becoming aware of the tablet in my hands, and shifting it in my grip, I added, "That's all right. I can always sleep in tomorrow morning."

Emmerson Ray gave me a slight smile. "Yes," he replied. "I suppose you can." He looked over my shoulder to Zachary, gave him a nod.

I watched on as Zachary took a few steps away from me and then turned around completely, disappearing through another doorway leading deeper into the caverns.

"What is this place?" I asked.

Emmerson Ray drew in a deep breath. He appeared to rise a full head and shoulders in height. "It's what I would term a 'command centre'. Or perhaps a 'nerve centre', if you wanted to get poetic."

"A command centre for what?" I asked. "Simple Sun?" And then, because I felt as though I was getting into the swing of how we were supposed to speak, I couldn't help but add, "I didn't think it was that sort of an organisation."

"Tonight is the night I welcome you into my cell, Marcus."

I couldn't help but feel the rampant homoerotic vibes resounding from this particular comment. This wasn't some sort of a jailhouse romp.

Was it?

"Recall our conversations about self-fulfilment," he said. "About how everyone should work on their own projects — do what they can to best further the goals of Simple Sun?"

I certainly remembered a lot of speaking — or, maybe, a lot of lecturing — but I wasn't certain I could recall all that much talk about organisational goals ... or maybe I had just drifted off for that bit. Perhaps that was why my marks at school had always been on the average side. I decided it was better to go with the flow. "Yes," I replied.

"Well, Marcus," Emmerson Ray said, "this is my particular effort — my ambition for advancing the cause of Simple Sun." He pointed at a screen. "Do you see? There?"

I tried to work out which of the screens he was indicating.

One of them was showing a map.

I was pretty certain that was the spot he was intending to draw my attention to.

"Uh, yeah," I replied.

I wasn't much of a geographer, or a "cartophile", or however you're supposed to refer to people who are obsessed with maps.

"That's the target," Emmerson Ray said. "That's where it will begin."

I shifted my attention back to Emmerson Ray. "Where what begins?"

"The revolution."

I looked back at the screen, then looked at Emmerson Ray again. "Ah," I said. "I see."

# THE KING OF COMEDY

E mmerson Ray was walking away from me, stepping closer to the screens on the wall. My heart had returned to something like a normal rhythm but I still had the feeling that everything could blow up at any second ... it was that sort of a place.

"When I started Simple Sun I always had this idea in my mind — that our governments are inadequate. And that our brains are no longer capable of managing the enormously complicated mess we have made of our world. We need artificial intelligence to take over. We need computers to guide mankind into the next phase of evolution."

As with that talk I had gone to see with Kelly, I could feel myself getting lost once again. I wondered whether I should try and walk Emmerson Ray back to some particular point where I could get a firm grip on things but — to tell the truth — I didn't want to seem like I was a complete and total idiot. I didn't want to rush to conclusions but the fact that he was saying all this stuff, that he had invited me into his "cell" — whatever that was — suggested that he hadn't yet made up his mind on my intelligence yet. At least he hadn't consigned me to the scrap heap.

Even if it was because he was using me in some way ...

The tablet felt especially heavy in my hands but I forced myself to stay sharp.

To keep my focus on the present playing out before me.

"But first, we need a testing ground," Emmerson Ray continued, and then waved his hand at the screen with the map. "This island, about fifty miles north, has a population of around a hundred thousand. Through-out the course of the past century, it has undergone successive corrupt governments which have systematically asset-stripped the island nation for their own personal benefit. That's what I'm talking about when I talk about human beings no longer being capable of carrying out rational decision-making once a civilisation has boomed in population to a certain size. Our brains are made for villages not metropolises, let alone countries."

There was a long pause while Emmerson Ray broke away from our conversation to say something incomprehensible to one of the people wearing headsets. I realised before long that I recognised all of these people from the Main Lodge.

Scripters.

Usually they had laptops in front of them, furrowed brows, as they knitted together line-after-line of code.

Once he had finished his conversation, and his attention returned to the map on the screen, I decided I should at least attempt to make this into a two-person back-and-forth rather than the lecture it was threatening to become.

"Uh, so," I started. "What's the plan?"

"The plan," Emmerson Ray continued, "is for us to take the island. To install our own government."

Emmerson Ray hadn't been wrong in implying that Simple Sun's ambitions were lofty.

I composed myself.

"You mean, like a ... uh ... *coup*?"

Emmerson Ray grinned. "I don't particularly like that word. It has the implication of violence. Of something being taken by unfair means, and unfairly held ... I prefer the term 'evolution of government.'"

"Ah," I replied. "So you're planning on evolving their government?"

Emmerson Ray nodded and gave a slightly giddy chuckle. "Uh huh," he replied. "That's precisely what we're planning on doing."

There was a long break.

And I decided that I was supposed to fill in the space.

"And how're you going to do that?"

Emmerson Ray hacked a laugh and for the first time I thought I detected the sign of mania in his eyes. That was different from anything I had previously witnessed in him.

In fact, I had reached the point where I would've believed it impossible.

I had come to believe Emmerson Ray was so level-headed, so logical in the way that he went about his business, that it was impossible for him to get swept up in emotion, to get caught out by something so base as excitement.

"One thing at a time, Marcus," he said, clapping his hand on my shoulder. "One thing at a time."

Emmerson Ray led me from the main room with all the TV screens and the Scripters. We arrived in a smaller, narrow chamber which had only a single computer station, a pair of widescreen monitors. There was a vacated chair in front of the blank screens.

"This will be your workstation," Emmerson Ray said.

I couldn't help my mind casting back to Lucas and LifeWare. "I get my own office?"

Emmerson Ray chuckled again. "You certainly do."

True, there wasn't all that much remarkable about the arrangement, save that we were perhaps a hundred or so metres underground in this system of caves. Actually, this was turning out to be a little too similar to what my first day at LifeWare had felt like ... from what I could remember, in any case.

Feeling obliged to do so, I sat in the desk chair, tested out the back support, and attempted to lever myself up and down a couple of times. Then I looked to Emmerson Ray with a sort of expectancy ... as if I had just turned up to my first day on the job and I was waiting for my supervisor to outline my duties. But Simple Sun — as I had well learned throughout my time on the island — wasn't that sort of an organisation.

344

Emmerson Ray appeared to have drifted away, thinking about some-thing else entirely while I had been inspecting my new workstation, but he returned to the moment now. "The island which we are intending to evolve is a perfect test case. They have no active military. Their IT systems are in the dark ages — a real white flag for any would-be hacker ... we won't have trouble wresting control from them."

Still sat in the desk chair, I stretched out my feet, wiggled my still-aching toe. "You don't think they'll notice that you, uh, take their government from them?"

"Oh, they'll notice. Sooner or later. But not until it's too late."

I scanned this statement for any signs of megalomania.

He had delivered the words so coolly, so crisply.

Almost as if it was an entirely normal, reasonable thing to say.

Perhaps it was.

Maybe, in a few decades, this would *all* be normal.

It might be that Emmerson Ray was controlling the whole world from this little bunker in the belly of some anonymous Caribbean island. And no one would know any better.

"How's it going to work?" I asked.

Emmerson Ray looked me in the eye. "They have presidential elec-tions coming up — in about a week's time — we have a candidate. Someone who has lived on the island their whole life but who is also a member of Simple Sun. They will stand, and they will win."

"Are you ... rigging the election?" I asked, wondering whether it was worrying that I was cottoning onto these undoubtedly horribly illegal activities just a little too easily.

"Mm," Emmerson Ray said. "Again, can't say I agree with that choice of language. It makes the assumption that the current system in place is fair and somehow legitimate enterprise, when nothing could be further from the truth. Throughout the history of this nation the ballot boxes have been fixed, votes tampered with." A thick smile fixed itself upon his mouth. "All we're doing is tampering with the system one final time. You have to operate within a system to destroy it ..."

My brain did some rattling around and my lips began to wobble before I could really do anything meaningful to stop them. "And what makes you think that the new system you put in place will be anything better than what's gone before?"

"Trust me, Marcus. A random-number generator could've done a better job governing than the particular assortment of politicians this poor island nation has had to endure over the past century. Fairness will make a long overdue appearance."

I glanced out through the doorway, to the main chamber where the Scripters were hard at work, coding their little hearts out. "And what makes you think that you can trust this candidate you've put up for election? What makes you think that once they get power they won't just turn their back on you — refuse to do what you say?"

"Well, Marcus, I honestly think we're well covered there."

"Okay."

"Because the candidate is me."

I wasn't entirely sure what to make of this latest development. For some reason, I turned my attention downwards, to the tablet which I still held in my hands. Almost as if it was a stuffed toy I had brought along to a therapy session to calm me down. Only this wasn't a therapy session and the tablet very definitely was not squashy or comforting to squeeze.

"I know what you're asking yourself," Emmerson Ray said. "You're wondering how I might be president of an island nation and still keep up with the rest of my work in Simple Sun — how I might continue to progress my projects with such responsibility?"

I had to admit that my brain hadn't actually got that far.

Perhaps my brain isn't like everybody else's.

Maybe it is just a little slower.

"We will be phased into all levels of government — all decision-making will use Simple Sun systems. Everything that can be automated *will* be automated."

I couldn't help but notice how emphatic Emmerson Ray was sounding. He certainly showed what I believed was the requisite amount of passion for someone who wanted to grab the world by the balls and show it who was boss.

"Now you're wondering where you fit in. Why I'm letting you into my cell."

Again, the weirdness of the terminology hit home.

Did we really need to go around calling things "cells"?

I looked to my workstation again. For the first time since I'd been on the island I was getting chills down my spine. Flashbacks to LifeWare. That was a chapter of my life which I had sincerely hoped was over with. Maybe Simple Sun was too good to be true.

As I had sort of expected all along.

"There's only so much that can be automated," Emmerson Ray continued. "We need content to feed into our systems — parts of the system which will require human feedback, and which will feedback to humans." He grinned. "I never did like the word 'user', I always thought human was a bit more ... accurate."

"And you want me to ..." I thought about what would be the correct terminology, but got stuck and decided to just have a stab at it "... *write* that?"

"Mm," Emmerson Ray replied, his eyes never leaving mine. "That's something you'd be interested in, wouldn't you?"

I looked out through the doorway again, to all of those screens.

I could just about make out the map of the island.

And I thought about what we were plotting.

No doubt about it, this was the sort of thing that got you locked up for decades. If what Emmerson Ray said about the governors on the island we were targeting was even halfway true I didn't imagine the prison system would be particularly welcoming.

And especially not to political prisoners.

"I ... sure," I replied, thinking about the alternative.

Or — more specifically — the absence of one.

Emmerson Ray clapped his hands together. The sound of flesh on flesh as loud as a thunderclap. "Then it's settled," he said, turning around, heading back to the Main Chamber. "You'll get yourself settled in. Someone will be by to show you around." He threw up his hand as if it was a trifle. "Essentially you'll have a stack of items that will require some words ..."

"And I'm the one to write the words?" I asked.

"Exactly."

As he turned to go, I recalled the tablet I was still holding. "Uh, Zachary told me to bring this along with me." I held it up as if I was some clueless school kid holding his homework up for the teacher to inspect.

Emmerson Ray flipped a glance over the tablet.

Smiled.

"You've still got it."

I thought that was pretty evident. "Yeah."

He nodded. "Take it to Zachary before you leave. I just wanted to make sure it hadn't fallen into ... *other* hands ... things will be a bit tense over the next few days. I want to limit any ... unforeseen variables."

I couldn't help thinking that this was the first time I had heard Emmerson Ray speak a bit like a programmer. Was that what he was? Some pumped-up programmer?

I watched him slip out through the doorway. Once he'd gone, I took some deep, cleansing breaths, and then turned to my computer screens. I guess it was time to get to work.

To see what I had got myself in for.

For some reason it just didn't seem to compute that it was the middle of the night.

My brain felt as though it was wide awake.

The upshot of having gone for a midnight walk. The pep talk from Emmerson Ray.

If talk of coups does nothing else then it sticks a hot poker up your arse.

Gets your attention.

One of the Scripters visited me, to give me a short tour of what were to be my duties. He remained disconcertingly vague about certain aspects and I didn't really see it as my place to ask too many questions seeing as I almost by definition of the phrase had absolutely no idea what I was talking about. After asking whether I understood everything okay — I patently didn't — he retreated, leaving me alone with my workstation and the tasks which awaited me. Once the Scripter had switched on the computer, we had immediately been greeted by a "stack". This was a whole list — disappearing off the screen — which featured various brief descriptions of things the Scripters needed some sort of text for. Despite everything, it still seemed a little dumb that people who were clearly so intelligent needed help actually putting stuff into words that other humans would understand. Because wasn't writing just another form of coding, after all?

Maybe it was *my* type of coding ...

With the Scripter, we had worked through an example. It had been a note requesting a sequence of descriptions to be added around traffic signals. It was requesting things like a written instruction on moving traffic from one lane to another. There was a utilitarian description of precisely what the code did. My task was to phrase the instructions in a way that would be halfway intelligible to normal humans. I thought it was just a bit of a stretch to presume that I resembled anything like a "normal" human being ... but I supposed I would give it a go.

Emmerson Ray *had* put his faith in me.

As I browsed through the list, wondering what I was expected to achieve this evening, I thought some more about the end users — the people on the island fifty miles from here that Emmerson Ray had mentioned. Emmerson Ray, I suppose, was also going to be one of those users, assuming that he managed to get himself into power. Not that that seemed all that big of a stretch given what I had learned so far about Emmerson Ray and Simple Sun.

I wondered if Emmerson Ray was planning on changing the form of the island's flag to the Simple Sun logo. That might be a decent opportunity. Jesus, was I already angling for a position in Emmerson Ray's Ministry of Propaganda?

I went through about half a dozen items on the stack before deciding rather arbitrarily that I had done enough for one shift. I guess I'd never make it as self-employed considering the lack of work ethic I have when I don't have a boss breathing down my neck ...

Just like when I would leave LifeWare, I powered down my computer, and made for the doorway. Standing in the way was Zachary. It almost brought up my dinner to see him standing there. He had taken me by surprise. I guess that anybody who works in the service industry develops that annoying skill of being able to go around near silently.

Seldom seen and never heard.

On instinct, my eyes fell to the tablet which I had set to one side while I had been working on the computer, but which I now cradled at my chest as preciously as if it was my first-born child. The most unnerving thing about the whole situation was how Zachary didn't say anything at all.

How he just sort of seemed to stand there.

Waiting.

... *Waiting* for me to hand over the goods.

For the first time since I had set foot on the island, I had to admit I was unsure.

... *Unsure* whether I should do what I was told.

Until now, Emmerson Ray's reaction to me having the tablet on my person had been so nonplussed. It seemed out of keeping that he was suddenly getting twitchy about it. But, then again, perhaps it was as he said and he just wanted to avoid any chance of there being any "unfortunate" breaches. He *had* allowed me into his "cell" ... whatever the hell that meant.

Now I had access to "privileged information".

That was how I read it.

I decided I was going to play it cool. Perhaps it was the geeing-up effect of being given a meaningful — *seemingly meaningful* — task to do. Something to contribute to Simple Sun for the substantial pay rise they had provided me with upon leaving LifeWare behind. And so, with what I thought of as a confident swagger, I strolled up to Zachary, smiling faintly, the tablet still clutched to my chest, and attempted to squeeze past.

Zachary, however, did not move from the spot. "Give it to me," he said.

His imperative tone was a stark contrast to his breezy Caribbean accent.

I hesitated a moment, instinctively feeling like I was making a mistake.

But what were my choices?

I was *on* Emmerson Ray's island ... I was currently in his *bunker*, or whatever the hell this place was ... surrounded by his Scripters ... now, admittedly, as with most coders, they weren't exactly the height of physical specimens, but they at the very least had numbers on their side.

And I didn't back myself in a physical fight with anyone ...

Looking over Zachary's slender but tightly wound physique, I knew who would come out on top if it came to blows. Let's just say there would only be one of us doing the blowing ...

I eased my arms away from my chest, drawing the tablet away from my body.

Zachary reached out towards me.

For a few seconds, we were stuck in kind of a stand-off ... neither of us willing to give ground. Until, finally, there was a low, persistent, *blep — blep — blep* coming from the Main Chamber. Some sort of an alarm. We both turned to look through the doorway.

As one, the Scripters were all looking away from their individual computer screens to the TVs mounted up on the walls. Every single TV screen had retuned to the same image. No longer were there several screens showing live surveillance feeds from either our target island or the one we were currently on. They were now showing the map of the target island.

One of the coasts had a throbbing red dot upon it.

A series of red ripples cascading out from its centre.

I think my mind had decided what this represented a few seconds before I heard the husky whisper sneak free from between Zachary's lips.

"Earthquake," he said.

I glanced about me, to the Main Chamber again, and everyone focused upon the image displayed on every single one of the monitors. I wanted to pick Zachary's brains about what this meant for Simple Sun, for Emmerson Ray's ambitions, but I reminded myself there were bigger things at stake. At least in selfish terms. I had decided I wanted to get out of this cave with the tablet in my possession if at all possible.

As we stood there with the same steady *blep, blep, blep* sounding Emmerson Ray appeared. As this seemed to be an evening of firsts, I wasn't entirely surprised to see him looking flustered.

His hair was sticking up and his eyes were veiny.

"Come on, Zachary," Emmerson Ray said. "We need your help."

Zachary turned to me, looked me over, and for just a second I thought he would wrench the tablet from my hold, relinquish it from my possession. However, after another cry from Emmerson Ray, he left me standing in the doorway, gurning at what was playing out before my eyes.

A few moments later I realised the universe had thrown me a bone.

This was my chance.

And I'd better take it.

So I bolted out of there, the same way I'd come in.

I was breathing heavily when I arrived back at the beach shack.

My heart was drumming in my chest.

And I felt as though my veins were filled with fiery sparks.

As I had jogged my way away from the cave — every fifteen or twenty steps stubbing my bare feet on something hard and/or sharp — I had expected to hear a shout on my heels, and to see Zachary emerging from the gloom, pursuing me, coming to claim the tablet.

Looking back along the shore, the calm seas lapping at the soaked sands, I could see the barest pink outline of the first of the day's sunrays beginning to inch their way up over the horizon.

When the tablet began to vibrate in my hands I nearly dropped it ... it was hard to believe — given my intrinsically clumsy nature — that I had managed not to drop it since that unfortunate day on the way to work on the bus. I reminded myself that this wasn't the original tablet. That I hadn't ever dropped this one. Maybe if I had dropped the original tablet hard enough none of the rest of all this bollocks would've come to pass. When my eyes fell upon the tablet screen, I saw there was a message in a simple, no-frills font:

*Black Pine Calling*

With a final glance around me and — seeing the coast was clear, literally — I ducked in through the curtain which hung across the entrance to my beach shack.

After swiping right to accept the call, the tablet took a few seconds to process the image.

I found myself staring at Kelly's face.

My heart sped up.

And I felt a chilly sensation in the pit of my stomach.

But I managed to get my visceral reactions back under control without too much fuss.

"Kelly?" I said.

"Marcus," she replied.

The video on her end was quite dark.

There was a golden light in the background, uplighting in a sitting room, that sort of thing. I thought there were others in the background, although it was difficult to be sure. The quality of the image was quite grainy and the connection wasn't particularly stable. I was treated to several seconds of frozen video frames while the audio continued to come through more or less clearly.

"Where are you now?" she asked.

"Uh, on the island," I said, and then, realising that this probably wasn't the most useful information I could impart at this particular time, had another go. "Back in my beach shack. On the shore, near the shore."

Kelly turned her head and muttered something to someone behind her.

They said something I didn't catch.

Most likely — if it was something even remotely technical — I wouldn't have understood what was being said in any case.

"You've still got the tablet," Kelly continued, a statement of fact rather than a question. "That's good," she added, and then, "We've been tracking you ... tracking your movements this evening. He took you there, tonight, didn't he?"

I filled in the blanks as to what she was suggesting by the "there" and the "he" in her sentence. There could only be two answers.

So I gave mine.

"Yes."

"Okay," Kelly continued, "and it appears that the disruption worked. Did you notice anything before getting out of there?"

I told her about the earthquake warning which'd flashed up on the screens.

This, apparently, was the right answer. Kelly became quite animated, smiling as she turned to speak to the others in the room with her. When she spoke to me again, she was positively jubilant. I couldn't help but feel a slightly warming sensation pass through my chest at my minor role in bringing out this feeling in her. "That's great, Marcus — great stuff."

I waited out a few beats, while someone was saying something to Kelly. And then I decided enough was enough, it was time for someone to fill me in on what was actually happening.

Explain things in terms I might be able to understand.

"Uh," I said, "what's going on?"

Despite myself, I felt a flush fill my cheeks.

It wasn't my completely my fault that I had become entangled with all of ... *this* ... whatever *this* was ... and neither was it my fault that I had decided in my infinite wisdom I would be better served throughout life to study medieval history rather than computer science.

Again, Kelly was conversing with someone else.

I overheard her saying something about this being a "secure line".

Clearly trying to advocate for bringing me into the loop.

I had to admit I was glad somebody was sticking up for me.

That somebody was trying to let me in on what was going on.

To make me feel just a modicum less confused than I felt right now.

Apparently having reached some sort of resolution, Kelly returned to the camera and replied, "We're satisfied the line is secure at our end. Are you sure you're alone there, Marcus?"

I was on the brink of telling her that I was when I heard the unmistakable sound of a cough coming from outside the beach shack.

Every nerve in my body fired.

And my heart skipped several beats.

Something told me to hit the Standby button on the tablet — to flip the screen off instantly so that whoever was out there wouldn't have the chance to see me conversing with someone else.

But something else told me to play if cool for the moment.

As if it needed to be communicated, I held my finger to my lips, indicating that Kelly and the others on the video call were to keep quiet for the time being.

I rose up off my bed and went to investigate.

I surprised even myself at just how sly I was in approaching the curtain which concealed the entrance to my beach shack. I never would've thought I'd have been capable of being quite so quiet — and intentionally so — for such a period of time.

I reached for the curtain.

Yanked it back.

And prepared to fight.

The night was a dark blanket embroidered with rhinestones. On the cusp of the horizon, I could make out the slightest wisp of cloud. It reminded me of when I first got facial hair. It had been all soft and curly ... and hadn't lasted too long, of course.

It had soon become wiry and uncomfortable.

Standing before me was a silhouette. It took my eyes a second or so for them to distil the features fully and take in who it was.

Riko.

Of course it was Riko.

Who else would it have been?

His eyes were wide with fright, his mouth slightly parted. "Jesus shit, man," Riko said. "You scared me half to death. I didn't hear you coming at all. You ever think of being a ninja?"

With my heart still doing its best to burst my eardrums, I gave him the glimmer of a smile.

I didn't say anything about the tablet, it would take longer to explain than just to show him.

And so I gestured for him to come into the beach shack.

The tablet was still lying on my bed, and Kelly's face was still there.

Riko gave me a questioning look as if it pained him on some level to be intruding on something private. I gave him what I hoped was a reassuring shake of the head.

No, not this time ... he was perfectly welcome to intrude upon my privacy this time.

With the curtain once more concealing the inside of my shack from the world outside, I told Riko to take a seat on the bed. The two of us focused upon Kelly on the screen. "So," I said, "as we were saying — what's going on?"

"Who's that?" Kelly asked, her brow furrowed.

"Riko," I said, as if this explained everything, before deciding it probably wasn't sufficient. "My flatmate."

Riko shot me a pained expression.

I corrected myself. "My *former* flatmate."

Kelly once more consulted with the others in the room behind her before turning her attention back to me. And now Riko, as well. "Is he …"

"Involved in Simple Sun?" I finished for her, giving Riko a sidelong glance as if I required his input at all … as if Riko's input at this particular juncture would be anything like a good idea. "No, not at any sort of high level. He's just a ground-level operative. Like me."

I searched for any sort of crack in Kelly's austere expression, but it wasn't to be found.

I couldn't help but think I had got myself tangled up in some very professional, very adult, games. Perhaps calling them "games" at all suggested I was well out of my depth. However, it appeared my explanation was sufficient because Kelly took a deep breath and began.

"I was contacted by Black Pine for the first time while I was still at LifeWare. They're a security systems company." She glanced back around the room to those behind her.

I still couldn't make out anybody else … it was too gloomy.

"They were interested in what had been happening with our servers. The attacks we had been undergoing. They were able to trace the attacks back to systems which appeared to belong to Simple Sun. As it happens, they're experts on Simple Sun — they've been tracking them for quite some time. That's why they're the ones who got in touch in the first place."

My mind felt as though it was pizza dough that a particularly bony-knuckled chef was giving a good kneading.

"They think that Simple Sun's interest in LifeWare had to do with John Horsham's work with them. From what I was able to work out during my time at LifeWare while doing John Horsham's job" — the way she phrased it was dripping with resentment — "Simple Sun believed he had stored some work he'd done for them on LifeWare systems, thereby using their robust corporate cyber security for protection. Not entirely ethical, or legal, by any means, but I can see the logic of why he might have done something like that."

My chest tightened.

I thought about the tablet which me and Riko were looking at right now.

And my mind's eye — on a completely unrelated note, of course — flashed back to that scandalous photo of my ex Olivia which'd appeared on the tablet screen when I had walked in on John Horsham's death scene. I started to speak.

"Did you ... uh, find anything he was working on?"

Kelly shook her head. "No," she said. "Nothing that stood out, anyway. Just standard LifeWare stuff. As far as I was able to see he just clocked in and did his work, like anybody else. Unless he was working on some other device."

I couldn't help butting in. "Like a tablet?"

Kelly smiled. "Like a tablet."

At this point, Riko nudged me in the ribs. He flashed his eyebrows at me. It took me a while to realise he was suggesting I was giving away some sort of secret. As if Kelly didn't already know about the tablet, despite the fact she was using it to communicate with us in a secure fashion.

"Yeah," Kelly said, in an off-hand manner, "*about* the tablet."

I prepared myself.

What was she going to say now ... that they had realised it contained some sort of a ticking bomb? That it might go off in my hands at any moment of the damned thing's choosing? Or was she going to ask me to do something comparably mundane, like destroy it.

"You may have already noticed but the tablet that you have isn't the one you originally picked up from John Horsham's office."

I breathed in deeply, and then cast a glance downwards. My eyes dropped to the smooth screen. The lack of the hairline crack from when I dropped it on the bus ... back when I had briefly wrestled control from the driver on my way to work that fateful Monday morning.

I had noticed that.

One of the few things on a very short list I *had* noticed ...

"When I took the tablet from you," Kelly said, "I decided the safest thing was to copy the contents of the drive onto another device and then give that to you." As if she needed to prove it for effect, she produced what was apparently the original tablet and held it up to the camera.

"Ah," I replied, wondering whether my lack of enthusiasm at this revelation was giving anything away. If it was giving something away then it probably wasn't anything of any importance. Deciding I needed to try my best not to sound like a surly teenager, I carried on making noises through my blowhole. "Have you been able to find anything out from the tablet? Anything that might, uh ... help what we're ... uh ... trying to do?"

Halfway through that sentence, I couldn't help thinking to myself just how ridiculous I was sounding. But once you've started speaking it's difficult to stop mid-flow without looking like even more of an idiot.

Kelly huffed out a sigh that spoke of the effort involved in summing up hours and hours of work in a meaningful way for the layman. "Not exactly," she replied. "That's why we're getting in touch with you now. We were hoping that you might give us some eyes on the ground — a better insight into what Simple Sun are up to."

I slowed down my thoughts — thinking through what had occurred this evening. I had been fairly certain that Kelly and co — since they had known about the earthquake, they had been the ones to sound the false alarm — would know a fair deal about what Simple Sun were doing and what they had planned. But from what she said it appeared this wasn't the case.

All of a sudden, I became a little self-conscious.

Perhaps I was thinking about the money going into my bank account.

The salary Simple Sun was paying me.

Simple Sun was — *officially* — my employer ...

But, then again, they were planning what amounted to a bloodless coup on an unsuspecting — if not undeserving — tropical island. And so I decided to spill the beans.

This, of course, led to yet more frantic deliberations on the other end of the call.

When Kelly asked me to repeat just what role Emmerson Ray had carved out for me, I felt completely ridiculous. I explained how I was supposed to be providing plain English explanations, or messages, or whatever, for the code that was feeding into the island's governmental IT systems.

Kelly's furrowed brow told me everything I needed to know.

That my job — and the tasks I'd been assigned — made not one lick of sense to whatever it was that they had worked out. Then again, I could only say it how I saw it ...

After yet more deliberation on the other end of the call, Kelly finally shifted her attention back onto me (and Riko) and outlined our next steps.

"All right, Marcus. Do you think you're in any danger?"

I couldn't help but think of the irony in how the tables had turned. I had thought I'd need to save Kelly and Fil from whatever was going on back in the UK. And things had completely flipped over. Now it was me who was — apparently — in need of a hero. "I ... don't think so," I said, considering the workstation that'd been assigned to me.

That had all the hallmarks of permanence, if nothing else.

Or perhaps it was just a ruse to ease me into a false sense of security.

Who was to say?

As always it was a case of all these high-level players with Little Old Me forever stuck in the middle.

"Good," Kelly said. "Then the only advice we can give you at the moment is to stay where you are, act natural, and hold tight. Okay?"

I thought this through. I wasn't sure I felt quite as confident as Kelly. But, then again, I didn't have all the pieces of the puzzle in front of me ... maybe if I had then I would've felt better.

"Okay," I replied, because there was nothing else really to say.

"We think we're on the cusp of a breakthrough," Kelly said. "The fact that we were able to penetrate Simple Sun systems, issue that false earthquake warning, gives us cause for hope. That we may be able to disrupt other plans they have. And that we'll be able to alert law enforcement to their activities."

A thrill passed through my blood as I thought of the implications.

Was I involved in criminal activity?

I guess that when someone talks about coups — stuff like that — there's a sort of assumption that there's an illegal element creeping in somewhere along the line ...

"What if ... ?" I began, but I could see the video had frozen.

The audio had been reduced to an indiscernible distorted hiss.

I waited another half minute or so before giving up and tapping to disconnect the call.

I breathed in deeply and then sighed out all the air in my lungs.

I only realised Riko was still there when he spoke to me.

"All right, all right," he said. "No reason to get hot under the collar about it — it could be worse, couldn't it?"

I looked him in the eye, unsure exactly how to phrase a response.

"I mean, look," Riko continued, and then, dropping his voice to a lower, more conspiratorial tone, "we're on a tropical island. We get cooked for. We've got shelter, a beach. Stuff like that." He nodded at me. "And you're, you know, getting a chance to give your dream a go?"

"What dream, Riko?" I replied, my tone of voice drier than I'd intended.

"You know," Riko said. "That whole thing about being the King of Comedy?"

I listened to the sound of my breathing some more — the gentle tickle at the back of my throat as my immune system combatted some minor tropical lurgy it had not previously encountered in bleak old Blighty — and then I responded. "I don't think there's much scope for comedy in what I'm doing — actually, it seems straight-faced as fuck, to tell the truth."

Riko shrugged, gave a slight frown, and then looked off out through the doorway of the shack to the dawning sky. "I don't know why you have to be so negative all the time."

# ACTING NATURAL

The weird thing about routines is how they just sort of sneak up on you.

When you least expect it, you're waking up the same time every day, eating the same thing for breakfast every morning, leaving your place of lodging at a certain hour ... and then going about the rest of your day in a sort of trance. It's definitely a trance because whenever you get back to wherever you live in the evening you try to remember what you've done that day and come up eerily empty. Like someone else was piloting your body all day and you've just leaped back in for the evening shift.

Given all that had gone on — all the Simple Sun craziness, Emmerson Ray, the tablet, Kelly ... — I should've been acutely aware, paranoid to everything going on all around me. But while it's true to say that I was somewhat on edge the day after the call with Kelly, after I got through with my duties — my first proper day, no less — I allowed myself to be lulled into a sense of security. That nothing bad was going to befall me.

Not quite yet, anyway.

It was an especially sticky day. One of those days which I'd learn to recognise came at the end of each of these patterns of hot weather. Soon — perhaps in as little time as a few hours — storm clouds would loom overhead and with a single, world-shaking crash of thunder, rainwater would come hammering down. Already, I could picture the scene, the Scripters dashing about the paths between the beach shacks — perhaps unadvisedly — using their closed laptops to shield their heads from the worst of the downpour. However, that wouldn't affect my day of work ... I worked indoors, underground, of course.

As I stepped into the system of caves, I was for a moment over-whelmed by the coolness of the air against my face. The gentle prickle as my skin puckered into gooseflesh and the hairs on my forearms and the back of my neck rose. I could still taste the woody flavour of the porridge I had had for breakfast that morning, tinged with toothpaste as I had hurried to diligently carry out that particular hygiene ritual. Most of all, though, I savoured the smell of the caves. While there was no doubting that above ground the rich smells of damp vegetation, the sweetness of gradually rotting fruits on trees, was calming, it could sometimes also be overwhelming. The slightly dank, earthly scent of the cave was a sort of pallet-cleanser. No matter where I would've been in the world, I could've dug down and found a stone chamber like this one.

Or so I imagined.

As I made my way through the Scripters, there was only the rattling of plastic computer keys, the odd sigh here and there breaking through the tinny buzz coming from the music in the headphones and earphones most of them wore.

Up on the cave wall, the TV screens remained.

They were tuned to the standard video feeds — the target island's surveillance systems.

They monitored comms on the entire island, also showing what was happening on the ground. Although I wasn't technically minded — and as I'd shown well at LifeWare, almost entirely ignorant of organisations and their power structures — it was pretty obvious that this showed the same sort of power and devastating control that a ten-year-old boy shows when he stands over an ants' nest with a jug of boiling water.

After a few half nods to people I sort of recognised, I took my place out of the Main Chamber, at my allocated work terminal. Slouched in the chair, I flipped on the computer with a practised gesture, only to hear Emmerson Ray's dulcet tones over my shoulder.

I nearly lost my breakfast. If taking control of that island required any degree of sneaking around then Emmerson Ray would be in his element. I swivelled in my chair.

Today Emmerson Ray was wearing a white shirt over a pair of black trousers. "Good morning, Marcus," he said, taking a step forward, that same wide grin spreading his cheeks.

After my heart had returned to its natural position in my chest — but with my pulse still throbbing madly at either side of my neck — I said, "You scared me half to death."

His smile expanded. "Never admit to fear, Marcus. I thought I had taught you that."

Feeling a migraine sparking into action, I reached up and massaged the side of my forehead. "I'm sure you did. In case you haven't heard, I've always been a bit of a dim pupil."

Shaking his head, but still smiling, he took more strides forward. "Always putting yourself down, too." He stopped smiling for a moment, his eyes meeting mine. "Don't do that."

I waited for the smile to reappear upon his lips but he continued to frown.

Something caught in my throat.

"Okay," I replied.

Finally, his smile returned.

He held out his hand to indicate my workstation. "How's it going? Everything in order?"

This was just like being back at LifeWare. I remembered when anyone — usually Lucas — asked me some question about what I was working on my mind would always go completely blank. Nothing would occur to me. I glanced back at my computer screen. "... Yes," I settled on.

"Excellent. I'm reliably informed that you have been doing stellar work."

I felt a slight glow through my veins but I immediately poured metaphorical cold water over it. If my working life had taught me nothing else it was to be as wary of praise as criticism ... perhaps more wary. One of the worst things you can do is do something right without knowing what it is ... because next time when the same situation comes along how're you going to know what to do? How to do it right again? I decided to play it cool, though, considering Emmerson Ray's chiding a few moments ago. "Okay," I said.

Emmerson Ray took a stride towards my computer screen.

I couldn't help but feel just a touch self-conscious about what I was working on.

I wasn't *precious* about the little descriptions I was writing for the bits of code which arrived on the stack minute-after-minute, hour-after-hour, but I was ... weirdly proud of them. I suppose you have to be slightly proud of the work you do otherwise you'll go completely crazy.

Nobody wants to be just a rat in a maze chasing cheese.

"Good work," Emmerson Ray continued, perusing the list.

My muscles tautened and I felt as though I was sinking downwards in my chair.

To tell the truth, I thought on some level he was humouring me. Why had he chosen me when he could have had his pick of the entire workforce? Especially with the whole "come-work-for-me-and-double-your-salary" pitch? There had to be something he had seen in me.

Something I had never seen for myself ... something which I *still* didn't see in myself.

"This one," Emmerson Ray said. "Right here."

I shifted my focus back onto the screen and to where Emmerson Ray was pointing.

It was a piece of code which — as far as I could gather — related to some sort of engineering controls. The labels that required "localisation" — the phrase in computer speak which referred to writing things in a manner normal humans could understand — I had decided to define as "Increase Flow" and "Decrease Flow".

"Do you know what this is for?" he asked, his stare intense upon the side of my face.

For some reason I was having flashbacks to a maths class long ago consigned to memory ... or so I had thought. I recalled Mrs Masterson — who used to go by the nickname "Mrs Ate-Her-Son" due to her rotund size — wobbling along between the desks in the classroom as we scrabbled to copy down her scribblings on the whiteboard. Her favourite demonic pleasure was to halt at a random student and ask them to explain — to the rest of the silent class — what they were writing meant. Most of the time, the student was unable to explain and with a wicked grin of triumph Mrs Ate-Her-Son would deride our entire generation as "copy-and-paste artists" as if it was our fault computers had popped into existence during our timeline.

It didn't appear Emmerson Ray was seeking the same pleasure. On the contrary, he seemed to actually want me to explain what it meant for his benefit. Only now did it occur to me Emmerson Ray might not have the time to read through every single line of code his Scripters were so busily producing and that he might actually rely on the annotations I was making so he could actually understand what was going on. Suddenly I started to see the scope of responsibility of my role and wondered whether I was truly worthy of this power.

And then I stopped thinking.

"Uh," I said, "I think it's for controlling pressure going in and out of some sort of water system?"

Emmerson Ray grunted to himself, neither an indication of acceptance or rejection ... it seemed to merely be a kind of quiet comprehension. "And this, here," he said, indicating another line of code on the screen.

I screwed up my eyes and wondered why I hadn't taken up the offer of those many vouchers which got posted through my letterbox to have a free sight test. It had to be impossible that my eyes were any sort of okay after the years of screen time I had put in. "Uh," I started in the same vein as the previous response, "that's an electrical system. Switches the mains off and on."

Emmerson Ray straightened up, backed away from the screen, nodding to himself. "Okay, okay," he said. "Looks like they've mapped most of the infrastructure. That's good news." When he rolled back his shirt sleeve to examine his wrist watch I realised he was shaking slightly. Just the fact he was worried about something was unnerving in itself. He nodded to himself again, and then fixed me with another stare. He flashed a smile but this time the smile didn't convince. "I've had good feedback, Marcus. You're doing a good job. Everything's going to plan. You will be a big reason for our success in meeting the objective." He stepped away, preoccupied with something taking place in the Main Chamber.

I thought he had forgotten about me by the time he was standing in the doorway, but he turned and said, "The election is tomorrow. Would you like to come with me?"

I glanced another time at my computer screen as if it was going to provide me with the answer to his question, and then realising I was being an idiot, I turned back to him.

I thought about what Kelly had said, that whole business of "being patient", or "going with the flow", whatever it was she had said. Wouldn't it spook Emmerson Ray if I gave him reason to be suspicious? Shouldn't I cherish the opportunity to be ever more confided in until the chance came to slip the knife into his back?

... Or maybe I needed to decide which side I was on.

In the end, my response was hardly as emphatic as Emmerson Ray would've liked.

"If you think I'd be helpful," I said.

However, thankfully for me, it didn't appear Emmerson Ray was all that bothered about picking me up on minor character flaws. He had bigger fish to fry.

"Good," he replied, his tone short, clipped, his gaze distant, looking out across the Main Chamber. Finally, he returned his attention to me. Gave me an unconvincing half-smile. "I'll have Zachary come by to your shack tonight — get you looking the business."

While I listened to Emmerson Ray's footsteps disappear off into the Main Chamber, I turned my attention back to the computer screen. More code that needed labelling.

More ways of saying the same thing only *better*.

In a way humans could understand.

In a way the *new rulers* could understand.

# A COUP BY ANY OTHER NAME

The sea breeze was pleasant as it blew back my lengthening hair. It dried up the sweat on my face almost as soon as it seeped from my pores. I was still feeling damp, as I had done ever since I had arrived on the island, but this was a different sort of damp.

A salty dampness.

Given that we were on the sea, in a motor yacht playfully dipping up and down upon the placid waves, the smell and taste of salt was thick in the air.

And I felt it exfoliating my skin.

Scrubbing all the old stuff away.

Making me new.

If it wasn't the first time I'd been on a boat like this then it was certainly the first time I'd been on a boat like this *and* dressed in a suit. I was wearing a white shirt under a jacket and straight, black formal trousers. Thankfully I had been allowed to forego the tie.

Emmerson Ray, who was half-hunched over the railing at the prow, peering into the waves as they dashed against the hull, was wearing the exact same outfit as me. Or, well, more accurately, I was wearing the same outfit as him. That had been the measure of things when Zachary had arrived in my beach shack about an hour before dawn with the zipped-up suit bag and a pair of smart-looking shoes. He had told me I had fifteen minutes to get ready after which he led me off on a maze through the jungle and down to the port. It was somewhere I hadn't had cause to visit before (I had arrived to the island on a small plane, at the airport a little further inland). There had been about half a dozen boats of sizes varying from a couple of inflatable dinghies up to three or four of what looked like recommissioned fishing vessels. Undoubtedly the crowning glory was the motor yacht we were travelling on right now.

The motor yacht was big enough to accommodate six or seven with space to comfortably sleep three or four within the cabin. Zachary hadn't mentioned anything further other than that I was to proceed to the port and board the yacht.

And I had done as I had been asked.

I had done my best not to spend too long staring at various bits and pieces of the yacht as if I had just landed on an alien planet. But it was difficult. This was a part of the world I had only ever seen on TV, on the internet, and so I felt as though I needed to fully absorb the experience.

There was a set of steps which led to the upper level on top of the cabin. This was where the captain was perched, on one of the pair of chairs in front of the navigational controls. The captain — although I probably should've guessed it by this point — was Zachary.

I had to admit I was impressed by the scope and variety of Zachary's skills.

I could see why Emmerson Ray kept him close.

There were three Scripters, too, including the blond girl with the glasses who I had seen in Riko's company. She was wearing a trouser suit, her blond hair tousled into corkscrew curls. I don't know much about hairstyling — and even less about *ladies* hairstyling — but I couldn't help but marvel that this must've been a gargantuan effort given the limited preparation time and the relative humidity. As with all the other Scripters, she had a laptop bag hanging off her shoulder. Ten minutes out of port the trio of Scripters set themselves up — laptops on laps — and beavered away on the bench seat at the stern of the boat.

One thing which I'd never quite thought through about boats was the amount of vibration caused by the motors. I had always thought it seemed weirdly retrograde to go sailing around the world with nothing more than the power of the wind to guide you, however, after about half an hour into our journey, I thought I was starting to see the reason why sails might be appealing. The boat engines hit a high-pitched, whining frequency which seemed to tap into the particular set of nerves and muscles which controlled my jaw. As I clung to the guardrail, it was almost as if someone was physically inducing stress upon me. Not that the boat — being an inanimate object — could be aware or expected to act on this discomfort.

Then there was the sour stench of the boat exhaust which seemed to penetrate everything. Again, once we were on the high seas, I wondered as to whether it might've been more prudent to get dressed once we arrived at our destination, rather than turn up smelling like a bunch of oily rags. Then again, I supposed that as with all else Emmerson Ray had carefully measured and calculated advantages and disadvantages before reaching a decision. Apparently smelling like oily rags wasn't going to be a deciding factor in whether or not we were successful.

The word "failure" didn't feature in Emmerson Ray's vocabulary.

I half expected Emmerson Ray to call us all together, to give us some sort of a briefing prior to the day ahead, however he remained where he was, standing at the railing at the front of the boat, hunched over, in self-reflection. I couldn't help thinking this was the most introverted I had ever seen him.

I heard footfall on the steps leading up to the bridge and saw the captain — Zachary — was descending. As he made eye contact, a shudder jangled down my spine.

There was something about him which put me on edge.

It was the feeling that he was a savage dog belonging to Emmerson Ray, willing to do his bidding. And all it would take was a snap of the fingers for the dog to descend into a wild rage.

Perhaps I was overthinking it a tad …

Zachary's smile took me off-guard. He leaned into me so he could make himself heard over the sound of the ship's engines. "Some snacks down below if you'd like." He jerked his thumb in the direction of the cabin.

I looked up to the bridge once more, seeing the ship's controls were unmanned. I didn't know an awful lot about sailing — nothing, actually — so I hoped it was normal for the captain to step away from the controls like this. Admittedly, the seas were calm, and the boat just seemed to be making mundane progress cutting through the Blue Yonder on its wavy line. Autopilot?

Zachary gave me a clap on the shoulder for good measure, and despite the smile which continued to stick to his face, I couldn't take my eyes off his the entire time. With a nod, he clambered his way back up the ladder and onto the bridge once more, returning to the controls.

Within, I breathed a sigh of relief.

I looked to the Scripters, seeing they were immersed in threading together yet more lines of code. Or doing whatever the coding equivalent is of dotting the i's and crossing the t's. I decided not to disturb them with earthly matters such as sustenance, venturing into the ship's cabin alone.

There was a pair of doors on hinges leading into the cabin, like in an old-style western saloon. As I made my way in, I have to admit I struggled for a few seconds against the force of the spring on one of the doors. Once inside the cabin, I was pleasantly surprised to find the rumble of the engines was much quieter, although I would've expected the opposite. The acrid stench of the exhaust was much less pronounced, too. Portholes gave glimpses out at the ever-perfect languid Caribbean seas — the sun glinting off the surface in a magical manner. There was a table with space for about six people, a cushioned bench on either side. The cabinets were all done up with a faux walnut finish — or I *thought* it was faux. Beyond, I could make out a door leading to the toilet, and beyond that one going into the prow. I had only to look around a moment longer to realise that the "snacks" Zachary had mentioned were located beneath the table in one of those large portable cool boxes people like to take on picnics.

*Normal people* ...

Until now I hadn't realised I wasn't actually hungry, and that it had been out of a certain fear I had obeyed Zachary's suggestion. Although he was an altogether different character to Emmerson Ray, I had a similar desire *not* to test his patience.

I would only end up coming off worse for it ...

I headed deeper into the cabin, realising I could no longer see the Scripters sat at the desk outside through the windows in the swinging doors. I thought again about inviting them in, feeling guilty to be gorging myself on whatever delicacies Zachary had prepared and brought with us for the journey. I decided against backtracking, though. Back in the cave, I had once interrupted a Scripter who'd looked particularly vexed by a problem they were working on. I thought that a nice warm cup of coffee might help them to start seeing things straight again.

I hadn't expected to be told to, "Fuck off" quite so unceremoniously.

I ducked under the table, feeling weird to be doing something mildly acrobatic in formalwear. I slid the container along the floor of the boat. It made an ugly scraping sound of plastic against wood but once I'd started I didn't see much point in stopping. Down on my knees on the hard wooden cabin floorboards, the lid of the cool box was difficult enough for me to prise free. Once I had managed to get the cool box open, however, a pleasant coldness wafted up from within. Smoky water vapour — like a genie spilling from the spout of a lamp — unfurled across the floor of the cabin. It took a few seconds for the water vapour to part and for me to be able to stoop over and see the contents of the cool box. I could see lots of tin foil wraps which I decided had to be sandwiches (by the size and shape of them they looked like they might be baguettes but I told myself not to get my hopes up too much just yet ...). Then there were a few large packets of crisps in there. Not that I would ever question Zachary's credentials as head chef — at least not out loud and definitely not to his face — I wasn't entirely certain crisps required this kind of preservation treatment, even in tropical climes. Below the sandwiches and the crisps, there was an array of drinks cans. They were all sorts of fizzy tropical juices. I had to admit I was *slightly* disappointed there weren't any naturally squeezed juices, but I supposed this was a coup after all and the provisions we'd packed were just that ... a way to keep us going to our goal.

Emmerson Ray's goal.

Simple Sun's goal.

... The first step on the road to world domination.

Over my shoulder, the boat engines got loud all of a sudden. The unmistakable fishy, salty smell of the sea breeze got into the cabin. Although I wasn't doing anything wrong, every muscle in my body seized tight. I felt like the proverbial child with his hand caught in the cookie jar.

"Marcus?"

I nearly leaped out of my skin.

I swivelled my neck, feeling the strain of my muscles against my throat.

It was the blond Scripter who Riko had been "going around with".

She held her laptop tucked under her arm and she released the cabin door she had been holding open, allowing it to swing shut behind her on the tropical world outside.

Blue sky, blue sea, and sunshine peeped through the windows in the doors, casting her in silhouette. I could see she was perspiring slightly and that her complexion was starting to turn a slight shade of red. I had a haphazard thought about asking her whether she had remembered to pack sunblock ... but managed to keep my mouth shut. She was wearing a cream blouse beneath her dark-blue suit jacket. She had on a pair of sleek heels the same colour as her jacket and I have to say I was impressed she managed to keep her gait so steady considering their height. Not that I've ever had an experience — positive or otherwise — of wearing heels myself ... I promise.

She stepped toward me and I gradually rose up from the cool box. "I don't think we've ever been formerly introduced," she said, nudging her glasses back up the bridge of her nose.

They had slipped down slightly due to her sweating.

"You know who I am," I said, soon realising how haughty this sounded even if factually accurate.

She arched an eyebrow. "My name's Danna," she said.

I opened my mouth to robotically repeat my name but caught myself at the last moment.

In the end, deciding I had to give something back, I said, "Raisin — Marcus Raisin's my full name." To fill the silence that followed, I reached my hand out for her to shake.

A few worry lines — so characteristic of Scripters — etched themselves in Danna's forehead. However, she gave my hand a shake. As we went to unclasp, our palms got a bit stuck together and both of us grimaced at the sensation. I took a step back, partially because of my social awkwardness, and partially because it was baking hot in the cabin and I could hardly bear the added discomfort caused by the body heat from another human being.

"What, uh ... can I do you for?" I asked, and then, glancing to the cool box, "I, uh, spoke with Zachary, and he said I should come down — get something to eat. Important to have ... *energy* for ... the ... uh, election?"

Nothing about the sentences — if they could even be called that — sounded in any way emphatic. I knew I sounded as if I was trying to hide something.

But I wasn't trying to hide *anything* ... was I?

Before I could add anything else, Danna glanced over her shoulder, to the doors behind her, then spoke up again. This time her voice was louder, though. "It's clear," she said.

My confusion — and not to mention panic — worsened when I heard the fumbling about coming from within one of the cabinets. Using those survival instincts faithfully passed down through year-upon-year of human survival, and supposed evolution, I turned to face the source of the sound. I pinpointed which cabinet it was, seeing a handle bobbing up and down vigorously.

"Wait, wait," Danna called out, crossing to the cabinet.

As soon as she squatted down I saw what it was that was impeding the door. There was a small wooden latch which had been engaged — I guess it was slipped into place whenever the cabinet was not in use so the door wouldn't loll open drunkenly while out on the open sea.

Now unlatched, the cabinet door swung open to reveal its contents.

Riko.

I should've fucking known.

Riko stumbled out of the cabinet, apparently still in the process of acquiring his sea legs.

If he hadn't stood out like a sore thumb simply by being there then he would've looked out of place. While we were all in formalwear he was bedecked in a Hawaiian shirt, baggy board shorts, and a pair of flip-flops. I guess it was a touch warm inside the cabinet because he was absolutely soaked in sweat. I caught a whiff of his perspiration mixed with deodorant. He looked wide-eyed, on the brink of panic. "Water! Water!" he said ... far too loud.

Acting in a motherly fashion, Danna, as all Riko's girlfriends end up doing, saw to his immediate needs, carefully but firmly taking hold of him by the forearm and guiding him over to the kitchenette and the faucet there. That was where her intervention came to a halt for the time being. Riko shrugged her off and stuck his head under the faucet, switching it onto full.

Powerless, I stood across the cabin from the two of them and watched as Riko soaked himself yet again ... this time in fresh water. I noticed the puddle beginning to seep into being around Riko's feet and at one point wondered whether he had stowed away on board in a guerrilla attempt to scuttle the ship. Why *had* he snuck aboard? Other than to make my life more difficult ...

Soon enough, that particular question was answered.

"Where is it?" Danna said, her face reflecting an inkling of the panic I felt.

Riko finally flipped off the tap and the splash of water ceased.

I glanced around, back to the doors leading onto the deck, sure this must have disturbed someone. But if anybody had overheard the slushing of water it hadn't been enough of a red flag for them to grow suspicious. Zachary did know I had gone below deck, after all ... and I supposed the Scripters knew Danna was taking a coffee break as well.

Riko straightened up, breathed in deeply, and then exhaled melodramatically. He pushed his fingers up through his damp hair, smoothing the thick dark strands down over his head. He puffed out another time and now his immediate survival needs had been met, he switched his attention fully onto me and Danna for the first time.

And smiled.

Never has a smile ever been so out of place at any time in history *ever* ...

"Christ! It was hot in there."

"Riko," I said, and then glanced to Danna. "What the hell are you doing here?"

Riko blinked another few times. Then he looked to Danna.

"Where is it?" Danna repeated.

"Uh," Riko replied, and then scratched the back of his neck. He looked beleaguered. His complexion was still red from being heated up in the cabinet. Finally, he appeared to return to something resembling the real world. "It's, uh ... oh ..." He trod past us back to the cabinet and leaned over, plucking the tablet from where it had lay concealed.

He held it up with a beaming grin. Like it was a trophy.

"You pinched that," I said. "Out of my shack."

Danna, however, was already on her way over to Riko. She gave him a severe stare and he relinquished his hold on the tablet.

I was fairly certain I was supposed to do something — the tablet was important, right? — but I wasn't entirely sure what ... it might've helped if Kelly, or anybody really, had clued me in on just what was going on. I could dream, I suppose ...

Now Danna had the tablet, her movements became more irritated. She held the device to her chest as if it was a pile of library books she was shielding from a raging downpour. She made for the leather sofa on the other side of the cabin and dropped down upon it. She immediately started up the tablet, her finger swiping the screen this way and that.

Feeling like an idiot standing to one side, I said, "Do you ..."

"Need your help?" she replied, without her eyes leaving the screen. Finally, she glanced up, flashed me a smile. "Thanks, but no thanks."

I gave Riko a slightly pained look and he gave me a smirk by way of response.

A few minutes passed and I was acutely aware of the world beyond the cabin. I thought about the others on the deck outside. Would they come and have a look inside? Would Zachary become suspicious about just how long I was taking to consume the subsistence provided?

"So," I began, the tension rippling through the room becoming too much for me to bear, "I guess you're ... uh, in league with" — I grimaced at sounding like a fifties superhero comic — "*Kelly* and the ... uh ..."

"You mean Black Pine," she replied, still remaining focused upon the tablet screen, her response more of an interjection than a question.

"Yeah, that's right," I said.

"Yes, I am."

Riko gave me a nudge with his elbow and dropped his voice to a husky whisper. "Kind of like a double agent," he said.

"Exactly like a double agent," Danna said out loud, apparently having overheard.

My natural reaction was to check for the doors leading to the deck, sure someone might've overheard. But of course it was near impossible to make anything out over the roaring engines, the shushing of the sea against the hull.

"It's okay," Danna replied, apparently a mind-reader, "it's a secret, but it's not going to be long now." This time she finally looked up from her tablet. "Soon this will all be over."

It felt as though the finality of this remark merited as smile, but her expression remained unmoved. Her face might as well have been carved out of granite.

She returned to the tablet.

"Okay," I replied, and allowed silence to overtake the cabin once again. Finally, I shifted my gaze onto Riko. "How come you know so much about all this? Why didn't you tell me?"

He shrugged. "I tried to find you, man, but you know how it is ... you've been busy ... doing whatever it is you've been doing. Whenever I went to your beach shack you were never there."

Whether or not this was the complete truth, it was difficult to say.

There wasn't much I could do even if I decided I didn't believe him. And what would it even change at this point?

I leaned into Riko and dropped my voice again, my gaze falling upon Danna who was working away in a borderline frenzied manner — tapping here, swiping there. "So," I said, "what's she actually doing?"

Apparently Danna overheard. "*She's* trying to stop Emmerson Ray's head expanding so much that it makes him rise into the air and float away."

A couple more seconds ticked by. "That sounds ... empathetic," I replied.

Still focused upon the screen, Danna pouted and tilted her head to one side, considering my comment. "It's one way to look at it."

I looked to Riko, and then back to Danna, and then to the windows which looked out across the deck. Because I couldn't help it, I blew out a long, continuous sigh. I picked out a spot on the cabin wall that didn't look particularly uncomfortable and leaned my shoulder up against it.

Riko mirrored my gesture.

I pressed the side of my skull against the wall, feeling the vibration from the ship's engines ploughing through me, rumbling through my entire nervous system. It made the tips of my fingers and toes tingle. I closed my eyes and recited what had become my mantra at some point in my mid-to-late twenties. It also happened to be what Danna had said a few moments earlier. She had plucked my thoughts from the air as if my brain was nothing more than a database to be hacked.

*Soon this will all be over.*

# ELECTION DAY

It was the strange motion that brought me around.

And the change in sound and vibration of the ship's engines.

The engines hit a throaty, low-frequency sound and I could hear the constant gush of water being jetted out of some mechanical orifice.

When I opened my eyes, I realised I was lying on my back on the sofa down in the cabin. The ceiling was an odd colour that seemed to shift from beige to vanilla depending on which I convinced my brain it was. I was still wearing my shirt and trousers but I had shucked the jacket and hung it off the back of one of the chairs at the table. Although there was a mild air-conditioning unit in the cabin, I still felt that familiar film of sweat covering the entire surface of my skin.

This was just how it was in the tropics, I supposed.

As I lay there, I realised that the boat was yawing slightly to the side.

I glanced through the porthole nearest me and saw only sea, but then I switched to the other side and was surprised to see a concrete wall:

The dock.

I eased myself up into a sitting position and then rubbed the sides of my head, doing my best to smother the fledgling migraine that threatened to squeeze my brain in its fist. When I looked around the cabin, I saw that nobody else was down here. The cool box, however, had returned to its previous spot beneath the table. I guessed that while I had slept the others had been down here and gorged themselves on its contents. There was no sign of Riko either, which meant he had either been discovered and very quietly taken prisoner by the others, or he had returned to the cabinet where he had initially concealed himself.

Knowing Riko as I unfortunately did, I was fairly certain they wouldn't have taken him quietly ... there certainly would've been enough noise to raise an entire street from deep sleep, let alone one anxious dozing man.

Even with the noise and vibration from the ship's engines.

There wasn't any sign of Danna and I supposed she had returned to the deck.

I heard shouts outside, up on the dock, and I watched a rope being hurled past the porthole and being pulled tight. The boat inched closer to the concrete wall.

Stifling a yawn with the back of my hand, I hooked the jacket off the back of the chair and threw it over my shoulders. Then I slipped out through the double doors and back onto the deck.

Immediately the full heat of the sun struck me. Its brightness blinded me afresh. As I brought up my forearm to cover my eyes, I realised that while the ship had been at sea, the wind had rushed across the deck, creating a pleasant breeze. But as that breeze was no longer being generated the sun had the chance to have its say.

"Here you go, mon."

I hardly had time to get my bearings before I felt something land on my head. Instantly there was shade all around. When I reached up, I realised it was a sunhat, of course, and when I looked around some more I saw Zachary handing out wide-brimmed straw hats.

I picked out the others standing on deck.

The other two Scripters.

And then there was Danna.

I attempted to catch her eye but she was having none of it ... I suppose it might only raise suspicion if the two of us were to commence being matey-mates after never having exchanged a word. Thinking about it, I was glad I hadn't been called into action as a double agent.

I was fairly certain I wouldn't have been a good one ...

Further up, on the bridge, I saw Emmerson Ray was standing upright, his chest puffed out, none of that previous posture where he'd been collapsed over the rail and looking somewhat defeated at all present now.

Up on the dock, I watched a pair of workers wearing short shorts and t-shirts tattered from long hours of working with heavy equipment in the hot sun, tying off the ropes to the bollards embedded in the concrete. Another one of them appeared bearing a wooden walkway which — with the assistance of Zachary — they placed between the side of the boat and the dock. I looked around, to the other two Scripters, their laptops tucked into their armpits. Although I wasn't a mind reader I was fairly certain they looked twitchy. Danna, however, looked confident, unshaken.

Once the walkway was in place Emmerson Ray strode over to it and then gestured for us to come to him. With the other three, I ambled my way along, headed for where he stood. I'm not sure quite how it happened, but I ended up being the first to arrive. When I made eye contact with Emmerson Ray, I was certain I saw something. A glimmer in his eye? It sent a quiver through my belly. Before I had time to dwell on the sensation, the others had arrived behind me.

I looked out ahead.

Zachary was still on board, his foot pressed firmly upon the walkway, keeping it secure to the boat, while the two workers manned the other end up on the dock.

Thinking of Riko, I resisted the urge to glance back at the cabin, knowing it would only raise suspicion. And so I looked forward, immediately finding myself confronted with the narrow plank of wood barely connecting the boat with dry land. The sea water was about two, three metres below. Through the kaleidoscopic film of spilled fuel, I could see fishes swimming. I looked up again, to the men holding down the plank, knowing all I had to do was put one foot in front of the other and I'd be there in no time at all. As I took my first step, I heard Emmerson Ray's voice on my heels. "Go on, Marcus. Show us how it's done."

A large black car with tinted windows picked us up almost right on the dock.

We all piled into the back seats — me and Emmerson Ray sitting facing backwards while the Scripters were facing forwards. I could see the boat through the tinted rear window.

Zachary was going about his business, doing all the mooring tasks.

I felt a slight heaviness in my gut to think that Riko was still stowed away in the cabinet down in the cabin. I wondered why he was actually on board ... thinking about it he had never answered the question directly. But when did Riko ever?

At first, the air conditioning within the car seemed a long-awaited mercy — a salve for the desperate heat we had endured during our voyage. Soon, though, after about ten minutes of driving our way along winding, poorly asphalted roads with rocks scattered across the surface and the odd pothole for variation, it felt as though I was standing in an ice-cold stream.

I started to shudder.

When I looked over the Scripters, I saw they too were struggling with the temperature.

Emmerson Ray, however, was entirely unmoved. His gaze fixed on some point in mid-air, completely focused on achieving his goal. Or so I thought.

"Danna?" he said.

This seemed to surprise Danna as much as it did me.

She stirred from the semi-catatonic state we had all slipped into. "Yeah," she replied.

"Did we ever discover the source of that glitch? The earthquake warning?"

Danna blinked rapidly several times. Emmerson Ray missed this re-action as he was looking out the window. She glanced at me briefly, but then composed herself and returned her attention to him. "Pietr narrowed it down to a faulty ambient temperature sensor."

Emmerson Ray didn't react.

It felt as though everybody in the car — including the driver, over mine and Emmerson Ray's shoulders — was holding their breath.

Finally, Emmerson Ray nodded vaguely and mouthed, "Okay."

I thought about the earthquake warning. The alarms that had sounded. On the call afterwards Kelly had claimed it as a victory. It had been Black Pine behind the whole deal.

And Danna was their person on the inside.

Even though I knew I was being ridiculous, I couldn't help but feel a little put out.

What did that make me?

Just some idiot being washed along — making up numbers?

I recalled how Kelly had said that my job was to "act natural".

It all felt as though I was being treated like a child.

Emmerson Ray stirred from his thoughts once again. He glanced around as if he had just woken up from a disturbing dream. He took stock of our surroundings outside the car.

The road was well tarmacked here, smooth. The buildings on either side of the road were a variety of pastel shades — faded salmon, teal, olive paint. The telephone or electrical cables drooped down in a defeated manner in between their wooden pylons.

"We're about ten minutes away," Emmerson Ray said. "It's nearly time."

He focused his full attention on me.

And I felt my stomach gurgle.

"Have you got the speech, Marcus?"

It felt as though everybody's eyes were on me. I reached into the inside pocket of my jacket and removed the piece of paper that I had folded in two and which bore the contents of Emmerson Ray's election victory speech. For a second, I felt somewhat paternal about its contents, wanting to shield them for as long as I possibly could. I recalled Emmerson Ray's calming words, how he had told me that nobody ever remembered victory speeches.

That there was no pressure on me.

Now we were actually here, though, now that we were actually doing this, I couldn't help but feel a large amount of anxiety.

I handed it over to him.

Emmerson Ray held the paper — still folded — between his fingers. Some time passed. I wondered what he was waiting for — when he was going to unfold the paper and look at what I had written. In the end, though, he just gave me a nod of what I suppose could've been interpreted as gratitude and tucked the paper into his suit jacket's inside pocket.

We turned several corners, rising up a steep hill, passing through a thick patch of jungle — trees clustered together on either side. If we had cranked the windows down, I know the air would've smelled thick and fruity, just like the island we had left that morning.

Inside the car, though, with the air conditioning blowing, it felt almost like we were passing through a museum. Like we were one stage removed from the real world.

Not that I was complaining that I wasn't having to hike up this hill in formal wear ... and my smooth-soled black leather shoes.

A smattering of three- or four-story bright white buildings greeted us at the top of the hill.

The landscaping surrounding the car became more pristine.

It was the well-organised result of human hands.

There were neatly pruned bushes and a series of flowerbeds alongside the road. The thick foliage which we had passed through on the way to get here had been cut back to leave exposed rock. Only weedy grasses growing up through the gaps had been spared the strimmer.

The car came to a halt outside one of the buildings.

By that time I had had counted them.

There were five in all, clustered into what I decided was the shape of a pentagram.

Whether or not that was an omen, I was unsure.

I had always been somewhat undecided about the devil.

... In more ways than just one.

The driver came around to open the back door of the car, and he doffed his cap to Emmerson Ray as he clambered out. I looked to the other Scripters, my eyes crossing with Danna ever so briefly, before I followed Emmerson Ray.

The sun's reflection off the bright white buildings was almost blinding now that I didn't have the shading quality of the tinted glass from inside the car. The heat, too, hit me like a crashing wave. It felt as if I started to sweat instantly. The car had stopped in the spot at the centre of the five buildings ... well, not quite in the centre. At the very centre of the asphalted circle, there was a statue about three metres tall which depicted a Caribbean islander, dressed in what I thought was probably seventeenth-century ship captain's garb, his chest thrust out proudly, a telescope held at his waist, the other hand at his brow shielding his eyes from the sun as he looked to the horizon.

As I followed his gaze, I saw it stretched out to encompass the settlement below.

What I supposed was the capital of the island. More of those pastel-toned, single-storey buildings interspersed with sprouting emerald trees. It was a weird view because it was almost like looking over a ghost town. The trees hid most of the roads between the buildings, with only the odd space, here and there, giving away the ponderous light traffic meandering along.

"Algerknot Summerby," Emmerson Ray said, standing at my shoulder.

I realised he was talking about who the statue represented.

I gave Algerknot another look over as if this new information might make me see the statue in another light. But, no, it was just a statue.

"One of my ancestors," Emmerson Ray said. "I am a direct descendent, actually, something which has been of great assistance in my campaign."

This time I did examine the statue with that in mind.

Trying to see the resemblance.

Was it just my imagination or did they have the same chin?

"Ah," Emmerson Ray said. "Looks like the welcoming party is here."

My eyes followed his to the entrance of one of the buildings and I saw a suited woman flanked by a pair of younger male assistants, similarly formerly dressed. I wondered if they were only dressed that way today because it was an important event. I could never quite get my head around the idea that someone could dress in a suit and live in a hot climate. The woman had braided hair and a complexion of hazelnut butter. She walked with purpose and wore something between a smirk and a frown. An expression to keep you guessing.

"Emmy," she said, her accent lilting, almost affectionate. "How was the trip?"

Emmerson Ray met her with a beaming smile. "Smooth sailing, all the way."

She flipped a gaze over me, Danna, and the other two Scripters. "I see you've brought along all your merry men."

Emmerson Ray shrugged. "You've gotta have back-up sometimes." He turned to the four of us. "This is my sister, Clara," he said.

I started to feel a strange tickle at the bottom of my gut. It seemed somehow even more of a family affair with Emmerson Ray's ancestor — in statue form — looming large over us all too. I guess that this whole election business hadn't been so much of a long shot after all.

I was beginning to wonder just where Simple Sun fitted in.

"Well, then," Clara said, turning on her heel. "You'd best be following me."

As Emmerson Ray, Clara, and her two assistants, headed for the building from which they had emerged, I looked over Danna and the other two Scripters.

We exchanged a glance but none of us said anything.

With a hard swallow, I fixed my eyes upon Emmerson Ray's heels and placed one foot in front of the other. I hadn't taken half a dozen steps before I heard the engine thunder back into life as the car pulled away, leaving us stranded.

The lobby of the building smelled strongly of disinfectant and floor polish. It was all white tiles. There was a reception desk with a young receptionist examining her well-manicured red fingernails. When she heard our footfall, she looked up and her eyes widened as she took stock of Emmerson Ray. Her mouth formed a small, dark circle. I looked a little closer at her as we passed through the lobby. Her eyes never left Emmerson Ray. I guess he was something of a celebrity.

We took the lift up to the top floor of the building.

This turned out to be an open-plan area the size of a football pitch with windows occupying every wall, giving a three-hundred-and-sixty degree view out across the entirety of the island. I gazed down at the capital stretched out below and then to the dock where I could just make out the wooden jetties. I wasn't able to identify the exact location of the ship we had arrived on earlier, but I couldn't help imagining just what Riko was getting up to *down there* ... When I got to thinking about whether or not Zachary might have discovered him by now, my thoughts were cut off by Emmerson Ray calling us all together.

Clara — Emmerson Ray's sister — had apparently pressed a button somewhere and a large cinematic screen was lowering into view, grumbling mechanically to itself as it went.

I looked about the others, seeing Clara's two male assistants and wondering vaguely to myself whether they might be some sort of security personnel.

Were they armed?

That sent a thrill through my bloodstream.

I could really do without there being guns involved ...

Standing alongside Danna, close enough so I could hear her deep breathing, with other Scripters to my side, I fixed my attention upon the screen. The picture flickered into life. It was barely possible to make out the image. The sun shone in brightly through the windows. As if Clara — or one of her assistants — had read my mind, the sunshades began to lower, blotting out the sunlight and steadily plunging us into gloom.

Emmerson Ray arrived standing beside me, folding his arms across his chest.

The screen flitted onto a TV transmission — a news report.

It was a female reporter, about in her early thirties, her hair carved into cornfields. She wore a businesslike, serious expression as she stood with a beach in the background, the fronds of the palm trees blowing gently in the island breeze. Like Clara, and her assistants, she seemed unfazed to be wearing a fully-fledged trouser suit even in this tropical climate. "Yes," she said, apparently responding to someone back in the news studio, "people have been filing into polling stations all day long, casting their votes. However, as polls closed five minutes ago, we are now able to give first indications of the result. What we are looking at is an extremely close-run race between the incumbent Hendricson Hendrick of the Modern Liberal Party and Emmerson Ray of the Simple Sun Party — a big surprise given the high-polling majority for Hendrick prior to the campaign. However, as everyone watching will well know, Emmerson Ray saw a surge in popularity leading up to election day. Still, we can safely say we did not expect to see a race this tight."

I shifted a glance at Emmerson Ray, worried about the obviousness of the name he had chosen for his political party. I'd thought Simple Sun was supposed to be a borderline secret organisation.

Emmerson Ray met my gaze. I sensed the tension he had emanated earlier in the day had dissipated somewhat. As if his worst fears had been assuaged by this reporter's words.

There was an unseen voice onscreen. Apparently from the studio. "And, Jenna, do you know what time we'll have the official results by?"

The reporter, Jenna, replied with the same firm expression fixed upon her face. "We'll have official confirmation by nine o'clock this evening."

The camera flipped back to the newsroom, a suited man and a woman, both of them with shiny-looking complexions in the studio spotlights. The sound muted as an infographic appeared on the screen, showing the voter turn-out by locality or parish, or however the island was organised. Nobody in the room said anything.

And then Emmerson Ray spoke up.

"So," he said, "nothing left to do but wait." He glanced back at Danna and the two Scripters. "Clara, do you think we could set up somewhere?"

"Of course," Clara replied, now wearing an easy smile I would've thought impossible earlier on. She gestured for the Scripters and Danna to follow, one of her assistants going with her.

I watched on, Emmerson Ray and Clara's other assistant beside me, as they ventured back into the lift and disappeared behind the sliding doors.

Emmerson Ray bowed his head and strode over to the windows which looked out across the capital, and the whole island below. He rested his forehead against the glass, his arm also pressed against the glass over his head.

I went to join him.

At first I was unsure whether Emmerson Ray wanted me to be anywhere near him, however, as he sensed me approaching he gave me a slight smile and beckoned me closer.

Looking over my shoulder, I saw Clara's assistant had taken up a position by the lift.

It felt almost as if he was standing guard.

To keep someone out. Or to keep us in.

"It's almost over," Emmerson Ray said. "One way or another ..."

I wondered if he was wary of putting his doubts into words. He appeared to have spent a good portion of his life attempting to completely obliterate negative thoughts from his mind's lexicon to the point that it was a reflex.

I allowed a few more seconds to tick by before I dared speak up. "And then?" I asked.

Emmerson Ray held his breath in for a long moment before sending it back out again with a hard exhale. "It'll be the beginning we've all been working for — the greatest base that Simple Sun could have hoped for. We shall be more than an organisation. We shall be a sovereign nation."

I resisted the urge to repeat the same question, childishly, as much as because I was afraid of giving away my own naivety over the whole situation.

Why was he apparently willing to trust my victory speech wasn't a hunk of shit? We would have to wait and see what happened in the election before getting to any victory speeches.

"You're still not convinced, are you?" Emmerson Ray asked.

I pursed my lips, peered down over the buildings spread out below. The green puffs of trees. "I ... don't know," I replied. "I guess I'm still not sure what I want to achieve, what I want to do ... I mean, what am I ... some sort of admin assistant?"

I didn't intend the words to come out as bitterly and bluntly as they sounded.

Emmerson Ray drew back from the glass, still remaining focused on the island spread out below. I wondered if he was thinking about how this might all fall under his control in a matter of hours. And perhaps he was considering the hundreds, thousands, of issues he would be required to address if he did succeed in obtaining the power he sought.

His gaze fell across me. "Is that what you want, Marcus? Is that what you want to be?"

I was taken off guard by the direct nature of the question. "No," I said. "I don't think so."

"Then don't be."

Emmerson Ray remained straight-faced for another few moments and then his lips cracked into a smile once more. He clasped my shoulder and steered me away from the window and the view looking out over the island capital. "Come on," he said. "We'll find out soon."

To tell the truth, it was nothing of what I had expected an election day to be like, especially when in the camp of one of the serious contenders. I had built up an idea of brewing tension with the odd stab of chaos here and there; that there would be people, advisors, party supporters swarming around a warm energy that threatened to burst into a blaze at any second ... but like everything else Emmerson Ray did, everything appeared to be under control.

We had all ended up in an IT suite with about half a dozen machines. The blinds were pulled down leaving the room in air-conditioned darkness. There was an empty whiteboard up on one of the walls and an unblemished calendar that showed the current month. A faint smell of coffee clung to the whole room. The only sound was the distant mumbling of the TV screen on the wall set to a low volume, talking heads within the news studio, blabbering about this or that, with an update every five or ten minutes on the latest batch of votes that had come in. There was also the familiar clacking of computer keyboards and the occasional huffing sigh — the sounds I had grown so used to while I had been working in the cave, "tagging" those bits of code, or whatever it was that I had really been doing ...

Emmerson Ray had slipped out of his jacket, hanging it up on the back of one of the unused computer workstation chairs. He stood with his arms crossed over his chest, a picture of perfect calm. I would have paid a lot of money to find out what was going on inside his brain. Or maybe I just didn't want to know. Unlike Emmerson Ray's cool exterior, however, his sister, Clara, was pacing back and forth, hands folded at her waist, every so often looking up at the TV screen.

I got the idea that something was going to happen at any moment. I noticed that Clara's assistants were standing at either side of the IT suite doors as if they expected someone to come bursting in at any second. "Turn it up," Clara said, finally, cutting through the silent room.

One of the assistants obeyed. The TV volume cranked up a few notches. The same presenter — Jenna? — was standing with her microphone outside a building that looked austere with its white stone and tinted windows at the entrance. It took me a moment to realise she was standing outside the building where we were currently located.

"We have just received official confirmation," she said, her eyes fixed upon the camera, and by extension, the viewer, as she spoke. She glanced down briefly to the cue card she was holding. "Hendricson Hendrick of the Modern Liberal Party returned thirty-eight per cent of the vote, while Emmerson Ray, of the Simple Sun Party has managed thirty-five per cent."

A vein throbbed in my temple.

Unconsciously, I sank my teeth into my lower lip as if I expected someone to give me a whack on the back of the head. When I looked at Emmerson Ray, I realised everybody else in the room was doing just the same. However, he was smiling — appearing to be on the brink of breaking out into laughter, actually. "Well," he said. "I guess this tells us something."

There was a swollen quietness in the room as the TV screen flashed to scenes of the other candidate — incumbent, Hendricson Hendrick, apparently.

Nobody thought to turn down the volume.

Nobody dared move a muscle.

Not until the tension was resolved.

There had to be a hundred or more people packed into the hall on the screen. There were balloons floating everywhere and streamers firing off from all angles. Someone had let off a bright-red flare. People were jumping up and down, celebrating victory.

In the end, Clara broke the silence.

"What does this tell us Emmerson?"

Emmerson Ray's eyes wandered the room, came to me, hesitated and then drifted onto the Scripters. He held up his hands, as if in surrender. "That someone isn't telling the truth."

The room was completely still.

Everything quiet.

I expected Emmerson Ray to spin around and point his finger accusatorily at me. I wondered if he might be carrying some sort of weapon. This day had felt strangely ominous, like it might well be my last day on Earth ... who could tell? At least I was dressed for the occasion. I was wearing a suit so my corpse would look respectable when my parents travelled to identify it.

Somehow, it was me who spoke first. "What now?" I asked.

Emmerson Ray was halfway through turning to me to respond when there was some commotion in the hallway outside. I watched on as Clara's assistants each produced a handgun they had been wearing strapped onto their thigh.

My heart rose to my throat and beat so hard I was worried it might end up in my mouth.

I didn't want to get myself caught in the middle of cross-fire ...

I wanted to extract myself from this situation as fast as I possibly could.

If escape was still an actual possibility.

Someone was thumping their fists against the other side of the door.

Clara's eyes widened as her assistants looked to her for a clue as to what they were supposed to do next. Finally, Emmerson Ray spoke.

Somehow, he was still smiling.

"Ask who it is," he said.

One of the assistants did so.

From the other side of the door, we all heard, "It's me — Zachary! Let me in!"

Emmerson Ray hesitated long enough for me to wonder whether he suspected Zachary of mutiny. As far as I knew Emmerson Ray treated him as his right-hand man ... as his most trusted advisor, or assistant, or whatever he was ... but perhaps all was not as it seemed. In the end, he gave one of the assistants a definite nod. Holding his gun by his thigh, the assistant opened up.

Zachary stumbled into the IT suite. He had never looked anything other than calm, but right now he certainly looked flustered. As if he had seen a ghost. His eyes flurried about the room, taking stock of faces. His scowl eventually fell upon me.

And that was when the accusatory finger came.

"Him!" Zachary said, finger extended, pointing squarely at my forehead.

Not really able to escape the limelight, I shuffled my feet a little.

"His *friend*!" Zachary continued. "He was on the *boat*!"

Emmerson Ray pressed his lips together. The jovial expression had softened now, become more neutral. And I was beginning to get awfully twitchy about Clara's armed assistants.

He looked at me.

I forced myself not to look at Danna.

"Riko?" Emmerson Ray asked.

"That's right," I replied.

Emmerson Ray cast a glance at Zachary. "How did it happen?" he asked.

Surprised that the line of fire was being directed away from me and towards Zachary, but not entirely disheartened, I allowed my stomach muscles to unclench just a little. Perhaps it was going to be okay. Perhaps a reasonable explanation would come out of all this.

Maybe I'd finally learn what was going on.

Maybe I should just keep on dreaming ...

Zachary looked outraged to be challenged. His nostrils flared as he stood his ground, square-shouldered, proud. He sneered as he spoke. "No idea how he sneaked aboard — I found him down in the cabin, in one of the cabinets."

"Did he have it with him?" Emmerson Ray asked.

Zachary held still for a long few moments. And then shook his head.

Emmerson Ray became pensive. He cast another look at me. "Do you have it, Marcus?"

I decided I should play the fool.

At least for a little while longer.

"Have what?" I asked.

Clearly this was the wrong thing to say because Emmerson Ray barked for Clara's assistants to come to attention. And they obliged without delay.

They approached me. While one of them stood with their weapon pointing to the ground, the other patted me down. I couldn't help but think that it was somewhat fanciful thinking that I might be able to conceal something as bulky as the computer tablet in a suit jacket.

Not finding anything, of course, the assistant shook his head and backed up.

There was some more silence, and then Clara spoke up. "What now?" she said.

Her voice was croaky.

Almost defeated.

I wondered just what else might have been on the line with Emmerson Ray losing the election. I guessed that whatever contingency plans had been put in place for Emmerson Ray failing to win over the populace would now need to be tried out.

Emmerson Ray took a few steps across the room, staring at the carpet tiles, as if they might contain scriptures — something to guide him through the next few minutes of his life.

"I don't like it," Emmerson Ray said. "It's too ... convenient."

"What's convenient?" Clara replied, her eyes wide.

"There has to be someone," Emmerson Ray said. "Someone inside. Someone close. Someone giving everything away."

"Didn't you hear what I said about his friend?" Zachary replied. "It's him!" He pointed at me as though he had a laser in his fingertip. I had a strange sort of tickle in my ribcage.

More uneasy silence ...

God, what I would've given for a car going past blasting reggae, or whatever the music staple was on this island. It would have been impossible to hear any car going past given that the windows were all double-, maybe triple-, glazed and clearly soundproofed.

Emmerson Ray cocked his head to one side, again focusing upon those carpet tiles. He took another few steps. And then, head still bowed, he clicked his fingers at one of Clara's assistants.

When the assistant didn't appear to recognise what it was he was being asked for Emmerson Ray simply clicked his fingers more insistently.

Finally, the assistant cottoned onto what he was attempting to communicate.

He handed over his gun.

It took me aback just how expertly Emmerson Ray examined the gun.

First he held it up in his grip, squinting, looking at the barrel, the black grip. I don't know anything about guns but I was pretty sure this wasn't the first one he had held.

Once he was done with his initial inspection he snapped the chamber, or whatever the top part is, and then held the gun down at his thigh. Finally, he raised his head, as if seeing his surroundings properly.

I glanced about the room.

Frightened eyes.

Something within me told me to look at Clara. She was the one who knew Emmerson Ray best ... she was the one who would know for certain whether or not we might have something to fear. Her eyes were wider than I had ever previously seen. And she was taking subtle steps backwards ... headed in the direction of the door.

My heart thumped percussively in my eardrums.

A voice at the back of my head told me to drop to the floor.

But I ignored it for the time being ...

I would've thought people with genes like mine would've long ago been weeded from the genepool.

With a definite, decisive action, Emmerson Ray brought the gun up and aimed.

Without any hesitation, he squeezed the trigger.

And the world blew apart.

# PICKING UP THE PIECES

My ears rang horribly.

The worst tinnitus I could ever remember having.

I was lying on my front, on the ground, although I couldn't remember falling ... or dropping. But here I was. I felt the scrub of the carpet tiles against the underside of my chin. When I breathed in, realising my lungs hadn't been pierced by the bullet, there was a slight tang of sulphur in the air. There was another smell, too.

Something I couldn't quite place.

Not until I dared lever myself up onto my elbows.

Everyone else, I saw, was lying on the ground.

At first, I thought Emmerson Ray had gone on a killing spree, and that I had somehow managed to survive and black out the horrific scene. But as I spent longer looking over the other bodies lying on the ground, I saw signs of movement. Fear rippled through them as it did me.

I breathed in again, turned my head to one side.

And that was when I saw him.

Emmerson Ray.

He was about ten, eleven paces from me. He stood over one of the bodies ...

This one was different, though.

This body wasn't moving.

My chest squeezed tight over my ribs. I tried to breathe in deeper but it was no good.

My lungs just refused to take any more of this air.

That was when the images began to play out before my eyes in slow motion.

And the thoughts dribbled through my brain.

Because I realised the body belonged to Danna.

I stayed still, keeping focused on Emmerson Ray.

Certain he was going to snap back into rapid action once more.

And I was so sure I would be his priority target.

Zachary had already said so much ... and yet, Emmerson Ray hadn't listened to him.

He had decided Danna was the one ... not *me* ...

Not *yet*, in any case.

Emmerson Ray remained perfectly still, continuing to stare down upon Danna's dead body. I didn't think I would see two dead bodies so close together in time ... after John Horsham having been my first. Maybe I was getting to be something of an expert because this time I knew just from looking at Danna that she was dead.

Something deep within me wrestled my gaze upwards, back to Emmerson Ray.

I tried my best to read his expression — to second guess what he might be thinking.

But I came up completely empty.

It was Zachary who broke the silence.

"How did you know it was her?" he asked.

Emmerson Ray blinked once, twice, as if clearing a delusion. And then he fixed upon Zachary as if seeing him for the first time. When he parted his lips I loosely thought he might be about to ask him his name ... but then:

"She was the only one that asked."

Zachary cast a glare in my direction, looked to Emmerson Ray once more. "Asked what?"

"The tablet," Emmerson Ray replied. "When Marcus didn't give it to you ... she was the only one who asked what had happened. She knew about the tablet."

"What now?" Clara asked.

From where I still lay, my eyes scanned the room, finding where Clara was. Like me lying on the ground. She had spoken with a sort of otherworldly tone. As detached as if she had been reading a text thrust before her eyes.

Emmerson Ray breathed in deeply, his strong shoulders hunching back. Although it was impossible, it felt almost as if he had risen to twice his height.

That he had gained width too.

For the first time since he had killed Danna, he shifted a look in my direction. For a horribly long moment I thought he might arc the gun up and stick a bullet between my eyebrows. Instead, though, he held the gun by the barrel and offered it to one of Clara's assistants. The one who had given him the gun in the first place. As soundlessly as it had been given, the assistant received the weapon ... I could see even from my spot on the floor that he was visibly trembling.

I guess that simply having a gun doesn't banish your nerves completely.

And seeing someone killed before your very eyes isn't any kind of relaxant.

"It's time for Plan B," Emmerson Ray said, and then cast a glance in the direction of the remaining Scripters.

Their complexions had gone completely white. Blood drained from their faces. They seemed more like marble statues than actual living, breathing human beings.

I waited for Emmerson Ray to elaborate on Plan B ... however, Zachary merely nodded at the mention. I could tell that Plan B was something I wasn't privy to.

"On your feet."

Everyone did what he said without hesitation.

It didn't matter that he was no longer armed.

Perhaps it's true what they say.

Guns don't shoot people ... *people* shoot people.

I didn't know where to look.

As I followed Emmerson Ray out of the IT suite, I did my best to keep my head up, not to look down. And yet it was impossible.

I had to look back.

There she lay on the carpet tiles.

A lifeless form.

What the hell was I doing here?

What the hell had I got myself in for?

We'd barely got out of the room when I felt a strong grip on my forearm.

When I turned to look, I saw Zachary had grabbed hold of me.

His eyes were wide and watchful as if I might be about to show off some implausible karate skills. He didn't have anything to worry about. When I'd been at university, I hadn't so much as given the karate, or martial arts club, whatever it might've been called, a second look.

"Let him go."

Both me and Zachary looked to Emmerson Ray, who had spoken.

Apparently still jumpy from what had just happened back in the IT suite, Zachary let go of me immediately. Is it a good or a bad thing if a murderer trusts you?

Emmerson Ray offered no further comment as he led us along the hallway. He didn't need to command us to follow him — the situation implied it.

Sun beamed in through the windows.

Over the statue, in one of the other buildings, I could see people on a balcony.

I realised that it was the winning party.

The victor celebrating with his supporters.

The incumbent.

For some reason, I found myself almost on Emmerson Ray's heels, with the two Scripters, then Clara and her assistants trailing. Zachary was bringing up the rear. I could see his eyes flicking about their sockets, scanning the world around him for any sign of threat. One thing was for certain. This outing had proved once and for all that Zachary was more than just a skilled pair of hands in the kitchen.

"Here," Emmerson Ray muttered, turning sharply and heading down a flight of stairs, into what appeared to be a basement.

I hesitated a moment.

Glanced up ... saw a green emergency exit sign with that white shape of what I've always thought to be a jubilant person dashing for their life whilst being followed by malevolent flames.

Someone prodded me in the back.

One of the Scripters.

He leaned into me, spoke in a husky voice. "Keep going. It's all right."

I wasn't quite sure what to make of this comment. Whether he might be on the same side as Danna. Whose side was I on? I have never had the highest opinion of myself but I had at least thought that if it came down to backing a murderer or being on just about anybody else's side then it'd be a fairly obvious choice to make.

Realising that the others were closing behind me, I descended the stairs.

Heading into the basement.

Into the darkness.

Following a murderer.

The lighting in the basement was very different. There was no daylight, of course, only the dim flickering orange bulbs every ten metres or so. The corridors, too, were much more narrow, and they seemed to come to an abrupt end every so often and go suddenly off at right angles.

It was as if someone had planned a labyrinth below this building.

Finally, Emmerson Ray reached a room right at the end of the basement.

I wondered exactly where we might be ... and then all was revealed.

401

A red light gleamed on a card-scanner.

Emmerson Ray held his watch up to the device.

It bleeped twice and a lock disengaged with a mechanical grumble.

He plunged the handle downwards and shoved his way inside.

That was when the sounds of the festivities reached me.

Up ahead, there was blazing calypso music punctuated by the odd yelp of uncontained joy. Emmerson Ray cast a glance back over his shoulder. As we carried onward, I was sure to keep my eyes peeled for Clara's assistants. And for the weapons they carried. But neither assistant made a move to hustle their way to the front. Was this all going to end in a nasty cloud of blood?

Was this the revolution Emmerson Ray had in mind?

Following Emmerson Ray, we rose up the spiral staircase, going deeper into the belly of the building. The music got louder. And so did the hum of jubilant conversation.

Nearby a woman screamed.

My blood froze in my veins.

When the scream twisted into carefree laughter, however, my stomach untied itself from the knot it had wound up into.

I noticed the two Scripters were sticking close to me.

Lagging on my heels.

I wondered whether they were attempting to align themselves with me, recognising that I was clearly as non-homicidal as they were. And then, with a more cynical edge, I wondered whether they just thought sticking close to me was the best way to ensure their own survival.

Because if anybody was going to get greased next then surely it'd be me.

Emmerson Ray led us up a staircase to where the party was taking place.

It looked like the ground floor but I was disorientated from the journey this far.

A grinning man and woman staggered about the corridor.

They each had a drink in their hand.

For a moment, it seemed as if they would just walk past us, but then the man, as he passed by, stuck out his finger, thrusting it at Emmerson Ray's chest. "Unlucky, man. Maybe next time, huh?"

I held my breath, waiting for Emmerson Ray to strike.

Standing at the head of our column, Emmerson Ray watched as the man and woman staggered off, disappearing around the corner and out of sight.

But not out of earshot.

The woman's parting giggle bounced between the walls.

It didn't seem like anyone else was coming.

The coast was clear.

For whatever Emmerson Ray was planning.

It was Zachary who finally approached him. When he spoke to him, he kept his voice low, conspiratorial, making it impossible for anybody else to overhear whatever he was saying.

Once Zachary was finished, Emmerson Ray leaned away from him, shook his head decisively and then glanced back over the rest of the group — me included. As if I needed any more reasons to feel on edge, Zachary shot me a glance, picking me out from the bunch. And in his hushed voice he made his point to Emmerson Ray yet again.

But it was greeted with another shake of the head.

Had I had a reprieve?

And if so was it only temporary?

Emmerson Ray turned to the others and spoke so we could all hear him over the sound of the celebrations. "We're going to go and speak to the organisers — tell them that we have an issue with the result. That we want a recount."

I couldn't help but feel that I was being included in that "we". The idea sounded simple enough. But I had already seen what Emmerson Ray was capable of ... and it was impossible to wash that recollection from my brain once it had been sowed. But, then again, there were Clara's armed assistants to contend with. I might not have a lot of experience of real life but if there's one thing I've always understood on an intuitive level it's to take care with people who carry guns.

You never know when one might go off ...

Emmerson Ray led us along yet more corridors — the music and shouting getting louder the whole time. Finally, I could see the colours of the revellers up ahead. The bass was so loud that I could feel it shaking my shirt off my skin. I looked to one of the Scripters and he gave me a stern look in return ... as if he expected that I might be about to do something. Or maybe it was just simple resentment that I had had such a free ride up until now. Just sort of swanning about not really doing anything — not settling on anything — and ending up in this situation with the others.

A situation I had no business being caught up in.

As Emmerson Ray took stock of the room, apparently seeking out Hendricson Hendrick, I looked about those assembled for myself.

And that was when I saw him.

Riko.

# THE CHASE

E verything happened too quickly for me to take stock. To make any sort of sense of the scene.

People swarmed about. No sooner had I spotted Riko than he disappeared among the revellers. I glanced to the rest of my group, seeing that nobody was paying attention to what I was looking at. Or so I thought until my eyes fell upon Zachary.

Staring right at me.

Like a hyena which'd caught the scent of blood in its nostrils, Zachary snapped his head around, looking into the crowd below, attempting to see where I had been looking.

Riko appeared again.

My heart leaped into my throat and Zachary vaulted off his spot and into the crowd.

Before I could think clearly, I was after Zachary, following him into the collection of damp suits and dresses, the rustle of fabric against my skin. And the heat bringing on a sweat of my own.

I took long strides, doing my best to keep up with Zachary, and at the same time trying to keep sight of Riko — his target. I nearly bumped into Zachary when he came to a sudden halt.

Riko had vanished.

It was an almost comical moment as me and Zachary took stock of one another. Clearly both wondering whether we should be coming to blows ... and ultimately deciding that this was at odds with our mutual goal. Speaking of our mutual goal, Riko appeared again.

Up above the crowd, on a raised platform walkway, making his way down one of the corridors leading away from the main hall. Before I could think to look away, or perhaps he would've spotted him even without me providing him the clue, Zachary was after Riko — tearing through the crowd once more. He bumped a man up against a wall, and he cleaned knocked over an overdressed woman in what appeared to be a ball gown. I sped after Riko in Zachary's wake, waiting for my chance to slip past him ... to ... do whatever it was that I was planning on doing.

We were away from the festivities, although I could hear the sound of a voice through a microphone following me down the corridor from the main hall.

Emmerson Ray's voice?

Was he speaking to the crowd?

One thing was for certain, he wouldn't be giving the victory speech I had written.

Zachary was taking full, leaping strides now, rapidly gaining on Riko as he disappeared around the bend. Zachary disappeared too as I willed myself forward further — *harder* ... and then ... there were people up ahead.

All of them standing still.

Wearing what looked like black jumpsuits. Zipped up to the throat.

I did a brief body count — ten, eleven?

Before I'd even taken stock of the faces, the emblem of a conical-shaped tree stitched in white thread on the breast pockets caught my eye. Quite similar to the Simple Sun emblem, thinking about it. Not that I wanted to think about it ...

The next thing that registered was the weapons.

At first I thought they were guns ... but then I realised, with only momentary relief, that they were stun guns. As my eyes rose up the torsos, I finally absorbed the faces.

All of them familiar:

Kelly.

Fil.

... Lucas?

My brain stopped for a second. I thought about how Kelly had mentioned she had joined a company on Lucas's recommendation. Black Pine. That accounted for the trees stitched onto the breast pockets. There were other familiar faces, too.

Ones which surprised me even more than Lucas's.

Toby Horsham.

And Daymian with a "y".

I took sharp breaths, looking at their stern expressions, and the manner in which they pointed their stun guns. With great relief, I saw they were pointing them at Zachary, who was down on his knees, hands clasped behind his head. When I glanced up I saw Riko was just behind the first row of the black jumpsuits — Kelly, Fil, Lucas, Toby and Daymian. Riko was looking somewhat startled, clearly still running off the adrenalin.

Finally, Lucas spoke.

*God*, how I had wished never to hear his voice ever again.

"On your knees, Marcus."

For a few seconds I was in shock.

My lips might even have parted, like I was a cartoon character.

I looked across all the familiar faces, all of them wearing stern expressions.

Grey-faced as anyone I'd ever seen on the bus to work in the morning.

My gaze fell onto Kelly, as I instinctively looked for some sign of sympathy.

Something to show me that she *knew* I wasn't the enemy.

And in so doing put Lucas back in his place.

When Lucas spoke again, it was a bark. "Get down now!"

It sent a jolt through my stomach. Even though I had had Lucas angry with me at work before, this was a tone of voice I was unfamiliar with. It shook me enough to make me want to do what he said without question. But there was still one thing I had in my favour.

I looked over at Kelly.

Did my best to put on that most pathetic of expressions: "pleading eyes".

But Kelly was shaking her head.

407

I could see her eyes were slightly watery.

Her lips parted slightly but no sound came out.

When I looked back at Lucas, his eyes looked like they might bulge out of their sockets at any second. He had gone uncharacteristically red in the face.

I got down on my knees, feeling the fuzzy scuff of the carpet tiles against the knees of my suit trousers.

"Bag 'em?"

It was Daymian's voice ... no question.

I waited for someone to tell him to wind his neck in.

But Lucas was in charge. "Go ahead," Lucas said.

And just like that all the lights went out.

Nobody said anything as I was led away. In the darkness, able only to make out faint snatches of light which bled through the spaces in the black fabric of the hood I wore, I felt myself bump elbows with someone several times. I guessed it was Zachary.

Once I'd been "bagged", my wrists had been tied up with what felt like plastic cable ties. And because it was someone with a sadistic streak who had been entrusted with the task — namely, Daymian — they had been tied up so tightly that my fingertips were beyond numb.

I wondered when necrosis might kick in.

The voice — amplified by a microphone in the main hall — still resounded through the corridors, although it was growing fainter. I guessed we were being taken outside. This assumption proved correct because — not long after — I felt a waft of warm air against my cheeks.

It blew back my unbarbered hair.

Then there was the sturdy non-nonsense hardness of concrete beneath my feet.

The sound of a car engine starting up.

My thoughts going dizzy for a second, I wondered if Toby and Daymian had gone to the trouble of boating their old banger over from the

UK. However, this thought disappeared from my mind pretty soon after it had arrived. I was pushed down into a passenger seat. I could feel the familiar squishiness of leather beneath my bottom and I knew this was a level of luxury that wasn't present in Toby and Daymian's car. There was also a sense of roominess. A synthetic, recently-valeted car smell. Doors slammed shut, seatbelts clicked, and with a roar the car jerked out of its spot, hurling me into the window. When the car turned back the other way, I bumped up against Zachary, sitting alongside. We knocked heads and stars danced across my vision, speckling the darkness of my hood.

The car rose and fell with the undulating island hills. I tried to listen for any conversation between the driver and passenger sitting up front, but they kept quiet. We might've driven for twenty minutes or for as much as an hour. After a while, without the visual clue of the scenery passing by the window, we might as well have been on the Astral Plane.

As the car began to slow, I heard Zachary speak to me in a low, husky voice.

"Hey? These your friends, right?"

I didn't say anything.

Is someone who knows your name and recognises your appearance your friend?

And is "friend" an ever-present state or subject to change as circumstance dictates?

I settled on, "Yeah," keeping my voice equally low.

"You really weren't in on it or is this some double bluff?"

I was flattered that — after all he had seen of me — Zachary still thought I was intellectually capable of performing a "double bluff" ... whatever that meant in practice.

I strained to keep my voice quiet. "Believe me when I say there are creatures still-undiscovered by mankind that know more about this situation than I do."

"Shut up back there!"

I guessed it was the passenger sitting up front who had spoken.

Strangely, because of the bag over my head, it felt as though they were right next to me, speaking directly in my ear.

Zachary didn't appear willing to push his luck and we remained quiet for the remainder of the journey ... which was over in due course.

The car took another sharp turn, bumping me and Zachary awkwardly together another time, and then crunched its way up a gravel driveway before finally skidding to a halt.

Doors opened and shut again and footsteps sounded on the gravel.

Before I knew it, the back doors flung open.

Stilted tropical air seeped in through my hood.

Someone grabbed me firmly on the forearms and wrenched me upwards.

Because I'm a kind-hearted sort of fellow deep down, I didn't resist, doing my best to make their task as easy as it could be. From the sound beside me, I judged that Zachary was employing a different strategy. After a few swearwords — muttered both by Zachary and his handler — we were frogmarched across the gravel driveway, and then across a well-watered and tended lawn, judging by the pleasant softness underfoot and the fragrant, grassy air.

This was followed by what felt like functional concrete slabs.

"Watch your feet," my handler uttered as I caught what was apparently the front doorstep with the toe of my formal shoes.

I couldn't help thinking how it was going to leave a scuffmark on the leather.

Maybe I'm destined to be an office drone for life.

The house smelled heavily of elderberry cordial and cinnamon. The floor was hard and slightly slippery beneath the soles of my shoes. I decided it must be marble or something similar. I was led by my handler a few more steps before I was ordered to "Sit!" on a squashy sofa.

My head covering was removed.

In keeping with everything else during my being-kidnapped experience, it was done without attention to my comfort ... actually, I'd say the bag was emphatically *ripped* off my head.

For a few seconds, the world was blinding.

It felt as though I might've materialised in the centre of the sun.

Out of the blazing light, a silhouette formed.

To begin with it was blurry; an indistinct, changing form.

Finally, though, the image cleared.

And there, sat in an armchair before me, was Riko.

He looked just as surprised as I did ... if his wide-eyed expression was anything to go by.

It took me another moment to realise it wasn't Riko who had been doing the manhandling. That particular act could be attributed to the burly-looking dreadlocked gentleman wearing sunglasses and standing in the doorway with his arms firmly crossed over his chest. Looking at his muscles, I judged he could have quite easily hoisted three of me over his shoulders and back.

Good thing I didn't have triplets ...

I focused back upon Riko.

*Why* was it always Riko?

Riko attempted a smile but it died on his lips, slackening and turning into a scowl.

"Why didn't you tell me?" I asked.

At first, I thought Riko might attempt to distort and reframe, distract, as was his MO, but this time he appeared to have a laser-sharp focus.

I wondered if something had finally broken in him.

If the world had finally bitten him.

"I ... had to keep it secret," Riko said, unable to hold my gaze after the initial syllable. "That was the only way to get inside. We had to use you ... uh ..."

He appeared to be searching for a more suitable phrase so I decided to put him out of his misery. "It's okay," I replied. "Don't spare my feelings — I've just landed on a tropical island to take part in a coup, witnessed a murder and then been kidnapped. Oh, and I think there was an election today, too. But my guy — the murderer — lost."

Riko aimed a look at the man standing in the doorway — the one who had brought me in from the car, my "handler" — and I wondered just how much free will Riko was exercising in being involved in this whole thing. Whatever this "whole thing" was …

Riko turned his full attention back onto me. "They … *we* need to know some answers, Marcus. That's why they thought I should talk to you."

My heart was racing but from somewhere I summoned the ability to take a deep, cleansing breath. That helped slow down my thoughts. It was strange because although I felt right on the verge of hysteria, a gentle calm lay over me like a finely threaded bedsheet. Maybe it was the years of office work which'd finally sanded down my emotional responses to nothing much more than a primitive quietness. "The tablet?" I asked, my eyes falling on it, resting against Riko's outer thigh as he sat in the chair.

Riko blinked a few times as if I had just committed some masterstroke. He glanced about, patting the chair cushion, as if he might've misplaced it … he finally got hold of it. His steady gaze rested upon the screen. He flipped a glance up at me. "John Horsham told me to do it."

For a few seconds, I felt the prickle of blood in my veins.

My forehead throbbed.

And then I realised he was talking about the virtual-reality version of John Horsham, who would seemingly forever live on within the tablet.

"What did he tell you to do, Riko?" I asked.

Riko squirmed in his seat. He looked to the handler standing in the doorway and I wondered whether he might be about to nod to him, signalling that I was to be roughed up. However, Riko eventually turned his attention back to me. "He told me about … Black Pine … about what was going on … about what I needed to do …"

"Right …" I replied, feeling as though I was being sucked into a vortex.

"He said … he said … he told me about the Conclave. That you needed to go."

I shook my head, not quite sure I followed.

I half expected a few screws to rattle about my skull.

"Then," Riko continued, "there were more instructions. As things unfolded further. That I was … to leave you to it mostly … and that when the time came the tablet would find its way back into my hands."

I felt the beginnings of a migraine stabbing my frontal lobe — or whichever part of the brain it's supposed to affect. My whole body felt stiff as a board, the overwhelming heat replaced by a lifeless icy sensation. Then it came to me. And I felt brilliant enough that I dared a grin.

"That's not the tablet," I said. "Not the real one."

And that was the moment when I heard another familiar voice.

"No, Marcus, you're right, it isn't. But this is."

All my muscles squeezed tight and I turned to look.

Kelly wore a black jumpsuit, like the others who had intercepted me in the hallway. There was no trace of a smile. Indeed she held a near-identical tablet in her hands. I could see the hairline crack down the middle of the screen. I knew she was telling the truth.

Kelly flipped Riko a look which he didn't interpret right away. Finally, though, he appeared to get the idea and rose up out of his chair. I waited for her to order him from the room but instead he remained standing where he was.

Kelly tapped the tablet against the palm of her other hand. "John wanted to carry on going," she said. "He wanted to keep on living — forever. That was his dream. Although he didn't believe he would leave life as quickly. Just as Danna didn't expect to suffer a premature death."

I scanned Kelly's tone of voice, and her choice of words. I wondered if it was shock, or something else, because she didn't sound all that torn up about the death of someone who was apparently a close colleague, or co-conspirator, or whatever Black Pine were. She delivered her words with the same ruthless efficiency of a computer programmer building up their code one line at a time to its logical conclusion. "John wanted me to take on the tablet," she said. "That was his ambition. That was who he was speaking about in his message."

I looked to Riko, to the handler and then back to Kelly, unable to let this sit any longer. "I ... didn't know that you knew John that well, I ..."

Kelly shook her head. "I didn't — I doubt we spoke more than half a dozen words to one another during the course of our time there. But he decided that if anything happened to him then I was the one most likely to take over his role and the one who had the most appropriate skillset to suit the task." Her features darkened. "You see, John was planning on leaving Simple Sun. That was why he secretly founded Black Pine ... an organisation designed to destroy Simple Sun."

I drew breath, feeling as though the room was beginning to spin.

I tried to work out how I had got involved in this.

But then a more pressing question arose.

So I asked it.

"How did Riko get involved again?"

I thought Kelly might crack a smile at my base naivety — stupidity? — but it appeared that any sort of joviality we might have once shared had dissipated. She remained frozen-faced, unperturbed. "John's code is dynamic," she said. "AI. The same base layer Simple Sun uses. The same layer which they have built all their systems on. The tablet incorporates all user interaction, piles it away in databases for later use. It identified Riko as its most likely collaborator."

I couldn't help but feel slightly scorned at the idea that the tablet had chosen Riko over me for its "special missions", or however they might be described.

"John was far more important to Simple Sun than Emmerson Ray made out as his funeral. He was the keystone in everything. In fact, you might say Simple Sun *was* John Horsham. His life goals, ambitions, all encapsulated within a single entity. More crudely put, Simple Sun, without John, is a zombie, although Emmerson Ray fails to see that. Or maybe — as it appears from what's gone on today, the past few weeks — he always had different aims for Simple Sun."

"Like taking over a country?"

"Like taking over a country," Kelly agreed.

My heart was back to thudding at the underside of my throat now. My palms had gone clammy again. I consciously slowed my breathing ... forcing myself to be calm even though it seemed as though calmness was not called for. I decided as I had started out speaking frankly I might as well continue. "How did Black Pine come into existence? ... I don't get it."

I wondered if Kelly would give a look to the handler. Perhaps they would exchange a nod and I would be carted away for good to some dark space. However, she did what I least expected. She gave me a potted explanation. "John create an AI to work on the company. It involved moving funds, creating infrastructure. Making a living, breathing entity."

I flipped Riko a glance only to see he was nodding along ... although I was fairly certain that it was more in the way that a dog might nod along with its owner in order to get a treat.

Kelly continued, "He set up avatars — shell employees who would eventually give way to real ones. They had duties and responsibilities, everything that a company needed to act. It was a virtual company, running in a virtual world ... until his death changed all of that — his death was the trigger for Black Pine to step into the real world. A true counterpoint to what Emmerson Ray planned on doing with Simple Sun."

It seemed as though Kelly had finished talking and I wasn't of any mind to start asking questions. I was satisfied that I knew enough.

At least for now.

I wanted to lighten the mood — maybe switch it away from the slightly morbid overtones it was currently suffering from.

"Do Black Pine pay better than Simple Sun?"

Kelly gave me something approaching a smile, although it was more of a smirk. "John thought it all through — he pays everyone competitive with the market."

I shifted my focus back onto the tablet Kelly held in her hands, and then glanced over to the imitation one which Riko had — and which Kelly had returned to me before I had left the UK to arrive on the Caribbean island as a member of Simple Sun.

"What role does the tablet have to play?" I asked.

Kelly looked at the tablet she held in her hands as if she had forgotten it was there at all. "We need you to lay low, Marcus," she said.

This felt oddly familiar.

"Wasn't that what you said I was to do back when I was on the other island? Simple Sun's island?"

She wrinkled her nose. "And you hardly did what you were told, did you?"

I shrugged. "I didn't want to attract suspicion — it would've helped if I had even a little bit of information."

When Kelly spoke again, her tone was more definite than I could ever recall her sounding. "You'll know soon enough what your role is."

And I guessed that was all I was going to get.

Soon after, with my mind still reeling from what had happened, I was whisked off into a small bedroom with Riko. The white paint was flaking off the walls and the small window looked directly at the stucco wall of the house alongside. Thankfully, though, the room was in the shade so we didn't have any sun beaming in. From what I could tell so far from being here, I didn't believe that there was any sort of air conditioning. The door shut behind me and Riko. I was a little heartened to think that Riko, too, had been ushered off to one side ... out of harm's way ...

Riko still had the tablet.

That was something.

After the door had been sealed shut behind us, a long period of silence elapsed. Outside the door I could hear heavy breathing. I supposed the handler had been assigned to keep tabs on us ... to make sure we didn't stick our fingers wherever they shouldn't be stuck.

I decided I might as well go for the jugular.

"So," I began, innocently enough, "when were you going to tell me about John Horsham bossing you about from his digital grave?"

Riko met my eyes for a brief moment, then looked away. "I ... I was just doing what he told me. You know?" He shrugged as if I would understand but from my lack of response he twigged that it was going to take a little more effort. "When someone tells you to carry out their dying wishes, it's not something to take lightly." For good measure, he added another, "You know?"

I sort of knew ... but, then again, I also knew Riko seldom if ever took the time to so much as consider living people's points of views and feelings, let alone the dead ... I guess it's like all those self-help books say, you've got to give people the chance to change — however improbable and out-of-character those changes might seem.

"Why didn't you tell me before I headed out to the island? To the heart of Simple Sun?"

Riko made a weird wrinkly face, his lips like the mouth of a volcano. "It wasn't what John wanted," he settled on finally.

Again, there was that whole complete change in attitude.

Doing what someone else said.

I wondered if what other people might think — or want — had passed through his mind before he had taken off his clothes while quitting his job in a literal "streak" of passion.

I don't know where it came from — like some sort of a bolt from the blue — the question which I needed to ask at that exact point and time. "What does John want now?" I asked.

He looked flustered by this question and if I had had any doubt in my mind then it evaporated. I had chosen just the right thing to ask. Finally, he said, "He wants us to get away. As quickly as possible."

And it was right then that the explosion rippled through the air.

It knocked us and everything surrounding us to the ground.

# A WORLD TORN APART

There was something heavy lying across my chest. It took me a moment to realise the blackness I was experiencing was due to something soft lying across my face. I clawed at my face, casting away a cushion. When I opened my eyes I saw that dust swirled everywhere, that it was getting into everything. My eyes watered. And then something even more uncomfortable occurred.

I breathed in ... and took down as much grainy dust as I did air.

It took everything within me to force myself to breathe. I had no choice but to keep on breathing despite the fact I was turning my airways into sandpaper-lined tunnels. I spluttered several times, and saw through the plumes of dust that a bookcase or something like it lay across my chest. It wasn't particularly heavy looking — made out of some cheap wood, but it was wedged against the wall in such a way that it was keeping me pinned to the floor.

Across the room, I could see Riko.

He was lying face down.

Not moving.

Maybe it said something about me that my first instinct was to look for the tablet — to see where it had ended up ... it lay a few paces away from Riko, having come to rest at a skewed angle.

I dug my elbows in beneath me, attempting to push upwards against the bookcase lying on top of my chest. It shifted slightly. Another go at pushing and it lurched off me, tumbling to the ground. When I turned

418

on my side, the rough sensation of the dust in my throat was too much to bear and I coughed at the ground covered in rubble, spluttering out as much of it as I could — but only succeeded in breathing in fresh dust. Finally, with my eyes streaming, I forced myself up into a crouch and then straightened up. It took me a few seconds to analyse the sky poking through and the sun beaming in. Whatever it was — a bomb? — it had blown a hole in the side of the house. I listened for any sounds but heard nothing ... and so I turned my attention back onto Riko, lying face down across from me.

I've never taken any sort of first aid or resuscitation courses so when I got over to where Riko lay I was at somewhat of a loss as to what I should do next. To begin with I wondered whether I might nudge him with the toe of my shoe, but I decided that this — even for Riko — was a touch too devoid of sympathy. And so, feeling pains and aches in my back which hadn't been there before, I got down on my haunches once again, and clutched his shoulder. Then I squeezed.

Perhaps I'm some sort of miracle worker who's just never had a chance to come into his power, but Riko gave a murmur in response, coming around from the daze he had fallen into following the explosion. Moving slowly, he rolled over onto his back, looked up at me through squinting eyes. His black hair was thick with white dust. "Spark?" he said.

I couldn't help smiling.

"Yeah," I said. "It's me." I looked at the tablet, and then around us again, as if someone might be about to invade this placid little scene.

I could hear someone in the near distance groaning.

"Here," I said, offering Riko my hand.

He looked at me through bleary eyes for a few moments before clasping my palm with his. I hoiked him up to his feet, finding him much heavier than I expected. As he stood up straight, I noticed a trickle of dried blood running from his forehead — a burgeoning bruise just beneath the line of his fringe.

"What happened, Marcus?" he asked.

I made my way over to the tablet, stooped and picked it up. "Looks like someone was trying to blow us up."

Riko gazed around our surroundings. "Oh," he said. "Shall we leave, then?"

I looked Riko in the eye. "If we're free to go."

Riko shrugged. "Doesn't look like there's anyone stopping us."

Once I was outside and I passed by a neighbouring house — which still had its windowpanes fully intact — I caught a glimpse at my reflection. There's something about someone wearing a dishevelled suit which screams, "zombie", like the corpse has been dressed up for the funeral and diligently laid to rest in its coffin before being committed to the earth ... only then to arise once again, clawing and groaning, ready to make its mark upon the world one final time — until someone knocks its head off or otherwise disposes of it in the method *du jour*.

Riko, on the other hand, as he was still wearing his beach bum gear, looked altogether more normal. At worst he looked as though he had undergone a heavy all-night beach party and — from the ashy dusting in his hair — he looked as though he might've got too close to the blazing bonfire.

I expected there to be some rampant militia advancing along the road, making for the house where we had just come from — grave-faced soldiers bearing automatic weapons ... but besides the smouldering wreckage of the house, there was nothing altogether remarkable about the scene.

"Drone strike," Riko said.

"Huh?" I replied.

"Looks like it was a drone."

I glanced back over my shoulder as if this might give me a fresh perspective on the place where we had just come. But, no ... it looked pretty much like the fabled bombsite.

We carried on walking, making it around the corner. There was still no sign of any military presence ... which was something of a relief. I started to feel more comfortable — comfortable enough to start asking Riko some more questions.

"Why ... *who* would've done that?"

Riko flashed his eyebrows. "Emmerson Ray. But I suppose you knew that already."

I opened my mouth to respond, wondering whether I might be about to make an even bigger idiot of myself by admitting just how little I knew. Just how little Emmerson Ray, et al, trusted me. How I was the very definition of the naïve stooge just bumbling along unquestionably doing his master's bidding.

We got further and further from the scene, although I could still smell smoke on the air. In the distance, I could hear sirens growing louder. Deciding I might as well come clean with Riko, I said, "Where're we headed now?"

"To the rendezvous," Riko replied.

"Oh," I replied, and then, as it appeared he wouldn't fill me in any further, "Where's that?"

"Air strip."

It appeared that was the only clarification I was going to get.

And I supposed I'd have to be happy with it.

"Sparky?"

"Yeah?"

"Can I have the tablet?"

I had one of those weird moments of panic when I inexplicably thought I might've lost it somewhere. In the end, though, I still very much held it in my possession, dangling down at my side. Sort of relieved to get it out of my hands, I passed it back to Riko.

"Here you go," I said. "You're the expert."

We walked on for the best part of an hour through sprawling streets, improvised houses built out of cinder blocks and corrugated steel roofs. As a consequence of the explosion, I had acquired a hole in my right shoe. I felt every pebble and uneven portion of the ground on my sole. Riko pulled out the tablet at odd intervals, scrutinising the screen, modifying our direction — in several cases apologising and dragging us back to a previous turn in the road.

We attracted some attention from the locals, as I guess that anybody who was clearly a tourist, or not from the island was sure to do ... not to mention if they were dressed in a ragged suit and covered in dust and dirt.

Finally, the houses just sort of stopped and wide open fields commenced.

The grass was long and verdant and lush.

I followed on Riko's heels, making my way along the path flattened out of the foliage. A bright light caught my eye through a line of trees up ahead. The sun reflecting off something metal.

A shudder shredded my nerves. I quickened my pace. It felt as if someone might be intent on stopping us progressing. I bumped into Riko's back, sending him stumbling forward. He spun on the spot, gazing at me with wide eyes as if he was a puppy I had just kicked.

"Sorry," I said. "I thought there was someone following."

Riko looked about, shrugged, and then carried on his way.

When we reached the other side of the field, I could clearly see the small four-person planes all lined up in a row, each of them parked at the exact same angle, at rest on wooden chocks. Although all of them were a white colour, they had slightly differing shapes and designs — a sash of blue here, or a tangled design of red there. Beyond the planes, a ragged windsock which I suppose had once been a fiery red, but which was now a sun-faded peach-colour, flailed in the light breeze. There was what could only be described as a metal shed — racing-green but now showing its chipped black undercoating.

Riko glanced at the tablet once again and then held it up as if he was some kind of water diviner. Except his equipment was attracting him to aeroplanes rather than boreholes. After a couple of misfires, he led us definitively towards one of the planes. When I caught a glimpse of the screen over Riko's shoulder I saw John Horsham's all-too-familiar virtual face peering out at me. There was something oddly unnerving about John Horsham's virtual self — he never seemed to be actively frowning ... on the contrary, he wore a smirk on his face at all times, the closest Technomancer had ever got to smiling in life.

Riko led us up to the plane. Then he tapped something on the screen. Something within the plane made a *chuck-chunk* sound and the pilot's door inched open. Riko had unlocked it remotely with the tablet. I couldn't help but think back to my experience with the bus that fateful morning ... we weren't about to ...

"Spark? You wanna sit in the pilot's seat?"

To begin with I was wrong footed by the question. Finally, I settled on a response which accurately reflected my state of mind. "... Why?"

"It doesn't matter where you sit." He gave the tablet a pat. "John's going to do the flying."

I felt my stomach squeeze as I considered what Riko was proposing.

It was ridiculous.

Of course it was.

... And yet ... there was some part of me which was intrigued ... perhaps in a kind of morbid way. Maybe this was it — maybe my destiny all along had been to go down in flames. I gave Riko a steely glare and then stepped up into the cockpit.

It was much hotter inside than I expected. The suit I was wearing didn't help matters. Whoever designed suits didn't come from a hot place ... or if they did then they were a masochist.

The air smelled of oil and synthetic materials and what I thought was cigarette smoke. I couldn't imagine anybody being so deficient of brain cells as to light up a cigarette while piloting a plane. But, then again, I had seen worse things. That was the problem with the internet — always lowering the bar ... making the All-Time Worst even worse.

From behind the joystick — or whatever the technical name was — I watched Riko round the nose of the plane and arrive at the co-pilot's door. He yanked himself up into the chair beside mine and dragged his door shut with an almighty bang I would've hesitated to treat a robust hatchback to. He set the tablet on his lap and tapped away at the screen.

He swiped here and pinched there.

"What're you ...?" I began before being cut off as the motor thundered into life. The propeller, too, began to turn. "Uh," I said, slipping Riko a sidelong glance. "Do you know ... ?"

The propeller sped up so much that it sent a roar through the entire cockpit.

So loud that I could no longer hear a thing.

From somewhere, Riko produced a pair of headphones with a curly cord which he snapped on over his ears. He jabbed his finger in my direction, indicating the side of my chair. I looked and — sure enough — found my own pair. I put them on and was a little spooked to hear Riko's voice come over the tinny speakers ... a strange sensation to think that he was sat right next to me and yet from listening to him he seemed miles and miles away.

"It's going through pre-flight checks," Riko said.

By "it", I guessed he meant the tablet.

I snatched a glance at the screen, seeing it was a flurry with lines of code, windows opening and closing, a thousand calculations and decisions being made each and every second.

"I was wrong, you know," Riko said. "When I said it was hacking for idiots."

"Oh?" I replied, my voice being picked up by the microphone inches from my lips.

"Yeah. Not the computer kind. It's a life hacker. It handles anything you throw at it."

I turned to face out of the window ahead, seeing the propeller spinning faster and faster, the engine having settled into a grumbling regular rhythm now.

It was the motion that caught my eye.

Nothing more than the stirring of foliage.

I thought it might've been a strong breeze, but when I looked closer I saw the truth.

It was people ... two people ... dressed in those black jumpsuits.

A thrill ran through my stomach.

Riko, his eyes still fixed downward upon his tablet, hadn't seen what I had.

So I called his attention to it.

He looked up, wide-eyed, slightly bleary.

He stared long and hard. "Oh, shit," he said, his voice coming over my headset.

"What is it?" I asked. "Are they armed?"

Riko shook his head, mumbling something or other.

"I can't hear you," I said.

Riko met my eye. "The tablet ... John Horsham ... he didn't say anything about this ... this wasn't part of the plan."

"There's a *plan*?"

Riko didn't answer the question directly, busying himself once again with the tablet, tapping away at the screen.

The figures were getting closer now.

Two of them.

I recognised their faces.

Kelly.

Fil.

My heart throbbed up in my throat.

I turned on Riko again. "What're you doing?" I asked.

This time Riko did hear me. "I'm checking it's all right for us to have them tag along."

"What'd you mean?"

He looked me in the eye. "With John Horsham."

That shut me up.

What was John Horsham in his virtual form, now?

Some kind of high-tech fortune-telling eight-ball?

"Well," I said, "they're twenty metres away — I don't think we'll have a choice soon."

Riko shook his head but didn't reply, busying himself yet again with the tablet.

They were ten metres away now.

Close enough to see that they too were covered in dust and debris.

Riko snapped upright into a straight-backed sitting position. "All right," he said.

"All right, what?" I replied, my eyes falling onto the panicked faces of Kelly and Fil ... I could tell from their expressions that their intentions were not devious — they were afraid.

Just like me and, well, I assumed that Riko was scared too ...

"They can come," Riko replied, somewhat enigmatically.

I looked at the plane door where Kelly's face had just appeared. It was impossible to hear anything with the headphones squeezed on over my ears and the constant grinding of the engine.

"Uh," I said.

"It's fine to open the door," Riko said, anticipating my principal concern. He leaned across me and jabbed the handle down with the flat of his palm.

Hot air rushed into the cockpit and I felt my cheeks flush.

When Kelly continued to be muted despite the fact that she appeared to be screaming at the top of her lungs, I realised I was still wearing the headphones. I peeled the ear cups off, one at a time, feeling how their leathery contacts had got stuck to my sweaty skin.

"Come on, Marcus — we've got to go!"

As if to push this point further, she leaped up into the cockpit, brushing past me, making for one of the seats in the back. Fil sparkled with perspiration and was wild-eyed from the journey to reach the airfield. He piled in after Kelly. Realising I might be able to make myself useful for once, and that it was something within my skillset, I brought the plane door shut with a slam.

The engine noise was still bad but then I remembered my headphones and plonked them back on my head. In the back Kelly and Fil had their own sets. Now we were all on a closed audio channel ... like an antique form of video-conferencing.

"We need to go!" Kelly repeated over the audio.

Riko, however, took his time tapping the tablet ... putting through the "life hacks" required to get us into the air. It sent a fresh jiggle through my stomach to think we were relying on the tablet to get us into the sky. And to keep us there. To take us wherever we were headed. My own experiment controlling the bus had narrowly avoided disaster.

I was fairly certain aviation carried a whole other host of complexities.

Too late, now, though as I spotted men in uniforms bearing automatic weapons in the foliage surrounding the airstrip.

This could all end very quickly.

And with a lot of kerosene and ... spilled blood ...

Riko jabbed his tongue out of the corner of his mouth in a way that a nine-year-old doing his maths homework would've been proud of.

It looked promising at first. Riko tapped something or other and the plane jerked off its chocks. Its nose nodded up and down with a kind of defeated protest. Like a resigned yet stubborn old mule reacting to a hard day's work ahead. The plane felt about as substantial as a drained tin of prunes. As Riko or — more likely — the tablet guided the plane along the runway, the plane slipped and slid with even the slightest of breezes. I glanced over my shoulder, watching the uniformed men swarming from the foliage.

Kelly recognised the anxiety I was experiencing. "Don't worry," she said. "We're not in danger of them firing — we've overridden the government protocols. No authorisation."

Although I had been a pencil-pusher my whole life I had to admit that I didn't find this particular bureaucratic detail all that comforting. All the same, I forced myself back to face the front. And Riko, still with his tongue sticking out, working silently to guide the plane along the runway on its unlikely passage up into the air.

Suddenly, the plane came to a halt.

"Kelly, look!" Fil called out.

I'd almost forgotten about Fil, sitting in the back of the plane alongside Kelly.

When I turned in my seat, I saw he was pointing out the window at the airstrip behind us.

I saw a suited man standing amongst the armed uniforms.

A man I recognised all too well:

Emmerson Ray.

The expression on Kelly's face was all I needed to see.

A mixture of disbelief ... *terror*.

She stared long and hard at Riko. "Get us up and out now!"

Riko approached the tablet with renewed frenzy — stabbing away at the screen, smashing through menus, doing whatever it was that the plane needed to get us into the air.

Finally, the propeller buzzed louder, changing frequency.

Getting higher pitched.

And we began to inch forward.

At first I thought I heard a heavy raindrop fall on the wing.

Hail, maybe.

Once the realisation dripped through my brain, however, I realised just what it was:

A bullet.

It was too late for us to do anything about it.

The plane was picking up speed.

Sending us up into the air.

Or at high velocity into the trees.

My heart thumped in my mouth.

I gripped on tight to the sides of my seat as if securing myself to its cushion might save me from sudden impact. I heard another few raindrops, hail ... *bullets* ... Just as I was certain the coup-de-grace was about to come, that the whole fuselage would blow apart in a plume of smoke and flame, the tail lifted off the ground, and rocking back, the plane took to the sky.

We were flying.

There was a stunned silence while we surveyed the airstrip disappearing below.

None of the men appeared to be shooting any longer.

Clear, azure sea spread out below us. Crisp waves catching the daylight and giving off silver flashes. The plane was droning on steadily, much calmer now that it was airborne. After about ten, fifteen minutes flying, and fairly convinced we weren't simply going to drop out of thin air, I breathed in deeply and sank back in my chair.

This was the long-awaited moment of respite I had been waiting for.

"What's the damage?" Kelly asked.

It took me a second to realise she was asking Riko ... he was the one at the controls, after all. My stomach did a small leap as I thought about the wings. When I looked out the window I could clearly see a couple of bullet holes.

Riko furrowed his brow as the plane's joystick twizzled from side to side, righting the direction of travel. John Horsham was on screen. Only now did I realise Riko was wearing an earphone in one ear, hooked up to the tablet. I wondered if he had had it in all along — listening to John Horsham's digitally rendered voice from beyond the grave.

"It's running diag — "

The engine sputtered, whined, then sputtered some more.

We rocked backwards, the nose climbing an invisible hill and pointing us directly at the sun. I brought up my arm to shield my eyes from the dazzling light and clenched my teeth as I felt the plane dropping ...

# MAROONED

I hadn't had the foresight to roll up the legs of my trousers and so they were soaking wet as I waded into the shallows, making for the plane. As I approached the fuselage, rocking about the gentle swell, I wondered whether it was due to Riko or John Horsham that we had managed to land the plane in the vicinity of this island.

I had no idea when I had left the plane behind.

Or staggered out onto the beach, either.

Everything was blurred together and the welt on my forehead was throbbing even more — it seemed with every one of my strides.

I eyed the bullet holes in the wings.

And then I saw Fil's face in the window.

Pressed up against the glass, his complexion was pallid and his eyelids had a bluish tinge.

My heart squeezed cold blood into my veins.

And I wrenched my attention away.

My eyes followed the fuselage, moving gently all the time with the current. I turned my attention to the cockpit, and to where I had sat beside Riko.

There was no sign of him.

I looked about in a panic, as if he might've scurried off somewhere like I had apparently done following the crash.

I recalled the voice which'd called me here.

Kelly's voice.

I rounded the plane, nose stuck in the sand, and looked over the other side.

There I saw the broken window.

The shards of plasticky glass standing up jagged.

I thought about what I might find. My heart rose in my throat.

And thumped for several seconds.

I stirred from inaction.

Got over my initial fear.

"Kelly?" I said, my voice sounding husky, worn, although I felt strangely calm.

I guess the crash had shaken me up more than I realised ...

Feeling the water creeping up my thighs, I waded deeper into the sea, running my hands along the fuselage so I wouldn't lose my footing on the shifting sand beneath.

When I reached the window, I held my breath.

And peered in.

Golden sunrays flowed in through the egg-shaped windows, splashing the interior.

Water had got in, reaching about ankle height.

I saw Fil sitting across the aisle, his face pressed up against the window, still unconscious.

I switched to the foreground, the seat nearest me, the smashed-open window.

Kelly.

Like Fil, she was dressed in a black jumpsuit. And, like Fil, she was dozing away the shock of the emergency water landing. Or so I hoped. Seeing Fil and Kelly up close sent sparks through my blood. I leaped into action, heading for the closed door.

I stood and thought about it for a few moments, wondering how this had happened. I had to have left through this door ... but why would I have left everyone else — Kelly and Fil — still inside? Had I suffered temporary insanity? The word "insanity" drifted about my skull ...

Riko.

I reached for the metal handle, tugged on it and felt it give. I realised how weak I was ... it felt as though just lifting my arm up into the air was an effort. My jaw muscles tightened up. I yanked the handle downwards, feeling the unseen mechanism giving slightly. At the point when I was sure it was going to unfold on top of me, I staggered to one side, landing in the cool water.

From my place in the water, I watched the stairway unfurl before my eyes like the entrance to some forgotten tomb. I hoped circumstances wouldn't turn out to be so dire.

I had seen enough dead bodies.

I scrambled up, splashing water everywhere in my haste to get back on my feet. I've never quite been able to completely vanquish that childlike panic that there might be a shark, or something out to get me, lurking in the water.

It's that old fear about the unknown.

That which you cannot see.

What was I going to see now?

I took careful hold of the guardrail as I stepped up into the plane. When my eyes fell upon Fil, I saw his eyelid twitching slightly. I looked to Kelly. It was her voice I had heard calling out only minutes ago. It was difficult to believe looking at her right now.

"Hello?" I said.

Neither of them responded.

Despite the humidity, an eerie chill bit me.

I forced myself onward.

Beneath my feet the plane stirred in the currents. I braced myself, grabbing hold of the headrest on the captain's chair. The plane took gut-churning moments to regain its stable position. For a second, I was certain it was going to keel over ... that water was going to come gushing in.

I snatched a breath, tried to balance myself, and then squeezed Kelly's shoulder.

A firm, manly squeeze that under any other circumstances I might've been quite proud of.

She didn't react.

It was like trying to stir a ragdoll.

"Kelly?" I said. "Kelly?"

There was something — the twitch of her bottom lip — the slightest wrinkling of her nose — and she mumbled something under her breath.

"Come on," I said. "We've got to get out of here."

I shifted my attention over my shoulder, to look at Fil, still seemingly unconscious.

I turned back to Kelly. "I need your help," I said.

Finally, as if she had lead weights pressing down upon her shoulders, Kelly made the momentous effort to rise up from her seat. She had the bleary look of a sleepwalker as she caught her balance. I hovered my arm close by in case she toppled over. But she appeared to get a grip on herself and the focus in her gaze returned.

"Marcus?" she said, this time with the faintest of smiles on her lips.

A softness of tone ... completely unlike how she had spoken to me earlier in the day.

Before we had escaped the island.

"Yeah," I said, "I'm here — we had a crash, and we need to get out." I jerked my thumb in Fil's direction. "I need you to help me get him up and out, too."

Kelly's gaze was becoming crisper, clearer, with each passing moment. She shifted her eyes onto Fil, where he sat in his chair. "Okay," she said, her voice not much more than a murmur.

I leaned over Fil, seeing his chest rising and falling with heavy breaths.

"Hey?" I said. "Hey, Fil?"

No response.

He remained still as anything — unmoved by my words.

Maybe it was something I'd seen in a film or on TV — or perhaps I have some harboured, unspoken desire to be a stage hypnotist — but I snapped my fingers at him.

And waited expectantly for his eyelids to shutter open.

But, of course, he remained unmoved.

I looked at Kelly but she clearly wasn't yet in any position to offer useful advice.

It was up to me to use my initiative.

And so I did my best.

I clasped Fil beneath his arm and applied as much force as I dared, gradually elevating him.

I was surprised at my own strength.

... Perhaps Emmerson Ray had been right when he'd suggested I had "hidden depths", or whatever he had been insinuating when he had taken the decision to recruit me for Simple Sun.

Kelly shifted around to take hold of Fil from the other side.

Between the two of us we got him up onto his feet.

Fil had enough consciousness about him to steady himself standing and his eyes lolled open for the briefest of moments, showing off the sliver of a half moon.

When we brought him down the steps and into the shallows, he quivered slightly at the sensation of the water against his skin. I looked over to Kelly, checking to see she was still lucid.

When we got to the beach, and the fine sands, I saw there were two pairs of footprints.

Had me and Riko staggered out of the plane together?

I tried to piece together my memory, following the crash, but all that remained was the impact. And then the darkness.

"Let him down gently, Marcus,"

While I had been lost in my wonderings, I realised we had reached the upper edge of the beach. The palm fronds threw shade across the fine sand. Cool and refreshing.

We eased Fil down onto the sand. We placed him in an upright sitting position. While down on her hands and knees Kelly set about examining him with the competent eye of someone who had attended a first-aid course. She gave me the vaguest hint of a smile. "I wanted to be a doctor once," she said. "But I decided that machines were a better bet."

"Less emotional?"

She shifted back onto Fil. "Not necessarily." She paused. "Future-proofing."

I straightened into a standing position and cast my gaze at the horizon. I imagined a pirate ship looming there. A scene which might've occurred four hundred years ago. "It won't be long before we're all androids if Emmerson Ray has his way, I guess."

"I don't think Emmerson Ray thinks much past Emmerson Ray to be honest."

Kelly rose, easing Fil back into a lying position on the sand. She stood up, met my eye briefly and then cast her gaze to the sea ... perhaps to the plane banked in the shallows. She breathed out a long sigh. "What happened to Riko?" she asked.

"I was thinking the same thing."

She looked into the trees. "I never did get a good read on him. I was never really sure if he was ... really like the way he appeared to be or if it was just an act."

I looked to Fil, who appeared alive but in a feverish dream. "Well, I've known him for some time — long enough to know that ... however he acts ... it's not an act."

"I see."

Kelly's tone suggested she wasn't completely convinced by my judgement.

It also suggested something else which I decided I had to nip in the bud right away.

"You do realise I have no idea what's going on, don't you? That I've been lost pretty much right from the beginning? Look," I continued, feeling myself growing red in the face and not because of the heat, "think about things from my perspective. That offer, the one which Emmerson Ray gave me, what would you have said in my position?"

Without so much as pausing for thought, Kelly replied, "I would've turned it down."

"Really?" I said, growing increasingly frustrated or incensed or however I was supposed to label the pissed-off feeling. "Some dumb customer support advisor? No job satisfaction. Shitty pay. And only the prospect of more to come. No light at the end of the tunnel — no hope."

Feeling as though I had blown myself out, I took a couple of gulping breaths. I realised I was still dressed in a suit — an extremely soiled and wet suit but a suit nonetheless. Deciding it was time to act on my discomfort, I ditched the suit jacket and rolled back the shirt sleeves.

Finally Kelly replied, as always with a frustrating sense of calm and perspective.

As if I was the irrational one.

"Look, Marcus," she said. "I can see where you're coming from but you've got to take responsibility for getting yourself into that situation in the first place."

That felt as if someone had punched me in the chest.

Not that I could deny she was telling the truth.

Still, the truth hurts.

Kelly went on, "You made all the decisions that led you to that customer service rep role you claim you hate, just as I made the ones which landed me in John Horsham's boots."

As a gentle fresh breeze blew across the beach, I realised the sun had dipped quite considerably in the sky. It would be dark soon. Here the night came swiftly and methodically like a blackout blind winding down. Nothing like the ambush of British winter nights or the languid never-ending summer evenings. I wondered if we should start thinking about making a shelter or something, that was the kind of thing people did all the time in these situations.

On TV and in films, at least.

I drew breath.

"I didn't want ..." I thought about the scene I had witnessed earlier on this very long day — Danna's murder at Emmerson Ray's hand. "... It was an adventure," I said, "a way out of my life."

"I think, Marcus," Kelly replied, "you need to ask yourself why you were looking for a way out of your life at all."

I looked away then, not really sure how to respond.

What she said was sage.

Harsh ... but sage.

As night settled in over the bay, the waves continued to slop against the side of the downed plane, seemingly forever condemned to be banked in the shallows of the beach like some long ago erected monolith. Kelly was lying on her back, dozing, having heaped a pile of sand underneath her shoulders, back and head. She had Fil's head resting in the crook of her armpit, my folded-up suit jacket forming a pillow, his airways angled upwards. Although I didn't know much about medicine — or much about anything as it was transpiring — I guessed this was some sort of recommended procedure.

Just like back on the Simple Sun island, the moon and stars shone brightly. It set the beach in an eerie witching-hour glow. I wondered if there were such things as spites and gremlins in the tropics ... probably if you took the right kind of drugs.

There was still no sign of Riko.

And I was starting to get antsy.

I decided I was more concerned about the fact he had been conspiring away from me rather than the actual details of the plan he might've hatched in secret with the virtual John Horsham. It was better to have Riko where you could see him. That way you could be totally sure he was up to no good rather than second guessing yourself the whole bloody time.

With a final look over Kelly and Fil, deciding they weren't going anywhere quickly, I rose to my feet. As I strode away from them, along the beach, I noticed the air temperature. It was comfortable, like back on the Simple Sun island, no need for a second layer ... which was just as well because I only had my shirt sleeves and the thin material of the formal trousers I was wearing.

Feeling as though I was a detective solving a crime at an excruciatingly slow pace, I examined the footsteps running up from the shore, where the plane had come to rest.

Sure enough, I saw the two sets of footprints.

Mine — wider, deeper and smoother from the flat sole of my shoe — and Riko's which were shallower and a weaved design from the underside of his flip-flops.

I followed the trail up the beach and into the foliage.

The footprints were still running alongside one another.

I stepped into the palm trees and immediately felt the moonlight dim around me. Up ahead, I could hear the chirruping of what I imagined was a frog. More concerning, I heard the *rattle* of what I desperately hoped wasn't a snake, or something worse. When I breathed in, I tasted sweet water vapour clinging to the air — the dampness lined my air ducts, prickled my lungs.

I looked to the ground, mine and Riko's footprints.

We had gone together — that much was certain.

And I had ended up on the other side of the island ... with no sign of Riko.

Peering through the trees, out further ahead, I spied what looked like a clearing.

Moonlight poured in through a gap in the canopy.

When I reached the clearing I continued to track Riko's footsteps. It was becoming more of a challenge. The sand had become darker, mixing with scrubby dirt. To my right there was a loud *cackle* which near enough peeled me out of my skin. There was no sign of another clearing up ahead. I knew I should turn back. It occurred to me that we would soon need fresh water, and preferably something to eat. That was what my brain told me although my stomach still felt sickly following all the events of the day. It was hard to believe I had been on the boat just over twenty-four hours ago — jetting towards the island Emmerson Ray had decided would represent the keystone of the Simple Sun empire. Just as the reasonable part of my brain convinced me to backtrack to Kelly and Fil and wait it out until morning, I noticed a glimmer up ahead.

Something in the foliage.

The light was too bright to be moonlight.

Hurrying, stumbling a few times over tree roots hidden beneath tangled foliage, I barrelled towards my target. Although it was near total blackness some primordial part of my brain sensed movement. Some sort of fear receptor considering the way it sent a tingle down my spine.

My senses telling me it was time to flee.

I overrode their advice and continued on my way, getting closer still.

And then my voice emerged from where it had hidden away in my throat.

"Riko?" I said.

More movement out of darkness.

And the light flickered and disappeared.

"It's okay," I said. "It's *me*."

No response.

I felt the jungle closing in on me like a damp cloak. Hidden animals — frogs, mosquitoes, monkeys? — buzzed and chirruped and chippered away. It felt as though they were all perched above, organised by some higher power, and were readying to pounce. To show man his place was no longer amongst the animals but back in his cities — his manmade utopias.

I closed my eyes.

Listened.

Heard the crunch of footsteps.

Something snagging a branch.

Like a man possessed, I snapped my eyes open, hurtling forward, trusting all my ancient genes to guide me towards my target. I bounded onwards, and finally sensed him ahead, spiralling, weaving, trying to get away. Although I've never been much for any sort of sport I dipped into that well of forgotten knowledge and pulled from it a leaping rugby tackle, catching Riko tightly about the waist and bringing him tumbling to the ground.

I half expected Riko to struggle and squirm beneath me.

But he held still.

Defeated.

439

RAYMOND S FLEX

My heart thumped steady and low in my eardrums and gradually my eyes became more accustomed to the surrounding gloom. Out ahead, I could see the tablet, lying in the grasses.

Its screen switched off.

Realising there was no point in lying on Riko any longer, I rolled off him, and sat with my legs splayed out to one side.

Riko blinked to himself, clearing his daze, perhaps getting over the shock of having me attack him from out of the darkness. Then his gaze focused upon me.

"I didn't see you," he said.

"What happened?" I asked. "After the crash?"

It's always seemed a borderline inexplicable phenomenon the way that your eyes can grow accustomed to the dark. I could now make out more of the finer details of Riko's face — and I realised that a welt was rising out of his cheek.

"Did you bump into something?" I asked, pointing to the bruise.

Riko brought his hand up to his face, his fingertips lingering over the surface of the inflamed skin briefly. "No," he said, and then caught my eye.

That was all I needed to know.

"I did it?"

Riko nodded solemnly.

I searched my mind for any trace of memory.

For anything I might've recalled from my journey out of the plane and into the trees.

But it was all blank.

Until I woke up on the beach on the other side of the island.

Riko spoke again. "You wanted the tablet," he said. "It was ... I dunno, sort of like you were Frodo in Lord of the Rings ... you just flipped out and went for me."

Still, there was nothing registering in my memory, neither near or distant.

"I don't ... remember," I replied.

Riko's eyes darted about their sockets, searching my body as if I might be harbouring a concealed weapon. "After you ... *did it* ... you just sort of made a sound ... sort of like ... like ... a bull? And then you just sort of ... sort of stormed off through those trees ... swearing and stuff ... I thought you were going to tear the tablet from my hands — you could have done, I would've given it to you — but you just gave up ..."

It was strange to hear Riko speak in the way he was speaking.

As if he was frightened.

Or perhaps *because* he was frightened.

I realised I had never really believed that Riko was ever capable of it.

Now I knew different.

I looked away.

To the tablet lying a few paces from us.

"That's why you ran from me — just now," I said, "... but why didn't you put up more of a fight? If you were afraid I was going to do something harmful to you?"

Even through the darkness, I could make out Riko's non-committal shrug.

That was more like the Riko I knew and loved.

The Riko that just sort of winged every last thing.

"Shall we go back to the others?" I asked.

Riko looked through the jungle, back in the direction I had come at him from out of the darkness. When he spoke again, it was with a genuine sense of worry. "How are they?" he asked, and then, bowing his head, "I just ... I couldn't think of anything but getting out of there — I panicked ... I should've stayed behind to help ..."

This admission took me off-guard ... especially as Riko had hardly ever — if *ever* — shown he held other people's concerns close to heart.

"I don't think I did much better, do you?" I said. "I mean, I went after you like some wild animal and then passed out on the beach."

Strangely, however, Riko resisted my attempts at levity. "Are they okay?"

"Fil's not looking too good — but Kelly has some medical training, or something like it ... they're resting, back on the beach."

Riko nodded at this. "They're not ... not ... *pissed off* with me?"

As with everything else involved in this conversation, I was weirded out. I thought about letting him off the hook in the way his pitiful tone demanded but then decided to pull back just a little. "I think they're okay," I said. "Let's go back and see."

I got up and then peered off into the darkness, trying to identify that I was going to take us back the exact way we had come.

"Marcus?"

"Hmm?"

"The tablet, Marcus," Riko said.

"Oh," I replied, looking back over my shoulder, seeing it lying on the ground, almost lost amongst the foliage ... but not quite. There was a single, dim light glowing from somewhere, telling us it was still alive if currently on some sort of standby mode.

"I want you to take it," Riko said. "It's yours."

I was on the cusp of rejecting Riko's assertion but when I looked him in the eye I realised he was on the brink of tears. Just why, I wasn't entirely sure. And yet it was enough to throw me off balance. To tell me I needed to do what he asked. And so, as Riko rose up to his feet, I paced over to the tablet, stooped over and snatched it up. It was much heavier than I recalled ... or, well, as it was a copy of the original, it was the same weight as the other one.

"Come on," I said. "Let's go back."

# DESERT ISLAND LIFE

As the sun crowned the horizon, I watched the golden light splash across the calm Caribbean seas. There wasn't a cloud in the sky. A gentle breeze blew in across the beach. Palm fronds rasped against one another and sent sand skittering in low dusty clouds. If it hadn't been for the plane crash right before my eyes, scarring the otherwise flawless picture of tropical paradise, then I might've been able to convince myself I had died and gone to heaven.

Maybe I had died.

And this place was heaven ...

As I sat with my knees clutched up to my chest, my chin resting on my kneecaps, I caught a fruity whiff on the air. One of those fruity smells that is so sweet it's almost rotten.

I cast a glance over my shoulder, to the others — Riko, Kelly and Fil — further up the beach, all still dozing away. I stood, feeling aches and pains I hadn't felt the day before but which I imagined had been a result of our getaway from Emmerson Ray and the island.

It was surreal that I was still dressed smartly — as if going for a job interview ... only I'd been attacked by especially slobbery wolves on the way there. I thought about ditching my shoes and going barefoot but my snake phobia got the better of me. Although I knew logically that leather wouldn't provide much protection from a snake with an especially sharp bite — the sort of snake I had in mind — it gave me a crumb of comfort. As I trudged my way along the sand with a lopsided gait — one foot sinking in and then the other — I noticed bunches of

443

bananas hanging from a tree just beyond. I suppose, utilising my powers of logical deduction, it was a banana tree.

Despite their large size, the bananas were still almost entirely green. Then again, they still represented the closest we were going to get to anything resembling breakfast.

I looked back to the others, all of them still slumbering away. When my eyes fell upon Riko, I wondered just what had seized upon me that had made me think it might be a good idea to throttle him. I mean, which one of the reasons it might've been ... Whatever the whim had been, I had clearly suffered some sort of concussion since. I had turned the issue over in my mind, doing my best to draw out any memory I might've unknowingly repressed.

But there was nothing.

As I got closer to the banana tree, I was surprised at just how much it looked like a giant root vegetable. Like a radish or a beetroot. Still, the banana-shaped fruits — otherwise known as bananas — could be only one thing ... unless I was about to make some horrific mistake ...

After a few more steps, I realised there was a whole grove of banana trees before me. The tree I had initially spotted had large but mostly green bananas hanging off it. As I went further, I realised there were several plants with much riper, yellowing bananas. The bananas grew on a vine which sort of stuck out of the main trunk. They dangled down so the lowest banana scraped the ground. I couldn't help wondering whether it was a good or bad sign that no other animal resident on the island had thought to gorge itself on these bananas thus far. Or maybe we'd lucked out and there *weren't* any beasties on the island after all. That sounded far too good of an eventuality considering my luck. Well, I was still alive, I suppose ...

Deciding to take my and — by extension — the others' fate in my hands, I treaded amongst the banana trees, snapping off bananas as I went. The weight of them surprised me and a couple of times I dropped them upon my well-scuffed shoes with a *whoompf.* I wonder if under normal circumstances these impacts might've registered a little more but — as it was — I seemed to be operating on another plane entirely from my body. Once I'd got myself a good armful of bananas, I made my way back to the beach. I noticed Riko and Kelly had stirred from their slumbers, although Fil continued to lie on his side. They traced me with their gaze as I approached and I could tell that their mouths were watering at the sight.

When I got to them, Kelly was smiling from ear to ear.

"I see you got breakfast," she said.

Riko, however, wore something more akin to a frown. "I've never liked bananas," he said. "It's something about the texture." He aimed a look around me as if I might be concealing something else I had successfully foraged from the wilds of the island. But of course there was only the Caribbean sea. "No water?" he asked, with a tone of intense expectation.

Feeling perspiration dampening my forehead, I allowed the bananas to slip free of my arms and to fall into the sand. A touch of colour rose in my cheeks — the pride of the provider.

"There'll be a stream somewhere," I said, unsure quite where this streak of optimism was coming from. "We can go out and search for it later on …"

Kelly was on her knees, staring at the bananas. Finally, she glanced up, with a kind of weird — almost begging — expression.

"Don't stand on ceremony," I said.

Kelly snatched one of the bananas, ripping its peel and chomping on the soft fruit within.

It was only being here, with Riko, Kelly, and the slumbering Fil, that I realised just how unhungry I was. I wondered if it was a side effect of trauma, or something … like my body telling me there were more important things to consider than stuffing my face at this particular juncture. All the same, I settled among them, plucking one of the bananas up from the pile and casually removing the peel. I even noticed — out of the corner of my eye — that Riko was curiously inspecting a banana, as if it was some sort of alien species.

We remained like that — each of us lost in our varying levels of appreciation of our bananas — until I heard Fil give a murmuring sound from where he lay.

As one, our heads turned towards him.

I thought he might have just been talking in his sleep, or his coma, or whatever had befallen him. However, I realised his eyes were open a slit ... and that they were darting about, taking everything in. Finally, his focus came to rest on Riko.

His eyes opened fully for the first time.

And his lips parted slightly.

He let out a cry.

My heart leaped on a few beats.

We all stared at Fil.

When his voice finally died in his throat, his eyelids drooped low and I thought he might be on the cusp of fainting again. Of descending back into the coma, or whatever it was he had been immersed in. But then his eyes opened wider than they had done before. He attempted to shift himself up into a sitting position. Kelly couldn't help her medical instincts in wanting to reach out and help. Fil, however, stared at Riko, fixated. To be fair, I couldn't exactly blame him for his Riko-interest ... there's a lot to dig into there.

I'm sure any psychiatrist worth his salt would have a field day and a half.

With Kelly's aid, Fil managed to get himself up into a sort of side plank, resting on his elbow and knee for support. Apparently the rest had given him the chance to recover some of his former strength because he was able to sustain himself there with minimal help from Kelly. In fact, after a few moments it was as if the scene which'd just played out before us hadn't happened at all.

There was a stillness again.

I considered another chomp on my banana but thought better of it. For all the quiet and calm, everybody was still waiting on Fil to explain himself. When I snatched a glance at Riko he looked shifty, his eyes darting about.

I knew this was going to be good.

Finally, Fil spoke, his voice wobbling all over the place. "After the crash ... just after the plane landed," he said. "I hit my head when we ... set down ... but then everything was stopped and everything was nearly silent. Just the lapping of the water, nothing else. And then ... and then ... as he was getting up, out of his seat, he ... he *hit* me."

I looked to Riko, seeing how he was going to explain his way out of this one.

I readied myself to grab him if he tried to flee.

This was one situation he wouldn't escape from.

He was trapped on a desert island.

No, he had to face up to his problems now.

He had to face up to us.

He had to face up to *me*.

Riko jabbed his tongue into his lower lip, in thought ... always a very dangerous sign indeed. "He tried to take the tablet," Riko said.

As if we were watching a tennis ball bounce back and forth over a net, me and Kelly switched our focus onto Fil. He came around from his side plank position to kneel shakily. He narrowed his eyes as he focused on Riko. "I asked him where he was going ... and he struck me."

It was funny, I couldn't remember in all our time spent together at LifeWare a moment when Fil had even come close to losing the plot. Or showing any sort of emotion other than the happy-go-lucky kind. Maybe I was mistaken, though, and it was just the professional mask that we all wear. Then again, I guess that if anybody is going to break you, it's going to be Riko ...

Fil shook his head. Riko's eyes flashed, and he looked in my direction. He shifted his attention onto the tablet itself, shut down and lying in the sand a few paces away. Fil turned to me now. "You saw," he said. "You took off after him, while me and Kelly were in the back of the plane. And then ... then everything went dark again ..."

Kelly picked up this time. "... I was sort of in a haze, until I saw you walking along the beach, Marcus." She raised her chin slightly. "I thought you were ... *someone* else."

Not for the first time, I got a chance to experience what it was like to blush in a tropical climate. The double dose of heat in my cheeks. It was a simple thing but I had wanted to believe that I was a hero. *Kelly's* hero. Just for those few seconds ... until I reached the plane and the realisation dawned on all involved that she could very easily take care of herself — and probably me too come to think of it ...

Riko was becoming really quite unsettled now. He kept on glancing around as if someone might drop by to provide a welcome distraction.

Emmerson Ray parachuting in perhaps?

But there was no assistance for Riko from our immediate environment.

He would have to go it alone.

With only his wits for company.

"Listen," Riko said, holding up his hands as if he was attempting to calm a trio of feisty ponies, "if you just let me explain it'll all make sense." He paused as if one of us was about to interrupt him. His gaze fell upon the tablet once more. "I was doing what John Horsham told me to do ... after landing." He sighed long and hard as if this was an excruciating tale to tell.

Realising he was attempting to halt, and knowing Riko the best out of all of us, I stepped in. "And what did he tell you to do?"

Riko swallowed hard, looked to the horizon, and then to the shore. His focus finally fell upon his bare feet and shins which were covered in a mixture of dried sand and mud. When he spoke again, his tone of voice was low, pained, almost childlike. "He said I needed to get away from you all — that it was important ... that it was the next part of the plan."

"What *plan* Riko?" Kelly said, jumping in this time.

There was no trace of fatigue from what she had undergone in her voice.

She was sturdy — unshiftable.

And that was good because you had to be both those things when dealing with Riko.

Riko nearly smirked but appeared to lose confidence right at the very last moment. "Into the trees, into the jungle," he said. "There he said that I could hear what he had to say next."

"And what did he have to say next?" I asked.

Over by the banana trees where I had just got back from foraging our breakfast, there was an enormous explosion. It shook the island to its bedrock.

We all hit the sand, face down.

The smell of smoke coiled up my nostrils.

My heart beat in my throat — threatening to choke me.

Everything was icy cold for a few moments ... before the heat returned.

When I raised my head from my position on the sand, I surprised myself to see I was the first up and looking around. I had never pinned myself as brave ... or maybe it's just that whole thing about the thin line between bravery and stupidity. I was the only one with it in my genes to risk getting their head blown clean off. Right away, saw the plume of smoke rising up from between the banana trees. I switched my attention onto Riko, and then Kelly, both staring at the impossible-to-ignore sight. I waited for ten, twenty seconds, perhaps a little longer, and then said, "Emmerson Ray?"

Neither of them replied right away.

I noticed Fil stirring from where he lay.

Perhaps the explosion had done something to knock life back into him. Or maybe some elemental, hardwired evolutionary core of his brain had kicked in. Whatever the explanation, I was fairly certain he was back in the room ... the "room" in this case being a beach.

Fil arced his neck to look at Riko. "It was you," he said. "Wasn't it?"

Riko remained stunned by the scene for a little while longer. One thing was for certain, if he did have anything to do with it then he was just as startled by the outcome as we were.

Or he was doing a very good job of pretending.

"Uh," Riko began, "yes, well ... no, it was John — John Horsham."

"John Horsham's dead," Kelly said. "I think we've all come around to accepting that no matter how devastating it might be." She nodded to the tablet, lying in the sand a few paces away. "What's in there is nothing but an echo — a memory. A *very weird*, *interactive* memory, but a memory nonetheless."

"Is there more of it coming?" I said, deciding someone needed to ask the important questions. "Whatever that was?"

Riko avoided my eye either because he didn't want to lie directly to my face or because he had decided I was intimidating now I had proven my physical prowess in the jungle.

He shook his head. "No," he replied. "I don't think so."

"You don't *think* so?" Kelly said. "Or you're *sure*?"

Riko shrugged and looked out over the beach, making a conscious effort not to look at the smoke. As if it might just disintegrate into thin air if he stopped thinking about it. He nodded to the tablet. "I'm never completely in control of that thing. That's why it happened ..."

"Why what happened?" I asked. "The explosion?"

"Yeah," Riko replied, and then scratched his forearm.

"You were following orders?" Fil asked. "John Horsham's orders?"

Riko nodded.

And remained silent.

I decided to press him. "Riko?"

He didn't relinquish right away.

And I wondered if I wouldn't have to exert a mite more pressure.

In the end, he let loose a defeated sigh and spilled the beans.

"He said I wasn't to tell anyone about this. That it might get in the way."

"Get in the way of what?" Kelly asked.

"The ... plan," Riko replied.

"We'll come back to that," I said, "but what did John Horsham tell you to do?"

"John Horsham, or" — Riko shot Kelly a glance — "his digitally preserved memory, wanted me to get away from you all ... for safety reasons."

"Okay," I said. "That was very considerate of him — and it was to do exactly what?"

"What ... you just saw now," Riko said.

450

"A bolt from the blue?" Kelly asked.

Riko shifted his attention onto Kelly, giving her his full and undivided focus for the first time in the conversation. "Yeah," Riko said. "That's what it's called — 'A Bolt from the Blue'."

A few more seconds of precious life ticked by and I decided to speak up rather than miss out on yet more goings-on. "Is that ... something on the tablet?"

"Yes," Kelly and Riko said, together, both turning to me.

"Okay," I replied, holding up my hands in surrender. "Thanks."

"It's an app," Kelly said, taking pity on me, "that I couldn't quite believe when I got down to examining its coding." Her lips remained parted but she stopped speaking for several seconds — as if someone had suddenly stuffed an invisible cork in her throat. "It interfaces with, well, I don't think there's a way of putting this any more technically ... *space lasers*."

"Space lasers?" me and Fil responded, apparently our turn to speak at the same time.

Kelly nodded and then sneaked a look at Riko. "That was about the point where I decided the thing was beyond me. Or, well, that I didn't want anything to do with it. There're certain things you don't want to get yourself mixed up with in the IT world. Anything to do with either space or military — let alone both — is pretty high up on my list."

"But Riko didn't mind so much?" I asked.

"That's for Riko to explain," Kelly replied.

And the three of us all looked at him.

"I guess this makes me look pretty stupid," Riko said.

It seemed as though he was expecting one of us to deny this.

*Good luck with that ...*

"It's just," he continued, "if you knew the full story — it'd make more sense."

Behind our backs the waves sloshed into the shore.

Something on the downed plane creaked.

"We've got all the time in the world," I said, as if it needed saying at all.

Riko drew breath and scanned each one of us. Then he looked at the rising smoke. "John told me to get away from the plane quickly ... so as not to put the rest of you in danger. He said the priority was to destroy the original tablet, now it was no longer under Kelly's control."

I looked to Kelly for confirmation of this.

After all this time I had almost forgotten that the tablet lying on the sand a few paces from us was a duplicate of the original. And I also realised I hadn't seen Kelly bearing the tablet tucked beneath her arm on the way to the plane.

Someone else had it, then ...

Or so I thought.

Riko continued, "John knew Kelly had lost the tablet. And so he worked on a solution to destroy the thing before it could fall into the wrong hands. He had to guide me through the process because there were some manual elements which only a human being would be able to compute."

I couldn't help butting in. "And this ended with you firing a space laser?"

Riko's lips flapped open.

Then shut again.

He gave me a steely glare and a nod.

"But," Kelly continued, "you picked the wrong tablet?"

Riko scratched at his forearm some more as if attempting to escape his very skin. "I ... was looking over the list ... and ... I might've got fat fingers — just for a second!" He added the qualifier as if it made any difference to the physical results. As if it meant the scorched earth and rising smoke were less notable because of it. "John told me there would be a delay — for the satellite to get around to the right position ... but by then the tablet had moved."

Riko nodded at me.

This time Fil spoke up, briefly surprising me and the other two. "So the other tablet — the original one — it's presumably still back somewhere on that island ... did it get blown up too? Another space laser?"

Riko shrugged.

Which didn't seem quite appropriate, but still ...

"I guess," he said.

As the four of us absorbed the state-of-play, the duplicated tablet, having narrowly escaped oblivion, made a bleeping noise. As one we craned our heads to see what it was up to. Even from where I stood, I could see the digital avatar of John Horsham splashed upon the screen.

Riko glanced to us as if asking permission. He stalked off to the tablet and retrieved it from where it lay upon the sand. This time, however, instead of being all secretive about his virtual friend, he brought the tablet over. It was more surreal than I could ever fully appreciate to have the four of us standing around the tablet, on a desert island, the mid-morning sun beginning to bake the sands, staring at an avatar of the deceased John Horsham.

But, still ... there we were.

On the screen, John Horsham blinked to himself with something between a smirk and a frown lining his lips. He held his hands out of sight, clutched behind his back. As before, he looked much neater, more orderly — and not to mention a few kilos lighter — than he ever had done in real life. "Well done, Riko," he said, finally speaking. Although his voice was far chirpier than it had been in real life, it didn't fail to send a skitter down my spine.

Sort of like walking over someone's grave.

And maybe it shook me up to see that he was on first-name terms with Riko, too.

John Horsham's focus softened and I got the weirdest sensation that he was *looking* at all of us. "I have lost all signal of the tablet ..."

Riko glanced up at the three of us — clearly still finding it weird he was sharing his little secret with someone else. "We, uh ... had another strike. Not far from here. I guess the triangulation was a little off ... uh ..." he shifted his full attention back to the screen "... are you totally sure the other strike hit the tablet? There's no chance it might've just ... *missed?*"

The digital John Horsham furrowed his brow. "It is possible, although an explanation for the strike missing its target here might be the location and lack of signal coverage."

Kelly looked suddenly alarmed. "That island is densely populated ... and, well, if it did hit its target who's to say that it didn't deal some collateral damage to the surrounding area?"

John Horsham appeared to muse on this point a moment further. "I am unable to detect any signal from the other tablet — that's all I am able to elaborate on."

"Can't you," Kelly replied, "like tap into the news networks there, or something? Surely they would've said something about a laser beam sizzling down out of the clouds and burning a hole in the ground?"

If his silence was anything to go by, it appeared John Horsham took exception to being told what to do. I guess even avatars in digital prisons have a sense of ego.

At least this particular avatar did.

All the same, John Horsham responded a few seconds later. "I cannot find any news reports regarding this incident."

"That's reassuring," I couldn't help chiming in.

John Horsham flashed a smile as if he had picked up on my sarcastic tone. Then he said, "Now, as for what to do next ..."

Kelly interrupted. "How do we get off this island? And back home?"

John Horsham had stopped speaking when Kelly had started talking over him. I had to admit that the sense of reality about the way the digital version of John Horsham acted was more than a little eerie to behold. When John Horsham spoke again, it was with an unmistakeably biting tone. "I thought you wanted to stop Simple Sun? Emmerson Ray?"

Kelly parted her lips to respond, met my eye and then closed her mouth. She turned back to John Horsham. "I want whatever's going to cause the least amount of bloodshed. We've had enough already."

John Horsham appeared to consider this for a few moments — as if he was running some complex calculations. For all I knew, that was exactly what he was doing. "We'll send out a ping — bring rescue. You may have already noticed, but the battery on this tablet is running low. I have already identified several ships in the area and when you are ready

I shall send out a group SOS, bringing them to your rescue. Once you get on board you are to recharge this tablet and I shall examine our options from there."

I looked at the others' faces to see their reaction at being told what to do by a computer tablet. By the time I had done so the screen had gone blank.

John Horsham had run out of battery.

# ALL ABOARD

Everything stank of fish guts.

I thought I could feel the stuff seeping into my skin. It was hot, too, in the ship's cabin, with only a tiny porthole cracked open to allow in some of the fresh sea breeze. The boat glided from side to side as it cut through the placid seas, headed on a course guided by satellites or whatever technology they used to navigate boats with. There were four bunk beds for the four of us. The others — Riko, Kelly and Fil — were all sort of dozing away while I was lying on my back, on one of the top bunks, staring up at the scuff marks on the once-white ceiling.

John Horsham had promised us a boat to get us off the island and he had delivered.

It had been four, maybe five hours after the tablet had run out of juice that the boat had appeared on the horizon. A little while after the motorised dinghy had been launched to fetch us. The men aboard the boat all spoke with Caribbean accents and were clearly locals from the islands. They had been friendly when they had greeted us, welcoming us on board with grins and pats on the back and jesting comments asking what had happened to our plane. It appeared it wasn't the first time they had attended castaways. They had set plenty of drinking water before us. I hadn't realised how thirsty I was until one of the men had insisted that I take some draughts. As the water trickled down my throat, I had visualised all the parched cells in my body gradually reinflating. As they had shipped us back to the main boat — a fishing trawler anchored fifty, a hundred metres out from shore — I had wondered just how much longer I would've been able to bear without drinking. I told myself I would've found a solution soon enough — just as I had with the bananas I had foraged for our breakfast before the space laser had sizzled down through the heavens.

When we had got onto the boat itself, the captain had presented a far more solemn figure. He had asked us serious questions about the plane crash, about whether anyone had been injured or perished. After one of his officers inspected us for injuries, he had declared we were to remain in our assigned cabin till we returned to port. Although I hadn't said anything to the others I'd kind of felt like we had just been told off by the head teacher at school.

As if any of this was actually our fault ...

From somewhere, Riko had produced a charger for the tablet and duly plugged it into the closest available outlet. The power on board the boat wasn't as quick to charge as an outlet back on dry land but it was better than nothing. And it was that or nothing.

I tore my attention away from the scuff-marked ceiling. "Does anyone have any idea where they're taking us?" I asked ... a general question to the room.

Kelly, across from me on the other upper bunk, responded. "He was tight-lipped about everything — why would he tell us where he's taking us? One thing's for sure, there'll be groups of police lying in wait for us ..."

On the bunk beneath Kelly, Fil spoke up. "Is there anything we can do?"

"What?" Kelly replied. "Grab one of the dinghies and make a break for it across the Atlantic?" She paused another moment before summing up her thoughts. "No," she said. "It's wherever the captain's going or a lethal swim."

It was good to know exactly what our options were ...

Riko was suspiciously quiet, in the bunk beneath mine. When I flipped a glance in his direction, I saw he was busying himself with the tablet, flipping through a variety of screens, apparently trying as hard as we were to figure things out.

"How're you getting on?" Kelly asked.

Riko didn't realise she was addressing him at first and there was no response.

"Riko?" I said, hoping to get his attention.

"Hmm?" Riko replied, finally, and then looked up from where he sat on the edge of his bunk, ungluing his eyes from the screen. "Oh ... I think I've managed to get into the ship's navigation systems." It was only as he spoke the words that he appeared to acknowledge the gravity of what he had achieved.

It felt as though my eyeballs were bulging from their sockets.

When I looked to Fil and Kelly, I saw I wasn't alone in my disbelief.

"Can you alter our course?" Kelly asked.

Riko pouted and turned his attention back down onto the screen. "I ... suppose so."

Kelly kicked her legs out from beneath her, perched on the edge of the upper bunk, and peered down between her dangling ankles at Riko. "Where're we going?" she asked.

Riko did that weird two-finger gestured to zoom the screen out some more before we could see the whole picture. Seeing as I had seen next to nothing of any plans — let alone maps of the local area — it was essentially meaningless to me ... beyond the fact that I could tell the difference between what was dry land and what was sea.

However, as it happened, there was no need for interpretation, because Kelly filled us in. "Back," she said, and then glanced up, meeting my eye. "Back to the island."

There wasn't much for us to do.

Or, maybe to rephrase that, there wasn't much for *me* to do.

Until I heard heavy footfall outside the cabin.

And the steel door burst open, clanging against the wall.

The captain stood in the doorway.

His eyes were wild, his hair sticking up all over, his nostrils flaring. He looked like a picture of madness. His stare swept the entire room. When he spoke, his voice had that same maddening bark that teachers have. "The ship's course is stuck! Someone is at the navigational systems — and my bet is it's one of you!" He blew out his cheeks, his stare passing over me for a blood-freezing second before releasing me and drifting onto his next target, Fil. "Now, which of you is going to own up ... or am I gonna have to start tossing you overboard one at a time?"

My stomach seized tight. There's something about the idea of being unceremoniously hurled into the open sea that is unspeakably terrifying.

Thankfully, Kelly spoke up. "It's not us," she said. "But we know who it is."

The captain shifted his focus onto Kelly. I couldn't help thinking to myself that there was a touch of disappointment to his expression. Perhaps he was the old-school, not-quite-extinct, chivalrous type who believed women were all sweet-smelling roses and silky scarfs. However, if his expression was any softer for Kelly being a woman, then his threat didn't lose any of its edge. "Maybe we should start by throwing you over and see if that corrects the problem, huh? Allows me to take back control of my own damn ship!"

I decided I might have a say in this. "Riko," I said. "Show him the tablet."

There was some shuffling in the bunk beneath mine.

The captain's eyes flitted about all of us.

I could see he was bunching his fingers into fists down at his side — just waiting for the excuse to let loose some of that tension he had built up.

I leaned over my bunk to see Riko firing up the tablet — recharged via the ship's power. The familiar Simple Sun logo flashed up, making me feel a nauseous swell deep down in my stomach. I wondered if I would ever look at the sun in the same way again. He looked up at me, clearly attempting to throw the captain's ire back in my direction. "What now, Spark?"

I looked at the captain, who was of course now eyeing me with increasing suspicion. I knew one badly placed foot here might well see me tossed overboard. "See if you see anyone hacking into the ship's systems."

Out of the corner of my eye, I saw Riko stared at me long and hard.

I maintained eye contact with the captain. "Come on," I said to Riko, "you're the expert with that thing. Ask John Horsham about it if you don't know what you're doing."

This proved all too much for the captain to bear.

I guess we all have our breaking point.

He brought his left fist down hard against the wooden frame of my bunk, making the mattress and my bones shake. "Who is John Horsham and what the hell is he doing to my ship!"

When I spoke again, my tone was more rushed.

I could just smell that salty sea air in my nostrils.

I could almost feel the playful nibbles of the Great Whites.

"Look," I said, addressing the captain. "You've got to believe that throwing one of us overboard isn't going to help things. The person ... the organisation that's doing this ... they have nothing to do with us ..."

I waited, seeing if one of the others would interrupt unadvisedly.

Thankfully their sense of self-preservation was as strong as mine.

The captain took a moment — huffing a breath through his nostrils.

Some of the tension relaxed out of his shoulders.

He looked at me closely.

I could see the weariness just beneath the surface of his eyes. The kind of weariness that only comes from a lifetime spent out among the elements. I'd seen that look in the eyes of those approaching their pension at work. The look of a survivor.

And this was merely another battle.

"Who's behind this?"

I caught Kelly's eye, wondering if she might be about to fill in the gaps. But although her lips were slightly parted she didn't appear to be readying to bale me out.

I guess she was okay with me being the one to test the water.

"Emmerson Ray," I said.

The captain's gaze lingered upon me for a long while then he shifted his focus onto the floor. "Son of a bitch," he said, and then raising his eyes again, "The whole goddamn family — sons of bitches, all of them."

Despite the constant hum and vibration from the ships engines through the cabin, I could feel the silence opening up in the room as the four of us waited with bated breath.

The captain elaborated. "They've been ruling that island since ... well, you know, since the British left. They're down in the roots, rotten to the core. They've been wanting political power for so long ..." he shook his head "... I don't know." Finally, he looked us over. "Just what've we got ourselves wrapped up in?" His mouth turned upwards at the corners. He shook his head again. "Emmerson Ray."

"Marcus?" Riko said.

The fact that he called me by my full name was jarring ... but it was Riko all right ... albeit in a previously unknown "serious" mode.

I looked to him, sitting on the bunk beneath mine, the tablet laid on his lap, the virtual rendering of John Horsham standing there patiently, his hands clasped at his waist as though he was a computer salesman rather than a technician.

"He says that he can do a local override on the ship's system — reset our course."

I was just about to tell him to do just that, and by so doing stepping upon that most sacred of rights, passed down through the centuries, untouched by the heavy hand of time:

That on board a ship the captain makes all the decisions.

"No," the captain said, to the surprise of all of us.

There was no trace of the anger on the captain's face now.

Just determination.

It was one of those moments where you expect someone to twizzle their moustache with their fingers ... except the captain had no moustache to twizzle.

"It's time," the captain said. "Time I faced Emmerson Ray — that whole bloody family." He looked away, to the wall, to some undetermined spot. "It's been too long running."

As the captain had his introverted moment, we all exchanged glances.

461

No, we weren't sitting in the stalls at some hammy amateur theatrical production.

This was real life.

The rush of the sea breeze was a welcome relief after being cooped up at in a cabin. "Emmerson Ray" had been the key to unlock everything. I stood at one of the rails of the ship — it was either port or starboard, I've never really got my head around telling them apart — and peered out across the flawless sea to the green lump growing steadily up and out of the horizon.

The ship rocked back and forth steadily in the calm seas while on deck the fishermen went about their work either bare-chested in denim cut-offs or in soiled vests covered with fish guts. The muscles on the bare-chested men made me feel very inadequate indeed.

Thankfully the sea breeze was sufficient to sweep away the smell of sweat and fish and something extremely unpleasant and tangy that I couldn't — and didn't particularly — want to put my finger on.

Kelly arrived beside me, resting her elbows on the railing and leaning over with her hands clasped. Within a few seconds of her arrival she had already shown herself approximately a thousand times more at ease than I was.

"Do you think this is crazy?" Kelly asked.

I considered my answer, not wanting to sound like a complete coward right from the off.

To tell the truth, I think I went too far in the opposite direction to be entirely convincing.

"No," I said. "Definitely not."

Kelly gave me a sidelong glance.

And I decided to double down.

It was now or never.

"We have to face up to him, sooner or later ... I mean, he chased us off the island with armed men. What about that says that even if we did make it back home he wouldn't, you know … send someone after us … like Toby or Daymian?"

"Toby and Daymian are on our side."

"Oh, yeah," I replied. "Thanks for reminding me."

It really had gone out of my head.

… I guess when you see someone bearing down upon you with a stun gun in their hand the thought that they're evil tends to remain scarred into your grey matter.

Behind us, upon the deck, I saw Riko was examining one of the piles of rope, coiling it in his fist and then shaking it back down like he was some sort of floating adolescent wannabe cowboy. One of the deckhands said something to him as he passed by and Riko stopped what he was doing until the deckhand had gone out of sight.

Then he began doing it again.

Fil was being altogether much better behaved, at the stern of the boat, sitting there apparently without a care in the world … happy to go with the flow.

I wondered just how dangerous it was to go through life just "going with the flow".

… I was doing a good job of trying it out.

"What do we do when we get there?" Kelly asked.

I shrugged. "I guess the captain has something planned. It sounds as though this is a beef which hasn't just sprung out of nowhere. It seems like it's been simmering for generations."

Great, now I was sounding like a prophet in every bad film ever made.

Kelly sneaked a glance back over her shoulder, her gaze settling upon Riko who continued his rope tricks. "We've got the tablet — John Horsham on our side. And as best as we can suppose, the original got smoked by that space laser."

I still couldn't quite get my head around the space laser.

But, then again, perhaps I didn't have to.

It just *was* …

The ship's engines reached a higher pitch and I sensed the vessel cutting through the waves more quickly, carving through the water with a more determined line. The island was looming large with every passing second — emerging from the horizon.

"You think this is a good idea?" Kelly asked.

I resisted the urge to shrug ... there would be time for shrugging later ...

"I don't know," I replied. "I guess we'll see."

# BACK ON DRY LAND

The dock was about how I remembered it. I could even see the boat we had arrived in the previous day. I couldn't help my mind sweeping back to those memories. To all of us being carried along with Emmerson Ray, Zachary leading the way to our fates ... and to Danna's death.

The captain stood at the front of the boat as it rocked its way across the waves and closer to port. I half expected to see armed men emerge on all sides but it appeared there was nobody to greet us except for the seagulls. All the same, my heart pattered in my throat out of anticipation.

And my ribs squeezed my lungs making every breath a major effort.

There was nobody on the dock this time, so when we got close enough to the concrete structure, a couple of deckhands deployed buffers and then leaped up onto dry land bearing ropes which they tied off upon the pilings there.

I followed Kelly up onto the dock.

Back on dry land, I felt dizzy.

All at once the tropical air was too much to take.

The dense heat squeezing me from every side.

I felt a hand between my shoulder blades.

"It's all right, Marcus. Let's get going — follow them."

I turned to see Fil, a faint smile sketched across his lips. I told myself that if Fil wasn't perturbed by the course of events then I couldn't have all that much to worry about. Or maybe he — like me — was just naïve or even completely oblivious.

The captain led the way. All crewmembers stayed aboard save the four who went ashore with the captain, flanking him like noble knights.

We entered an area thick with foliage. Tropical-looking trees springing up all around us. It felt very much like we were undoing all the good work of our escape from the island.

As we went along the winding path, through ever-thickening under-growth the earth beneath my feet became softer, my shoes sinking into it more readily. I wondered if it was made up of clay or something like it. The path snaked around a long bend and I realised Riko was pacing alongside the captain, leading the shortest column, and that Kelly wasn't far off his heels.

Riko was holding up the tablet and — I imagined — conversing freely with John Horsham about our direction and ambition. I wondered if I wanted to know where we were headed or if I was all the happier for being oblivious. Probably the latter.

The path snaked the other way and Riko, the captain and Kelly slipped from sight, leaving only me and Fil bringing up the rear, behind the crewmembers.

I hoped we knew what we were doing.

When I came up against the back end of the group, everybody had stopped in their tracks.

I soon saw why.

There was a gap in the foliage ahead which looked out over what appeared to be some sort of highway. As far as I knew it was the same one I had travelled on at Emmerson Ray's side on the way to the building where we had awaited the election results. I thought again about how he had had the victory speech I had written for him tucked into his pocket.

That already felt like a lifetime ago.

When we'd left the island on the plane, beyond the overriding idea that we were probably going to die in a horrible — and most likely fiery — crash, I'd believed deep down I would never return to this island again ... but, well, as with most things in my life, it hadn't exactly gone the way I had planned it. And here I was again.

The captain was still deep in conversation with Riko, the two of them examining the tablet as if it possessed the meaning of life itself. For all I knew, it did.

Since he was standing beside me and possibly as beleaguered as me, I turned to Fil and asked him what was going to happen. But he was only able to give me a shrug. As I was glancing back over my shoulder wondering whether we were going to beat it back down the path, I realised there was a steadily growing rumbling sound in the air.

A low-frequency rumble in the ground beneath my feet.

The crewmembers looked at one another. It comforted me that they appeared just as unsure about what was going to transpire as I was. That it was a secret held between Riko and the captain.

When the rumble finally reached its zenith — the quaking beneath my feet was sending a jostling sensation up through the pit of my stomach — a sixty-odd seated bus rattled into view.

Its paintwork was non-existent, scraped right down to the underlying grey metal, and it was dented all over. I guessed it had to be twenty, or more, years old. As it came to a halt with a screech of brakes and a huff of hydraulics, thick black exhaust fumes puffed up.

I turned to Fil and somehow managed to raise a nonplussed smile. "Guess this is our ride."

On board the bus, it was difficult to shake the idea that I was going to school.

It didn't remind me of bus journeys to work because those city buses had always been in fairly good nick ... and reasonably clean, too. It seemed as though the bus companies reserved bombed-out, near-enough-falling-apart buses for the school runs — probably on the basis that kids defile everything they come into close quarters with.

It's impossible to have nice things ... at least around children.

Still, even the school bus services I'd been on as a kid had had windows. And the seats hadn't been completely devoid of springs, the fabric threadbare and seemingly bound together to a large extent by dust and stubbornness.

The only person on the bus was the driver, who was wearing a white shirt and a black tie, a pillar box hat resting on his pate. He nudged the visor up when he saw the captain and they shared a brief greeting and a chuckle. I got the impression they knew one another.

I managed to get me and Fil seats right behind Riko and the captain, who were sitting on the seats directly behind the bus driver. Kelly was on the other seat behind the driver, across the aisle while the crewmembers spread themselves out amongst the other seats on the bus.

Now I hoped we would get some sense of direction.

As the bus rumbled into life and gradually purred its way along, beginning to climb a curve going up a hillside — with trees still on either side of us — I could see Riko flipping through screens on the tablet. A virtual map opened out. It wasn't like the two-dimensional ones I was used to seeing on mobile phone apps or on computers. This one was a full-on, three-dimensional representation, updated in real-time. I shifted a glance at Kelly who had her lips pursed in what could only be an expression of concern. I remember her saying that as a personal policy she didn't like to get wrapped up in anything to do with military tech and I couldn't help but think that this was exactly what Riko was up to right now.

After about twenty, twenty-five minutes of driving along the meandering road, feeling the warm breeze blow against my cheeks through the paneless windows, we came to a village. The houses were all painted in bright colours and most had corrugated plastic roofs. The tarmac on the road crumbled into softer earth here, too, and there were several potholes that the bus had to swerve to avoid. The captain said something and the bus driver brought us to a halt at the side of the road as diligently as if he had been one of his crewmembers.

When my thoughts got giddy, I realised I was holding my breath.

Waiting to see what was going to happen.

The captain addressed us in his easy Caribbean lilt. "All right, everybody off."

It felt like the weirdest coach trip I had ever been on, to be picking my way down the bus steps to the dilapidated road. And it was made even more surreal still when I stopped to consider I was still dressed in a suit. Only now I looked as though I had been dragged through a hedge backwards. Two or three times. ... And in thirty-degree-plus heat.

The captain led us up the road and brought us to a stop outside one of the houses. The house didn't look any more remarkable than the others in the village. The captain strode up to the steel front door and rapped his knuckles. There was quiet as we waited to see what was going to happen. I couldn't help noticing Riko was standing at close to the captain, ready to be called upon. He held the tablet on standby dangling down at his thigh like a revolver.

After about half a minute the door opened and a doughy woman with cotton wool hair in her seventies appeared. She was wearing a dress in a multicolour pastel shades and went barefoot. She squinted up at the captain, who was a head and shoulders taller than her, head slightly tilted to one side as if she was attempting to clear a blockage in her memory.

Then — after a second or two — a wrinkled smile scored her expression.

She leaped forward with the vitality of someone four decades younger, throwing her arms about the captain's neck. The captain, apparently taken aback by the suddenness of this gesture, paused a moment before leaning over slightly. He laid one of his substantial palms on the upper back of the lady as she hugged him tightly. When they broke off their embrace, the woman leaned back, apparently to take in the entourage accompanying the captain. With another muttered word, she disappeared into the house. The captain gestured us all inside.

The room smelled sweet and fruity, and I soon saw why.

On her kitchen counter — assembled from what looked like drift-wood — she had a blender filled with tropical-coloured juice. When I say "tropical-coloured" I guess I am saying it was a sort of purple-blue. It was a shame it was clearly insufficient to offer to all of us, although she did offer the captain some which he refused with a polite shake of the head. Someone shut the door and the half dozen or so of us all assembled around the captain and the woman waiting to hear the next step in the plan. "This is my Aunt Agnus," the captain said, unable to keep his broad grin to himself.

It was the kind of inner-child grin that can never be absolutely erad-icated no matter how much therapy you go through.

"We thought we'd pause here," he continued. "Make plans before the big push."

I looked around the others, hoping someone might chirp in, asking what precisely this "big push" entailed. Riko was lurking about with the tablet close at hand ready to be called upon. With not much more than a nod from the captain, Riko arrived at his elbow, and the captain went on speaking. "We cheated the hack," he said. "With my friend here's help, of course."

I expected Riko to smear on a shit-eating grin but he remained strangely neutral.

Dare I say it ... *modest?*

"We used the device here to make them believe we had managed to escape their control — we disappeared from their tracking systems."

I looked to Kelly, hoping I might find some sort of confirmation from the only technically minded person I knew and trusted here. But she too was absorbed by what the captain was saying.

"We arrived incognito." Here the captain couldn't help but grin. "And my cousin Gus was able to bring us up here on his bus."

I looked around for Gus the bus driver but he was apparently still with his livelihood.

The captain went on, "From what we've been able to establish from looking at on-island communications — and my Aunt here has just confirmed — " the captain's aunt smiled at her mention " — Emmerson has seized control of the central government buildings. He has taken

470

control of military systems, crippling their organisation, forcing them to stand down." Finally, the captain looked in my direction ... or perhaps he was eyeing Kelly and Fil who were standing nearby. "Before that occurred he was able to raise an improvised militia, those armed men who pursued you off the island, shot at your plane. Since then, though," the captain continued, "there has been something of a stalemate. Both sides waiting to see what Emmerson will do."

Here Kelly spoke up. "And so we're just going to wait? Wait to see what he does? That's not very proactive."

Just like any good public speaker, the captain shifted his focus completely onto Kelly, beaming from ear to ear. It was the look of a public speaker who waits for someone to unwillingly fall into their trap. And to prove the very point they are trying to make.

"Who said anything about us waiting?" The captain took a step forward. Not just toward Kelly but towards his whole assembled audience. "No," he said. "Do not get me wrong — we will stop Emmerson ... and we shall do it right now."

It was here that Riko finally surfaced from his immersion in the tablet. Perhaps he was running some sort of report the captain had requested. Something top secret.

"How can you be sure," Riko said, "that he won't shoot the lot of us?"

The captain's expression darkened. He shifted a glance at his aunt, pursed his lips. "Emmerson has strayed a long way from being a reasonable human being — if he ever truly was one in the first place — but there is one thing I still have to assume. One thing that our efforts are grounded upon."

"And what's that?" Kelly said.

The captain breathed in deeply, flaring his nostrils. He puffed out his cheeks with his exhale. "That he wouldn't kill his own brother to get his hands on power."

# NIGHT-TIME RAID

M oonlight shone nearly as brightly as sunlight.
Rain hammered down upon the palm fronds above our heads.
It was a weird sensation.

Although the trees were largely keeping me dry, I felt soaked through with sweat from the humidity. I almost wanted to step out there into the gushing rainfall and allow it to wash me clean. Once I got out of this situation — if indeed I ever *did* get out of this situation — then the first thing I wanted was a hot shower and a fresh set of clothing. I was standing beside Fil while through the trees, and across the dirt track, I could see Kelly and Riko down on their haunches. They had two crewmembers behind them just as me and Fil had two crewmembers behind us. The captain, or Winderston, as he had introduced himself after his stirring speech, was on the dirt path, picking his way along, scoping out the route ahead. If Winderston — and Riko's — calculations were correct, and I had no reason to suspect they weren't, aside from the fact that, well, it was Riko we were dealing with, then we were about five minutes' journey from Emmerson Ray's location.

As I thought back on what had just transpired I wondered whether I shouldn't have drawn some clue from the fact that Winderston, the captain, was the only person I had come into contact with who referred to Emmerson Ray as "Emmerson" without the "Ray".

I couldn't help wondering whether we should've taken some precautions before coming here ... like maybe arming ourselves. Although as far as I knew the crewmembers might've been packing something. Who was to say they didn't have a concealed weapon or two about their numbers? The captain, Winderston, couldn't really be foolhardy enough to believe Emmerson Ray — who I had witnessed kill someone in cold blood — would buy a "brother, my brother" routine?

Then again, what did I really know about Emmerson Ray?

Whatever I did know about him, I knew even less about Winderston.

One thing was for certain, though, I was just as culpable for Danna's death as anybody else.

Black Pine had been right to treat me as a collaborator. That was what I had been.

As a raindrop sploshed its way down the back of the collar of my once-white, now-grey with sweat and dirt and whatever else, shirt I couldn't help thinking what had become of the others. My thoughts strayed to consider Toby and Daymian ... even *Lucas* ...

Someone whistled shrilly.

I looked through the foliage, seeing Winderston had risen up off his haunches, that he was striding along the dirt path. I looked to Kelly and Riko in the trees on the other side of the path.

They nodded to one another and stepped out from their cover.

"Come on," Fil said, gripping my shoulder. "We've got to go."

Everything within me — my survival instinct, I guess — screamed out for me to stay where I was. That I would be safe here. Or, well, safer than I would be going with the others.

I rose with Fil and the pair of crewmembers behind us.

We followed on Winderston's heels.

We plodded along for a good half an hour. I wondered why we hadn't come in some form of vehicle. The bus we had travelled on would've been preferable to the hard slog through the jungle. Maybe it was easier for the others given that they had more appropriate footwear than the dress shoes I had on. The dirt path widened and I was surprised to see the well-pruned hedge confronting us. Like ambling through the English countryside and coming across a mansion.

Only we were in the Caribbean.

My heart thudded against my ribs. I felt a chill pass up my spine. An out-of-place sensation. The humidity had to be close to a hundred percent and it felt as though every single pore in my body was expelling sweat.

The hedge was tall and performed the same task as its English equivalent — notably keeping the house and grounds out of view of the Great Unwashed. I couldn't really have complaints about being brandished as part of that particular group at this particular time.

Winderston led us along a dirt track and around a bend to a set of wrought-iron gates twisted into a swirling pattern ... again a design that would've been at home back in England. As I got closer, I heard Winderston mutter to Kelly, that this had once been the governor's mansion.

Beside the gate there was a telecom.

I expected Winderston to nod to Riko, to have him use the tablet to hack our way inside, but instead he jabbed the glowing orange button. The intercom emitted a distorted chirping sound. Like when you put a phone on loud-speaker mode. I turned to Fil who was close by. "Are we really just going to ask to be let in?"

Fil shrugged by way of reply.

A voice responded on the intercom and Winderston spoke evenly, calmly.

There was a long pause.

I sort of expected mechanical arms bearing submachine guns to poke out of the hedges and slaughter us where we stood ... but, no ... no machine guns.

Not yet, anyway.

And what was more, no longer than five seconds later the gate arced open, without so much as the hint of a squeak from the hinges, inviting our party inside.

Winderston peered back over us, his eyes falling upon me for some reason, and then he put one foot in front of the other and entered the grounds.

I took a sharp breath — lied to myself about having lived a full and satisfying life — and then followed.

The mansion was actually quite something to behold.

It was made out of white marble, or at least something that looked as though it was marble. Pillars held up the roof of the porch area at the front and there were blooming flowerbeds. Everything looked calm. And there was no sign of Emmerson Ray or in fact anyone at all.

I kept sneaking glances at Winderston, trying to get a read off him, to see whether he was in danger of panicking. But he gave absolutely nothing away.

I guess that's one of the properties leaders tend to have in common.

Good poker faces.

Excellent at not letting anyone see what they're thinking.

Capable of getting people to think what they want.

Without so much as pausing to take stock of our surroundings, Winderston strode his way up the staircase to the front door, grasped hold of the gargoyle-like brass doorknocker and gave it a couple of thuds. The sound echoed about the grounds surrounding us and it made me jump.

It felt as though I had suddenly appeared — completely out of place given the tropical climes — in a Gothic horror novel. The only real mitigating factor was that I wasn't wearing something skimpy, frilly and lacy.

A long pause followed — long enough to wonder whether there was anybody inside, although I could see the warm orange glow from within. I also thought I could hear murmuring voices. Finally, the door swung open to reveal a person in a black jumpsuit — the same clothing Fil and Kelly wore. The jumpsuit which was emblematic of Black Pine. As if this wasn't enough of a surprise, I took stock of the face sticking up through the neck of the jumpsuit.

It was Lucas.

Of course it was ...

Even despite my shock, I couldn't help but slip Kelly and Fil a sidelong glance to see what their reaction was. Their lips were slightly parted, eyes wide. On the other hand, Lucas didn't appear all that surprised, although his eyes did linger across me for a while longer than the others.

He stepped aside and allowed us in.

I did my best not to meet his eye as I passed him in the doorway, which wasn't actually all that difficult given the enormous opening.

Beyond, in the entrance hall, several chandeliers hung from the ceiling. A twin set of spiral staircases twisted upwards, mirror images of each other. They led up to what I supposed had to be a significant quantity of bedrooms.

Keeping close to the crewmembers — and their considerable muscles — I trailed in Winderston's wake. He appeared to know where he was going.

Kelly and Fil kept close to me.

I wondered if they thought I was some kind of lucky charm.

I suppose luck can be defined as "not dying".

Winderston led us through a series of hallways, replete with oil paintings; dark, matte colours of sombre scenes from centuries ago. Most of them depicted "traditional" British scenes, such as fox-hunting or banquets. I couldn't help feeling a slight snooze coming on as my eye passed over the paintings. They took me back to all those forced marches on school trips to museums and art galleries and the like while the art teacher droned on about the importance of "technique" or something or other. I wonder what you're supposed to do as a human being when you see no path in either the professional or academic world.

You just *are*, I guess ...

Or your name is Marcus Raisin.

Winderston brought us to a halt in one of the rooms just off the hallway. As he slowed, I got to peek in beyond the walnut doorframe.

The room was about two, three storeys high and must've occupied a significant corner of the house. Bookshelves covered the walls which were stuffed to bursting with leather-bound tomes. There was an ornately patterned rug adorning the floor — if it wasn't authentic Persian then it was an extremely high-quality imitation. A long window looked out across the grounds and because of the elevated position of the mansion it was possible to see the roads leading here. Now I could see why our arrival hadn't come as a surprise.

You could see the entire periphery of the mansion from this room.

A room where lofty arguments would be had and weighty decisions would get made.

In front of the window a figure sat behind a long desk. The figure was flanked by two others standing. Like Lucas at the door, the two standing figures wore Black Pine jumpsuits. I guess this was the cue for more gaping expressions of surprise on the part of Fil and Kelly. When I squinted enough to make out their faces my worst suspicions were confirmed.

It was Toby and Daymian with a "y".

"Glad to hear you made it back safe and sound."

The broad voice from the figure sat at the desk filled the room.

Emmerson Ray.

At first, I was certain Emmerson Ray was addressing me personally … apparently I wasn't beyond flattering myself. However, as I soon realised, from Winderston's advance into the room, I wasn't anywhere close to being centre stage right now.

"Brother," Winderston said, his own voice betraying his smile, "you didn't expect to see me back here?"

Emmerson Ray remained seated at the desk. He brought his hands up behind his head and leaned back in his chair. "We identified your boat," Emmerson Ray replied. "We got hold of you — we were towing you in."

Winderston took another step towards the desk and I noticed Toby visibly flinch. All it took from Emmerson Ray, however, was a sharp glance to have him stand down. In any case, I wasn't sure what sort of damage Toby might've been capable of inflicting upon Winderston.

Surely hardened sea captain versus nerdy coder was a physical mismatch for the ages?

"Why did you stop?" Winderston asked.

There was a certain bite to his question and I was fairly sure Winderston was the elder brother. He appeared to have that knowing dominant upper hand.

"We lost contact," Emmerson Ray replied.

There was no trace of bitterness in his response.

He was just stating facts.

He nudged his head in the direction of Daymian.

"I got my best boys on the job — but they just couldn't seem to get a handle on it." Emmerson Ray held up his hands. "Thought you'd struggled free of the net like a naughty fish."

Winderston smiled wide now. "Or a Great White Shark."

Emmerson Ray cocked his head to one side and narrowed an eye.

I wondered if he was truly vexed or if he was just playing the part.

"How did you get here on the island without me knowing?"

"So you didn't know?" Winderston replied, with a little bit more than a touch of cheek.

Emmerson Ray shook his head and gave something of a smile by way of response. "I'll admit we thought you'd outwitted us. We didn't know you were on your way here."

"You see," Winderston said, "that's the problem with technology. What you needed was a person standing up on the highest spot of the island, watching the seas. But that'd be too much like Olden Times, wouldn't it? The problem is that after you spend long enough staring at a computer you begin to believe it's your whole existence. You've got to get out into the real world, brother. See the world through your eyes. Not through some filter."

Emmerson Ray pouted. "All it would take is a camera," he said. "That would replace the human eye quite adequately."

"'Quite adequately'?" Winderston replied, arching an eyebrow. "Whose notes are you reading off, bro? When did 'adequate' become the measure of anything?"

Emmerson Ray didn't respond. It was difficult to pick up on whether or not he was becoming riled by the interchange, or if he was merely picking his moment.

The moment for what I was unsure.

I might not have known all that much about Emmerson Ray, but he was unpredictable.

He could turn on a penny whenever he chose.

Like he had shot Danna.

I hadn't seen that coming ... so what made me think I would see his next move?

I shifted a look at Fil and Kelly, standing close by, and noticed Riko was remaining near to Winderston's elbow, sort of like a street dog that's been fed by some stranger and is hopeful — *ever so hopeful* — of having found his forever home.

His forever master ...

Emmerson Ray's eyes passed from Winderston and onto Riko. Then down to the tablet dangling at his thigh. "That looks very much like a piece of tech that went ... *missing* quite recently."

"Word is," Kelly said, "that God hurled down a holy bolt of lightning and fried it."

Emmerson Ray's eyes lingered upon Kelly's before drifting off across the room. "The battery overheated," he said. "The thing blew up ... I wasn't there at the time but I don't imagine it was all that dramatic. These things never are." His eyes returned to Winderston. "In real life."

Winderston held his brother's gaze. "But *real-life* murder runs it extremely close, huh?"

Emmerson Ray didn't even flinch.

It was the moment that told me everything I needed to know.

That something ... something about Emmerson Ray wasn't entirely *human*.

When he spoke again, there was a coolness to his tone.

A machinelike quality.

"Every problem has a solution — all that stops you achieving it is *ethics*."

"'Ethics' is a funny way of describing human life."

Emmerson Ray shrugged and dipped his chin to his chest. A chillingly dismissive gesture. When I turned my eyes upon Toby and Daymian, I saw the blind devotion. Of course Emmerson Ray had been happy for them to run riot — they were just acting out what he would have been only too glad to do himself ... if it hadn't cost him the bigger picture.

This island.

"Are you happy now?" Winderston said. "They gonna make you prime minister?"

Emmerson Ray kept very still. "We need to await the outcome of the process. But I am quietly confident."

"Poor people," Winderston replied. "Poor, poor people."

I heard the footsteps to my left.

Lucas brushed past me.

Since it was a fairly large room, I was fairly certain he had taken pains to get as close to me as he dared. He sauntered his way up to the desk, to Toby, Daymian and Emmerson Ray.

As I looked at the four of them standing there, I couldn't recall having ever seen an uglier cabinet of monstrosities. What were they planning to do next? Did they each have a stun gun? Were they going to systematically torture each and every one of us?

Looking at Winderston, I couldn't see him coming quietly.

Or being any sort of victim.

Yet they still stood there.

And we stood facing them.

Who would break first?

Outside, in the grounds, I heard a whistle blowing.

Like one of those whistles that traditionally might've been found at a factory.

Signalling the end of the working day.

Or the end of one shift and the beginning of another.

But then I realised it was shriller than that. The tone was dulled somewhat by the thick windowpanes. It was some sort of a handheld whistle.

Like a PE teacher's whistle.

A wild thought sneaked into my brain.

That somehow Mr Daphies — my PE teacher from back at school — had stirred himself up and out of retirement to come and save me.

Absurd, of course.

And yet ... I couldn't help but cling to hope.

Finally, after what seemed like hours and hours of stand-off, Emmerson Ray rose from his seat. Even though they stood a fair way apart, I could tell Emmerson Ray was a smidge taller than Winderston. Suddenly, I wasn't completely convinced that a fight between the two of them would be such a foregone conclusion after all.

"Do you hear that?" Emmerson Ray said. "That is the sound of revolution."

# INTO THE FRAY

My whole body was shaking. I might not have realised if it hadn't been for my teeth.

They just started to chatter apropos of nothing.

The whistle grew shriller still and I remained focused upon the four figures standing before us, in front of the window looking out over the garden. Despite the sound, everything was still, dark ... until there was a bright white flash.

My brain leaped into life. My muscles seized tight.

I looked to Winderston. He had taken a couple of subtle steps back.

That was the opposite of reassuring ...

Riko was holding his ground. Either he was too startled or he thought we didn't have anything untoward to worry ourselves about. We would find out in the ensuing moments.

The whistling rose to a shriek.

I felt a strange tingle through my brain.

When it was too much to bear, I covered my ears with my hands. And then, when that was no longer enough, I doubled over myself, squashing my hands to the side of my head with my elbows. As I bent over, I noted Emmerson Ray and his cronies appeared entirely unaffected.

It made me wonder if ... they weren't human somehow.

And then, all of a sudden, without warning, the shrieking subsided.

I remained doubled over for several moments.

Catching my breath.

My heart beating against the underside of my throat.

Emmerson Ray was smiling broadly now.

It wouldn't have been possible for him to smile with any more villainy if he had tried.

His cronies — Toby, Daymian, Lucas — all beamed in a similar fashion.

"Evolution," Emmerson Ray said. "A marvellous thing." He pouted. "But ruinously slow — *achingly* slow. If only somebody gave it a nudge. To speed up our body's potential."

For some reason I felt as though I had been swept back to the Simple Sun Conclave. Emmerson Ray was employing the same speaking voice. Or maybe I'm just overly sensitive to marketing prattle. And just as easily taken in as anybody.

Winderston appeared to have recovered something of his former composure. "What're you talking about? How was that sound anything to do with evolution?" His eyes shifted between Emmerson Ray's cronies and then over the others who had come with him here.

"It wasn't the sound exactly," Emmerson Ray replied. "It was our *reaction* to the sound." Emmerson Ray was reading aloud from the supervillain playbook. "Or weren't you watching? Were you too busy covering your ears? Protecting yourself?"

Winderston said nothing.

Emmerson Ray went on. "No," he said. "The human body is capable of so much more when we have absolute control." He smirked. "Our brains are remarkable contraptions but they are ... they *lack* the structure of a computer system. Often when you want to switch something on or off the programming of the brain gets in the way."

Kelly broke in. "You mean the human being gets in the way?"

Emmerson Ray glowered.

Kelly flushed slightly.

He went on. "How might we mould ourselves if we had complete control of our bodies — all of our facilities? Pain, for example, can be a useful sensation. Its main purpose is to keep us from causing ourselves harm. But there are times when it is a distraction. When it can get in the way of what we are attempting to achieve."

Winderston broke in. "Like looking strong and powerful in front of everybody? Showing that you're not afraid of some whistling?"

Emmerson Ray snapped his fingers. "Exactly — that I'm not afraid of whistling ... amongst other things."

There was a pause and then Winderston spoke again. "So, what'd you do? Put a chip in your brain? Rewire your synapses?"

The corners of Emmerson Ray's mouth turned up in a smile. "I like that phrase. And yes, it was a lot like that." He nodded to Riko. A split second later I realised he was nodding at the tablet he was holding. "When John first showed me that device I thought it was such a pity the functionality was trapped in circuit boards, behind a screen." He tapped his temple. "Why not put it in a brain? And release a person's true potential?"

My heart thumped percussively.

I felt the beats at the pit of my stomach.

Emmerson Ray's smile descended and an altogether more serious expression took over his features. "You might say it would create the first generation of true *supermen*." His eyes flashed briefly to Kelly. "*Superwomen*."

"What're you saying?" Winderston asked.

Emmerson Ray smirked.

"You've got computer chips in your brain?" Riko put in ... wholly unnecessarily.

Emmerson Ray breathed in deeply. He began to wander from one side of the room to the other. The urge to play the supervillain had become impossible to resist. "It was John Horsham's last project," he said. "We had to enlist help, of course. A specialist neurosurgeon."

"Is he dead too?" I asked, unable to keep quiet any longer.

My comment was met with a glare. "No," he replied, belatedly, "he's still very much alive — and still very much a part of Simple Sun. Part of the movement. Part of the future." He paused melodramatically. "Soon there will be no past."

"That sounds ..." Kelly butted in. "About right ... except, well, there's only the present. That's the only thing that actually exists in reality. If you want to be technical, the past doesn't exist but neither does the future."

Emmerson Ray said nothing to this. It was difficult to tell whether he was smouldering or gathering his thoughts. Whatever the answer, when he spoke again his tone of voice was just as measured, unflappable. "As I was saying," he continued, "John Horsham was very much a part of this stage. But this would also be the last part he would play. His time had come. He had ... other plans. Different plans. Ideas that were incongruent with Simple Sun."

"So you killed him?" I couldn't help the words spilling out of my mouth.

My mind swept me back to that day which felt like years ago now. When I had walked in ... and seen Technomancer dead. ... Dead in his boots ... and — as his father had pushed to clarify — "definitely not wanking".

Emmerson Ray glanced over his shoulder, catching Lucas's eye. "Sometimes there's no other way."

"A personal touch?" I added, deciding that since I was pushing my luck I might as well stick my head right in the noose.

"You could say that," Emmerson Ray replied. "Or you could call it 'assurance'."

"Then," Kelly started, "Black Pine? What about Black Pine? I thought John started it when he decided that Simple Sun ..."

Lucas broke in. "John was a bit overeager to recruit some ... people for his venture. He needed someone on the inside. Somebody within LifeWare, to help with what he had in mind."

Everybody was watching Lucas now.

In a weird way it was satisfying. Everybody else was getting the opportunity to see just how much of an arsehole Lucas was. It wasn't just me on my own any longer. But that was little solace given what emerged from his mouth next. "John never was all that much of a people person, or, well, more accurately, he was never a *real-world* sort of person. He saw people as fixed constants rather than variables ... binaries rather than hexadecimals. That was his downfall in the end." Lucas snatched a glance at Kelly.

She gave him a poisonous look in return.

"He didn't think about stuff as fluffy as 'due diligence'. He took everything anybody said at face value." Lucas smirked. "In exchange for playing his game I got him to help me with a personal business venture ... local models."

Here he sought out my eyes and I did my best to bite my tongue.

This was a situation I knew couldn't be improved by me opening my mouth.

"I even thought I'd introduce him to a few of the models. Give him a chance at companionship." Grinning, Lucas shook his head. "He really was clueless. I set him up with a nice girl and he showed up in his stained work shirt stinking of BO ... He brought her a bunch of wildflowers that looked like they'd been picked from the roadside." He raised his chin. "Thought I'd give him another go, give him some tips, but that first experience broke him. He lost interest." Lucas focused upon me again. "I thought I had just the girl to switch things around for him."

I felt an unnerving wrenching sensation in my stomach.

If I had been blushing previously then I was positively glowing now.

"Who?" I asked. "Olivia?"

Lucas gave me a sly grin.

As everything unravelled before me, I tried to make sense of all that had been said. The countless dizzying revelations swirling about my head. I wondered if one day — perhaps not in the too distant future — I would understand. That I would *just* understand.

Everybody's got to have a dream I suppose.

Lucas was wearing the slimiest grin I had ever seen. "That night in the pub, when we bumped into one another, when you saw ... the two of us together. I had arranged to tell her what happened to John — one of those things you have to tell someone in person. One of those things that just seems so *inappropriate* to say over the phone, although at times needs must."

It was strange. One of my enduring memories of that night had been my disappointing plate of fish and chips. All the interruptions had caused them to go cold. There had been the pleasant interruption of Kelly ... but then there had been Lucas.

Ruining my spare time just as he did my working day.

At least I had definitively terminated my contract with LifeWare. He no longer had a hold over me. But then I thought it through just a little further and had a horrifying realisation.

Were the two of us working for the same organisation? If Black Pine and Simple Sun were one and the same then didn't that make us ... *colleagues* ... ?

Lucas continued, "She and ... *Technomancer* ... had a date together a few weeks back. They had a good time, or so I thought, from John's feedback. However, as it turned out, the experience was somewhat one-sided. Olivia had no interest in a second date."

Lucas looked me in the eye, daring me to speak.

I felt the weight of everybody staring at me, but in particular Kelly.

I wasn't sure why I was so disconcerted by what she might think.

Perhaps somewhere in the deepest, darkest depths of my soul I believed the two of us might have a chance. At what, exactly, I wasn't entirely sure.

When words finally did come, I pleasantly surprised myself with my apparently selfless concern. "Is Olivia okay?"

Lucas blinked a couple of times as if he was put off balance by the question. "Yes," he replied. "She's fine. I think."

"You haven't seen her recently?"

Lucas shook his head. I wondered if he was disappointed about this. He inspected the cuff of one of his overall sleeves. "Not since that night in the pub actually. She ... seemed quite shocked about what happened."

I couldn't help but think about the scene when I had walked in. "John," I said. "When I ... walked in on him. He ..." my eyes fell upon the tablet still dangling from Riko's grasp "... There was a picture of Olivia. He'd hacked into my phone. Got hold of it somehow."

I hoped nobody was going to call me out on still having pictures of my ex-girlfriend on my phone. I told myself it was an embarrassing fact that I just needed to lay on the table.

"Mmm," Lucas replied, looking at the ground.

I snatched a glance at the others in the room, wondering what they were making of mine and Lucas's exchange. When I looked at Lucas this time, a hot streak of anger ploughed through me. "What does that mean?" I asked.

"I ..." Lucas met my eye again briefly. "There was ... well, something before that. An issue, I think. After John saw some photos of Olivia — he seemed to take a particular liking to her. I ... think ... perhaps an *obsession*."

My skull squeezed my brain. I thought my eyes might bulge from their sockets.

But somehow I managed to keep everything together.

"What're you talking about?" I said. "When did this happen?"

"Oh, some time ago ..."

"When you showed him pictures?"

"I ... didn't show him the pictures."

Now this was getting ridiculous.

It was one thing to be dicing with death — expecting Emmerson Ray to put a bullet between my eyebrows at any moment or else to switch that impossible-to-bear whistling back on ... but it was another to be standing up in front of everybody else.

Going through all *this* with Lucas.

But I wanted to know the answer.

"*Who* showed him pictures?" And then I felt as though the ground gave way beneath my feet. "When did he see the pictures for the first time? Were me and Olivia still together?"

Lucas didn't answer. But he looked extremely glum. On any other occasion I would've taken it as a victory for him to appear like the proverbial rat caught in a trap.

But not right now.

I just wanted to hear the truth.

"I ... don't know for sure," Lucas began. "But I imagine he saw pictures of her for the first time at your desk — where you had them pinned up."

My mind whirled as I considered this.

I didn't have to consider it too long.

Of course that was the logical explanation ...

Another thought occurred to me — back in the Sermon.

The scene I had tried my very best to scrub from my memory.

"In the pub," I said. "You and ... Olivia, looked very ..."

The trace of a smile caught the corner of Lucas's mouth. He raised an eyebrow ever so slightly. "Touchy-feely?"

I said nothing, feeling my cheeks burning brighter still.

I felt like such an idiot.

Everybody in the *room* must've thought I was an absolute idiot.

Lucas looked to Emmerson Ray, as if apologising for the delay. That this discussion between the two of us had wasted enough time already.

*I* wasn't about to apologise for anything.

Lucas let loose a sigh. "I ... suppose there was something between us, maybe a spark, but it didn't go anywhere, Marcus. Especially not after I gave her the news. She was horrified, as you might well expect. She needed space. And things were busy at work. And with Simple Sun."

I wasn't sure whether Lucas was speaking honestly or whether he was employing high-level emotional manipulation. I had seen him keep a straight face telling bold-faced lies.

Nobody said anything and Lucas took this as a silent cue to continue his diatribe.

"I was the one who caught John, one day, with the tablet, hacking into someone's phone — not yours on that occasion, Marcus. And I shan't speak anymore to what I exactly saw. All that matters is that I was sure what he was doing was illegal and against all sorts of company policies ... I expected John to beg me not to report him, to plead that this would just stay between the two of us. But instead he took a whole different tack. He started telling me about the organisation he was involved with. Simple Sun. And then he began to jaw all about what he was doing with his own creation, Black Pine. That he was planning on dismantling the organisation from the inside. When I pointed out that this wasn't much of an excuse for accessing other people's devices without their permission, he told me he had to test his theory somewhere — somehow. In the end, he offered the tablet to me. Said I could take it home for the weekend and 'have a go.'"

The room was so quiet I could hear the ticking of a clock coming from somewhere. When I looked over at the mantelpiece, I saw a carriage clock rather than some cartoon time bomb primed to go off and turn this already crappy day into an unashamedly awful one.

Lucas drew breath and sighed it out, taking another step forward as though he was an actor treading the boards in some amateur theatre production. "I admit I got up to some mischief. But it hadn't gone unnoticed. That evening I was intercepted on my way home by Toby and Daymian."

This was the signal for Toby and Daymian to look shifty.

Lucas went on. "I had just got to the front steps of my flat when I got the feeling someone was following me. But ... nothing ... I was through the lobby, the key in my front door before I noticed the car parked out on the street. I thought nothing of it. Just a delivery person working for one of those parcel-slave companies. When I heard the knock at my door not five minutes later it was something I expected subconsciously. I wasn't expecting a package but it's not uncommon for delivery people to knock on my door with parcels for my neighbours since mine is the first door you see upon entering the building."

I wondered when Lucas was going to get to the point.

... Or, perhaps, more exactly, when Emmerson Ray was going to reveal our fate.

"When I opened up, however, I saw Toby ... pointing a stun gun at me. He wanted to see the tablet. He knew I had it. Daymian was standing at his heels, grinning in a creepy way."

A smile flickered across Daymian's lips.

"I thought of screaming out, something like that, but I suppose the diplomat in me convinced the more survival-focused parts of my brain to calm down. And it was a good thing too, otherwise there might have been a much worse outcome."

"I don't know about that," Daymian said, speaking up for the first time in this showdown. "I like to think we would've used our common sense."

Toby spoke this time. "I'd only have tasered you till you were on the ground. Once they hit you stop — that's the rule, only reason to have a stun gun."

"Well," Lucas replied, "perhaps I would've reacted differently had I known." He drew breath. "I made Daymian and Toby's acquaintance and they educated me about Simple Sun, suggested I attend a Conclave. Of course I obliged ... and that was where I met Emmerson Ray. A true revolutionary for our mundane times."

The last part seemed tacked on, although with Lucas it was difficult to gauge his sincerity.

Silence in the room followed.

Lucas went on, "When I returned the tablet to John a few days later he thought he had converted me — what with its ability to hack into just about anything ... its ability to *see* or *do* anything. But Emmerson Ray got to me first. And it was his vision I believed in. Not that I wasn't going to take everything John was offering." He shrugged. "It's a mean old world, you have to take what you can get when you can."

If I'd been a cartoon, my jaw would've latched open and my tongue would've lolled down my chin. It was just so extraordinary to hear Lucas voicing all of my concerns out loud — confirming my very worst suspicions. Never in my wildest dreams would I have believed it possible. And yet ... I wasn't dreaming ... or if I was then someone had given me some extremely potent drug — something to make me trip complete and absolute balls.

Nobody said anything further and Emmerson Ray used this as his opportunity to retake centre stage. "Without wanting to sound too melodramatic," he said, "I hold this entire island in my fist, and soon I shall hold the world."

I don't think he could've sounded more melodramatic if he had tried.

"Are you with us? Or are you against us?"

No sound. Not even the gurgle of water through the building's pipes, or the rustle of the breeze in the trees outside, or the honk of a distant car.

All I could hear was my own heartbeat throbbing in my eardrums.
I waited to see if one of us would step forward.
Make the first move.
And it was then that the tablet — still held tightly in Riko's hand —
began to make a series of "pips".

# RAISING THE DEAD

"**S**hut that thing down," Emmerson Ray said, turning on Riko. Suddenly finding himself the centre of attention, Riko flushed and jabbed at the screen. I could just see over his shoulder the stocky — but not quite stocky enough — figure of John Horsham. His mouth was jabbering open and shut ... although the only sound coming out was the series of "pips". The sound reminded me of sonar "pips" from those submarine films.

Ghostly ... but not altogether uncomforting.

Then again, I've never knowingly met a ghost, so who am I to judge whether or not it would be a comforting or unsettling experience?

Riko wasn't having much luck in shutting the tablet off.

For the first time since we had invaded the mansion, Emmerson Ray lost his temper. He gritted his teeth and let loose an, "Argh!" snatching the tablet off Riko and hurling it at one of the bookcases which lined the walls.

I half expected the tablet to strike the bookcase and bounce up off the floor as if made of rubber. As if John Horsham might've designed the thing with Emmerson Ray's rage in mind.

But ... no ... it struck the hard wooden floor and splintered into half a dozen pieces.

I guess the tablet wasn't as spectacular as everyone had initially believed.

"There we are," Emmerson Ray said, glowering at the broken pieces. "It's over ..." He slowly turned around to face the four of us.

Riko's courage finally buckled. He came over to join me, Kelly and Fil.

I wondered if losing the tablet was a form of emasculation.

I glanced over my shoulder, realising that a familiar figure — Zachary — was standing in the doorway. I wondered how long he had been there.

Just watching.

Waiting.

What caught my attention, however, was the gun he held down at his thigh.

I found myself caught between the stares of Emmerson Ray and Zachary.

I didn't know where to look.

Where the most immediate threat was likely to come.

Before I knew it, I had my answer.

The shrieking sound came again.

Unlike last time when it had been a cloying, borderline annoying tinnitus, this time it developed into an all-consuming echoing ring, as though I had my head inside a church bell while someone beat on it from the outside with a mallet.

Whereas before it had gradually worn me down until I doubled over in discomfort, this time I felt my knees grow weak. Before I could help it I tumbled forward — somehow finding the presence of mind to hold out my arms and have my elbows break my fall.

The skittering sensation through my nerves from the impact coupled with the insatiable ringing in my brain made it feel as though my body was twirling through a whirlpool. I wondered if it was because of all the time I had spent by the sea — if that was what had caused me to think I was being sucked down into its seemingly never-ending body.

Everything went black for a few moments.

... And then ... there was a shot.

I thought I was dead.

I thought that the blackness, the fact that the ringing in my head had subsided for a few merciful seconds, meant I was being swept along on the tides of the ever after. I even thought that — on balance — this was at least a dramatic way for me to go. It would be in the news.

Maybe someone would even write a book about it.

However the illusion was shattered when I opened my eyes and realised I was very much still harnessed to this mortal plane.

Slowly, I stitched the elements of my existence back together.

Everything was blurry, but I could see.

Everything was still ringing dully, but I could hear.

I was in a weird tangled sort of a heap but I could feel the hard wooden floor against my left cheek. I had the vague taste of blood in my mouth, the smell in my nostrils.

*Still alive.*

About as alive as I ever got.

I had to take a moment to remember the gunshot.

That it had cracked like a broken bone.

I narrowed my eyes, hoping to get a better view of the scene surrounding me, my circumstances. And I wasn't entirely disappointed.

Even though my eyesight was still blurry, I traced the only figure standing.

It took my brain another second to register that this was Zachary.

That he was the one I had seen standing in the doorway.

And that sent a pulsing sensation through my gut.

Was he coming for me next?

I focused on him. Thinking through the sight I had seen only a matter of hours ago.

Emmerson Ray standing over the dead body of Danna.

This scene was a lot like that one.

Almost an intricate reconstruction.

Except this time it was Zachary who was standing over the body.

The body of Emmerson Ray.

My heart throbbed beneath my tongue.

I felt a giddy nausea swill through my veins.

A million different thoughts skidded through my brain.

Was he ... dead? Or was it my overactive imagination?

Everything felt as though it was moving in slow motion.

The others were coming around.

Realising what had just transpired.

But I couldn't understand ... and the underlying fear remained.

It was then that I noticed Daymian rise up from behind the desk. His eyes wide and his complexion even paler than usual. He brought his hands up slowly to his face, flattening his palms against his cheeks as his gaze fell upon Emmerson Ray's lifeless body.

His focus moved onto Zachary. "What ... what the ... *fuck* have you done?"

Despite the profanity, there was no anger.

More like desperation.

As though he acknowledged who held the power here.

The person who was holding the gun ...

Zachary continued to stare down at Emmerson Ray's lifeless body. And then he nudged it with his bare toes, poking through the strap in his flip-flops.

I only thought people did that in films ...

Daymian aside everyone was very much keeping to themselves.

Holding their breath.

Zachary finally lifted his head.

And he grinned.

"Got the bastard!" he said.

My body felt weightless.

It was undoubtedly Zachary's voice I had just heard, and yet it sounded ... different.

Too spiteful.

Zachary was nothing if not obscenely calm and collected.

It was out of character for him to interject so bluntly.

Zachary wasn't proceeding on a killing spree, however. Rather, he was holding out his arm, flexing his fingers with a confused look on his face. After a few seconds he glanced up with an expression suggesting he was seeing us for the first time. No longer on the ground, and clearly trying to soak up the unbearable ringing in their heads, everyone else had got back to their feet.

Behind the desk, I could see Lucas and Toby standing beside the inconsolable Daymian.

Closest to me was Kelly, still dressed in the same black jumpsuit as Lucas, Toby and Daymian. Fil, too, wore the same clothing. Riko was in his Hawaiian shirt and flip-flops and he was perhaps the only one not staring at Zachary ... he was apparently heartbroken by the sight of the shattered tablet. Everyone wore an alarmed, slightly shell-shocked expression.

I imagine my face didn't look much different.

God ... I really had come a long way from LifeWare.

I wondered if breaking free had really been worth it after all.

... What the hell was I saying to myself?

Perhaps I needed another dose of LifeWare misery to remind me ...

The grin on Zachary's face gradually disintegrated. He turned slowly so his full attention fell upon Riko. It was more than him just *looking* at Riko. It was like his eyes were *burning* right through him. I wondered offhandedly if Riko was going to be his next victim.

If Riko would be next to bite it.

But as if to assuage Riko's fears — if indeed he had any — Zachary allowed the gun to slip from his fingers. It landed with a clatter at his feet. I don't know much about guns and how likely they are to be dangerous if dropped but I considered it a miracle that the thing didn't go off.

This gesture, however, did not seem to assure Riko.

Riko remained rooted to the spot, mouth agape, waiting for what was going to happen next.

Zachary closed in.

I readied myself to leap in and ... well, do *something ... anything ...*

Zachary halted when he was about half a dozen steps away from Riko. He breathed in deeply, his shoulders hunching backwards, and ... held out his hand.

Riko stared at Zachary's hand as if he'd never seen one before.

I wondered if Zachary was going to grab hold of Riko and perform some sort of elaborate flip, breaking his back in the process. Maybe by dropping the gun he had decided it was time to get physical. Time for him to press flesh to flesh ... and then flesh to floor.

Maybe I have a future as a pro wrestling commentator ...

Finally, well-advisedly or not, Riko accepted Zachary's hand.

I waited for the acrobatics to ensue.

For Zachary to hurl Riko across the room.

But after a few seconds of normal hand shaking it was all over.

Zachary withdrew his hand, arched his shoulders back and let loose a long exhale. "Thank you," Zachary said, the word so hushed it was almost under his breath. He massaged his scalp as if a migraine was beginning to bother him. "I ... don't know ... how long I can hold on."

"Hold onto what?" Riko replied, the only one capable of speech for the time being.

Zachary winced. "Hold onto ... hold onto this body ..."

Nobody said anything. Even Daymian was engrossed by Zachary.

Outside, a motorbike blazed by. Its ripping engine sent a jolt through my gut.

Zachary continued, "I ... didn't think I would get to see the real world again ... at least not like this ... but ... but ... it seems as though my code worked." Zachary's speech became more and more pained. He shifted his attention onto Kelly. They exchanged a knowing glance.

And even I was fairly sure I knew what was going on ...

"You never really know," Zachary went on, "whether your code's going to work until it goes out into the Big Bad World."

Kelly's mouth formed a tight "oh" shape. She looked as though she was going to say something but then sealed her lips tightly once more.

I realised it came down to me to vocalise the absolutely bleeding obvious. "John?" I said, the name sounding alien in my mouth. Probably because I'd never addressed him directly before.

Whenever I had been forced into interaction with one of LifeWare's IT department's finest, it had followed the format of me lingering awkwardly about in the doorway and saying something like, "Oh, hey?" as if I'd just stopped by to shoot the breeze.

Zachary sighed and his whole body seized tight as though someone had suddenly jabbed him with a cattle prod. I shifted a glance in Daymian and Toby's direction.

But there was no sign of their stun gun.

Zachary breathed in deeply, closed his eyes, swayed on his feet.

Perhaps if it had been a different situation then one of us might've gone over to support him. To prevent him from crumpling to the ground. But there was the not-so-small matter of Emmerson Ray's body lying between us, a pool of dark blood beginning to ebb out from beneath.

That made three dead bodies I'd seen in my life.

Knowingly, anyway ...

And although I had seen my first gunshot victim a matter of hours earlier, this one was definitely more grisly ... I had more time to focus. Zachary ... or as I was gradually coming to terms with ... John Horsham, was standing before us, his eyes looking as if they were going in and out of focus. "On the tablet," he began, "I ... downloaded as much of my ... myself as I could manage ... I never ... never truly believed it would be possible to ... to do this. There was no way to test out the theory. Not until ... not until now." He took a honking breath, spluttered a couple of times, and then staggered to one side, catching himself on one of the bookcases lining the walls.

"I ... don't get it," I said. "How're you? How's that even ... possible?"

Zachary remained in the same position, apparently immobilised by his current struggle with ... well, John Horsham ... or perhaps it was the other way around. Finally, he straightened up once more, stretching out his neck to assume his full and *imposing* height. Still leaning against the bookcase with the flat of his palm, he eyeballed each and every one of us as if expecting an attack to come at any time from any side.

I recognised that look.

Zachary was looking back at us, not John Horsham. Then, seemingly as soon as I recognised this, Zachary took a back seat once more. A smirking ugly smile wormed across Zachary's mouth and I could tell we were back in the room with John Horsham.

John Horsham, driving Zachary's body, reached up a shaking hand and pointed his trembling finger at his temple. "They all have chips," he said. "In their brains. One of my final innovations." He smirked wider. "They used it against me — *killed* me. But what they didn't know ... they didn't know ..." Here his gaze swept across the room, drifted over Daymian and Toby before coming to rest upon Lucas. "... They didn't know I had a contingency plan. That it was all prepared for." He shifted to look at Riko. "All I needed was someone good ... or, no ... someone who was *simple* to manipulate — conducive to following instructions."

Just how Riko had ended up being that person was lost on me ... that familiar IT-guy sense of superiority was crossing over from the digitally reanimated grave.

"Black Pine was only the start," John Horsham said. "I hoped it would be my legacy, if it came to it ... but ... it also ... served as ..." He gasped between words. He reached up to his throat with a pained expression, his hand lingering there before dropping away once more.

"A life raft?" Riko put in, startling everyone.

John Horsham — in Zachary's body — could only nod. It looked as though he was choking on a chicken bone. I wondered if one of us should go help him ... I decided that if no one else was going to then I wasn't ... that was a lesson I had learned during this whole Simple Sun process.

John Horsham-cum-Zachary was really struggling now.

Doubled over, choking.

Every breath was a fight.

I saw the struggle playing out over his face.

At times I imagined seeing Zachary emerging from within, fighting for control of his own body, before John Horsham bludgeoned him back down inside. He — whoever *he* was right now — dropped to his knees, hands back around his throat making unpleasant rasping noises. Again, I wondered if someone was going to step in, and specifically whether that someone should be me.

I resisted.

I wasn't going to die on this particular hill.

I had decided that much.

"He jumped from the tablet," Riko said. "And into his brain. I ... never ..."

But Riko's voice just kind of floated away.

We all just stood there, watching.

As John Horsham choked Zachary — *and himself* — to death.

# AWAY

The woozy engine vibrated through me in a maternal fashion as the bus ploughed past the morning traffic in its rush-hour immune dedicated lane.

This was one of the perks of taking the bus to work.

Or it was supposed to be.

No traffic.

There was of course, the matter of dozens of human bodies packed into this tight metal box. Some, like me, on the face of it, fortunate to have located seats; and the rest having to make do standing, gripping tightly to handrails or whatever they could get hold of to keep from tumbling over with the bus's jerky movements as it swayed in and out of bus stops or hissed its brakes suddenly to avoid whatever blockage had materialised in the road ahead.

Among the passengers, there were the coughs unconvincingly suppressed with fists, sneezes implausibly caught by penitent hands. Mumbled chattering droned up and over the hands-free kits used to communicate with parties unseen. Tinny audio rattled from the headphones exposing whatever entertainment my fellow commuter happened to be consuming.

There was that unpleasantly moist warmth of body heat.

And of course the smells.

Through the misted-up glass, I watched raindrops spatter the bus window.

I rubbed a small circle in the condensation to see out. I'm not sure why, because outside everything looked grey and grimy. Perhaps I thought the world beyond would be better than the one immediately before me. Men and women dressed in work clothes shuffled about on the pavement. They jostled into one another, beneath their umbrellas, aiming their gazes at the toes of their shoes, trying to keep them clean of splashback from puddles. Some clutched disposable coffee cups which puffed steam up into the frigid morning air. That sent a tang through my stomach. I thought about how a cup of strong black coffee might be just the pick-me-up I needed. This realisation was checked, however, whenever an umbrella would rise high enough to see the pallid complexion, the consumptive bags drooping beneath the eyes of the commuter.

Coffee wasn't an elixir, it was a poison.

Yes, I was very definitely back in Blighty.

And back in gainful employment.

Technically I had never been *out* of employment. True, there had never been a contract — at least not one I had ever seen. If it did exist I suppose Simple Sun had an extremely complex and satisfactory reason for never having served me with a paper copy. All the same, Simple Sun had paid me on time and in full each and every month up until about six weeks ago.

That was when I knew the game was up.

Like, really up.

And that it was time for me to return to the real world.

There was only so long I could go on without earning ... even a few months at double my previous salary at LifeWare wouldn't stretch that far. And so here I was — another temp thrust out into the world of work. Just what the world needed. Another admin person pushing paper from here to there. "Dropping" emails and "actioning" ... whatever needed to be actioned.

I raised my eyes up to the sky, to the clotted slate-coloured cloud, the white light of the sun promising to break through at some unspecified time in the future.

It was still up there all right.

But we might not see it today ... or even this week.

As the bus descended the hill, I thought about the morning when I had seized control of it from the driver via the tablet. And I thought about how I might've caused a horrible bus wreck.

On more cynical days — as I made my daily trip to Daphne's Magic Estate Agent, which neither belonged to Daphne or was magical — I told myself that if I ended up causing a crash then it would at the very least have given the survivors and their colleagues something to talk about besides printer jams and unmanageable email inboxes when they reached the office.

Didn't anecdotes, or more broadly entertainment, add *some* value to the world?

Weren't they supposed to make everything just a little less dull?

Already I could tell people were getting antsy to get off the bus.

Shuffling their way along the aisle, headed for the doors which would soon open.

As I did every morning, I asked myself just why they were in such a rush.

Did their bosses stand on the door, stopwatch in hand, eyes twitching up to see the faces that dared arrive so much as a minute after their contracted start time? ... I considered my own experience, thought for the best part of a second, and decided that yes, most probably did ...

When the bus hissed to a halt I waited as politely as I was able, picking my moment before slipping out into the exodus. Ready to get stuck into the beginning of Yet Another Workday.

A steady sheet of drizzle unfurled like gossamer. Some part of me enjoyed the freshness of the rain. As a rule, the concept of baptism is overused. Nevertheless, I couldn't help remarking — even to myself — that it did indeed feel as though the rains washed away some of the scumminess of the world. Mother Nature licking herself clean.

Not that it would last long.

Soon enough dry weather would return and the human world would get back to work, putting its sooty fingerprints over anything and everything that dared get in its way.

*I* was part of that world.

The irony didn't escape me.

One good thing about working at Daphne's Magic Estate Agent was the dress code. At least for me. The temp agency had told me I was being brought in to help on a short-term basis with a "filing backlog" that had accumulated following the sudden death of the previous post holder. When I'd joked on the phone about the person having perhaps died beneath an avalanche of paper, the pleasant lady had made a sort of noise between a cough and a "huh?".

In all my time gallivanting off on desert islands and the like, I realised I had forgotten that whole workplace thing of how jokes either fly or drop like lead balloons.

When I'd hung up and got to thinking about practicalities, I realised I'd never asked what the dress code was. In the end, deciding this was my New Life, I had determined it wasn't a risk to turn up in jeans, a ropey old jumper and some battered trainers.

What was the worst that could happen?

Anna — the manager at Daphne's — might send me home.

Or I might get a stern telling-off from the temp agency ...

Long-term I wouldn't *progress* ... which was exactly what I was aiming for.

As it had happened, though, Anna had barely looked me up and down when I rapped the front door at quarter to nine. Her words had been, "Oh hi, Marcus?" before adding, more quietly and apparently mainly to herself, "You'll mostly be working in the back room ..."

She had been dressed in a smart trouser suit herself and I saw that her half dozen or so estate agents — or whatever their rank was — were dressed in a similarly formal manner: immaculately coifed, straight-backed, perched on the edge of their seats, pecking at their keyboards and mouse buttons. When I'd walked past, trying not to tread on the backs of Anna's high heels, they had murmured greetings, wearing smiles that made me feel a little like a leper.

That if I got too close to them they might also become "unaspirational".

True enough to Anna's remarks, and my own expectations, I spent most of my time in the back room. I was tasked with copying tenancy agreements, inventorying keys to properties and scrutinising polite — but slightly threatening — letters to renters behind on payments. All of the letters carried the same grinning cartoon character — and perhaps one-time owner who I presumed to be Daphne — stamped in the top right-hand corner. Anna's signature was facsimiled onto the bottom of each as well. A few specks of dirt which'd got into a copy-run long ago in the annals of history definitively gave the signature away as a photocopy.

Yep, this was my life. At least for right now.

But it was how I was paying my way.

Besides me, Anna had taken on another temp, similarly tasked with tackling the Mont Papier, otherwise referred to as the "paperwork mountain". Rick was a man in about his mid-fifties and despite finding out on the very first day that we would be in the back room scratching through dusty paperwork, he still turned up every morning dressed in a suit. As he explained to me on the first day, entirely unelicited, as the two of us worked together in close-quarters — his suit jacket hanging off the back of a desk chair — he had worked at a bank for the best part of three decades before some "irregularity", as he termed it, had arisen, and he had been made "redundant".

He hadn't gone into any more detail.

If there's anything I've learned in my working life it's that there's nothing more boring than having to listen to someone else's career history. Only when it involves "dismissal" rather than "redundancy" does it start to get a little more interesting.

Rick was definitely on a different sort of a trip to me. Suddenly out of work, he was desperately searching for another permanent role. And so he was doing what any Boomer with a sense of self-worth does ... he was hoping to make a "good impression" on Daphne so she would give him the job full-time. Daphne, of course, as I had soon established, did not exist ...

While I'd been scanning in an insurance claim for a break-in, he had muttered something about the importance of "dressing for the job you want". I had just sort of smiled back, in side-profile, not wanting to admit there wasn't a job on the face of Earth I truly "wanted".

Well, there was *one* ...

The sense of satisfaction you get from performing even such a basic task as paper-wrangling is palpable. I had realised early on in my tenure that there was a distinct difference between the sense of relief I used to feel after a day answering phone calls at LifeWare, versus the feeling of just having "tidied up", made sense of a large stack of papers that had previously been nothing but noise. Once when Anna had stridden into the back room, gazed around her as if inspecting a pristine Alpine landscape and proclaimed, "Well done!" with a beaming grin aimed in my direction, Rick had emerged from being down on his hands and knees, concealed behind a filing cabinet, and shot me a scowl.

Whenever the clock rolled around to five in the evening, I surprised myself at just how fresh my mind felt. As if I had just come around from a peaceful — if a little boring — dream.

When I returned to the room I was renting and dropped my bag in the corner there was the novelty of having unallocated energy — unallocated energy which I could use for such tasks as reading or going to see friends for a beer or taking a walk ... or ... well ...

It was strange.

This particular Thursday afternoon — when it came — I actually felt a strange aversion to the minute hand twitching its way ever closer to the hour, and the five o'clock closing time.

However dreamy my job was in its lack of responsibility, there was another reason for not wanting to leave that particular afternoon. It was because I was afraid.

Afraid of what was to come.

It was a short trip back to the room I was renting. I bummed about, not quite sure what to do with myself. The room was literally just a single unmade bed with an MDF desk topped with fake pine. I had acquired a transparent plastic box where I stowed my clothes. There was a toilet bag on the floor by my bed containing a toothbrush, toothpaste, bar of soap and an optimistic condom.

There was a bathroom down the hall I shared with seven others.

This was pretty much the extent of my life right now.

Because it seemed the right thing to do, I took a quick shower and put on one of my old work shirts over a t-shirt. I pulled on the jeans I had been wearing all day. I tried to sit at the desk and review the pile of paper — the only thing that could be classed as "clutter" in my room — but my vision blurred before I could so much as finish a sentence.

Anyway, the words were all solidly fixed in my mind.

I had read through that pile of paper more times than I could count.

My phone buzzed in my pocket sending a jolt up my spine. I nearly leaped out of the chair ... before I finally checked myself and gradually unfurled to assume my full height.

When I reviewed the screen I saw it was one of those completely unnecessary reminders I had set to go off an hour before the actual event. Sort of like setting a reminder notification for an appendectomy appointment ...

I swallowed hard, realising I had a lump in my throat. I steadied myself, squared my shoulders. I peered out through the small window with its view of a brick wall outside.

It was time.

I wondered if the Drunken Dive Pub had been named in jest. It was located in the basement of what looked like a former bank. Like so many other high-street former perennials, it was now a trendy high-street coffee shop. There were stories — myths and legends? — as to whether there was a secret passageway between the café above and the pub below. And many unfunny jokes had been cracked about whether the café staff might be constantly half-cut or that the pub staff appeared to be permanently perky. It was that time of year — heading into deep Autumn — when it was getting very dark around seven in the evening. The steady drizzle which'd fallen throughout the day had greased the concrete steps. The odd raindrop spattered the slick surface.

When the door swung open, the warm orange glow within subsumed the cool functional white light from the streetlamp outside. The rumble of conversation drifted out of the pub, seemingly carried on the smell of spilled ale and lager.

My mouth felt really quite dry.

The punter who had opened the door staggered his way up the steps, away from the pub. He was about my age. Judging by the way he was doubled over clutching his stomach, he was the worse for wear. The pub door swung shut again, leaving me in the clinically white street lighting.

I took a deep breath.

And then trod onto the concrete staircase leading downwards.

When I reached the door, I hesitated. Over the chattering and laughing behind the door of the Drunken Dive, I heard my acquaintance retching the contents of his guts in a nearby back alley.

It was like entering another world.

The music — too loud, distorted — and the general clamour of people all squeezed inside.

The only way to tell where the bar was was by observing the people all knotted together around a focal point ... otherwise known as the barman.

I flipped a quick glance about the place:

Raised wooden stage.

Microphone on a stand.

A circular spotlight shining.

Tonight's weekly event — "Chuckles" — was printed large and proud upon the black backdrop and featured a pair of caricatured smiley faces in white. One face laughing with open eyes and the other with them closed from the force of their chuckling ...

My very first proper comedy gig.

"Marcus?"

The voice came out of the thrall.

And yet I recognised it instantly.

Even so, I was surprised when I turned to look and saw Olivia — my ex-girlfriend — standing there. As I always seem to do when I am mildly startled, I blinked rapidly and felt a slight flush fill my cheeks. "Uh, hi ..." I managed to jabber out.

"Drink?" she asked.

I took stock of her for the first time in the filmy air. There seemed to be an undercurrent of pounding vibrancy to most everything. She was wearing a leather jacket cropped just above the waist. Beneath she had on a V-necked white t-shirt which showcased her chest in a fashion I was sure Technomancer would've found extremely alluring ... I certainly did ... Her black hair complimented the black leather jacket while her slightly pale complexion provided a neat contrast.

"Uh ..." I carried on before seeing over her shoulder Kelly appearing amongst the crowd.

"Come on," Olivia said, linking her arm through mine as if we were the very best of girlfriends. Or as if I was an elderly man she had taken pity on and was helping to cross a road. As Olivia led me on, I realised she was taking me in the same direction as Kelly. Kelly, though, hadn't yet noticed either of us. She had taken the completely understandable approach of heading for the bar. In the dim light, Kelly's hair appeared more red than the blond colour it actually was. She was wearing a baggy black band t-shirt hanging loose over a pair of tight-fitting jeans. As we continued on our way towards the bar ourselves, Olivia kept on speaking. "I saw your name on the poster."

"The poster?" I managed to blurt out.

Olivia nodded, grinning wide.

Maybe my memory was fuzzy but I couldn't remember her ever smiling like that when we had been together. Perhaps our separation had been good for her.

What did that say about me?

Olivia gave me a playful tap on the chest. "Yes, you know, pasted up around the place? Chuckles at the Dive? You're third on the bill ..."

But Olivia didn't get the chance to finish what she had started. We had arrived at the bar, sidled up alongside Kelly, who had noticed me. "Nervous?" Kelly asked.

Just hearing the word sent a tremble through my nerves.

My heart pounded.

"No," I lied.

Olivia leaned across me. I might've been mistaken but I thought it was a defensive manoeuvre. Or a controlling one. She laughed, almost in Kelly's face. "I suppose when you're born to do something you feel it in your blood." She shifted back to me as if expecting agreement.

In the end what she received was far more uncertain than that ...

Nonetheless, Olivia continued, "I always said you were funny."

Funnily enough, that didn't make me feel at all better. But the hollow sensation I felt inside at least subdued the raging nerves.

Kelly smiled politely, then the barman tapped her on the shoulder, gesturing at the pint of lager he had poured. He held the card reader primed in his other hand. Kelly busied herself with her purse, giving Olivia enough time to yank me away a few paces. Before I could get so much as a word out, Olivia fluttered her eyes at the barman and said, "Vodka screwdriver. Two."

The barman nodded and turned his back, setting about his work, the bottles hanging on the rack behind him. I did my best to focus on him for as long as was possible — until it proved impossible not to pay attention to Olivia. Who was speaking again.

"Tell me a joke," she said, an uncharacteristic, possibly faked, gleam in her eye.

"Uh," I managed to get out.

"Spark?"

Never in all my life had I been so glad to hear Riko's voice.

511

I turned on my heel, facing up to him. He was wearing a black shirt over a pair of what looked like work trousers. In the course of the past few months he had reinvented himself as a sort of life coach, procured a bunch of business cards ... disturbingly not entirely unlike Emmerson Ray although hopefully without the same openly evil intent.

"Riko!" I bellowed ... just as uncharacteristically as the gleam in Olivia's eye.

I must've been just a tad overeager because a couple of men standing in a group looked away briefly from their conversation even despite the music throbbing through the speakers.

I managed to prise myself free of Olivia's arm although I could tell that she was already busy plotting her next move.

Riko appeared to register my false enthusiasm as authentic. A welcome change from the usually quite grim-humoured Marcus "Sparky" Raisin ... albeit somewhat less grim-humoured since I had started on my new career as a temp at Daphne's.

"Sparky!" Riko said, this time with a broad smile and his arms stretched above as if he was offering himself up as a sacrifice for some mighty god.

Acting on impulse, I embraced him.

He smelled strongly of cologne and a little of sweat.

There was also that rubbery bus smell on him.

When we broke apart, I looked back at Olivia to see her frowning at the screwdrivers which'd arrived upon the bar counter. Seeing me looking, she turned that proverbial frown upside down. She picked her way through the crowd jostling the bar, moving closer to me and Riko. When she handed over my screwdriver, her arm brushed mine more than a little bit seductively.

Just what was the charm?

Was temping really *this* sexy an occupation?

Finally, it appeared Olivia was willing to show her hand. "Oh, hello, *Riko*," she said, surprising both me and Riko that she knew his name. Come to think of it, I couldn't clearly recall a time when the two of them had actually been in the same room ...

"You're here to see Marcus's act?"

Riko looked me up and down as though I was a wax model in a museum. "Yes. Yes, I am."

Nobody said anything and I wondered if it was supposed to be my turn. But if it was then nothing provided a bridging connection between my brain and my mouth.

Kelly joined us — bearing a pint of lager.

Apparently she was unmoved by Olivia's attempts at shaking her off.

I took a sip of my screwdriver, tasting the bitterness of the vodka at the back of my throat, not quite offset by the sweetness of the orange juice.

"He's going to be wonderful," Olivia said in a voice so cloying I couldn't quite believe it.

I could never remember her speaking that way while we had been together.

Perhaps she believed it was "attractive" for some reason?

I flushed — a pretty standard response to anything resembling a compliment.

Riko looked me in the eye. "Oh, I dunno, I've seen Spark's stuff. It's ... *regular.*"

"Hi guys, hope I'm not too late."

Everyone turned to look.

It was Filly.

He wore a white shirt over a pair of smart black trousers. As always he had on a broad grin despite the trauma he — *all* of us minus Olivia — had been through.

"Have you been on yet?" Filly asked.

Everyone turned to me with a certain expectation.

I took another swig of screwdriver.

Gulped it down.

"Nope," I said. "Not yet."

Filly nodded to my screwdriver. "I'd offer you a drink but someone beat me to it."

Another sip of screwdriver.

"Yup," I replied.

The attention of the group shifted in the direction of the stage.

I realised everyone — Olivia, Kelly, Riko, Filly — had turned to watch someone clambering onto the raised platform. It was a woman in her fifties wearing what I could only describe as a "hippy cloak"; a woollen cloak dyed all the colours of the rainbow. She wore thick square-framed glasses and squinted at everyone through the spotlight from where she stood at the mike. Somewhere out of sight the soundman turned the music right down.

All I could hear in the Dive was the sound of people excitedly chattering.

Bottles clinking.

Liquids slopping.

Feedback squealed through the pub speakers.

"*Ahem*," the woman said. She unfolded a piece of crumpled paper, cleared her throat another time, and then started speaking in a deep, throaty voice I would've thought belonged to a man about the same age if I hadn't physically seen her standing before us. "Good evening ladies and gents and welcome to another evening of Chuckles." She paused, glancing up at the audience, as if this was supposed to raise some sort of reaction.

Someone near the front — inexplicably — broke into fits of laughter.

"First up we have Ghanaw ... Ghanawar ... Ghahanawa ..."

"Gwyenda!" someone called from the crowd.

The woman on stage glared into the crowd. She would've been unable to identify the perpetrator because of the spotlight shining directly into her eyes. She shook her head and grumbled something indistinguishable, and then, "First up is ... *her* ... next we have Michael Rodan ... then it will be Marcus Raisin ..." My stomach tied into a knot . "And then finally ..."

Someone in the crowd gave a haughty shout.

It was almost a yodel.

It was either a true fan or else someone who had overindulged of the evening.

This time the woman wasn't as disturbed by the interruption. "... Heinrick Lee!"

The whole crowd let out whoops and whistles.

My stomach unknotted itself and did a backflip. There was nothing like striding out upon the boards with my childhood hero. I guess the weirdest thing about childhood heroes is that by their very nature you outgrow them — as I had outgrown Heinrick Lee. And yet the mere mention of his name still had an effect on me. Realising Olivia was much closer than I realised, I flipped her a swift glance and then necked my screwdriver before brushing past her to the bar once again.

The other stand-ups passed in a blur.

I'm sure what they said — some of it any way — was funny, and yet I struggled to raise so much as the merest hint of a smile. A couple of times Riko nudged me in the ribs with his elbow, apparently wanting to check I still possessed all the reflexes of a normal human being. It was only when I caught Kelly's look — Olivia's arm draped around my shoulder didn't prevent my wandering eye — that I realised what was about to happen. What I was about to do to myself.

I peered down at the pint of beer I had ordered from the bar.

All its fizzing orangey badness.

Cheap lager really was the bottom of the barrel — in more ways than one — but I had decided in a fit of pragmatic thinking that I shouldn't indulge myself in any more spirits before I took to the stage. In the course of the past week it felt as though I had watched every second of footage available of comedy nights varying from amateur to professional and it was always obvious when the performer had been at the sauce ...

And I was going to be better than those unprofessional, *sloppy* comics.

I was going to be ... and it was right then that I felt the urge to be sick.

That, at least, was what caused me to throw off Olivia's arm and shove my way through the crowded pub towards the exit. When I got outside, the air was fresh and clear. It felt as though invisible freezing-cold hands massaged my face. The sky had cleared up and thousands of stars clustered among the inky blackness.

"Marcus?"

I turned on the spot, seeing Kelly standing there.

My throat constricted and I took a sharp breath.

"Uh huh," I replied, in that weird place of believing that I wasn't going to be sick imminently and yet not wanting to tempt fate too terribly.

"You're on in five minutes."

This time I doubled over. I'm not sure why if my intention was not to vomit ... everything just felt better in that posture.

"Try rocking back and forth a bit too," Kelly said.

I did as she suggested. It did actually feel better. I wondered whether Kelly had once been a sailor, in addition to that whole would-be skate-boarding career.

I breathed in deeply.

Exhaled hard.

I wondered how long I could remain like this.

Maybe a little bit more ... just a ...

"Sparky?"

I had no need to look up to see who it was.

No one else other than Riko.

"Yeah?" I replied, doing my best to pretend I wasn't there at all.

"They're calling your name. They want you to go up there."

"Oh," I said, feeling a crawling numbness. "I see."

"You all right there, Spark?" Riko said.

"Yeah."

"Okay." Although I didn't look up, I imagined Riko exchanging glances with Kelly. "See you on stage then, huh?"

"Yeah."

Riko left me and Kelly alone.

Doubled over, my heart thumped my ribs more than I could bear. I realised I couldn't stay like this forever. I would need to square my shoulders and return to that straight-backed posture so favoured by society.

"It's fine to be nervous," Kelly said. "You wouldn't be human if you weren't *nervous*. But it's how you handle it. You've gotta get up there and give it a go."

My mind drifted back to that student night all those years ago. How I had stood on that stage. Felt the warmth from the spotlight — the audience an obscure shadow — and how I had promptly turned on my heel and beaten a retreat.

I knew what giving up felt like.

It felt like nothing ...

Did I want to feel more ... *nothing?*

My mind swept back and forth until after a little while — it might've been as long as a minute — I felt the flat of Kelly's palm on my back. And she started to stroke me.

To stroke me the same way someone might stroke a cat.

Or perhaps a pet iguana.

Her voice was much closer now. Its vibrations reverberating about my eardrums. It sent a warm fuzzy feeling through my blood and a not-unpleasant crackle of electricity over my bones. "You'll be fine," she said. "I promise. If you feel born to do it then *do* it. The longest journey starts with the first step. Etcetera, etcetera ..."

Gradually, still feeling Kelly's hand on my back, I straightened up. Her hand drifted away. I met her eye. We met one another's eye. And then we just seemed to come together.

Everything was warm, and perfect. Just for that moment.

Inside the pub, the crowd was much more hostile than when I had first set foot within.

It was jarring.

Everything had been so relaxed — everyone had been having a good time — just moments earlier. It made me wonder whether all barroom brawls started out with a feeling like this. If it hadn't been for Kelly squeezing my hand tightly, sending her distinct *feminine* warmth through my skin, then I might've turned on my heel and left this all behind.

But I had made my mind up.

Out there, on the grim little basement staircase, with Kelly's lips secured to mine, I had decided to cross the threshold and embrace whatever awaited me.

It was then that I saw the faces of all those who had come today.

*Olivia.*

As she took stock of me and Kelly, as the pieces of the not-too-complicated puzzle slipped into place, her face shifted suddenly from a try-too-hard grin into a bulldog grimace.

I moved on ...

Filly was next.

He clenched his fist and pumped the air in a way which I supposed was meant to represent some kind of solidarity or support. Or maybe he'd seen it in some teen film from the eighties.

Riko had a full pint in his hand and was deep in conversation with a girl with cosmic-blue hair which sheened in the bar light. However even Riko's natural self-absorption was unable to keep him from catching my eye. He lifted his pint glass.

Kelly released my hand from her grip. I turned to her. She gave me a quick peck on the lips. My heart gave a sudden lurch. My blood started to hum.

As Kelly slipped into the crowd, going to join Riko and Filly, I shifted my attention onto the stage and the woman in the hippy coat becoming more flustered with each passing second as the audience heckled. I reached the steps leading up to the side of the stage and took my place behind the curtain. The noise from the crowd got louder and louder but once I was behind the curtain everything was muffled. I was surprised at how dark it was.

It was then that I became aware of others around me.

Of *someone* near.

"Marcus?"

A familiar voice ... and yet ...

Heinrick Lee?

That was who it was.

Suddenly, even seeing snatches of his face in the gloom, I realised the truth.

Ridiculously, the only thing that emanated from my mouth was, "You know my name?"

Heinrick Lee chuckled.

At least *he* found something funny about me.

"I kind of assumed you're the one the compere's been banging on about for the past ten minutes while dodging bottles."

"Oh," I replied, flushing slightly. "Yeah, I guess so."

"Are you ready?" he asked.

"I ..." I replied, and then my gut squeezed a little.

In the darkness behind the stage it felt as though I was closer to the fabric of the universe.

Lost against its inky black smear on the canvas of existence.

"Yeah," I replied, my voice stronger now. "Yes, I am."

Heinrick Lee clasped my shoulder.

Gave it a squeeze.

"Good luck," he said.

When the spotlight shone momentarily in through a gap in the curtain, I could tell his appearance had changed. He now had grey patches in his previously lush head of hair. And his skin which had been stretched tightly over his firm cheekbones had leathered a little, turned saggy.

It was like he was coming to me from the future.

Like I was back to being a kid.

And we were here.

On the same stage.

Well, we were now ...

I took a deep breath, squared my shoulders. "All right," I said to myself. "All right."

I trod out through the curtain.

Out of darkness.

And into light. The clamour of the crowd.

# THE END

# AUTHOR'S NOTE

Thank you for taking the time to read one of my books. If you would like to hear about my latest releases you can sign up for my newsletter here: www.raymondsflex.com

Thanks for reading!

*Raymond S Flex*